DEAD LIZARD'S DANCE

A Tale of Murder, Love
and Witchery in Old Santa Fe
1782

Pamela Christie

Pamela Christie

Lone Butte Press
Santa Fe, New Mexico
2009

Lone Butte Press
P.O.B. 28214
Santa Fe, New Mexico 87592

distributed by

Wild Dog Books
7 Balsa Court
Santa Fe, N.M. 87508
wilddogbooks@cnsp.com

Cover illustration Christopher C. Clow & Pamela Christie

ISBN 978-0-9666860-9-8
Library of Congress Control Number 2009934202

Printed in the United States of America

This book is dedicated to my father

Alfred H. Stoloff

with love.

The people in Dead Lizard's Dance are entirely fictional, with the exception of Governor Juan Bautista de Anza and his wife Anna Serrano. Reference is made also to the Commander General of the Internal Provinces, Teodoro de Croix, and to King Carlos the Third of Spain, each of whom was far too important to be impersonated by another player.

A brief overview of the historical period and a glossary of Spanish words used in the text may be found at the end of the story.

The maps in this book were adapted from a map of New Mexico drawn in 1779 by the Spanish surveyor Don Bernardo de Miera y Pacheco.

The Characters

Nando: Fernando Aguilar, half-breed recruit in Governor Anza's spy network. Son of Benito Aguilar, deceased, and Benito's Ute slave, Nan.

Marisol: Nando's girlfriend

Luz de Gracia:
    Widow of Benito Aguilar, Nando's stepmother

Carlos: Luz and Benito's elder son, Nando's half brother

Francisco: Second son of Luz and Benito, also Nando's half brother

Luisa Piña de Diaz:
    Francisco's bride, niece of the felonious Alcalde Duran

Governor Juan Bautista de Anza:
    The governor of New Mexico in 1782

Anna Serrano: Anza's wife

Sebastian: The governor's right-hand man, a sergeant at the Casas Reales

Don Crespín Olivas and his colleagues:
    Investigators sent by **Commander General Teodoro de Croix** from Arizpe, Mexico

The Priests:
> Padre Miera
> Padre Domingo
> Severiano, a lay brother
> Gabriel, an orphaned boy at the convent

The Santa Fe Merchants:
> Don Alfonso Vial, the chief merchant and
> caravan master
> Aurelia Inez, his wife
> Facundo Salazar, a rival of Vial, also the
> Commissioner to the West
> Celedonia Griego, his wife

Nando's Ute family:
> Nan, his mother, daughter of Ute chief Cedro
> Segundo, Nan's second son by Benito Aguilar
> Nanita, Nan's daughter by Benito

The Medicine Women:
> Juliana
> Agapita, her sister
> Beatriz, another sister
> Cruzita
> Melchora, Celedonia Griego's Pueblo servant

Toribio: A Local thug

Navajo raiders:
> Nyol
> Tse

Pecos people:
> Tuqué, formerly an elder at the pueblo
> Gabriel's grandmother

Various soldiers, maids, drivers and drovers:
> Amado, Francisco's ranch manager
> Miguel, Nando's young friend
> Leonardo, a drover on the salt train
> Estrella and Feliz, servants at Luz's
> Paulina, tavern owner
> Baltasar, a soldier at the presidio
> Juan and Eloy, Celedonia's servants

Deep in the Kingdom of New Mexico
~ 1782 ~

Maggots in Carrion

My braid, whipped by a raw gust of wind, batted against my face. I was leaning back, envious, watching a hawk slide across the sky. She traveled the easy way.

For us it had been one foot in front of the other, pulling the horses most of the day. We still clutched our one musket and two lances, following the king's orders, never mind that we were out of powder and the tip had snapped off one of my antique spears.

Even so, our bootstrap outfit had made it through neatly. We'd sneaked past the official caravans and raked up the sparkling salt at a distant, hidden playa. We'd loaded our skinny burros high with the harvested bounty and managed to cross half of New Mexico without Comanches, Kiowas or even the Apaches realizing an unlicensed caravan had just trotted through their territory.

Riding Rosinante, my little Comanche mare, I led five mounted men who goaded and guarded twenty-one burros that carried a ton of first-quality salt. My packers and I had been jabbing at the donkeys for seven days now. There'd been no rain. We'd sucked dirty water out of puddles, hurrying before our thirsty animals churned up the slime. The sun was so hot during the day we peeled off mantas and vests. At night, frost silvered the grasses and we lay shivering in our blankets.

I, Nando, insignificant half-breed, who'd unexpectedly landed a position in the governor's intelligence service; Nando, who as recently as last summer had lounged in cushioned chairs at the palacio smoking cigars with the grandees, could forget all that now. My companions were no longer the colony's leaders, but flea-bitten asses and cranky drovers.

I leaned harder into the red, gritty wind and trudged across the land, darkened now by the shadow of a scorpion-tailed cloud. No doubt about it, I'd fallen off the face of the earth as far as the governor was concerned.

Governor Anza wasn't against me, but he had troubles of his own—fending off his rivals who wanted him recalled to Mexico, men like old Vial, who strutted his velvet-clad bottom at the head of New Mexico's caravan each year, and Santa Fe's other esteemed merchants, each of whom fought off the governor's reforms as steadily as they enriched themselves by the Indios' labor.

And if the merchants weren't nuisance enough, Anza's quarrels with the Franciscans never ceased. Our smug friars, wallowing in piety, refused to understand their costly missions had failed. Too, there were the local mayors, the self-serving alcaldes. The governor might as well herd coyotes as keep the alcaldes in line. No, Anza had his hands too full to worry about one of his lesser spies, me, Nando.

I had to face it: no more chummy days at the palacio. I needed to get this salt to the capital before the wagons left for Mexico and I was cutting it close. If we made it in time, my men and I would eat this winter and I would finally have enough money to marry Marisol.

Beasts and men, we were all fed up with the journey, but with any luck this wind would quit and we could make it over the pass before dark.

From Santa Fe, some other foot-sore merchant could take my cargo on the long trip to Mexico, to flog it as table salt to the ricos of Chihuahua and Parral. All I wanted was to drop my filthy hat on a hook, eat a bowl of hot stew and laze by the fire with Marisol in my arms.

I climbed back on Rosinante and gave her a kick, urging her toward the blue spike of mountains that promised we were almost home.

We had barely dropped over the last high ridge before Santa Fe when the light gave out. We found the stream we'd been heading for, but it was nearly dry. I left Miguel and the others scraping the sandy bottom, trying to eke out enough moisture so we could camp. Alone, I walked up the empty bed of Deer Creek looking for a better source of water. I followed a vague memory from childhood of pools back in a rock canyon where toads boomed out their love songs.

It was nearly dark now, but I didn't mind. The wind had stopped and it was good to be away from the men and animals, to walk slowly by myself, smelling the cooling trees.

It wasn't long until I heard the toads in a steep side canyon, calling to each other from their mossy pools. I climbed up the slick granite face and at the top found a trickle of fresh

3

water slipping over the stone. I made a small dam of pebbles, let the water puddle, and drank slowly. In time I filled two gourds, then managed a cursory wash in the meager thread of water. I rolled onto my back, felt the cold granite press against me, and waited for the stars.

When my heartbeat stilled, and before the wary toads started croaking again, I heard a clicking sound.

A riffle of wind passed over me and I heard another click. Branch knocking against branch? I sat up to look. Even though there was still a faint glow in the western sky, it was too dark to see much, so I hooked my fingers into cracks in the slippery rock and moved toward the sound, following a thin ledge that ended in the soft dirt of the woods.

Barely discernible in the gloom of the forest, a structure loomed, one of those brush-roofed ramadas the Indios build for their summer camps. I moved toward it through the pines.

This shelter was old and rattled in the wind. Forked posts held a roof frame of tree limbs. The once leafy branches that covered the place were now bare sticks. I'd come to a ghost house, eerie, and no place at all for a lone man to visit on the brink of dark.

Click. Click. I looked inside. Some black bundle hung from a roof beam. I crept closer, but stopped when I smelled the stink of maggots rotting in carrion.

Jesús Maria! Through the gloom I saw the open-eyed face of a man peering toward me. His head hung forward over his rigid body. Two long braids swung loose, and a foul smell permeated the air.

Sour spit surged in my mouth, but sticking my nose in the crook of my arm, I moved toward the hanging corpse.

The clicking came from a long, peeled stick lashed at its midpoint to the man's wrists. The stick kept the corpse's arms locked together behind him. Someone had hung this wretch by his elbows over a roof timber. Strapped him there. In the light wind that kicks up just at dark, the rotting body swayed and when it did, the stick knocked solemnly against a juniper post.

Christ in heaven! I launched myself out of the ghastly place and hurtled down the rocks to the creek trail.

Who was this person, hanging by his arms the way they kill witches? Who hung the old man so he would never touch the earth again? Was he alive when they did it, leaving him to die in his excrement and pain?

My knees caved in. Dropping to the ground I retched onto the dirt. My hands trembled as I held my head. After a time I drank from my gourd, pushed myself onto my feet, and began the walk back to camp.

Indio, from the looks of him. Pecos, probably. Their pueblo was near here. The corpse's stench clung to the inside of my nostrils. Did my men and I have to cut him down? Were we obligated to bury the man?

I moved warily, realizing that more than one person had been in on this death. A solitary killer couldn't string a man that high off the ground, particularly if the victim was still alive.

I would inform the authorities in Santa Fe, but I would leave the body there. The officials needed to see the horror of it. They needed to smell the stink and feel the fear at the death place.

I heard the thump of pounding feet and sank behind a boulder, waiting to see who was rushing up the trail. The killers returning, or worried people searching for their dead?

I took a breath. Two of my own men were hurrying to find me now that dark had fallen. They carried a firebrand, and its light bounced up and down as they ran through the trees. I stepped onto the path, relieved they hadn't discovered me heaving up my guts.

"Hola. You okay?" panted Miguel. The firelight reflected off his boy-boned body and his wise man's eyes.

"Sort of," I mumbled. Could I stand to go back to the ramada to show them what I'd found? I'd have to, because the government needed to be told.

"I've got to show you something. Come on and stay close. It's ugly," I warned. "But you won't believe me unless you see this for yourselves."

I took the burning pine knot and turned uphill into the forest. Lanky Miguel and the muscled, dark-skinned Leonardo followed close on my heels, breathing harder as we climbed. I held back when we got closer to the ramada, knowing the foulness in there, but Miguel and Leonardo went right inside and nearly bumped into the stiffly hanging corpse.

Miguel whistled softly through his teeth. "Pew."

"Who *is* that?"

I held the light close to the dead man's face. The two boys backed away. "Let's get going," Leonardo shivered. "His ghost's here."

"No. We've got to do this right. The officials in Santa Fe need to see the corpse, tortured like it is, because this looks like something a lot of people were in on, like an execution, in fact."

My stunned companions nodded. Leonardo's eyes darted toward the woods. "His killers are gone, right? They're not out there watching us, are they?"

Miguel shook his head. "They wouldn't stay around. Whoever killed this man never thought he'd be found way out here." His voice faltered. "Jesus, look how they broke his arms. How long did it take him to die, do you think?"

I didn't answer. It's hard to talk when your heart is slamming against your ribs. By the light of the torch, I'd just noticed thickly caked blood all over the crotch of the dead man's pants.

Miguel said, "We'd better bury him or animals will eat him before anyone from the palacio gets here."

"At least cut him down." Leonardo's eyes shifted toward the woods again. "His ghost might leave us alone if we let the man lie natural again."

I agreed. "We could put him on the roof, lay him on those old branches."

"The roof's better than nothing," shrugged Miguel, "but it means we've got to hoist the body up there. We're going to stink when we're done."

"So? We already do." I pulled out my knife to cut the thongs. "Let's get it done."

I kicked a hole in the dirt and wedged the burning pine-knot there to light our work. I pulled my neck cloth over my nose and moved toward the corpse. "Look, his manta's still here, bunched up behind the stick. We'll roll him in it. He can wear that while he waits for the government to show up."

Leonardo leaned his shoulder against the body to keep it from swinging. Miguel gave me a leg up to where I could slice the straps that bound the man to the beam. We eased the corpse down, sliding it off our backs, so it didn't plummet to the ground.

Leonardo untangled the rolled up poncho and spread it on the ground. We fumbled through the next part any way we could, wrapping the corpse, tilting the body and hoisting it high enough to ease the head and shoulders onto the lowest part of the roof. I wedged the dead man there against a viga, while Miguel and Leonardo pulled themselves into the dry branches. From there they dragged the remains to the center of the roof. I flung up pieces of rope and waited while they tied the body to a roof beam.

"Hurry up!" I called. "Let's get out of here."

"What's the rush?" Miguel asked, dropping to the ground. "This bastard's been dead for days."

"Maybe the killers *are* still out there," I replied.

Leonardo shinnied down a post and stood beside Miguel and me, holding the torch higher, trying to ward off the black night. "For sure that ghost is."

"I know, I know, and this is horrid, but we're almost done. The sergeant will be mad as Comanches if I waste any time letting him know. Let's get back to camp and try to sleep for a couple of hours. I'll ride for Santa Fe before first light. You and the other men will have to hide with the salt until I get back."

Leonardo was sour. "Damn it, Nando, we're awfully close to Santa Fe to have to wait around while you sort this mess out."

I was sick of him and his incessant mouth, but I couldn't afford to lose a worker. "Cut the whining, Leonardo. I didn't plan to stumble over a dead Indio hanging in the woods. Remember we talked about hiding half the cargo anyway, to skip out on taxes. One or two days, that's all, until Sebastian's finished with me. I can't afford to miss the caravan, so you can trust I won't be long."

I looked at the two of them, filthy before we started this job, and now smeared with tarry blood.

"Dios, you reek!" I said, and we tore out of there, hell bent for the water below.

Body Redux

The sky was pinking up when Sebastian found me in the palacio's stables, brushing straw off my third-best pants.

"Come to my office, Nando. I've got a few minutes to hear the whole story now."

"All right, if you feed me."

I'd ridden into Santa Fe just before dawn and slept a couple of hours, batting off the mice that ran through the hay beneath me. Still, staying near the government offices was easier than going home where I'd have to steer clear of my stepmother. Luz would love to have the news of a dead body to spread all around town. As for sneaking over to see Marisol, there wasn't time to make a visit worthwhile.

In his frigid office the sergeant handed me some bread and a wedge of goat cheese, which I hate. I tore into the bread, while Sebastian pulled his chin whiskers and asked more questions than I wanted to answer. Every detail brought back the victim's smell. After getting the facts out of me, Sebastian left to tell Governor Anza.

The sergeant returned as I was splashing my face and rinsing my mouth at the horse trough. His voice was sharp. "The governor wants a word with you before we leave. Get going. There's plenty I've got to arrange to start this party riding to find your alleged corpse."

"The governor wants to see *me*?"

9

"No doubt he's been missing you."

We watched as pueblo boys worked fast in the chilly air to saddle horses for the men going to Deer Creek with Sebastian and me.

"How many are coming?" I asked while I dried myself off. I was amazed the officials at the palacio took a story of mine seriously.

"Me, two soldiers from the light troop, the new lay brother Severiano, and the army's surgeon."

"You're joking. A surgeon's not going to help the corpse I found, and the man's long past prayers."

"Anza wants a report on the manner of the death. That's the doctor's job. The brother is coming along to make the Franciscans feel like they're being included."

"Why Severiano? Why not Padre Miera?"

"Miera's too old and fat. He'd have a hard time making the trip. Besides, Severiano's feisty and needs to be exercised."

"Maybe so, but you can rely on old Miera's judgment."

Sebastian gave me a shove. "Stop your confounded questions and get in there. Don't let Anza keep you long. We take off the moment the sun comes over Atalaya."

"As though I can tell the governor what to do," I called over my shoulder as I hastened across the courtyard.

Juan Bautista de Anza's furry eyebrows lowered when I entered his office, never a good sign with this governor. I stood at attention.

"You again," he greeted me.

I summoned my humblest smile.

Anza didn't return it. "You came across a dead man hanging in the woods," he stated, "not far off the road to Pecos, pinned by his arms, apparently tortured. On your word alone, Nando Aguilar, the word of a penurious half-breed, I remind you, I'm letting five men leave their duties for the day to

10

examine this corpse. I hope you haven't exaggerated your report."

"No sir."

"An execution, you believe?"

"It would take more than one person to hang a man that way," I replied to the top of the governor's head. Anza was shuffling through papers.

He seemed to find what he sought, then looked up and said, "It used to be that no one knew you worked for me, but it's clear from the gossip that your role's been leaked. Sort of the town hero, after the alcalde's arrest, eh?" Anza grunted as he rose from his chair.

"Which is why I've ignored you these past months, to give their memories time to fade. Now if anyone asks, we'll have to admit you're an aide to Sebastian. You're back on with us, at the same thirty pesos a month, Nando, in spite of the depleted state of my treasury. You discovered this mess. Now find out who the dead man is and who killed him. Here's your letter of employment and a permit for travel, so you can move around as you need to. But Nando, as much as possible, keep this quiet."

"Thank you, sir." I took the scrawled note, proof that I had paid work again.

"There's too much at stake in my domain right now," the governor frowned, "to have a group of killers on the loose. This death is distasteful and appears to have been premeditated.

"Report to the palacio," Anza continued, "as soon as you return with the body. And keep your mouth shut about the details, particularly in front of your esteemed stepmother. I don't want the people of Santa Fe upset by women's rumors at the very moment the Commander General's inspectors are riding into town."

11

I cocked my head in question. The governor took note, but said, "Ask Sebastian. He'll fill you in while you ride. Go. If I don't get you back to the stables, the sergeant will be storming my office. You have a knack for turning up corpses, young man."

The governor softened enough to shake my hand. "Nando, why do we always have to work on such sordid matters together?"

I accepted the handshake, even though he'd called me a penurious half-breed. It was the governor's own fault I was penniless, because he hadn't paid me in three months. But I had to yield to the half-breed description. For a certainty, it wasn't Anza's doing that my father once took a fancy to the beautiful slave woman he'd brought to his home.

The small cavalcade turned up Deer Creek canyon at noon. The men hurried to reach the ramada, to witness the corpse rotting on the roof. They wanted to pronounce judgment fast and get back to town before dark. I held back, unwilling to get to the scene in the woods any sooner than I had to.

Earlier, when we were riding side by side on the broad Pecos road, I'd asked Sebastian why Governor Anza took this so seriously.

"I didn't think anyone would care," I said, "since the victim is an Indian. I knew I had to report the death, but I didn't expect to be summoned by the governor. Now you've put together a whole procession. Why?"

Sebastian looked around at the other riders and decided no one could overhear us.

He kept his voice low when he said, "Commander General Croix, the man in charge of all Spain's provinces north of Mexico, is sending men to Santa Fe to investigate the transgressions of Alcalde Duran. A little fart named Don Crespín Olivas, whom I've had the displeasure of meeting in Arizpe, is about to arrive with a delegation of six sharp-nosed investigators.

"Croix has given Don Crespín and his councilors authority to look into the alcalde's felonies. I'm sure you're aware that the man you fingered as a traitor, Nando, was one of Anza's best friends. I suppose you had to do it, but it was hardly a diplomatic move. Now we're getting the repercussions. Because Alcalde Duran worked closely with Anza on government business, Olivas has permission to pry into Anza's private accounts and to scrutinize every aspect of our governor's administration of the colony.

"A courier arrived yesterday saying the investigators' party had reached El Paso del Norte. Croix's men travel slower than the messenger, but even so, they'll be arriving in Santa Fe any day now."

I nodded. "So the governor wants no freshly killed bodies hanging around to upset Señor Olivas."

Sebastian's full cheeks sagged into his brushy beard. "Officially Croix's spies are coming to probe the matter of the alcalde's treason. Croix authorized them to seize the former Alcalde Duran's homes, papers, and anything they believe should belong to the state. It's well known a man who commits treason forfeits everything to his monarch."

I thought about my half-brother Francisco living with Luisa, his bride, at her Uncle Tomás's hacienda. Tomás Duran, the accused alcalde. It looked like the luck of the newlyweds was about to run out.

13

"Unofficially," Sebastian continued, "Croix's been trying to unhorse Anza as Governor of New Mexico for a long time. But our governor's too clever. So far Croix hasn't been able to get him, but now the alcalde's trial gives the Commander General all the tools he needs to dig into the details of Anza's command. He's hoping to uncover enough to pry Anza from office."

"Why would anyone want Anza out?" I asked.

"The Commander claims it's because of what Anza's friends at Yuma did, but it's a stickier web than that. Croix fears Anza's strength. The Commander wants a weaker man up here, one his government can fully control."

The canyon narrowed, effectively ending the briefing, as we rearranged ourselves single file along the stream. In places the creek held no water, in others there were clear pools trapped in limestone basins. When we had to climb the cliff, we tied the horses and Sebastian gestured for me to lead the way up the rock face. Looking at the wall ahead, the soldiers discarded their leather jackets and long swords, but hung on to their knives. Brother Severiano tucked his blue skirts into his belt, revealing sturdy, white legs.

We used our toes and fingers to get up the cliff, squinting through the sparkling sunlight, trying to glimpse the body on the roof. I couldn't make out the ramada until we passed the last trickle of water. I climbed ahead, to where I could see the sagging rooftop, but I still couldn't spot the corpse.

"Come on," I told the rest of them, "Move closer. The woods are too thick here."

Sebastian gave me a doubting look and pushed ahead. "Dear Jesus," he said to me under his breath when I caught up with him. "You lied to your governor, Nando. You never cut that man down."

I stared. The body hung in the ramada, as though we'd never struggled to lay it on the roof. As before, the man's thin arms had been drawn up behind him, his elbows crooked tortuously over a roof beam. But this time there was no stick banging against a post and the body was tightly wrapped in a man's dark cloak.

Jesus, Mary and Joseph! Someone had returned the corpse to its original position, hanging it from the roof of the ramada. For some incomprehensible reason, the killers had come back while I'd ridden to Santa Fe.

Last night, when I'd been gagging onto the dirt, and later when Miguel, Leonardo and I had stoically laid the body out of reach of animals, the murderers must have been watching. I felt for my knife.

The soldiers, lay brother, and surgeon trudged the last distance through the woods to behold something entirely different than what I had sworn to. The account of a half-breed was worthless without witnesses. Where were Miguel and Leonardo when I needed them? The doctor stood there gaping, the soldiers held their knives unsheathed, while the lay brother crossed himself and launched a prayer. Shoulder to shoulder, the intrepid delegation from the palacio inched closer to the strung up victim.

Sebastian snapped, "Nando, what's your game? What's all this about cutting the body down and tying it on the roof?"

"That's not the body I told you about," I protested in a hoarse voice. "It's not the same man I saw before." It was beyond reason, but it was true.

Sebastian boomed over the chanting of the brother, "What in the name of Mary and the Blessed Saints are you telling me? What makes you say this corpse isn't the same one?"

"The body doesn't stink."

15

Every man turned and stared at me. Slowly they became aware that what I said was true. There was no rancid smell coming off the victim, none of the rank maggot stench that had caused me to vomit last night.

The doctor and Brother Severiano approached the dark bundle, the brother holding his cross in front of his face and muttering a protective litany. The rest of us drew a little nearer, but not too close.

"Nice cape," the physician said as he pulled at the tightly wrapped cloak. He poked, probed and stretched to feel the tied hands, but they were too far above his reach. The doctor gestured to the gaping soldiers. The younger of the two grasped a post and climbed into the roof branches to cut the leather thongs, while the second soldier stood by to support the body as it dropped.

Even so, the dead man fell hard upon the ground. His cape flew open. We looked on horrified as one of his arms snapped off. The soldier on the roof, braver than the rest, slid down and, seeing that no one else had budged, picked up the limb.

Puzzlement flashed to amazement when he held up a twisted juniper stick instead of a fleshy arm.

The group broke into jittery laughter. The doctor pulled the dead man up by the front of his blue jacket, reached in to where the man's heart should be and pulled out a handful of glittering straw. Our laughter grew bolder.

I noted the construction of the effigy: a bag of hay, juniper twigs for hands, with, oddly, a fat ring made of yellow grass wound around one finger. Old pants had been stuffed with grass, and there were no feet, which defect had been covered by the long cape. It was a much better cloak than the one Leonardo, Miguel and I had wrapped the original corpse in.

Now the "body" wore a short coat, old and tattered for sure, but with one tarnished silver button still attached to the blue wool. The jacket was an antique remnant of the uniform of a Spanish military officer. A tidy, dark peruke replaced the braids of the original victim.

"Not the same body," Sebastian agreed.

"Not a body at all," added the physician.

"Where's the real corpse?" the sergeant turned on me.

"I told you, Miguel and Leonardo tied him in the branches." I pointed to the empty space on the brushy roof.

Sebastian grilled me in front of the other men.

"Nando, you have an obligation to tell the truth. Isn't this the figure you saw here in the ramada yesterday? A fake then, and a fake now?"

"No sir." I prayed the sergeant would believe me. "The dead person I saw was gory and stank to high heaven. The only thing the same was the real victim had been hung this way too, by bending his elbows over that beam."

"You're saying the original body vanished?" The doctor's voice rose to a higher pitch.

Brother Severiano made the sign of the cross before suggesting, "Carried away by spirits. It has happened before, but this time, not by angels."

"The killers must have realized their victim had been discovered, so they got rid of the body," argued a soldier, a practical man. "I've never heard of spirits leaving footprints and there are tracks all over the ground. Let's start searching. If there's truly a corpse, it won't be far from here."

"But why would they leave this effigy?" Sebastian was flummoxed and pressed me for answers. "You're sure the man you saw was an Indio, Nando?"

"Yes, in poor clothes, not an officer's jacket. He had braids, like I told you. There's not much the same between the effigy and the dead man. Except, maybe," and I paused and pushed aside the spilled straw with my foot to look at the front of the effigy's pants. "Yes, sergeant. That part's the same."

I pointed at the black smear of gore at the crotch, only this time it was a painted embellishment, not the true blood of the victim seeping from inside the man's pants.

Mud and Gore

A cold-running ground wind streamed through my blankets and slipped along my spine. The wedge of flint under my hipbone stayed beneath me no matter where I moved. My legs hooked around stones to keep the sloping ground from tipping me into the arroyo. Dawn was imminent, but not yet here. I turned sideways to the ledge and pulled the rough blanket over the top of my head.

Yesterday afternoon, late, by the time the soldiers had given up their search for a true corpse and lashed the effigy onto the back of a mule, I'd finally convinced Sebastian to let me go back to my pack train for a few hours. I pleaded with my boss that I had packers and mules waiting and argued that he didn't really need me to show the governor this travesty we'd found in place of the dead man's body.

Sebastian wasn't smiling. "You can stay out one night. That's all. Get back to Santa Fe tomorrow before dark, or the governor will have you brought in."

I grimaced. I'd only just been rehired and I needed the money. But my salt was worth a substantial amount too, and I wasn't going to abandon my venture simply because Anza had temporarily reinstated my thirty pesos a month.

Sebastian let me go at the foot of the narrow canyon where I knew my friends hid with the salt. When people accused me of lying about the dead man, I could bring Miguel and Leonardo to the palacio, but later, when money matters weren't pressing.

I turned Rosinante toward the slot in the hills. As I rode up the narrowing arroyo, my nose told me my men were roasting a rabbit. I passed by the tethered burros, then ascended the yellow talus slope to their fire and greeted them, but I could tell that my packers were cross at being delayed only hours from the plaza. I tried to appease them with the small cone of chocolate I'd slipped into my pocket before I left town.

The disgruntled men showed me the only place they'd found to make their camp, on the slope beneath an overhang. It was a rough place, but at least Miguel had found a pool of water between two boulders in the streambed.

All night I'd breathed my own dank breath in the cave of my blankets, shivering and cramped. Finally, I'd found Marisol in a dream. My hands had been warm, crossed over her soft belly. I had the earth and piñon smell of her in my nostrils. Marisol was telling me a story, as though I were a child. I dozed off and on to the lilt and tumble of her words and kissed the fine nape of her neck, keeping my lips on her skin.

I lost her when morning came. I did not want it to be daylight yet, did not want to rise in the cold to work with frigid fingers, saddling stubborn animals. But here came the insistent light and the memory of the horrible discoveries above Deer Creek. My dream was in shreds. Reluctantly, I straightened my legs, preparing to get up.

It was then my Comanche mare screamed. I'd never heard Rosinante scream before. I threw off my blankets and ran toward the tie lines, remembering that cold wasn't the only reason I slept fully clothed.

My horse reared and shrieked again, tearing at her line so hard that the other horses reeled in terror. Rosinante crashed to the forest floor. Her hooves beat the air as she struggled to get off her side, to regain her feet. I reached into the gusty maelstrom and seized the broken lead rope under Rosinante's chin, dodging hooves and her thrashing head.

Fish and Mercury tore free, their ropes flailing. The fleeing horses rushed away down the arroyo, kicking up dust and fallen branches, as they careened toward the tall ponderosas. The men jumped up and were at my side. Leonardo sped to retrieve the animals, following the churned up track.

Ignoring the runaways, I pulled the rope hard to steady Rosinante and hung on until she calmed enough to gather her forelegs and bring herself to standing. My mare was blowing hard and her red coat was dark with sweat. I noticed a swath of blood on her chest and a black lump in the leaves by her hooves.

Muddy gore stuck to her. I moved in to wipe it off, but my foot caught on a fleshy ball of blood and feathers, muddled with dust. A raven, a mangled, blood-dripping raven, with fat talons and one shining eye, was dragging by a loop from Rosinante's neck. The agitated mare skittered sideways while I sliced the thong that held the mutilated bird.

First I snubbed my quivering mare to a sturdy tree, then I examined the raven.

I held it by a scaly leg. One blue-black wing hung slack and wild to the side. A long wooden pin pierced the bird's breast and protruded from its shining back. A looped leather thong dangled from the raven's broken neck.

Miguel stood beside me, staring at the filthy creature I held between my thumb and forefinger. Together, we examined the stick driven through the raven's flesh. It was the snapped shaft of an arrow.

I handed the bird to Miguel and went to stroke Rosinante, running my hand over her quivering back. There was caked blood on her chest and one gleaming wound on her withers that still bubbled wet and red. At first I thought she'd been punctured by a branch when she fell, but when I examined the wound I saw the cut was knife-blade clean.

Miguel used the thong to hang the raven from a tree limb. The dark bird twisted in the morning sun, dropping beads of blood onto the forest floor.

My men and I had traveled together for weeks. They were fond of Rosinante. This attack couldn't have come from them, but who else would there be in this hidden canyon? Miguel bent his lanky body under the tie line and ran his fingers over the ground, feeling for traces, for a hint, of how this had happened.

Rosinante's ears twitched and her eyes gleamed wild and fearful. I crooned and stroked her, felt her knees and checked her hooves. Her cut still oozed bright drops of blood. I fingered the edges gently, trying to imagine her terror. Only a sick mind would torment an animal in order to scare its owner. I pressed my forehead against Rosinante's heaving side.

Miguel brought water for her from the deep pool in the arroyo. Then he filled the leather bucket again for Leonardo to use when he returned with the other horses.

Miguel slipped into chest-high oak brush and disappeared down the dry creek bed. Sunlight filtered into the canyon, but the silvery morning light on the pine branches did not ease my worry. Someone had been following us, someone who had no qualms about terrifying my horse. Was it the killers who had watched us find their victim on Deer Creek? Were they warning us to stay away?

I skidded into the arroyo to look for Miguel, leaping over flat, lichen-covered stones, through the tinged oaks. I'd tracked him in the dry creek no more than a hundred yards when I saw foot holes where he'd climbed a dirt bank. I grabbed a clump of brush and pulled myself after him.

Miguel stood on top of a house-sized boulder, looking up, scanning the yellow cliffs below the red rim of the mesa. I scrambled to join him. Looking east into the full glare of the sun, we saw someone so unusual, so out of place, we knew at once she figured into what had happened to Rosinante.

Far above us on the staggered ledges, a lone woman in a long, dark dress strode swiftly, making her way steadily upward and east, toward the flat mesa top and the open country beyond.

At the final lip of rim rock she turned and looked down into the canyon below, but only briefly. She climbed quickly and soon disappeared at the place where the sky meets the tips of the tallest pines.

Santa Fe

The Governor's Charade

It wasn't often the Governor of New Mexico got to be alone. Juan Bautista de Anza found himself sitting still at last, watching a beam of sunlight move up the posts of the portico, as the sun dropped toward the western horizon. The governor's eyes ached.

Anza shifted forward in his chair and began shoving papers over his desk, searching for a specific page.

'Croix's lying,' he muttered, plowing deeper into the pile. 'From all the way down in Arizpe, I can smell the stench of the Commander General's lies. The same autocrat who bid me ride five hundred leagues to govern God-forsaken New Mexico. The very bellyacher who bestowed a pinché eighty soldiers on me, expecting us to hold off twenty-thousand enemies.'

Anza snatched a fistful of dun-colored pages and read in a mocking voice, "Investigator Don Crespín Olivas en route. Departing El Paso 22ⁿᵈ September. My trust in you dictates you will cooperate with my representative in every possible way."

The governor shot to his feet and paced his office. 'Send me your toady, Señor Croix. I'll go head-to-head with your Crespín Olivas, and I'll side with the devil before I'll yield to the schemes you two are concocting.'

Anza flung himself back in his chair and dug his fingers into the grizzled hair at his temples. 'God forgive me,' he added under his breath.

Through the watery glass of the narrow window, the governor watched a Pueblo man stride down the street in the last glow of the sun, leading a team of draft horses to drink at the acequia. Anza ached to have a simple job like the Indio's, to be tired by the end of the day, but not frayed, to look forward to an evening with friends.

A few men remained on the packed dirt plaza, scurrying to cram extra bales of wool onto an old wagon. The governor's eyes skipped over the scene, then focused on the closed façades of the flat-roofed houses that fronted the town square.

How he missed passing the evenings with his old companion, Alcalde Duran, never mind how disgraced the man was.

'I wonder if Tomás has reached Mexico, if they've locked him in a cell yet?' he said to himself.

The governor tipped his head back, closing his eyes. He could almost taste the putrid air of a distant dungeon.

'Tomás Duran lied to me for years. The alcalde trafficked with all my worst enemies, but damn it, he had the only decent wine in Santa Fe, and no one could beat the man at chess.'

Anza's scarred hands rubbed his neck. 'I couldn't believe it when that half-breed exposed Duran.'

The governor shook his head, remembering. 'All I said to Nando was, "Take a look around. Stay quiet like that lizard hiding on my mantelpiece, then let me know what you find out," and damned if the youngster doesn't finger my best friend for treason, proving beyond all doubt that Alcalde Duran was spying for the British.'

'And now here's Croix's using the alcalde's trial to unseat me, even though I arrested my old friend, and this same wily half-breed is stumbling over fresh-killed bodies in the woods.'

Anza's fingers stopped kneading his neck. He raised his eyebrows, surprised to be talking to himself. He leaned forward to glimpse a corner of the street market. No women remained. They had rolled up their bright blankets. The hanging bundles of vegetables, slabs of meat, and bushels of corn had been taken home as the chill night air began to settle.

The room darkened. The governor listened to the muted voices of people going to the private chapel down the hall.

'Evening prayers,' Anza murmured. He heard a tinny bell ring. 'Priests! The last thing I want to do right now is hear a priest talk.'

He reached for his punché. Anza stuffed his pipe with the tax-free, local tobacco substitute. 'Sorry King, sorry Old Carlos, no penny for you today.'

The governor lit his pipe with a splinter from the fire, then threw more logs into the corner fireplace.

"Sebastian?" he called, but not loudly. Anza leaned on the windowsill and peered into the gathering gloom. 'Where's my sergeant?'

"Sebastian!" he boomed.

The sad-faced aide poked his head into the room.

"Sir?"

"Do you have a cloak?"

"Yours is here, sir."

"I want to know if you have an old cloak, something on a peg by the door, something the man who brings in wood might use?"

Sebastian cocked his head, not sure why the governor was insisting on this.

"Well, bring it!"

Anza sat down to wait. The damn pipe hadn't lit. He dropped it on his desk and leaned back to watch the logs burn.

Where had Sebastian taken himself? The governor reached for his oldest boots and pulled them on. 'It's good to have the half-breed working for us again, even if he is part Ute. Figuring out who hanged that Indian by Deer Creek is a long shot, but it should keep Nando busy while Crespín Olivas is in town.' Anza snugged his heel firmly into the boot.

Sebastian pushed the door open without tapping and laid a shabby, homespun cape on the governor's desk.

"Where are you going, sir?"

Anza swung the cloak over his uniform and pulled the collar tight, looping the string around a wooden button at the neck.

"Sebastian, I wish to hell you and I could be friends. I wish we could drink huge cups of filthy wine together. But I'm the governor and it's not allowed. So please, sergeant, don't ask, and don't follow me either."

"Your wife, sir? Your supper?"

"Give Anna Serrano my regards, then make something up." Anza headed for the door, but Sebastian stood in his way.

"It's the hat, governor. You'll never get away with it."

Anza tossed the regulation governor's hat onto his chair, snatched the shapeless cotton one off Sebastian's head, and disappeared into the rutted darkness of Santa Fe.

The moon poked its round edge over the Sangre de Cristo Mountains. Free for a while, Anza wandered in the night along the far side of the plaza, peering into courtyards and doorways, listening for music, for any sign of liveliness. He skirted hitching rails and piles of dung, and then, for no particular reason, made his way to the steps of the church.

The fortified adobe stood shuttered and dark, with not even a candle's glow from one of the inner rooms. The bell tower blocked the rising moon.

The governor frowned. The whole town was silent as a cemetery. Only a nanny goat bleating behind a wall broke the deep quiet. Footsteps sounded down the street, and a door opened and shut. More silence. Anza looked up and noticed that the moon seemed to shrink as it rose higher in the sky.

Footsteps again, coming toward him, hurrying between the mud brick walls of the narrow alley at the governor's back. Anza slid his hand under the old cape and grasped his thin-bladed knife.

"No need, governor. It's only me," a light voice reassured him.

"Christ, woman!" He shoved the Toledo steel back in its scabbard. "You get me every time." The governor and the Pueblo lady laughed. The smile on her face was as wide as her second chin.

Anza peered down at the plump Indian standing beside him. "Come, Ayapita, how did you know it was I?"

"Your coat's humble and that hat's garbage, but you stand so erect, sir, and you're very tall. The paymaster's at it again, governor."

Anza leaned down to hear his informant's words. "Well?"

"Vial's hustling before the wagons leave. A dozen men enter Don Alfonso's house after dark each evening. Their packets bulge. Sometimes whole carts full of goods leave Vial's back gate between midnight and dawn, but mostly the men have only got mules with panniers, one or two beasts at a time."

Anza's voice coarsened. "Vial. Padding his purse as always. Selling the presidio's goods before he takes the caravan south, making sure he'll have plenty of funds to cut his own deals in Chihuahua. Meanwhile, my soldier's guns won't fire for lack of replacement parts, and the men's jackets are threadbare."

The little Pueblo woman tipped her face up toward her patrón. "Can't you stop him, governor, before he travels out of the colony?"

The governor shook his head. "The Commander General has my hands tied. If I move against Vial I'll be standing in front of Croix's tribunal within six weeks."

The governor straightened and gently took the elbow of his spy, steering her toward the river road.

"I wager I'll come up with something. Do you like to gamble, Agapita?" The woman nodded eagerly. "Keep your eyes on me. If I don't put a stop to Señor Vial, then you'll owe me a drink."

The woman giggled at the thought of treating the governor of New Mexico to a mug of aguardiente.

"Let's find one now, Agapita, to seal the wager. We can manage it at that dirty tavern behind the military chapel, if we stand at a table out in the dark. I'll buy."

"Honored, Señor. Rotgut, though."

"Sorry. Can't be helped."

"You don't want anyone recognizing you, sir. Can you slouch a little?"

The governor curled his back and dropped a shoulder, eyeing her for approval, but Agapita wasn't sure. This man would always look like the governor to her.

"Poor Agapita, working late nights to keep me informed, and in return I make you drink swill. But one has to keep a restless governor entertained."

"Oh, you pay me well, sir." Agapita stumbled on a loose stone and danced a few quick steps to regain her balance. Anza

caught her arm and she smiled up at him. "It's fine to work for you, governor. Plenty of people would stand in line for my job if they knew you paid in coin."

A grin spread over the governor's face. "I appreciate your candor, woman, but even though my silver's real, the work's dangerous. Vial would toss you in the river, should he discover you watch his gates."

"A little Indian woman like myself? Why, we're everywhere and nobody ever notices us."

"Keep it that way, my friend."

Anza propelled the woman by her elbow around the corner toward the riverside tavern, hanging back a moment before the turn, just long enough to catch a glimpse of Sebastian tailing him.

Good man, he thought. Doesn't obey orders, but my sergeant knows his job.

A Prince of the Land

We got the horses calmed down, salved Rosinante's wounds and were on the road again. I was heading into Santa Fe with my first cargo of salt, and no matter what we'd just been through, I had to be sharp.

I only wanted to get home and curl up beside Marisol, but I had to report back to the palacio first, and somewhere along the way we could expect to meet up with the taxmen who waited on the road into the plaza.

Miguel rode up beside me. "We could hide part of this you know."

"Not any more, now that the sergeant knows all about us, but I suppose, if you really want to take the risk and save a few pesos, you could go cross-country and take a few bags down to my brother's hacienda."

Miguel didn't bite. "It's more important for me to go into Santa Fe, to be there when they ask you about the body. You'll need a witness with a tale like that one. Are you going to say anything about that woman on the mesa?"

"Sure. Why not give Sebastian yet another piece of information that will convince him I'm crazy?"

I figured the long silence that followed meant Miguel was intent on guiding his horse down the stony hillside, but it turned out he was gathering his nerve to ask, "Nando, permit me, how does someone like you have a brother with a hacienda?"

Explaining our mixed-up family could be a challenge, but since Miguel had ridden all this way with me, he might as well know

"You remember when the governor arrested Alcalde Duran?"

"Who in Santa Fe doesn't?"

"Soon afterwards Francisco married the alcalde's niece, Luisa Piña Diaz."

"So. Who's Francisco?"

"My brother," I told him, enjoying this.

"They let a half-breed Ute marry the alcalde's niece?" Even Miguel with his bare feet and ragged pants knew enough about the importance of bloodlines to be shocked.

"I'm the Ute. Not Francisco."

Miguel rode closer and stuck his face under my hat. "Stop fiddling with me!"

"Me," I expounded, holding my arms out to the blue-green prairie, "I'm a true prince of this land. My father, Benito, was a wealthy man with a huge grant above Abiquiú on the Piedra Lumbre. He married Luz de Gracia, of purest Spanish blood, and they had Carlos; you know, the wounded lieutenant at the presidio. Their next child was Francisco. He's the giddy, unpredictable one, who somehow came up with enough sense to marry a rich girl, Duran's niece. She came with a hacienda, the largest one south of Santa Fe. You'll meet Francisco and Luisa sometime. Prepare to be dazzled."

Miguel kept his mule stepping in unison with Rosinante, while I told him our family's bizarre history.

"Up there above Abiquiu, many years ago, something went wrong. Benito and Luz didn't have any more children. But that didn't stop my father. There was a Ute woman on his ranch, a woman he'd captured when she was little, all grown up by then and too beautiful to ignore. Nan. She's my mother. Somehow Luz put up with Benito's behavior and Nan bore all the rest of Benito's children, me, Segundo and Nanita.

"But after sixteen years with him, my mother decided she didn't want to be anyone's servant any more; slave, concubine, whatever you want to call a woman in her situation. Nan sneaked home to the Utes, taking Nanita, her youngest child, with her."

"And leaving her first-born behind," Miguel said pointedly.

"As well as her second son. I don't think my mother had a choice. Benito was weak by then from his long sickness and the Comanches were raiding our ranch. Nan knew she needed to leave me there to help my father, and after all, his was the only family I knew. Segundo was big enough by then to stay with father too."

"Did you ever see your mother again?"

I nodded. "Often. I found Nan up north after Benito died. I took Segundo to her and I stayed with the Utes for a year. Nanita and Segundo are still there, living with my mother. I might never have returned, but word came that Luz needed me.

"The governor ordered our family off the ranch, but to make up for it, he sent Francisco to Mexico to study surveying and took Carlos into the army. Luz was a widow with nobody left to help her, and since she'd been a mother to me too, if you can understand that, I came back to do what I could. Say what you like, but last spring when Nan visited Santa Fe, Luz welcomed her as though they were sisters."

"You'd think two females would murder each other, sharing the same man."

"You'd think. But it didn't happen. Luz couldn't have any more children and she was smart enough to know Benito wasn't going to stop at two. By sharing her husband, she kept her home and her health, and got a hard working companion too."

Miguel and I crossed the mighty Rio Galisteo, all three inches of it, before my friend asked, "So are you Ute or Spanish?"

I shrugged my shoulders. "Don't know. I'd make a piss-poor Ute, living in a brush hut and fitting into a tightly run tribe, but sometimes dealing with the Spanish drives me wild. Times like those, I want a fast horse and a thousand leagues to ride it in."

Miguel couldn't contain his curiosity. "Do your Spanish brothers treat you well? Does your stepmother?"

"Francisco and Carlos are typical older brothers. They give me a hard time, but they help me out too. We were kids together. Luz forced all the same things into my head that she beat into theirs. Reading, numbers, history. She taught the same lessons to every child under her roof. We're family. You're nobody without your family."

If I could have snatched back those words, I would, because the day I met Miguel, Apaches had just slaughtered everyone in his home. Our friendship started when I picked up a shovel and helped bury them.

Miguel went silent for a while, and then to cover his feelings, jabbed, "But Francisco has a hacienda and a wealthy Spanish wife, and Carlos is a lieutenant at the presidio. Looks like Nando didn't get a cut of all that."

Standing high in my stirrups, I opened my arms to the endless sky. "But I'm rich, Miguel. I've got thirty bags of salt and a sweet woman with my baby in her belly. Like I told you, a prince of the land!"

Fever

By the time our pack train came down the hill, crossed the ford at the river, and approached the plaza, Santa Fe was in an uproar.

Word of the missing corpse had gotten out, even though the two soldiers who went to Deer Creek had been sworn to silence and the doctor promised he would keep mum about the disappearance of the murder victim. Sebastian surely followed his plan to hide the effigy in the cold north wing of the palacio. Even so, someone blabbed and the town went crazy.

I figured it must have been Brother Severiano, because no one thought to warn him. Clerics are supposed to be discreet.

Smoke rose from burning sheds behind a house where a witch was said to live. The fire had been knocked down, but black smoke drifted in a gauzy layer over the Barrio Analco. As we crossed the ford, I saw two presidio soldiers steadying a lone woman, fully clothed but drenched to the skin, helping her up the riverbank. Women who usually sat placidly in the plaza stood in an agitated knot beside the river, their skirts wet to their knees. The market place was empty.

An extra detail of soldiers marched through the town. Maybe this explained why I hadn't been stopped by any taxmen. Gates to the larger houses near the plaza were shut and barred, but business at the cantinas boomed and their patrons spilled into the streets.

I sent Miguel with the packers and mules down to Luz's cornfield, looped Rosinante's reins over a rail, and went to buy myself a drink, something lacking from my diet for weeks.

A single topic filled the bar, bruited about the smallish room by militiamen, petty merchants, and even the muleteers bound for Mexico with the caravan. Men huddled in clusters over rickety tables.

"They said the effigy was smeared with blood. All over its crotch," croaked the town's carpenter.

"You mean . . .?" Heads turned toward the little man.

"Damn right, *I mean*." The diminutive carpenter had never gotten so much attention in all his life. "And I'm guessing that's what happened to the Indian, too."

"The bitches cut his cojónes off?"

The carpenter nodded with a grim face. "And more. The whole thing, I bet."

"Jesús Cristo!" the men exclaimed in unison. There was a contemplative silence while each man took a long drink from his mug.

The bartender's deep voice cut into the quiet. "Stolen by witches. That's how bodies disappear."

"But the man was a witch himself. You can tell by how they hanged him."

"Someone wanted that Indian dead."

"Had to be a bunch of them to pull it off. How many would it take, do you think?"

"More than a couple to get him over the beam, and later to put together that fake body."

"In a pig's eye. That bastard never saw a dead body. Made up the part about the effigy to cover his ass. Corpses don't run away."

I kept my face behind my mug. So far no one seemed to know I was the half-breed at the center of this story.

A man with a huge mustache shook his head. "There really was someone dead up there. An Indio from Pecos, most likely. Old guy. Deer Creek's pretty close to the pueblo. The half-breed had witnesses."

"So where are they now?"

The men looked at each other like they had the goods on my story. I swallowed another gulp of the sour wine.

"What about this effigy?"

An off-duty palace guard blared to the crowd: "Wearing Facundo Salazar's second best coat and an old army officer's jacket! I was there when Salazar's wife recognized the cloak. Screamed her head off. Thought her husband was dead, but the body was a sack of straw, painted with pig's blood."

"Now you've got Salazar mixed up in this story, but in truth, it reeks of witches," piped a little man with a quivering goiter. "Had to be them. Who else but witches murder in bands?"

"Indios, you fool," replied another.

"But who can travel and not be seen?" the quivering goiter insisted.

"No sign of anybody," said the carpenter. "Flew in, flew out."

"Witches change their shape anytime they want," the off-duty guard concurred. "Turn themselves into cats, or owls. They favor owls. A witch woman could fly away over the hills and in minutes be sitting at her kitchen table, looking as innocent as one of her kitty cats."

I drained the dregs, thinking I *had* seen a witch, a real witch. Not a cat, not an owl, but a flesh-and-blood woman in a black dress, walking on a ridge top, far away from town. And I had seen the nature of the woman's work: knife cuts and the black, gory bird that terrified my horse.

I set the mug on the bench and slipped out of the cantina. I headed into the smoky street to report to Sebastian, leading Rosinante. Being back in town made my already skittish mare even more nervous. Her hooves danced on the stony road and she kept butting my shoulder with her muzzle. I pulled her past a corral jammed full of sheep waiting to be transported south, and then through the growing jumble of parked carts and wagons on the plaza.

What were they saying? That the fancy cloak wrapped around the effigy was Facundo Salazar's? Salazar, wealthy merchant, member of the town council, a man whom Anza often appointed to important posts in the colony? How could the murderers have come by that man's cloak, even his second best one?

I crowded into the doorway of the sergeant's littered office in time to see Brother Severiano standing toe-to-toe with Sebastian. The lay brother who'd been at Deer Creek jabbered away, stabbing his finger into the sergeant's face.

Standing beside the cleric was a youth I didn't recognize, partly Spanish but with a little Indio mixed in, red faced and hard-eyed, his wrists roped together with strong rawhide. A guard stood near Sebastian, musket at the ready.

"Mark my words, sergeant," Brother Severiano shouted. "I too witnessed every bit of what you saw there beside the creek. How can you ignore evidence of the devil's work? A dead body spirited away, and by whom? Replaced by a figure of a man with blood smeared on his pants! Only agents of the devil would put their hand to work that vile."

Sebastian stepped back from the ranting brother, whose voice, trained in oratory, rose to overcome the two-foot distance. Severiano demanded, "Remand your prisoner to me and the protection of the church. You cannot accuse Toribio of a crime, when he has only done his duty by denouncing the women who participated in this murder."

Severiano saw he was at risk of being evicted, but stood his ground and seethed, "Your whole colony is lax. Everyone in New Mexico encourages the devil's arts. You call these medicine women healers. Those of us from the Christian world call them evil. Not a single person here stands up to the usurpation of souls by the dark one. I've even seen Santa Fe's curanderas receive the sacrament in church."

Sebastian had heard enough. "Get out of here, Severiano. This is not your jurisdiction. Guard!"

Severiano unleashed his deepest voice. "The supreme judge of my jurisdiction rules all of heaven and earth. You will regret this action, sergeant!"

The guard was clever. He moved the man along, but not by force. Severiano bumped against me as he left, yanking his hood over his head.

Sebastian exhaled noisily, before rounding on the young man called Toribio. "You burned the old curandera's pigsty; then roused a mob to move into the barrio and harass solitary women. Why would any thinking man hold Margarita Chacon's head under water? You might have killed her, or torched the whole bosque. And you were in possession of a hawking blade, illegal weaponry."

The sergeant backed off for a moment and turned to me. "In his delusion this thug insists Cruzita is one of the witches involved in Deer Creek," Sebastian explained.

"That's impossible." I scowled at Toribio. "Cruzita wouldn't hurt anyone. She's too old to leave her hearth.

Besides, when she was younger, that woman was mid-wife to half the babies in this town. Probably you too," I told the ruffian.

"That's a pack of lies!" Toribio retorted. "Cruzita lives in that hut near those other brujas. Did you see where the vultures roosted today? On the dead cottonwood right above Cruzita's shack. And Margarita threw the evil eye at Damiana Bustos at the well."

Sebastian turned on his prisoner. "Birds roost in a tree, so you burn down an old woman's byre!" The sergeant was almost yelling. "A girl has dust in her eye, and because of you, the town crazies try to drown her. Corporal, take this jackass away. Lock him up where he won't be hurtful to the parish."

Toribio threw back his head. "Throw me away, mister, but you need to know something. There's a woman in that barrio who had the means to be in possession of Facundo Salazar's cloak. It's clear to everyone but you that local females are involved with this Deer Creek murder. Cruzita, Margarita, Juliana, her sisters, the whole flock of them. You'd better open your eyes. You know witches steal their victim's garments and put a curse on the clothes. You should be tying those women up, not me."

I backed out of the way while the guard cinched another cord around Toribio's wrists.

Sebastian wasn't eager to rise to the fellow's bait, but he needed any information he could get. "Who's the woman who got hold of Facundo Salazar's coat?"

The man looked straight at Sebastian. "I don't know her name. But it's easy to find her. She's the pretty one, Juliana's youngest sister. Puta!"

Sebastian slapped his hand on the table and shouted, "Enough! Just because a woman turns you down, you don't call her names and accuse her of being a witch. I'm arresting you for burning Cruzita's shed."

Toribio kicked the doorframe as the soldier led him away. Sebastian ignored the outburst and leaned over his desk toward me. For the first time I noticed the weapon Sebastian had confiscated resting against the wall, a hawking blade, illegal anywhere in Spain's dominion because of the torment it causes animals. The shaft was longer than I was tall, topped by an upward facing, curved metal blade that would sever the Achilles tendon of a buffalo with a single downward thrust.

"Toribio carried that? He was going after women with a *hawking blade*?" I took hold of the hefty shaft and lifted a finger to feel the crescent blade.

"Don't touch it! He's sharpened it like a razor. See what happens when you find a stinking corpse in the woods, Nando? The worst in mankind erupts. I'm familiar with this man. Toribio hates women. Any excuse will serve. Whenever he comes in from his family's placita at Agua Fria he makes trouble, but this is the first time he's carried a damned hawking blade. Weapons like these were supposed to be surrendered years ago."

I leaned the hawking blade gently against the wall. "Toribio's one thing, but I think you've got more trouble with the trumpeting lay brother," I told him. "Severiano's feeling pious, all right."

I sat on a bench while Sebastian paced and muttered.

"The whole Deer Creek incident is eerie. Unusual. Anything unknown and the first thing people do is blame it on witches."

"It had to be Severiano who told Santa Fe the dead Indian was missing," I said, "but sergeant, who came up with the notion the effigy was a figure of Facundo Salazar?"

Sebastian rumbled, "Where did you hear that?"

"Doing my job, sergeant. I stopped in the bar to get news. The missing body and the replacement effigy were all the crowd talked about."

Sebastian raised his lip in a silent snarl.

"How did Facundo's wife see the effigy, anyway," I asked, "since we wrapped the fake corpse up in order to keep it out of sight?"

The sergeant settled behind his desk. "By the worst luck, Facundo's wife paid a call on Anza's wife yesterday. Celedonia Griego was leaving by a side door just as we were carrying the effigy in. The lady recognized the cloak. Nothing we said would keep her from sobbing and tearing her hair. Poor Celedonia thought it was Facundo, her husband, dead and wrapped in his cape.

"To get her to stop shrieking, I had to let Celedonia in on the secret. I unwrapped the effigy and showed her it wasn't real. When the wife finally calmed down, she remembered that Facundo couldn't find that cloak a week or so ago. They thought one of his nephews had borrowed it, and then they forgot all about it."

I stayed put on the bench, tired to the bone. I wasn't sure how much I cared about any of this. All I wanted was to get to Luz's and gather Marisol into my arms. It had been six weeks since I'd had that pleasure.

"Do you need me any more?" I asked. "Does the governor want to speak with me?"

"All the governor asked was to know you came back. A matter of trust." Sebastian was on his feet and pacing again. "You understand that nothing went as Anza asked. He's furious about the town flaring up, particularly at this moment. The Commander's investigative party has reached Albuquerque and is nearly on us."

I sat still, pretending to care.

"Now that the whole town knows there was a murder and the body is missing, Anza needs to find out who died and who covered it up. Facts, verifiable facts, are what will help him face down the investigator's inquiries. You're the one who laid this mess on his doorstep, Nando. Provide Anza with solid information and you'll be serving yourself, as well as your governor."

"I'll do my best, Sebastian. Night and day, nose to the ground without letup, I promise."

I took a deep breath before adding, "That brute wasn't all wrong. This murder might have something to do with a woman."

Sebastian's gloomy face perked up. "What are you saying? You know more, don't you, Nando? Something you haven't told me. Out with it."

"Miguel and I saw a woman up on the cliffs the day after you and your men were at Deer Creek."

"A woman by herself, all the way out there?"

"All alone and keeping her eye on us."

"Any interaction with her?"

"She ran when we spotted her, which was right after someone attacked my horse."

"Rosinante? What do you mean attacked?"

"Cut her flank," I answered.

"Not an accident? Not torn while riding through the woods?"

I shook my head. "Cut with a knife, and then whoever it was hung a dead raven from Rosinante's neck."

"A dead raven?" Sebastian stared at me.

"My mare went crazy. When I finally got her calmed down, I saw where a broken arrow had been shoved through the bird's body. Rosinante was terrified, and not long after, Miguel and I spied this woman up on the rim rock."

Sebastian scrubbed his head with his fingers, whether from itching or worry, I couldn't tell. "Bunch of weirdness," he said. "What are you thinking?"

"A witch."

"This government doesn't believe in witches."

"This government should have seen the condition of my horse. And there's the interesting matter of the disappearance of the body from the ramada."

"If you insist on talking about witchery, then I'd say that from the manner of the man's hanging, it seems like it was one witch against another," Sebastian conceded. "They gang up on each other, you know."

"I thought you didn't believe in witches," I challenged.

"That's the official position and mostly I agree with it, but what I think isn't relevant. Most inhabitants of this colony live their whole lives dreading witches, and I've seen what happens when the people go after a supposed witch—like if they believe they've been given the evil eye, for example."

I could tell by the furrows on his brow that Sebastian wasn't convinced by the government's position. "*If* it was done by a woman," he said, "I don't believe any ordinary female could have hanged that man by herself, nor would she have gone back into those woods alone, hidden the corpse, and strung up an effigy either. Everything you're telling me is strange, but I'm going to bear it in mind. Bear it in mind."

My head ached with weariness. "May I go now? I've got packers to pay and a lovelorn lady at home."

Sebastian waved his hand, brushing me away. "Get out of here, but stay close. Find out what the kid meant when he said Juliana's sister got hold of Facundo Salazar's cloak. The sister's name is Beatriz. Follow up on that."

I knew full well her name was Beatriz, but owing to the reason for my knowledge, I wasn't about to share that with Sebastian.

"Lock your doors tonight," he advised. "Witch frenzy's the worst. Take care, Nando. No one seems to realize it was you who unearthed this mess, except your own boys and the men who rode to Deer Creek. But if there are witches working this one, Nando, you'll be first in line for that evil eye."

I'm sure Sebastian winked when he said it, but the light in the room wasn't good and I was already heading for the door.

Luz's house was dark. I stood in the yard and looked for any sign of life. In a minute I found it, curling faintly out of the chimney against the evening sky. So, rather than break in, I knocked, and after calling back and forth, Estrella opened the door. The Pueblo servant smiled.

"Nando. You're back."

"I'm glad someone noticed. Where's Marisol?"

Estrella shrugged. "Not here. No one's here. Luz is in Santa Cruz visiting the Silvas."

The maid stood aside and I walked in to stretch my hands above the remnants of the fire. "Did Marisol go with her?"

Estrella shook her head. My raised eyebrows asked the obvious question.

"Those two aren't talking to each other. They're all tight mouth and cold eyes. Marisol left before Luz started her trip."

So much for my longed-for homecoming. Worn out, I dragged my sheepskins from the corner and let them flop open on the floor.

"I can't believe you don't know where Marisol is."

With the quiet force Pueblo people bring to a secret, Estrella shut her face. I took hold of her wrist, fairly gently, but still the girl didn't yield. "I promised not to tell."

"Even me?" I looked straight at her.

The servant shrugged and pulled her arm out of my grip.

I turned as though I were finished with her and pretended I was about to shed my shirt and pants. "Go back to bed. I'll take care of the fire."

Estrella hesitated.

"Well? Are you going to tell me or not?" I asked, not all that pleasantly.

"Marisol's fine. She's in good hands."

"Whose hands?" My voice was taut.

"Your brother's." With that the maid left the sala for her shed off the kitchen.

Depending on which brother Estrella meant, this might not be good news. Or it could be. Carlos, even though he was the oldest, wasn't married yet. He was subtle about ladies, but I was sure they figured in his life. Now that Carlos had nearly recovered from his wounds, women wouldn't resist the lieutenant's uniform or the light brown hair that fell past his shoulders when it wasn't braided tight for battle.

But would he pursue his little brother's woman? I didn't think so. Still, Carlos was human, single and male, and Marisol a lovely girl.

Marisol's sunny face rose before me: the way she looked right into my eyes with her inquisitive, teasing look, laughing at me softly, the way color rose on her skin and gave away her feelings. Most men would be moved by Marisol's special brand of enchantment.

The safer choice for Marisol would be Francisco, even though he usually was considered more risky, being the pretty brother with the dark curls and high color. Thank God Francisco was under control these days. He'd just married Luisa, the alcalde's niece, and Francisco was still stunned by his good luck. Spirited and handsome, Francisco used to attract ladies in flocks, but Luisa was a sensible woman of the gentry who wasn't about to let her husband stray.

I stretched out on the thick, smoky sheepskins to think. Carlos, off soldiering, wasn't in a position to harbor a woman. Marisol must have gone to Francisco's hacienda.

If I wanted to be with her I'd have to keep riding. First thing in the morning I would deal with customs and taxation. Next I'd pay something to my pack crew with the few coins left to me, hoping my men would accept promises of real pay coming soon.

'Stay close,' Sebastian had ordered, but I needed to put my own life together. I'd leave for La Ciénega by noon, gather up Marisol, and be back lurking around the plaza, hard on the case, before anyone even realized I'd left.

Luxury's Lap

The hacienda was in full hum when Miguel and I rode down a crease in the tawny hills toward the sprawling adobe compound. The spotted housedogs barked, geese and chickens scattered, and the ever-curious goats looked up when we rode in. Women stopped their chattering around a huge, open fire in the courtyard, ignoring their pile of washing to stare at us.

"Francisco!" I yelled through cupped hands, and my brother came out from under the wide portál in front of the main house, waving his hat and calling Luisa from inside. We dismounted beside the trough in the courtyard, and spent the next few minutes watching Rosinante and Fish trying to suck the water dry.

Francisco thrust a cup of wine into my hand. "You're back! Did you get the salt?"

By way of answer, I handed him a leather bag full of the best table salt. "Try this."

Francisco glanced at the bag, murmured thanks, but didn't open it. "Let me guess why we're honored with a visit. Could you be looking for a friend of yours?"

"You know where Marisol is?"

"Here with us and full of life, so to speak."

This was music to my ears, but my pleasure faded when Francisco said, "Our mother was not on her best behavior with Marisol. Luisa and I thought Marisol should come and stay with us. In any case we were happy for some diversion."

Francisco forced a smile. My brother's usual enthusiasm was missing. "Countless officials have been here, pestering us. In and out of the cellars, examining everything, right down to our underclothes in the chests. The government sent them to assess the extent of Alcalde Duran's wealth."

Luisa stood at his side now. "And everyone of them expects a lavish dinner, rustic songs on the portál after dinner, and afterwards a fresh bed. My desire to be the gracious Señora is wearing thin, but Marisol helps me."

I kept an eye on the doorway while they explained their grievances, hoping to catch a glimpse of my lady. "So the inquiry hasn't let up," I began. "What . . ."

"Marisol!" My favorite woman in the whole world stood in the doorway, one hand on the jamb and one on her apron, an impressive frown on her face. She was tiny, sweet, perfect, and swelling at her middle, like a woman who has swallowed a cantaloupe. I stood dumbfounded, appreciating her unexpected grandeur. I wanted to bury her in an embrace, but there was something about that frown.

"Hello, Nando."

"Hello, Marisol." I couldn't keep the smile off of my face.

I was moving toward her when Francisco said under his breath, "You can see Marisol's expecting. Luz hit the ceiling, said she wouldn't put up with fornication under her roof."

"What?" I stopped in my tracks.

"We tried to reason with mother, and Luisa reminded her that Marisol was very recently widowed . . ."

"But, that's my baby!" I cried.

Francisco and Luisa dropped their linked hands to stare at me.

"Amazing," said my brother. "That's what Luz said. That she was ashamed some male under her roof had caused this. We argued with her, but she said not to take her for a fool, that she could count, that she might not look like it now, but she once had a certain proximity to these matters."

"Was she rough on Marisol?" I asked them.

I liked my stepmother, but Luz could be severe. I looked from one face to another. Marisol still waited in the door, with maybe a twist of wryness at the corners of her mouth. Francisco was giving Luisa an 'I told you so' look.

"Luz wasn't exactly mean," my brother said, "but she made it clear that Marisol was not to be in Santa Fe right now. 'You boys sort it out and let me know who's accepting responsibility here. I conduct a Christian household.' "

I put up my hand. "Enough."

Marisol hadn't let go of the doorjamb, so I walked over and threw my arms around her. She more or less tolerated the hug. There was even less response as I pulled her against my side.

"Meet my *novia*," I announced. "There will be a wedding long before this baby needs christening."

Marisol's fingers tapped on mine behind our backs, but I couldn't read the code.

Then she undid me. Clear enough for everyone in the courtyard to hear, family members, laundresses, Miguel, the chickens, dogs and burros, Marisol turned to me and said firmly, "We'll talk about this later, when we're by ourselves."

I looked down at her, dumbfounded. What a way to receive my offer of marriage! But Marisol unwound herself from my grasp and walked over to the pile of clean linen where she made herself busy folding a sheet. Luisa pulled something

51

dainty off the line, took Marisol by the hand, and led her into the house.

I turned to Francisco. "Was I just rejected?"

My brother rotated his palms to the sky.

Not sure where I stood with any of these people, I retreated to formalities. "Do you mind if Miguel and I put up here for the night?"

Francisco fumbled a few words to cover my awkwardness. "What do you mean? You're always welcome in my home. We're so bored down here, and worried, and no one can leave the ranch without permission."

"A rich man's captivity?"

"You named it. Christ, Nando, it's grand to see you, but what on earth is wrong between you and Marisol?"

I shook my head, feeling darker by the minute. "I've only been gone six weeks. Everything was fine when I left. Francisco, did Luz punish Marisol?"

"She didn't beat her, if that's what you mean, but Luisa decided we'd better get Marisol away from her. Having your girlfriend here has been good. Marisol hated town and my wife was lonely."

There was a firmer set to Francisco's face than I was accustomed to. "I do what I can to please Luisa Piña Diaz, but these investigations and our isolation are wearing on us," my brother admitted.

"I can see why, having to sit in the lap of luxury." I waved my hand toward the cluster of servants attacking the laundry, the spread of harvested fields and the munching herds beyond the hacienda's walls. Francisco didn't respond.

"When did Marisol start to show?" I asked.

"You know men don't notice these things."

"Or talk about them either," I added.

"More than a month ago," he conceded. "She's getting bigger fast. Luz hasn't seen the most recent increase. The women are wondering if maybe the father is *not* one of the Aguilar boys."

I clamped my lips to keep from blurting words I would regret.

"I'll go talk with Marisol, but not until I've pulled myself together."

Francisco nodded.

The happy reunion was long gone. My brother and I stood together feeling glum. How had everything gotten so complicated? I'd planned to tell Francisco about finding the corpse at Deer Creek once we were alone, but now I didn't want to add to his burden. Besides, I wasn't sure how many people I wanted to know that I was back in the governor's employ.

I'd risked this new job to rush to La Ciénega to get Marisol, but the woman wouldn't even let me touch her. I was supposed to be tracking down a clutch of murderers somewhere east of Santa Fe, but how on earth was I going to figure out who the dead Indian was when there wasn't even a body any more?

I needed time to think. Alone, I led our horses to the creek and stood beside them awhile, watching the golden leaves speckle the dark surface of the running water.

I left Rosinante and Fish to graze with the hacienda's herds and was walking back to the house when I heard Francisco's voice shouting again, hallooing over the fields. I hurried to the top of a hill to see who followed so hard on my heels. Could this be about Deer Creek? A clutch of indistinct riders soon turned into a dozen uniformed troops. Our brother Carlos rode in the fore, leading them to Francisco's hacienda

Carlos showed off his recovered strength by springing down from his long-limbed gray. No one had expected him to get past the injuries he'd sustained last spring, but he'd done it.

I watched the happy family greeting from a distance, while I made my way across the lumpy fields. Carlos grasped Francisco, and with an expansive sweep of his arm admired the fine ranch his kid brother now possessed. He hugged Luisa in a reserved sort of brother-in-law way. When Carlos saw Marisol, I took note that he planted a bold kiss on her glowing cheek and she beamed up at him. Someone must have pointed me out, because Carlos leaned back and bellowed my name, urging me to hurry across the stubbled pasture.

It had been a month and a half since I'd seen this brother. I waved at him, pretending I didn't mind at all that he'd just kissed my girl.

"So they finally let you out," I said, clasping his hand.

Carlos was downright gleeful. "I'm meeting Facundo Salazar. Anza's made him the Commissioner to the West. My men and I are accompanying him to Zia, Laguna, and Zuni. Anza's in the process of shutting down three missions, and after that we're going west to pressure the Navajos."

So I wasn't in trouble for leaving town. "That's a sturdy looking group of men there."

"Closing missions isn't a popular move of the governor's, but his orders come straight from the king's exchequer. Economize. Minimize the expense. The king of Spain has been pulling all the quilts onto his side of the bed for years now, leaving the Church out in the cold. He wants more for himself and less for the clerics, so of course there's resistance. The Franciscans give lip service to compliance, but they've had no problem firing up their Indians before."

"You expect trouble?"

Carlos steered us away from the servants and said in a low voice, "Maybe. Salazar's tough. Knows his stuff, but he can be harsh. You'll see when he gets here."

Francisco stepped back and asked, "The Commissioner's coming here?"

I wondered whether Francisco was worried or impressed. Myself, I was eager to get to know the man whose cloak had so recently been draped around an effigy.

"About an hour behind me. I'm sorry to spring this on you, but it was the best chance I had to visit you before heading west. As for Salazar, I think he is curious to see the alcalde's home; probably has his eye on it for his own family," Carlos laughed. "You do have extra rooms, don't you, enough to put him up?"

Luisa was counting on her fingers. I'd just shown up and there was Miguel. Facundo Salazar would require a private room, and Carlos, a full lieutenant now, was too high ranking to be put out with the sheep. It looked like I'd be in the barn with Carlos's soldiers.

Where did Marisol sleep? I doubted Miguel would squawk if I disappeared from the hayloft during the night.

While waiting for Salazar to arrive, my brothers and I sat at the long table in the dining room. We each lit one of the alcalde's cigars and shared a bottle of wine that was much better than the crude red I'd endured in the bar yesterday.

"You left after I did, Carlos. How were the barrio women faring after the flare-up yesterday?" I asked.

"Turns out that poor old crone lost her pig in the fire. It was about the only thing she owned," Carlos frowned. "Other than a gritty feeling in the air and some nasty talk, Santa Fe's quiet for now. The soldiers locked the town down tight from dusk to dawn, and there were still patrols in the streets when I left."

"Locked down the town? Women attacked? What's going on, Carlos?" Francisco asked.

I listened to Carlos while he leaned back in his chair and explained about a vicious hanging not far from town and the resultant search for witch women. He didn't glance at me, which made me think he didn't know the role I'd played.

Next Carlos shared less sensational news from town. "Word came in a special packet that Croix wants the governor to get the north opened to settlers again. Now that Anza's Comanche friends have sworn off further attacks, people will be able to return to their ranches. Maybe even we Aguilars."

Francisco and I listened eagerly. This was the piece of news we'd wanted for years, ever since the Comanches forced us off our lands above Abiquiú. We'd scarcely seen our home since.

"As part of that same order," Carlos went on, "we're supposed to convince the Navajos that they are no longer Apaches, that they aren't even cousins to the Apaches, and furthermore, Croix won't have any Apaches tolerated north of Zuni. If the governor can push the Apaches out, it'll mean more land for the peaceful tribes. He's supposed to turn the Navajos into farmers."

Francisco nodded his agreement with aggravating complacence.

Maybe the wine had loosened my tongue, but I couldn't stomach what my brother was saying.

"What does *convince* mean?" I burst out. "If I were Navajo, I'd slaughter every last Spaniard who rode west of the Puerco, steal their horses and attack any soldier who came within a hundred leagues of Navajo soil. And I'd marry all my daughters to Apaches!"

"Christ! What burr's under your blanket?" Carlos put on his patriarchal look.

"Every time the government relocates the Navajos, half of them die of the pox and the rest starve to death," I replied, refusing to let him intimidate me. "All that bringing them onto farms means is the dons along the Rio Grande don't have to ride so far to get slaves for their spoiled daughters."

Both brothers stared at me as though I'd lost my mind. I didn't care.

"Look, I want the ranch back as much as you do, but can you blame a man for trying to stay alive? Face it, we haven't left the Indios much, and we punish them cruelly when they try to do anything about it. Our herds and crops will always tempt raiders. I think the Navajos are lucky they're related to the Apaches. Anza knows what he's doing when he whittles away at that kinship."

Carlos sent a sour look in my direction. "I'll thank you to remember that I'm the Spaniard riding into their territory, the one you'd have them murder."

"Sorry, brother, figure of speech, but think about it. Didn't you love riding on the high grasslands around the ranch? You were heartbroken when that was taken away from you. You'd better believe the Indios feel the same way."

My brothers knew what I was talking about, but by then things had shifted for them. Or maybe I'd never realized how much their situation had always been different from mine.

Here sat Carlos, now a senior military official. On the banco stretched Francisco, charming and indecisive, but just this summer he'd married the heir to the former alcalde's extensive ranchlands. What a lucky accident for Francisco. He'd had no idea Luisa was a rich man's niece when he'd helped her make the trip up the Camino Real.

Both my brothers were sitting pretty in the Kingdom of New Mexico. It behooved them to toe the government line. I, on the other hand, didn't have a thing to lose.

To placate me, Francisco refilled our cups. "We can always count on Nando to keep things lively. Now tell us, Carlos, did you talk with Anza? Did he say anything about when we'd get the ranch back?"

"I'm not allowed to say."

"Hah! Then you've got news. Give!"

"We met today before I rode out. Once more I expressed my right to have the ranch restored to the family. Anza acknowledged that the ranch was father's through all the proper licenses and years of hard work. But the governor was so vague about our returning, that I divined his real message. We Aguilars are competing against someone else. I suspect there's a new petitioner for the lands of the Piedra Lumbre. Someone important, whom the governor can't ignore."

"I thought we'd run the main contender out," Francisco said.

"And his son to Kingdom Come," I added.

"We all thought so," Carlos agreed, "but the Durans aren't the only opportunistic people around here. Plenty of officials have risen high enough to become landed gentry now, and I can think of some up-and-coming merchants who'd like more property than the patch their warehouses occupy. Also, we have to assume the governor owes favors everywhere, even inside his own family.

"Truth is," Carlos summarized, "we Aguilars are small players and Anza keeps all three of us on the run working for the colony. Which of us has time to even visit Abiquiú, much less start that rugged life all over again?"

"I do," I exclaimed.

Both brothers turned to regard me, but neither looked me in the eye. Eventually, Carlos spoke what we all knew. To my brother's credit, he said it with kindness.

"I know. I know that's what you want, Nando, but it isn't how the world works. Under the law, Anza can't possibly grant the best grazing lands north of Santa Fe to a half-breed, even though he's in your debt. He simply can't."

"But," I argued, "he could give it back to *you*, and I could be your manager. At least I'd have a living, we'd recover the property, and there'd be revenue for us all; for Anza too."

Memories rose of the soft green meadows beside the stream, and of the encircling red rock cliffs that protected our home. High on those ledges, beneath the soaring flat-topped mountain we called Pedernal, sprawled the ruins of the old pueblo where we'd roamed as boys, playing games in the evenings after we'd penned the sheep in the ancient stone corrals.

I must have let my longing show, because Carlos leaned forward to appease me. "Nando, can't you see, because the governor's got me serving in other parts of the colony, Francisco's otherwise engaged, and because you're not viable as an heir, Anza has every excuse *not* to do what's right? A governor needs to keep all his options to curry favor and pay off political debts. When it comes to honoring our claim, the governor will take any out he can find."

Carlos looked at something deep in his wine cup before saying, "At least he brought the matter of our ranch up with me, face to face. That meant he wasn't dodging us altogether. I think it was his way of getting me to understand the predicament he's in."

Pamela Christie

Another Man's Child

Before I went to find Marisol, I dove in the pond to wash off the trail dirt and to clear the alcalde's wine out of my brain. When I came up from under the dark brown water, Marisol was sitting alone on the bank. I took it as a fine omen she hadn't let me get too far away. Marisol needed to talk too.

I pulled on my shirt and pants and walked over to her. I sat behind my lady on the grassy bank and wrapped my arms around her. I patted Marisol's round belly and nuzzled my face into her thick hair. My finger gently touched the faint birthmark on her forearm, wanting to trace its familiar butterfly shape. Embarrassed, Marisol pulled her arm away.

I was warming up in the sun and started to turn Marisol toward me, eager to take advantage of our first moment alone together. I didn't understand why she sat stolidly on the grass, refusing to soften into my embrace.

"You shouldn't have done that," Marisol finally said, in a sharper voice than I had heard her use before.

I massaged her shoulders slowly before I answered, "Done what?"

"Asked me to marry you in front of all those people. Told them this is your baby."

I waited to hear more, rubbing her back in the warm sunlight. I was encouraged that she went on letting me.

"But I want to marry you, and it *is* our baby, isn't it?"

Marisol's voice was quiet but firm, as she straightened me out. "My counting was wrong, Nando. I can't pretend this baby is yours. Look how big I am! It has to be Arsenio's child I'm carrying. I can't make you change your whole life when you're not the father."

My hands slowed their movement across Marisol's warm back. Even my fingertips were listening to her words.

"If I had a choice, I'd go home now to my farm on the Chama, but I don't have a choice. I need to be with people until the child is born. I'm sorry to burden your family, but there won't be anyone to help me within leagues of my old place. I'll leave soon after my baby is born. Then you won't have to trouble about me any more."

Mother of God! Why hadn't I whisked her off to the padre three months ago when Marisol had first told me she was having a baby? Why hadn't I made it impossible for her ever to leave?

"But Marisol, I don't mind if the child came from your husband. The man is dead. I want to be with you . . ."

I don't think Marisol heard my words. She had risen to her feet and was walking toward the house. Her sturdy little body took the slope without pause, so goddamn strong and righteous she was making me furious.

I jumped to my feet and yelled after her, "I'm going to Santa Fe tomorrow. I'm selling my salt to the captain of the caravan, so I'll be able to pay the padre for our Mass the moment you change your stubborn, irrational mind!"

Marisol stopped and turned, put her hands on her hips and shouted back, "What do I care about Marriage Mass and Christian households, anyway? I know what I'm doing, Nando. Leave me alone!"

I wasn't giving up. Yes, I had to get back to town, and fast, but it could wait until tomorrow. For now, my best plan was to stay close to Marisol and convince her she was wrong. Somehow I would ferret out Marisol's real reason for rejecting me. Had she realized, now that she'd been exposed to town ways, how dim my prospects were?

Commissioner Facundo Salazar was due at the hacienda any moment, one of the most prominent merchants in town. I'd stay and get to know the man. Maybe Salazar could help me get a start in this salt trade. I needed to make as much money as I could in order to marry and set up a decent home.

And just what had Luz said to Marisol that evoked that bit about Christian households? My stepmother and I would definitely be having a conversation, and when I was done with Luz, I needed to talk to a few ladies who knew about babies. Couldn't some women puff up like a piece of fry bread earlier than others?

Marisol once told me that her late husband, Arsenio, barely knew how to do it. Marisol had been decidedly eager for my attentions when I found her last May. Hadn't she told me right in the middle of that wild night when the alcalde was arrested, that I had made her a baby? And now Marisol had the boldness to deny all that?

Christ, if I weren't so tired and sore after the salt trip, I'd grab Rosinante and be out of here at a dead run. Someone had better write a guide to women's souls. They're as changeable as weather. More!

At least with the distraction of Commissioner Salazar arriving tonight I could hide in a corner and lick my wounds without everyone watching me. I found a patch of shade under a piñon tree on the ditch bank and spread my manta there to rest. But every time I forced my eyelids shut, I saw the face of the dead man in the ramada, pleading with me to cut him down and return his dangling feet to earth.

Slapping at mosquitoes, I fell into a hot and troubled sleep.

Self-Righteous and Arrogant

The man who rode in to the compound right after sunset was lean, tall, and handsome. There was no gray in his hair or beard. Facundo Salazar sat proudly on a sleek Arabian with his escort riding deferentially behind him, ribbons fluttering on their lances.

Facundo Salazar, Anza's appointed commissioner to oversee closing missions in the west, bespoke aristocracy. High cheekbones, an aquiline face, glossy boots and a gleaming coat with no dust on it, never mind the leagues of travel, made each of us in the yard ashamed of our own frowsy appearance. Even my handsome brothers started brushing themselves off and Luisa sped into the house to tweak the arrangements for the commissioner's comfort.

It was clear from the way Salazar dismounted, and the manner in which he strode toward the small group that awaited him, that the man was fit, though he may have been as old as forty. Carlos had told me that this commissioner, one of the richest merchants in Santa Fe, slept on the ground beside his men and tolerated no vices in those who rode with him.

Salazar left with my brothers to talk in the dusky sala. They were being so stiff around each other I was relieved when they asked me to oversee stabling the horses and finding pallets for Salazar's men.

I recognized one of the soldiers, Baltasar Bernal, and we took a few minutes to smoke together in the shade behind the barn. I told him what I'd been up to at the salt lakes, then asked, "Baltasar, is this Salazar the man I need in order to market my salt?"

"Depends whether you're going to sell it locally or ship it south. If it's for local use, you couldn't do any better than getting on Facundo Salazar's good side. If you want the higher prices in Chihuahua, you'll have to lick the boots of Alfonso Vial who runs the caravans to Mexico.

"Let me tell you how to play this." Baltasar poured a little of my punché into a cornhusk, fussed around lighting it, then took a deep draw.

"You've got to make Salazar think he's putting one over on Vial. Any chance he has to one-up his rival will get Facundo's undivided attention. Salazar intends to become the most successful merchant north of Chihuahua and it rankles him that so much depends on Señor Vial and his cronies down south.

"I don't know why Salazar fights to keep adding to his fortune. His wife's barren. The man has no heirs, just a house full of warring nieces and nephews. You'd think building a dynasty wouldn't matter, but I've never seen a man so eager to get ahead."

The field workers were coming back now, stacking their tools by the barn, and Pueblo boys were urging a small herd of good-looking horses into a corral where the animals would be safe from raiders through the night. I pinched out the remainder of my smoke and returned the butt to the pouch at my waist.

The sun was gone. Now red and gold silhouetted the pointed, black mountains just west of us. Ignoring the shouting beauty, we turned toward the house.

"Coming?" I asked Baltasar.

"Wait a minute, Nando."

Baltasar caught up and said, "I'm going to let you in on a secret. Señor Salazar instructed me to find someone in the household who could help keep this under cover."

"This?"

Baltasar beckoned. I followed him into the barn, and through the dusty gloom made out what the soldier's finger pointed toward. Sitting primly on the hay was a friend of mine, someone from the wilder days of my youth: Beatriz, a pert young woman who had helped many of the young men in Santa Fe rid themselves of the inconvenience of their virginity.

Beatriz wore a close fitting jacket, reminiscent of a soldier's uniform, above a long black skirt. Serviceable boots poked from beneath the hem, and her broad-brimmed soldier's hat lay by her hand on the straw. There was a pair of rolled up trousers on the hay. Apparently she had ridden in as one of the troop.

Beatriz had the good manners to pretend we'd never met. She sat archly, clutching her skirt around her ankles.

"We need assistance," Baltasar said. "Señor Salazar requires the company of this lady for his last night in civilization. The girl is dear to his heart and it's his wish not to be parted from her until the last possible moment."

Curly black hair fell in a thick tumble over Beatriz's shoulders. Her lips were slightly rouged with the stain of a crimson flower. She looked at me and lowered her eyelashes.

"What would you have me do?" I asked.

"Since the commissioner is a married man, he wishes her presence to remain a secret. Could you see that dinner is brought to the lady in some place more suitable than this barn, and after the family has retired, escort her to Facundo Salazar's bedchamber?"

It was shaping up to be a long night, but I could barely keep the smile from my lips. This could give me leverage with the richest merchant in town, and then, too, Beatriz's tantalizing companionship had never been a problem for me.

It dawned on me why Toribio suggested that Beatriz could indeed have been in possession of Facundo Salazar's cloak, the one found draped around the effigy.

"I may be able to help Salazar, but there are risks."

Baltasar pressed several coins into my hand. I felt their weight and added, "I'll do what I can to facilitate the Commissioner's comfort. Baltasar, let's you and I escort this lady to a better place."

That couldn't be my own room, since it had been commandeered, but I remembered a little casita where Alcalde Duran had once housed travelers. The hut was a poor jacal, made of upright juniper posts dug into the ground and plastered with mud, but it was surprisingly roomy. There were tallow lamps at the ready, a banco with blankets and a sheepskin, and a table strewn with the ranch manager's papers. There wasn't a window, so it would be safe to light the lamp.

"Baltasar, my kit, please," Beatriz ordered politely. The soldier scanned the cabin with his eyes, nodded and left.

As soon as he was gone, Beatriz had all the privacy she needed to work her magic on me. "Thank you Nando." She extended her hand, and not knowing what else to do, I kissed it.

"I heard that you came back to live in Santa Fe. Is that true?" she quizzed.

Was Beatriz asking why I hadn't looked her up? Her absolute beauty, the fragile Spanish rose kind of beauty, assaulted me, and I pressed my heels into the dirt floor to keep myself anchored.

"I came down from Abiquiú a while ago, but I've mostly been traveling since then."

"Are you avoiding me Nando?" Beatriz was looking down, fumbling with the silver buttons on her nicely fitted jacket, as though she might need help unfastening them.

I kept my hands at my side. "No, of course not. It's just that if I'm to bring you supper and not be noticed, I need to go back to the house now. Will you be comfortable if I'm gone for a while? I'll have to be careful, to not take any chances with your secret."

"I'll be fine. You'll find a guard posted nearby. I would like a little wine with my supper too, if that's possible." She looked up into my eyes from beneath her thin, shaped brows.

"I'll see to it." I backed out the door, as though she were some kind of royalty, then I stopped and cried, "Beatriz, friend! This is ridiculous!" I strode over and threw my arms around her. "Are you all right? Is this good for you? Is Salazar treating you well?"

She hugged me back and smiled.

"Nando, he adores me. I didn't really want to travel in this costume, but he insisted I come. Facundo's desperate because he has to be gone from me for weeks." She set my arms gently aside and regained her former composure.

I looked her over carefully, "Are you sure?"

"Almost." She tapped her boot on the floor. "Bring me two cups of wine, will you? Being with Facundo takes some getting ready."

"I may be able to find a whole bottle. Alcalde Duran left a trail of jugs behind. Maybe you and I can share some later."

She put her fingers under her chin and assessed my face.

"Not in the old way," she said.

"No, not in the old way. But we're friends aren't we?"

"Always. You were wonderful, Nando."

I laughed and asked, "How can an eighteen-year-old virgin be wonderful at anything?"

"Oh shut up and get my dinner, will you?"

And I was gone.

Making arrangements for the commissioner and Beatriz gave me something to talk to Marisol about, other than the treacherous topic of our future. Having enlisted Marisol, the danger that she would find me sneaking around with another woman was neutralized and I'd gained an accomplice. It was Marisol who carried supper out to the casita and much later, under the thin sickle of moon, she escorted Beatriz through the house to Facundo's bed.

When I joined the family in the sala, I saw that the atmosphere around the commissioner and my brothers had eased now that they'd emptied a jug of wine. We unrolled sheepskin mats in front of the blazing fire and even Salazar stretched out on one, using the wooden bench as a backrest. He sang the praises of his lovely wife Celedonia, lauded her excellent housewifery and boasted of her ability to oversee his business in his absence.

Having just hidden his mistress, it was clear to me that Salazar was a liar. I also didn't like how the commissioner crowed about pitting himself against both the governor and caravan master. Salazar formed the third side of a triangle of animosity between the forceful Anza, and Vial, the chief procurer for the government. And why not? By his own admission, Salazar was the owner of the most significant warehouses and weaving factories in the kingdom.

Salazar took a hearty gulp from his cup and continued on about himself. "Of course, I will not allow this business of being Commissioner for Indian affairs to interfere with my role as the main purveyor of goods in the colony. I have outlets not only in Santa Fe, but near the garrison in Santa Cruz, and even in the village of Albuquerque."

Wine ruddied his cheeks. "If you wish to purchase something in New Mexico, you purchase it from Facundo Salazar. Without me you haven't got a prayer."

As the budding salt merchant, I made a point of refilling Salazar's cup.

"Who handles your affairs while you are away?" asked Francisco.

"I have excellent factors whom Celedonia oversees. She is teaching my nephews matters of finance against the day one of them must inherit from me."

Carlos paused politely so Salazar's drama could be appreciated by all, then asked, "Do you suppose Anza will ever forgive Vial for supporting the men who traveled to Arizpe to file a complaint about the governor?"

Salazar smirked. "Anza would have hanged Vial on the plaza in a heartbeat if Commander General Croix hadn't backed the protesters. It was Vial's horses, Vial's equipment and Vial's contributions to their commissary, that enabled that mission."

"But Alfonso Vial didn't go with them?"

"Of course not!" the commissioner blared. "Vial's far too lazy to ride hundreds of leagues across a trackless desert. When he leads the caravans south, he travels in a huge wagon crammed with comforts and doesn't emerge for days. But it's no secret he provisioned the men who went to Arizpe in blatant defiance of the governor. Vial didn't care one bit if Anza repositioned the garrison on the other side of the river, but by underwriting those who did, the chief merchant made certain the governor got a serious reprimand from the high command. Anza has no reason to forgive him. Ever."

Salazar drank deeply from his cup. The long, elegant bones of his face gleamed in the firelight. "Vial's family's not much. He's got a weak little wife whom he recently wed, not like the strong life companion I'm blessed with. His children war with one another other, since each of his sons was born by a different mother. Gad, the man's been married four times and has buried every wife so far. This new girl had better look to her well-being. She appears to be barren, or so the women say, but I think my old compadre just doesn't have it in him any more."

In this negative vein, the man growled on. Fortunately the evening broke up early, though only I knew why Salazar was willing to relinquish center stage and go to his room.

I offered to escort the merchant out of the long, shadowy living room, to catch the opportunity to get a word in about having first-rate salt to sell.

"You are called Nando?" Facundo Salazar stopped in the hall and looked down at me.

"Yes sir. Half brother to Carlos and Francisco. I live in the capital with my stepmother Luz de Gracia."

He massaged the side of his face with a long hand, scrutinizing me.

"I understand you have done me a small favor," the commissioner said.

"I believe I have."

"I require another. Faithfully done, I will assure you that your salt will receive the proper attention from my wife, who handles my business during my absence. There will be a letter to that effect waiting for you in the morning. Should you betray the trust I vest in you, there will be consequences."

I waited.

"You must accompany Beatriz to the villa first thing tomorrow and return her safely to her sisters in the Barrio Analco. Carry this out so no one knows where she has been."

Given my unsettled state with Marisol, escorting Facundo's mistress back to town wasn't how I intended to spend the following day. Neither did I think it wise to travel on a lonely road for hours with an old girl friend.

Noticing my hesitation, Salazar stretched out his hand and placed two clanking coins in mine.

I examined them and let him watch me do it. "I'll take her home, sir. I wish you success in your campaign to the west."

Salazar was done with me. Clearly his mind was on more pressing matters as he disappeared into his bedroom. I hoped my friend Beatriz knew what she was doing. I hoped I did too.

The next morning, after Carlos and Salazar left, I found the two women asleep together on a pile of sheepskins. Using the mayhem of the expedition's departure for cover, Marisol had sneaked Beatriz out of Facundo's room before anyone could discover her and hidden Beatriz under her own blankets.

The women presented an intriguing picture, their two heads sharing the same pillow: Beatriz, typically pale and serene, Marisol glowing with her tawny high color. Rogue ideas of further adventure flickered behind my eyes, before I ruined the vignette by awakening them to get a start on the new day.

Uncomfortable Tenancy

At breakfast the common sentiment was relief that Salazar was gone. Luisa brought two letters to the table, which the commissioner had left in his room.

The first had instructions on the sealed envelope that I should present it to Salazar's wife, Celedonia. Presumably, Salazar was telling her to assist me in selling my salt.

The second bore Francisco's name. Luisa handed them to us while we ate our tortillas and eggs. After a glance at the seal, I pocketed my envelope, but Francisco opened his right then. He read the letter slowly, then silently handed it to Luisa. Being a lady of the gentry, she was able to read and did so.

The next thing the upper class lady did was hurl a handsome glazed pitcher onto the hearth. The broken shards clattered across the flagstone floor.

Francisco dodged the flying pieces and roared, "That sneaking son of a bitch! Why couldn't he have been forthright and told us face to face?"

"A roasted pig!" Luisa spat. "Fresh apples in a pie. My uncle's best wine! All the while that he stuffed himself at my table, Salazar carried orders to evict us!"

I retrieved the letter from Luisa's trembling hand and recognized the unmistakable rubric of my friend and employer, Governor Anza. Slowing down for some of the longer words, I read:

This is to inform you that the Commandant General of the Internal Provinces, Teodoro de Croix, our most devoted minister to his blessed majesty King Carlos the Third, has dispatched his representative, Don Crespín Olivas, who will arrive next week with appraisers and liquidators to oversee the disposition of the accounts, lands, and all chattels of the recently convicted felon, Tomás Duran.

Señor Olivas is to catalogue said possessions that they may be duly received into the estate of His Majesty the King, to be disposed of at His Majesty's sole discretion, in the time and manner that our Most Puissant Monarch deems proper.

As denizens of the former alcalde's estate, you Francisco Aguilar, with your wife Luisa Piña Díaz, are hereby instructed to vacate the premises of the hacienda within which this missive shall find you, as well as any and all other properties formerly owned by Tomás Duran, by the fifteenth day of October, taking only those personal possessions and servants of yours which were never within the estate of Tomás Duran.

This ruling by the hand of Commandant General Teodoro de Croix, was received by me, Juan Bautista de Anza, on the ninth day of October, year of our lord, 1782. I am hurrying his directive to you, courtesy of Commissioner Salazar, that you may be in compliance with the deadline.

May this letter find you and your wife in excellent health and may our most munificent Lord guide you to submit with good will to the ruling of your Monarch.

Juan Bautista de Anza

Luisa sank into a chair and Francisco bent over her. Marisol had entered the room while I read and looked at our family with sorrow. The dining room had grown cold. Clouds filtering in slyly from the west had blotted out the fresh morning's light, making everything look shabby, but whatever the condition of the rooms, the barns, the fields and animals, it was no longer my brother's affair. In five days he had to be out.

I hoped to God that Francisco had married Luisa for love, and not because she was an heiress. It was reassuring the way he wrapped a beautifully woven shawl around her shoulders and wiped tears off her face with his hand.

"It was an uncomfortable tenancy at best," Francisco stated defiantly, "except for being here with you, my dear. We'll go to Luz, I suppose. How far along is the addition to the house, Nando?"

"Exactly as far along as it was last time you were there. Remember, I've just spent over a month traveling to the salt lakes and back. Two new rooms, almost roofed, not yet plastered. No doors, no window shutters, no furniture and only dirt floors. The fireplaces are started, but not finished. The spaces are big. I think you and Luisa could set up household in one, and I . . ."

I looked at Marisol who was pointedly not looking at me, "and Carlos, can share the other."

I shrugged, knowing it wasn't much compared to the lavish hacienda Luisa and Francisco had enjoyed since their wedding in July. I wondered what kind of surroundings Luisa had known when she lived in Mexico? Grander than our drab mud rooms, I was certain of that.

Francisco was already making plans. "Carlos needs to be told immediately before he becomes further embroiled with Salazar. Besides, our older brother will be our best influence at the palacio. Nando, is there any chance you could ride to Carlos with this news, but without letting Salazar know?"

I thought of Beatriz waiting alone back in the chilly casita and shook my head. "I'll miss the caravan if I do. Find someone else to go; one of your servants maybe?"

I paused, regretting the job I had undertaken for the commissioner. That was when I decided not to cover up for Facundo Salazar any more.

"I'm afraid there's another Salazar secret going on around here. Marisol, will you go get her?" Luisa and Francisco stared at me.

Marisol whisked herself out of the sala and returned with a beautifully turned out Beatriz. Salazar's mistress was smartly dressed in trim riding clothes, broad hat, and veil. How different she looked from when I had known her before.

"Who is *this*?" Luisa rose from her chair, gaping at the strange woman standing in her dining room.

Beatriz stepped back. Did she actually feel shame?

"My name is Beatriz, ma'am." Her pale Spanish beauty, dark eyes and hair were oddly akin to Luisa's.

It was time I told the family what I knew. "She's Salazar's paramour. He sneaked her in last night. Couldn't bear to part with her any sooner than he had to."

Beatriz stood proudly at this description.

"The audacity of it!" Francisco, now at his wife's side, peered down at the girl who stood alone at the edge of the carpet.

"Imagine!" Luisa exclaimed. "And after being bored to death listening to Salazar's songs of praise to his unsuspecting Celedonia. What rot!"

Luisa turned to me, "What are we supposed to do with her?"

"Give her a lift back to town on your baggage cart, I suppose. Salazar dropped these into my hand to assure she was returned in secrecy to her sisters." Sheepishly, I set the two silver coins on the mantle.

"And a promise of help with my salt enterprise." I added the letter to the coins.

Francisco picked up the envelope. "Let's have a look. Our friend Salazar is so full of surprises, I wouldn't hand this letter to Celedonia thinking he's about to do you a favor. With your permission?" My brother ripped the seal apart and read the message.

"Well what do you know?" My beleaguered brother was actually laughing.

I didn't wait until he'd finished, but snatched the paper and read the commissioner's instructions to his wife. First the man spewed a great moan of hypocritical misery at not being able to remain with her, because of having to ride on the governor's mission. Then: "as to this bastard half-breed, extend him basic courtesy, but on no account offer to engage in his salt business. Push him off on Vial however you can. It must look as though we've made an effort, but Vial is even less likely than I to want to do business with a Ute. Nando's father's widow unaccountably includes him in her household, so please, my dear, conduct this with some appearance of care."

Now I was the one in the chair while someone kneaded my shoulders. I looked up hoping it was Marisol, but it was my brother's wife seeking to comfort me.

"Listen," I said, my face between my hands, "let me take Beatriz back and get her out of here. It's not entirely her fault what's happened, and her presence will only complicate matters. You can send my friend Miguel west to tell Carlos. Marisol can ride back to town with Beatriz and me."

"No she won't!" Luisa put her foot down. "She's too far along to travel on the back of a mule. She can help me pack and then ride on a cart."

"And where will you unload me?" Marisol asked with anger in her eyes. "Luz made it clear that she doesn't want one of her sons' pregnant lovers under her roof."

Francisco and I looked at each other, completely lost on this one. Luisa stood with arms crossed, waiting for one of us to come up with a solution.

Beatriz said, so timidly that at first none of us heard her, "I know a place where Marisol can live."

"And where might that be?" Luisa's tone was unpleasant at best. "You may be wearing fancy clothes, Beatriz, but aren't your sisters the witch-women of the Analco? If Nando is claiming this baby, that is no place for an Aguilar to be born!"

Tempers were flaring. Beatriz looked ashamed, Marisol, desperate, and my brother frazzled at the abrupt change in his life. I had no idea how to protect my baby and its mother when Marisol wouldn't let me near her.

"Luisa, is there any more chocolate?" Francisco suddenly asked, his first bright idea of the morning. "Let's all sit down, even Beatriz, and figure this out. There's no point in attacking each other just because the government has seen fit to put us in the street. And besides, Luisa, in our new circumstances, we might be very glad ourselves of a bed under the witch-women's roof, so take care."

His wife, having received the first reprimand of her married life, used fetching the chocolate as her excuse to quickly leave the room.

Before long, Francisco and Luisa resumed their places at the head and foot of the table.

Francisco began. "Luisa, forgive me please. Enough's happened this morning to shake up even the happy-go-lucky fellow you married.

"Beatriz, what you were offering was kindly meant. Do you indeed have a place where Marisol could stay for at least a few days until we get Luz's rampant morality under control?" Luisa smiled at this and the atmosphere began to improve.

"You were right," Beatriz responded. "Marisol shouldn't stay with my sisters, though they're healers, not witches at all. Not after what just happened to the curanderas in Santa Fe.

But I know a woman whose husband will be leaving with the caravan and who's afraid to be left alone. She'd like a companion."

Rising to my feet I blurted, "Marisol will not become any woman's servant!"

Marisol responded to my outburst with a scornful laugh. What other kind of life had she ever known?

"Who is the woman?" Francisco asked Beatriz.

"Doña Aurelia Inez, wife of Don Alfonso Vial," she said simply.

Luisa exclaimed, "The rich merchant's wife! *You* are a friend of hers?"

Beatriz nodded meekly. "Aurelia came to my sisters for a love tonic. Don Alfonso hasn't been himself. I was the person who delivered the medicine for them. The man's wife is very lonely, so we started talking. I felt sorry for her and came more often. Aurelia is quiet and kind. Marisol has been to Aurelia's house too, so I think this could work."

It sounded plausible enough, if you could accept the wife of one of the wealthiest men in the colony befriending a prostitute. Was Vial out of his mind?

I looked at Beatriz for a clue, and there it was, all over her pretty face. A beautiful, experienced tart, someone who could take over repugnant duties from the shy, child-like wife. Someone who could administer just the right tonic. Oh, dear Beatriz! The two strongest men in the colony, and archenemies? No wonder Salazar brought her with him. He didn't dare leave her alone. I had to act fast to disentangle my family from Beatriz's love mischief.

"I'll take Beatriz back to Santa Fe now, this morning. I'd like Marisol to travel with you, Luisa, when you come. Luz will soon be more accepting. Haven't you noticed how babies make her melt? If you can spare a couple of men I'll hurry to make one of the new rooms habitable for you."

"Unfortunately, our servants belong to King Carlos now," Luisa replied flatly.

Francisco stepped in. "However, they haven't been counted yet. I'll ask who wants to return to the pueblo and who might consider a life in town. Nando, why not let us visit Doña Aurelia and make a decision then? We'll see that Marisol is properly taken care of. We've grown very fond of her."

Would curanderas be better than a lecherous old potentate? I had reservations about putting Marisol anywhere near Vial, but out of options, I said nothing more.

Everyone stood, cleared cups, grabbed cloaks and hats and disappeared into various areas of the hacienda. Whatever could be saved from the grasp of the king's liquidators had to be gathered and sequestered right now. I was certain that a fair portion of the alcalde's personal effects would find their way into the carts, baskets and saddlebags of all who were counted among my brother's friends.

From what I knew of Governor Anza, he had most likely arranged it this way, giving us a few days notice, unsupervised, before the official thieves moved in.

Padre On the Rocks

Only a few hours after the revelations of the morning, Beatriz and I were riding side by side over stony ground. We wound around the base of a small mountain, sometimes catching shade from clumps of blue-green piñon trees. I led a pair of mules draped with old leather bags and shabby wicker panniers stuffed with riches from the hacienda.

Not long ago, two people on horseback would never travel this back route, but the natives close to town were friendlier now. Thus far we hadn't encountered anyone, but when rounded a massive red boulder, my gentle mare's ears rolled back and then she nearly threw me. Square in the middle of our track sat a hooded man.

I clung to the saddletree, just managing to hang on. I eased us toward the sprawled traveler, whose long legs jutted well into the narrow path. I pulled up and greeted the man with a sunny smile. The hood of his faded blue cassock fell back, and a silver cross twinkled on his breast. We had tripped over a sleeping padre.

The recumbent man's response to my pleasantry was a burst of expletives. He was hot, tired and cranky.

Close up, I could see he was at least twice my age, grizzled at the edges and weather-beaten. The hood of his cassock protected his tonsured head, but not his jutting cheeks or nose. The man's jagged face was peeling except for the part under the scruffy, red beard.

"It's my feet," he finally admitted. "Torn to shreds. I didn't have time to find a mule. We were told the commissioner would be arriving in a matter of days to make certain we had complied."

"You were right to get out of there. I recently met the Commissioner to the West. The man's a lying backstabber. Why no mount, padre? Apaches?"

"Not them. Navajos. They raided every western pueblo this summer. Zuni was hit twice. Cleaned us out."

That was nothing new, so I turned my attention to his ravaged feet.

"Your problem is no socks. Did they take those too?"

"No socks, no mules. Hadn't had a good meal for eons, until I stole one of their sacred turkeys before setting off. Never stole anything before. Decided it was time to learn how."

I offered the man water from my gourd. While he guzzled it, his pack tumbled onto the road, spilling a tattered pile of old blue rags and a collection of tidy linen bags.

"Altar ornaments," he grunted. "I brought them with me. Commissioner's orders. Secure the silver. Close the mission. Hie thee to Santa Fe for further instructions. Two hundred years of service and the bastards win. Franciscans to the rear, Bourbons to the fore. Long Live King Carlos!"

It was occurring to me this priest was drunk.

"Come on padre, let's get you into the shade."

All of us were tired, so I found a lone cottonwood, shimmering yellow in the afternoon sun. Before we settled on the thick cushion of leaves, I nodded in Beatriz's direction and said, "Beatriz, a friend of the family. I'm escorting her back to town."

"Beatriz," he repeated, bobbing his head at her, then proffered grumpily, "Padre Domingo, of the Franciscan Order."

Snores soon rumbled in Domingo's nose. Beatriz and I rummaged through his pack, and with a certain sense of righteousness, we tossed down the last of the sacramental wine that had so addled the man's brain.

I looked at the rangy figure, asleep there with his red face in the tawny duff, and I felt sorry for him. It must have been a hard servitude, alone at the distant mission, trying to convert unwilling natives, getting only hindrance from the government.

When the man awoke, I shared my jerky around, and tugging at a piece, the padre explained, "Twenty years I worked in the missions, mostly alone, and I made headway, I saved their souls, by damn! Until these devilish changes ordered by the governor, this consolidation of missions. Once the proclamation to close us down was read, there was no way I could remain. Within five minutes I was a thing of the past. The boys wouldn't ring the bell. No one came to my rooms in the morning to light my fires. I ran out of food.

"Just when you came along," he said, "right there where you found me, I was deciding whether to go up to Santa Fe like they told me, or turn my back on this whole thing. I could go south, you know, be in Mexico in a little while, with flowers, sunshine, poetry and plays! Intelligent conversation for a change.

"I would make Padre Domingo disappear. I could take a new name. Find a woman who'd let me live with her."

"Wait a minute. You're a priest. Women are forbidden."

"Do you think, youngster, that we aren't still men? Among all that the Franciscans forget to teach you, basic things like the native tongue, turkey stealing and sock knitting, they never mention what you're supposed to do about the lump under your garment when the pretty serving girls come to do the cleaning. No one mentions *that* while they're pounding Latin and liturgy into your skull."

Beatriz, sitting in the cool shade, flashed me a wink.

"And to cap it off they send you out to the mission field alone and unprotected, expecting you to save souls. Who out there wanted saving, anyway? Only me!"

I perched the swaying cleric on top of my mare and plodded along at his side, listening to him rave on, this time about needing to hurry up, needing to see to unfinished business in town, which seemed incredible to me, after twenty years away.

I watched the pile of mountains above Santa Fe get nearer far too slowly. It was turning into a long trip. Beatriz slept as she sat on her horse, exhausted by her exertions with the commissioner during the night.

"Bastards got us in the end. Brought us to our knees, thanks to Governor Anza, bowing and scraping to the king, eliminating missions, our precious Cities-of-God, the only civilization we've got in this colony."

Padre Domingo leaned so far off my mare to whisper his next point that I had to position my shoulder under his bottom to keep him balanced up there.

"You watch, my friend. Take the priests out of the picture, and these rich Spaniards will lose the only protection they have. Damn drums hurt my head. Glad to get out of there."

"I think you'll feel a whole lot better, Padre, once we get you back to town."

When we finally trudged into Santa Fe, the padre sneaked away and Beatriz wrapped herself like a mummy in her shawl. We hurried between mud-brick buildings down the narrow lanes, making our way to the Barrio Analco. The pitchy smell of household fires, crowded animals and urban sewage assaulted my nostrils. I'd forgotten the noxious stink of town.

My obligation to Salazar was fulfilled when I deposited Beatriz at the front door of her sisters' house. The woman was exhausted by the time we arrived and didn't stop to thank me before she disappeared inside.

Even though it was late, carts still rumbled on and off the plaza. Everyone was in a hurry to meet the deadline of the caravan's departure. Through open doors I saw wheelwrights straining in their workshops by torchlight, refitting the giant wagons. Smoke poured from the blacksmiths' chimneys. Bales of goods lay stacked under the portál by the palacio. The thump of looms was ever-present like a drum beat in the city, as merchants tried to force a few more yards of woolen cloth from the hands of the Indian laborers.

Alfonso Vial, master of the caravan, he who conducted all trades in Chihuahua for the government and most of Santa Fe's merchants, had a fat bottom. That was how I recognized him at the heart of a gaggle of self-important men, strutting into the palacio's courtyard.

His posterior notwithstanding, Vial was my main hope, now that Facundo Salazar had made clear his disdain for me and my enterprise, but there was no point trying to meet the chief merchant tonight. I was a road-weary peon whom he would brush off like a fly.

On my way home, I caught a glimpse of our reluctant padre heading straight for the parish church. In spite of his complaints he ran to get back within its walls.

The clang of hammers on iron slowed. Mothers called their children indoors. I scanned the sky above the round, dark mountains looking for weather, saw nothing to worry about, and turned for Luz's house, noticing that even though night had fallen, the pounding of the looms never stopped.

Along the Rio Grande, Just North of Albuquerque

Dawn Runners

In the starry dark, Niyol made out the gleam of his friend's smile. Niyol and Tse, with four other young Navajos, rode hell bent for a certain place by the river. They were painted, armed, and needed to be in place before dawn.

The men cantered down the leaf-littered road, between the huge cottonwoods of the bosque. Their horses' hooves drummed a song on the hard, chill, air. The Navajos bypassed the cutoff to the large hacienda on the Rio Bravo.

Head Investigator Crespín Olivas slumbered in his bed a quarter of a mile away at the fortified adobe compound. Only a yellow dog on the portál heard the running horses. The rangy animal lifted its snout toward the jagged granite mountain and howled. Dogs began to bark all across the hacienda. Muttering, Olivas rolled onto his left side and yanked the quilt over his head, trying to drown out the noise and the coming day.

Niyol, Tse, and the youths who rode with them, had no interest in the investigator sleeping in the high-ceilinged room. They leaned their horses into the long bend that moved them toward the river and the junction of two trails.

The Navajos pulled to a stop at the smell of cold campfire. Tse slipped to the ground and moved through the leafy willows. Niyol and the others took advantage of the break and put their mouths into the Río and drank. Niyol's lips were still dripping when he filled his gourd with silted water.

A man nudged his toe against Niyol's calf and pointed toward the woods. Tse stood in the willow brush waving at them, gesturing toward the east. The Navajos rose and barely making a sound, led their horses through the forest gloom. The sun had not yet risen above the Turtle Mountain.

The six young Indios crept through the woods, circumventing the leafy camp where Carlos, Salazar and the troopers slept wrapped in their blankets on the golden ground.

Niyol elbowed Tse and they snickered at the snoring sentry, his cheek pressed against the gray bark of a wide cottonwood.

Well beyond the hacienda, and now safely past the camp of the Commissioner to the West, the Navajos sprang onto their animals' backs. They rode a fast league south, before Niyol's hand dropped and they halted. Sun struck the prominent planes of his face and made his eyes gleam.

"Smell the cook fires?" he addressed his friends. "They'll be harnessing the oxen by now. You four wait in the cleft between those two sand hills. Catch your breath. I'll survey their camp. Tse, you ready?"

Tse didn't turn to nod, but kicked his paint toward the river and the ford. The Spanish party traveling from the haciendas to the west, on its way to join the larger caravan from Santa Fe, had spent the night on the western side of the Rio. The wagons were loaded with finished hides, sheepskins, spun wool, honey, tallow, and woven blankets. Riches.

Shrouded by leaves in the top of a young cottonwood, Niyol watched the encampment. Eight wagons. Pueblo Indian drivers.

Boys and women worked around a smoky fire, knocking something out of a pot, and carrying buckets to the wagons. The drivers yelled at mules and oxen, forcing them back into yokes.

From the branches of the twenty-foot tree, Niyol observed what he had come for: armed Spanish men standing by the tailgate of the second wagon, watching two Navajo girls climb into the back. Niyol noted the markings on the wagon, then his foot felt for the next smooth limb down, and the next. Without shaking the tree, he descended, and signaling Tse, they jogged back to their friends who waited in the purple shadows at the foot of two sunny hills.

Niyol lay low on the pinto's back. The horse's breath matched his own hard huffs, as hooves slammed against the earth and Niyol's bare chest felt the beat of the horse's pounding withers. His best friend, riding fast at his side, turned his head under his arm and grinned.

They hit just as the first wagon pulled to a stop beyond the ford, and the front wheels of the second wagon, the one with the girls in it, rolled out of the river. The Indians' one musket blazed a lick of fire. A mounted Spaniard let out a cry and seized his shoulder. The other wagons and riders were still struggling through the river. Arrows flashed in the sunlight. Men shouted and rearing horses churned the brown water.

Niyol, Tse and their men ignored the single shot a Spaniard got off and headed for the second wagon. The driver was a Pueblo man. He read the situation and took his chance. He stood on the wagon board and cracked his whip. His head snapped back as his mules got purchase on the gravel bank and the rig sprang forward. Wagon number two raced east out of the river, swerving onto the cart path into the bosque.

The mounted Navajos surrounded the wagon. A girl's arms stretched out the opening at the back. Niyol rode closer, leaned down, and in a clumsy struggle, dragged his sister out of the wagon, clutching her anywhere he could until he was able to sling her in front of him across the pinto's shoulders.

Tse, at full gallop, pulled a second, scrambling girl from the back of the wagon, and she, more nimble, wound her way around and over him, until she clung to her clansman's back. The double-mounted horses kicked dust into the air and disappeared in the direction of the black lava cliffs.

The Pueblo driver, eager to be free of servitude, made a gesture showing he would pass the reins to the Navajo who thundered along beside the wagon. The rider jumped, the Pueblo man grabbed him, and together on the driver's bench, they swung north into denser thickets where they could stash the trade goods as soon as the girls were safe.

The Spanish party had barely gotten their footing on the round river rocks, had scarcely found their weapons, much less any that were primed and ready to fire, before the raiders disappeared.

A burst of arrows from the last of the Navajos dissuaded the scattered caravan. One man wounded on the riverbank was enough. The travelers formed no pursuit.

Niyol let his pinto slow. The hand he'd clamped on the girl's back now took hold of her shirt and he tugged her upright, so she could lean against his chest as they rode.

"We've got you back. You're safe," he crooned to his little sister.

The girl nuzzled her head against Niyol's warm skin. She took a deep breath and said, "Thank you, brother." The freed girl leaned forward to grip the cantle, because they were plunging back into the Rio Bravo del Norte, heading for home.

Beet-Red Rage

Luz was still away. Just as well. She was going to be overwhelmed to learn that her entire family was coming to live with her in a matter of days.

I rummaged around for food and a cup of her wine and dropped onto the sheepskins by the fire. Too much was crowding my brain for me to sleep. Marisol's big stomach and closed face competed with serious worries about coming up with something to report to Sebastian soon. Scenes of tomorrow's anticipated meeting with the caravan master Vial also played behind my eyes. I tried to envision the merchant as a congenial person handing me credit slips for the salt with an uncle's fond smile, but in a swift turnabout the kindly man became a beet-red official, kicking my bags in rage until they burst and the salt spewed onto the street. Longing for sleep, I used my fists to squeeze the images out of my eyes.

Morning came. Not long after sunrise I stood in line along with other petitioners in the entrance to Alfonso Vial's courtyard. I carried a neatly wrapped package of top-grade salt.

My clothes were clean and decent moccasins covered my ragged feet.

The sun had climbed over the walls of the hacienda and was beaming its warm fall heat onto the packed earth of the courtyard by the time the portly merchant walked out of his private quarters. Vial spent a good half hour in conversation with Tito Bustamente, his trail captain. Only after the women of the household started coming into the yard and beginning their work did he even glance at the growing cluster of men who waited along with me, politely holding their hats in worn hands.

My stomach was growling for more breakfast by the time Tito came over to the man at the head of the line. The two of them disappeared through the dark doorway of an office. It didn't take long for the first job applicant to emerge. Disappointed, he slouched past the rest of us without speaking, carrying his battered musket low by his thigh.

Tito spoke to the group of us. "Anyone else here to get hired on for the trip?"

A number of sinewy fellows nodded. Tito shook his head at them. "Caravan's full. No more places. You're all too late. Should have been here months ago. And give the others waiting out there the same piece of news."

There was grumbling and hats were shoved back on, as most of the applicants went back to the road. That left two others and me.

Tito turned my way.

"What do you want with the patrón?"

"I have thirty bags of top quality salt, cleaned and properly graded. I wish to speak to Señor Vial about selling them in Chihuahua." The creases between Tito's eyebrows deepened a notch.

"Wait then. You others? What's your story?"

But the other two were no longer paying attention to the teamster. A woman had just entered the courtyard carrying a small basket. That she was saucily dressed was only barely concealed by a workaday shawl draped over her hair and shoulders. The fact that she was Beatriz wasn't concealed from me at all.

The little heels on her shoes tapped across the flagstones. She stopped in front of Tito and twinkled at him.

"Please tell Aurelia Inez her delivery is here."

Tito cocked his head in question.

"Don't worry. She's expecting me. Beatriz," she added, letting the shawl slip off her head and her hair fan out in the breeze.

It looked like someone else may have been expecting her as well. Alfonso Vial stepped into the sunlight outside the office, looking for the source of the lilting voice. Did his old face become softer, boyish even, when he located Beatriz in the shadows of the entrance hall?

Beatriz crossed the courtyard to enter the house, with only the slightest nod to me as her fresh blue skirt brushed past my legs. Alfonso Vial stepped forward so his path would cross hers, but Beatriz allotted him only a polite tilt of the head. Vial started to speak, but swallowed his words, finding it hard to have meaningful conversation with a woman's back.

I believe the almighty caravan chief was flustered and trying to cover up that fact when he strode over to me, all business again.

"What have you got here?"

"Salt for Chihuahua, sir. Top grade. It's table quality. Good enough for Mexico City, sir."

"Your name?"

"Nando Aguilar."

His eyes narrowed as he scrutinized my face.

"Luz's stepson," I ventured.

"I know who you are," Vial growled, not entirely under his breath.

"Just up from the Salinas Lakes, sir. I have thirty bags of salt."

I lifted the neatly sewn bag and pulled the drawstring at the top. I tipped it to pour a few granules into Vial's palm, but he seized the bag and poured the salt in an overflowing stream through his fingers. The chief merchant let the contents of the bag run out onto the horse dung that littered the courtyard. He flung the sack on the ground and kicked it into a patch of shriveled weeds.

My dream come true.

"Not the quality I want. You'll have to bring me better if you expect to do business with this company. Next!"

He turned to a new group of waiting men, who continued to gather in hopes of finding jobs. A full dozen of them stood silent, watching Vial humiliate me.

What did I have to lose? I spoke so all could hear and hoped my voice came through firmly enough.

"There's nothing wrong with this salt! You can make a handsome profit for yourself."

Vial delivered his venom straight into my face. "No. You're right, Aguilar. There's nothing wrong with the salt, but I don't do business with half-breeds. I don't do business with bastards either. Or Utes. Get your pestering ass out of here."

Alfonso Vial wasn't going to associate with Benito Aguilar's by-blow and he let the whole town know it while I stood there feeling like feeding him poison.

I woke up the first time that night when Luz returned home with her Pueblo servant, Feliz.

The second time I awoke was much later when a string of laden burros moved quietly into the yard. It was after the moon had set, and before any light of dawn. Muffled whispers and an aborted snort from a donkey brought me upright in my bed.

I stood in the doorway and watched Francisco's ranch manager, Amado, direct the unloading of the panniers, sending some items to the pole barn, others into the house.

I moved into the yard so as not to awaken Luz. "Good God, man! What does Francisco think he's doing? This is the first place Anza's people will search."

"All these here," and the manager swung his arm to encompass the bundles that were being dropped onto the ground, "they're household items from the alcalde's, horse equipment, things that will blend in with the Señora's possessions."

"And those?" I asked pointing through the darkness at three carts that waited in the lane.

"We're not talking about those. All but one are going north."

"You must have drenched those axles in fat. I didn't hear them come in."

"Right. Francisco made sure. He and Luisa will arrive in three more days."

"Where are you taking Duran's silver and wine?" I asked. "How do you plan to hide the alcalde's pistols, port and Spanish boots?"

"Are you sure you want to know?"

We laughed and I made my guess. "Francisco wouldn't risk going back to the ranch. Abiquiú, then. Our grandmother's abandoned house. It's in ruins, you know."

"True, but at your grandmother's house there's still a root cellar, pig sties and a cistern that's only partly silted in."

"Looks like Francisco's got it all figured out. It'll probably work. Where's Marisol?"

Amado looked uneasy.

"You do know Marisol don't you?"

"Of course."

"When's she coming up?"

"She's already here."

"Here?" My anger crackled. "Where's here exactly?"

"She went to Juliana's house, where Beatriz lives with her sisters."

"The medicine women? Francisco allowed her to go to *brujas* in the barrio?"

"Marisol will be mad if you call Juliana's family witches. She says they're her friends, important curanderas." Amado added, "She asked me not to tell you where she was going."

I rolled my eyes at the moonless sky.

"Look, Nando, I know how it is and I'm not the kind of person to keep a man worrying. Francisco's men brought Marisol in comfortably on one of the carts. They arrived just after dark."

The ranch manager must have seen frustration building in me, because he added, "The driver told me she was fine. Happy, even. Juliana and her sisters came out right away and wrapped her in a warm blanket. Marisol will be all right."

While I was taking in this piece of intriguing information—that Marisol had chosen not to live with me—silent servants moved chests off a cart and the rest of the panniers into Luz's cow barn. A bed and a table were carried into the empty shell of a room that would soon house the alcalde's heir.

Amado shook my hand and left. There was a brief squeak from a cartwheel and the rattle of a loose chain as the load bound for Abiquiú stole out of Santa Fe.

I lingered in the chilly night, fingering the edges of the blanket I'd wrapped around myself. The house stood dark and silent behind me, waiting to be completed, waiting to become home not just to a solitary old woman, but to a whole family.

My own included? Or had Marisol really finished with me? I prayed to the Christian's God only when a Spaniard forced me, but I might get on my knees soon and ask for help wherever I could find it.

A Harmless Bit of Fluff

The first part of wisdom was to finish the roof over our heads. My mind chipped away at my problems while I split wood. Thank God Sebastian had come with me to see that putrid business in Deer Creek. Anza might not be sure of me, but Sebastian had seen the effigy and seemed willing to believe there'd been a real corpse, even if it had gone missing. Still, the sergeant wouldn't put up with me stalling much longer.

And what to do with my salt now that both Salazar and Vial had turned it down? Like Vial, Salazar had refused my salt, not because of its quality, but because of who I was. Why was I surprised? People of the gentry always draw the line against upstart half-breeds, but a fine idea was taking shape as my ax spun wood chips into the autumn air.

Three good whacks and an entire limb laid itself open. A few more bursts like that and I'd have this roof covered by noon. Then I could clean up, find Salazar's laudable wife, and see what I could pull on her. After all she'd never gotten the chance to read her husband's letter, the one telling him to send me packing, that so vividly described my illegitimate birth.

Feeling better, I took time to look around me. From the roof I got a bird's eye view of the frantic preparations for the caravan's departure. Men ran rather than walked, while a woman shouted the length of the street. I smelled bread burning in an oven somewhere. At one point a herd of sheep squeezed down our lane leaving wool dangling from the rough adobe walls, and for a moment I thought I saw Beatriz and Marisol hurrying together toward the home of Alfonso Vial.

It took longer than I thought to start packing dirt on the roof. Toward evening, tired from crouching and pounding all day, and wondering when Luz would get around to delivering some promised laborers, I came down the ladder, devoured a bowl of beans and walked to the plaza. It was a few minutes before evening Mass and everyone was waiting for the church doors to open.

A tangle of weavers, released from their looms for now, stood in a cluster by the steps, along with the carters, blacksmiths and soldiers of our town. I saw Sebastian standing beside Governor Anza and the governor's wife, Anna Serrano.

Luz stood with her two serving girls under the yellow trees, chatting amiably with our neighbors. The poorer people from the Analco kept to their own group and laughed at two boys trying to tie a pig to a rail. Vial and his wan Aurelia sat alone in a carriage. Celedonia Griego, esteemed wife of Facundo Salazar, stood among family members, pointedly ignoring the Vials.

At first only one or two heads turned, then all moved at once, to observe the ruckus happening down San Francisco Street. Domingo, the pious padre, looked like he'd been drinking again. What was different was he had Beatriz in his clutches.

Shouting and prodding, the priest pushed the woman into the plaza as though she were a herd animal. Beatriz cried and tripped over her skirts, trying to get away from the man. I looked for Marisol, but praise God, she was no longer in Beatriz's company.

"Not in this parish you won't!" The priest swatted Beatriz's backside and dragged her toward the church. "I saw where you were going! Few people mistake it for a mercy mission, my girl."

Beatriz howled as the ageing, yet vigorous, Padre Domingo smacked the top of her head.

"If you won't stay home and work, I'll see that you're put in a household that makes you. And it will be a home without a husband to seduce!"

The priest was surely drunk and oblivious to the whole town watching him shame Beatriz. The padre raged at the girl who most people, except maybe the woman-hating Toribio, considered a harmless bit of fluff. People gawked as the two lurched across the wide expanse of plaza. Seldom were we treated to a spectacle like this.

"Let go. Let me go!" Beatriz pleaded with the gangly man who gripped her with one hand and thumped her with the other.

"I knew who you were the moment I saw you," he yelled. "La Bella. La Bella. Profiting by your name. As wanton as your fancy bitch of a mother! Sleeping with every man in town. Santa Fe is a Christian city."

Padre Domingo slapped Beatriz's streaming cheek, wrenched open the church door and shoved her inside. The big door shook when he slammed it.

Astonished, the onlookers started gabbling, some nodding, and others looking worried. Sebastian fidgeted uncomfortably, wanting to go to Beatriz's rescue, but he had to wait for orders. I made a note to find Domingo's victim after Mass, to see if my friend was all right.

I knew of two wives in the crowd who were paying special attention to the priest's implied message about Beatriz and husbands; women who had to be praying no one would turn to look at them.

The men and women of the upper crust began to take their place on the steps of the church ahead of the commoners. When the bell rang and we were allowed inside, there was no sign of either a battered Beatriz or the fanatic priest.

Deliberate Entrapment of His Senses

As dark closed in, I left the main town and crossed the narrow bridge to the Barrio Analco, to see how Beatriz fared. I left behind the eerie chapel of San Miguel and sped behind the jammed-together houses, past the privies, woodpiles and manure heaps that stank the same as in the better part of town.

Juliana's casita huddled in the bosque on a bank of the river, a forbidding place at twilight. Nevertheless, I needed to go there. Beatriz was my friend and had been publicly humiliated, and besides, this was where Marisol had been dropped off the day before.

Most people of the Analco were afraid of the house full of medicine women. Even though Juliana came from Cochiti Pueblo, anyone could tell her father was a Spaniard and a tall one at that. Plump Agapita, whom Juliana called sister, lived there with a child, as well as Beatriz, who had grown up in Cochiti too, but who radiated classic Spanish beauty.

Juliana sold philters and tinctures for healing and brought her medicine to anyone who asked for help, but people feared curanderas. They never looked at them directly, fearful of the evil eye, and some muttered protective holy phrases when they approached. I wondered that Juliana didn't take offense. Myself, if people treated me like that, I'd slip something into the mix, something to make them love-hungry, or to loosen their bowels, or maybe both at the same time.

I didn't knock on their door, but left the lane and entered the brushy woods. It was dark enough that my feet had to feel for the path to the old, leaning shed behind the curandera's house. I found it easily enough, and thinking I could get a clear line of sight to Juliana's only window, I slipped into the dark and slumped to peer through a chink between logs. I hoped the women would light their fire or a candle, so I could see them. I was kidding myself about coming to check on Beatriz. I really wanted to see Marisol.

It was only after I stopped moving that I noticed a discordant sound. I couldn't see my hand in front of my face, but my hearing worked fine. Something shifted behind a manger. I tensed and listened. It wasn't an animal. It was human. I held my breath.

Whoever it was held theirs.

Someone still out to get the witch women? An Apache looking to steal his supper?

My first thought was to get the hell out of there. I tiptoed fast toward the doorway, stepped outside, stopped, and listened again.

No noise came from the back of the shed now, but a man can't hold his breath forever. Hay rustled and there was a hint of a moan. Was someone sick in there? Or could it be lovers?

I stuck my head back in, just long enough to make out a figure crouched against the wall. We each froze. He made a dash for the opening. I flung my arm out and caught him in the stomach. We fell hard and I found myself wrestling with a stranger on the ground.

Skirts! The long hair of a female fell onto my face. Startled, I pulled my knee out from between her legs. Before I knew whether to hit her again or apologize, the woman simply gave up and collapsed under me. Somewhere she had learned to cry quietly. She whispered something like 'sorry,' and sobbed that she would go.

I jumped to my feet and stood so that I blocked the doorway. The woman stayed on her knees, pushing her hair back and dragging strands of straw out of it.

"What's going on here?" I asked.

"I'm sorry. I'm leaving." I still couldn't see much of anything, but her quiet voice was cultured.

"Perhaps you'd better explain." I continued to block the doorway.

"Explain yourself first!" she retorted in a coarse whisper. "I've as much right to be in this barn as you do."

"I'm sorry I knocked you down, but you scared me."

The woman kept crying and I relented. "Perhaps you should tell me what's wrong."

My eyes got used to the dark and a little light seeped into the shed from the in-and-out moon. I realized I was talking to a lady who was a lot better dressed than anyone in our household. I helped her up from the ground.

She hesitated, deciding if she could confide in me. "Do you know a woman named Beatriz?" the lady finally asked.

"Are you looking for her? I can assure you, she isn't in this barn."

"I need to find her, I need to talk to her."

"Why?"

The woman took some time before giving her answer.

"She has bewitched my husband."

"Señora?"

She sobbed, "Ever since Beatriz brought medicine for our nephew, my husband has not come to our bed. He refuses to speak when I ask why, ignores me when I beg. Beatriz has cast a spell on him. I know she has the means, because she lives with the medicine women."

"Is that why you're spying on Juliana's house?"

Perhaps there was a nod.

"I don't know if Beatriz lives here," I lied. "What are you planning to do when you find her?"

Knowing Beatriz, she had probably gone too far this time.

"I would plead with her. And if that didn't work, I suppose I would try to buy her off."

"Who is your husband?"

She hesitated. Being discovered at this was an embarrassment to her.

"There's not much I can do to help if I don't know. What's your name, madam?"

"Never mind my name!"

Tears were apparent in her voice. "He left without saying goodbye to me. He spent his last night elsewhere. I can't bear it any longer. I decided this morning to gather my courage and confront this woman. When that priest made his scene, I knew it had to be tonight."

"Why did you use the word bewitched?" I asked. "Accusing a person of witchcraft can lead to serious trouble."

"Because I know there are medicines that can do this. I know the Indians make drinks from plants that can turn a man away from his wife. My husband and I have been so in love! There is no other explanation than deliberate entrapment of his senses."

We both heard the door of Juliana's house open.

"I'm going," the lady exclaimed. "Forget you saw me. If you see Beatriz, don't tell her. This is my problem. If you encounter me in town, you must pretend we've never met. Forgive me!"

"I couldn't possibly tell anyone we've met. I haven't a clue who you are."

"Good," she said as she pushed past me.

She crossed through a scrap of moonlight before she entered the woods. Her face was lit up long enough for me to notice a livid bruise on her face, and conveniently, to see whose face it was. Celedonia Griego, the wife of Facundo Salazar. Of course!

I moved where she could see me. She needed to know to whom she owed a favor for silence. She paused briefly, and then the lady became a dark figure running into the night.

I whispered, "Fernando Aguilar. Oh so glad to meet you, madam."

Tongue and All

That took the breath out of me. I didn't knock on Juliana's door as planned, but came straight home. I lay on sheepskins in my unfinished room, thinking what it would be like to live here one day with Marisol and our child.

Her child. Possibly her late husband Arsenio's child.

No. This baby was mine. I knew that with certainty. How could Marisol have any doubt?

I looked at the vigas overhead and remembered where they had stood as trees, before we cut them in the forest. Marisol and I would make our home in this room someday. I had to believe it.

By my count, Francisco and Luisa had only two more days to vacate their home. I had to risk Sebastian's displeasure and stall another day or two, to buy time to get their bedroom roofed. Time, too, to talk with Luz and see if she would approach Marisol, make herself more biddable and invite my woman back to our home.

My mind wandered to the padre's shaming of Beatriz. What did the priest mean when he yelled, 'Just like your mother?' Who in Santa Fe had any idea whose daughter Beatriz was? Hadn't she come to town with Juliana years ago, straight from the pueblo downriver?

'La Bella, La Bella,' he had shouted. "As wanton as your fancy bitch of a mother!" I couldn't remember ever hearing Beatriz referred to as La Bella.

Beatriz was harmless; she was kind, but she had also slept with many men in this town, including me, and not so long ago. No one truly wished her ill; men adored her for a little while and then she moved on. Even the wives of her lovers knew she presented little threat. Most of them, anyway.

But Beatriz was operating at a higher level now with Commissioner Salazar, and probably the wealthy Vial as well. These weren't youths in a lusty mood. Beatriz was playing over her head, and now that the padre had attacked her, naming what the town had chosen not to see, she would most likely be forced to leave Santa Fe, or to withdraw to a dark hearth somewhere.

The light of the moon poured down the rough adobe wall in a waterfall of white, making sleep impossible. I reached for a bag of piñons and began mindlessly cracking the nuts between my teeth, thinking about Beatriz. When I first encountered her several summers ago on the path through the bosque, Beatriz wasn't much past girlhood. It was a hot afternoon during one of my few trips to the capital. My older brothers were moving my stepmother to Santa Fe after the death of our father. I wandered off, because I was tired of being ordered around by everybody, including the servants.

I struck out on my own and stayed away for hours. I found it easy enough to sneak through the wide gate into the Casas Reales, the palacio. I watched soldiers in front of their barracks, cleaning muskets and refitting their lances, and then I drifted back to the dim stables and leaned against the wooden rails, taking comfort in the presence of the horses.

I left by a back gate and followed the palacio walls, my hand brushing along the building's mud contours as I counted my steps, trying to judge its length. The wall was so long I lost track of the numbers before I was back on the plaza.

I delayed my return to Luz's by exploring a variety of streets. I peeked into the open doorways of the smaller homes and tried to peer over the walls that surrounded the grander ones. The houses stood solidly together, without a break between their walls, their pine roof beams jutting out of the rough mud walls.

Bored with town, I wandered into the cottonwoods by the river. The río was only a narrow stream, not at all like our plunging rivers up north. Sunlight filtered through the leaves and I got lost going no place in particular, so long as it wasn't home.

Beatriz was on her knees by the river. Because of the playing water she didn't hear me until I was already in the grassy place beside her. Her blouse was off and bright water trickled down her tanned breasts. It was a few seconds before I could take my eyes off them and look at the woman who thought she was bathing in private. When she raised her face to me, I lit out for the woods, but the pretty woman laughed and called out, "Stop!"

Which I did, but without turning around. Other than mothers feeding their babies, I had never seen a woman naked.

"Come here, boy."

"Uh, uh."

"You must be lost."

Her voice was friendly, teasing. I turned and saw her smile. She was leaning back on her elbows now, her bare feet in the water, her full, lovely breasts still uncovered. Her skin was browned all over by the sun. I stood there stupidly. No words were able to take shape in my mouth. I was eighteen and I hadn't slept with a woman yet.

"They call me Beatriz," she said. "Do you like me?"

I choked out something like "Yes." It was a start, anyway.

"Come here then."

This was promising beyond my wildest hopes.

I walked over, and because I felt awkward looking down at her, even from my not very tall height, I dropped to my knees on the spongy ground. She reached out one arm, pushed my long hair aside, put her hand behind my neck and drew me to her. She kissed me full on the lips and I was done for.

Looking back, I'm sure she knew it was my first time, but as I fumbled with the bundle of her skirts, and started learning how to kiss a woman, she never let on that she found me ridiculous.

I remember sunshine on my bare back, the warmth of her around me, and an explosion of light. She probably wanted to laugh out loud at me, but she didn't, just went quietly to work, showing me how to use tongue and teeth, fingers and toes, in the business of lovemaking.

When a scrim of clouds covered the sun and a slight wind lifted the leaves, we finally untangled ourselves. I helped pull her blouse back on and her skirts down, though I took my time doing it. I looked into her dark brown eyes, totally in love, and she, delicately, let me think the feeling was real. She brushed my shirt off as I pulled grasses and little twigs from her luscious, long hair. Cleaned up, we walked into the woods, arm in arm, bodies touching. She was tiny, smaller than I, so I was able to lean down to kiss her. What kind of magical apparition was she?

"Let me walk you home," I begged, and she tucked her hand into mine. We went through the cool woods, turning onto ever smaller paths which I tried desperately to memorize, and in a few minutes came to the back of a house. A small gate led into a garden filled with rows of vegetables and herbs.

"Welcome to Casa Juliana," she said. She turned and rose onto her toes and kissed me, tongue and all. I was leaning into her, clutching her waist, ready again, and eager for more, but her small hand pushed on my chest and made me stand back.

"Don't tell a soul," she said, "but I think you should come again soon."

I beamed at her and said, "So do I!" Beatriz went through the gate and shut it, leaving me on the other side.

Late that night, I sneaked out of Luz's house, threw my shirt over the head of one of my stepmother's fat hens, clamped the protesting fowl under my arm, and jogged along the labyrinth of paths until I found Beatriz's secret gate. I released the bird into the yard, stood there for a while, and then reluctantly went home. In the morning our household was in an uproar over a missing chicken, but coyotes are wily and bears prowl the edges of town, so I was never a suspect.

My level of experience had gone from zero to spectacular within an hour. Beatriz was a better teacher than I had ever known, no matter what the subject. I kept the salt smell of her on my skin for days.

I remember one more, quick tryst with Beatriz. I spotted her in the market packing up her medicines under the portál by the palacio. She let me know with a look that I could follow her. The circumstances, though sweet enough, were fleeting and couldn't match the magic of that first time along the stream.

Before we got another chance, I had been sent with the carts back up to Abiquiú and from there I traveled north into Ute country to stay with Nan, my birth mother. When I finally got back to Santa Fe, some years had passed.

By the time I encountered Beatriz down at Francisco's hacienda, my heart was locked to Marisol's, and I was very nearly a married man, one with a baby on the way. God bless and protect Beatriz though. She certainly never did me any harm. Not one bit.

The Agreed Upon Price

Facundo Salazar's wife, Celedonia Griego, was all business. An Indian woman, dressed in black, led me to the company's office within seconds of my arrival, past two chunky Pueblo youths who stood guard. I looked the Señora directly in the eye, as I clutched my sample bag and announced my plans to sell my salt to her enterprise, declaring that it must be carried on this year's caravan to Chihuahua.

Celedonia returned my boldness with an impenetrable look of her own. No emotion was in evidence, and the bruise on her face was covered with a powdery paste. The woman who had been hiding in Juliana's barn last night had made an effort with her makeup this morning.

She reached for her quill and in ink the color of dried blood wrote out an invoice, accepting my thirty bags of first quality salt. With a gesture of her ring-covered hand, she ordered the Indian woman to bring a small metal chest to the paper-strewn desk.

Sitting in the light from an open window, Celedonia counted out exactly fifty per cent of the agreed upon price of the salt in round silver coins and dropped them into a leather bag, which she handed to me. The invoice stated that the rest was to be paid in merchandise when the caravan returned the following spring.

She watched in disbelief as I signed my name to the document. My signature was neatly formed and had a distinctive air, not the usual X from a half-breed. I enjoyed watching peoples' surprise when I did a miraculous thing like write my name.

While the lady brushed sand over our signatures she said, "Word came that the caravan's departure has been put off for at least a week. Even so, deliver your goods to the warehouse before sunset. Directives from the caravan master change by the hour."

"Do you know why the delay, Señora?"

She looked up, annoyed. Celedonia Griego, preoccupied, had returned her attention to her work and was finished with me. Then she remembered she was courting my compliance and softened her expression.

"Pueblo men attacked wagons coming in from the western haciendas. Stole all their trade goods, including two women. My husband's courier rode without sleep to get word of the raid to Governor Anza and Alfonso Vial. The situation is unclear at the moment."

"I see."

The light from the window was not kind to Celedonia's face. Despite the make-up, her age was evident. The black silk of her shawl contrasted sharply with her overly white skin, and her eyes were as red as a bird's. Commissioner Salazar's wife dressed like a woman half her age, but this morning it worked against her. I thought how tender her stomach must feel where I'd slammed her with my arm the night before, but any sympathy would be out of place. She held tightly to her chosen role and I obliged her by doing the same.

"Melchora, show the man out. I have work to attend to."

Melchora wasn't tall, but she was sturdy and had a set look to her that qualified her as a good guard dog. Celedonia turned her back and didn't look up again. Melchora led me through an arched doorway, across their tiled courtyard, and out the door to the street.

"Your salt had better be good," she barked.

"I brought a sample to show the Señora. She declined to look at it."

"And you'll keep your mouth shut about last night too. No matter what transpires."

"As long as I'm paid."

"What's that in your pocket?" Melchora retorted.

"One half the value of my salt. And a piece of paper."

"You question the word of the Salazar Company?" The woman's eyes were the deep brown of piñon shells and brighter than a magpie's.

"We're in this together, Melchora. I might even be able to help."

"You got what you wanted. Now stay out of it."

I shrugged to show her I could care less about her mistress's marital problems.

Melchora declined to react, but said, "Give me that sample."

She poured some of my salt slowly into her palm, rubbing it against her fingers.

"It's good. I'll keep this and show it to the Señora later. She's likely to have second thoughts. Seeing this will calm her down. Your salt's fine enough all right. She won't lose on you."

Except for the fact that Facundo Salazar will surely be angry with his wife for buying my salt, I thought. But it wasn't my fault they were estranged, and maybe if Celedonia made her husband enough money, Beatriz's grip on the man would loosen.

I'd never had so much silver in my pockets. I almost wished the formidable Melchora would accompany me through the streets to protect me from thieves, though I doubted I could make her heel. I hastened across town to my new room, not saying a word to anyone. Pretending to be laying the hearth, I dug a deep, narrow hole in the damp ground. I put all the silver pieces in it, except for Miguel's share and enough to pay the other packers once they delivered the shipment to the Salazar warehouse.

A Downtrodden Man

I had barely covered the hole when soldiers knocked on my door and announced I was to present myself to Sebastian's office at the palacio.

Without preamble, the sergeant led me down the long length of a dark passage in the north wing of the palacio. We stumbled over crumbled adobes and made our way through a hundred years' of rubble, guided by the dim light from the cracks around the rotting vigas. Most of this so-called palace was a dilapidated wreck.

Sebastian opened the door to a cold, north cell and ushered me in. He pointed at a pile of rubbish against the wall. He had brought me here to examine the effigy.

"So real!" I said as my eyes moved quickly over the gory pants.

I picked up one of the fabricated hands, observing their construction and the hank of rope that bound them. A long piece of pale yellow grass was twisted several times around a finger, suggesting a broad, gold ring.

"Crude and cunning," I said slowly. "The woman on the cliff saw me. She knew I found the ramada and what was in it. She tried to drive me away, because she was afraid I would alert the authorities. When that didn't work, she replaced the dead man with this sinister thing."

Sebastian watched me with keen eyes, then concurred. "Someone's sending a message, one with menace. Those clothes on the dummy are a Spaniard's, and the symbolic castration is no joke. Even though you tell us the tortured man was an Indian, the threat from this effigy is to the Spanish."

I set the hand back down and Sebastian asked, "Are you aware that people really do this to witches? They hang them by their arms from a beam and leave them to die."

"Aware? Sebastian! Didn't I cut down the man on Deer Creek?"

I remembered Luz's stories about the witch days in Abiquiú. There had been screaming accusations, people dying with swollen bellies, suspects jailed or forced into servitude. The government threatened the alleged witches with hard labor chained to looms if they ever practiced their black arts again, but none of the suspects had been tortured to death.

"Governor Anza knows this murder reflects badly on his administration. So does the uprising in the west with the resultant delay of the caravan, and all at the time Croix's investigators are arriving, fervent to discredit our man.

"Get busy, Nando. You and I know blaming witches is ignorant peoples' sport, but something serious could be in the offing, and at the worst possible time."

Sebastian allowed himself a thoughtful scratch behind his ear. "Knowing you, you'll trip over the person who did this before the palacio has paid you your first peso. I'm surprised you haven't come to me with something already. Anza's been asking. I know your family is pestering you, but get them settled, then no more delays."

Resigned, I bent down and kissed the grass ring on the effigy's hand.

"Anything you say, sir. Happy to be of service, anytime I can."

Carts bearing Luisa, and all that remained of her worldly goods, rumbled into Luz's yard two days later. Francisco rode at the head of the procession.

By the time Luisa walked into her new quarters, I'd gotten the roof on, good enough for now as long as it didn't rain, and had laid flat stones at the threshold of the outer door and around the fireplace.

Luisa didn't say much to any of us before she went to her room. She worked by herself, then hung a blanket over the doorway. Luz and the rest of the household kept their voices down while the woman slept.

The following day, Francisco hauled more dirt onto the new roof with me, laboring alongside the Indian men. Soon though, he climbed down, cleaned up and walked to the plaza. Even dressed in his finery, he was not his usual self as he headed toward his interview with the governor. I was watching a downtrodden man.

The sky was clear and cold when the Indios and I stopped work for the night. There was no veil of cloud, or rising wind to keep me from sleeping in my unfinished room. I would stay dry this night, though there were still many latillas to cover.

I found Luisa, Francisco and Luz sitting by the fire. Luz bent over the long hearth, pulled out a pot of spicy chocolate and ladled some into a bowl for me.

"How did it go with the governor?" Luz asked my brother.

"I don't think he has it in for me," Francisco answered, "but Luisa's lawsuit to retain her share of Duran's property will be adversarial to the government. We and Anza will be on opposite sides." Francisco shrugged. "What else could we expect?"

Luz shook her head and reached over and patted Luisa's arm. "Praise God you're safe with us in Santa Fe."

I thought it sweet how she coddled my brother's wife, when she had driven my own girlfriend out of our home. Furthermore, Luz had been avoiding me. My stepmother had given me no opening to discuss Marisol's situation ever since the old woman and I had resumed life under the same roof.

"It was a discouraging journey," Luisa replied, "and it's left me tired."

Luz planted a kiss on her daughter-in-law's cheek, and pushed two pieces of oak together in the fire. After touching the little figure of the Virgin in the niche, she left the sala and went to bed.

I poured the chunky dregs from the chocolate pot into my bowl and scooped them into my mouth with my fingers. Francisco stroked Luisa's hand where it rested against her skirt. The three of us sat in comfortable silence.

Luisa finally asked, "Have you seen Marisol?"

"From a distance."

"I'm sorry, Nando," she said.

I shook my head. This was too embarrassing to talk about.

"Where did she decide to stay?" my brother asked.

"At the curandera Juliana's house. When I saw them from the roof, Marisol and Beatriz look like best friends. The mother of my child, and the town prostitute."

The silence grew.

"Would you rather she took that position Beatriz suggested, as companion to Aurelia, Vial's señora?" Luisa asked gently.

I growled, "That's a horrid place for Marisol! As far as I can tell, Beatriz is tupping the old merchant, who is duping his little Aurelia, and all the while Beatriz is double-timing him with Commissioner Salazar. Marisol should take one look at the situation and run for home." I didn't care whom I shocked; anyway, Luisa was no prude.

She was still considering the problem. "The caravan will set off soon, and Señor Vial along with it. Marisol might be well-served to become a companion to Aurelia."

"No! Marisol belongs here, married to me. When you've got Luz under control, I'll find Marisol and bring her home. Francisco, please sort this out. Thump your arrogant mother into shape," I stabbed my finger toward Luz's door.

"Francisco," Luisa said, turning her lovely eyes on my brother, "that's your job. She's *your* mother. I'll do what I can by paying a call on Aurelia tomorrow."

"You're on your own with that," I told her. "Old man Vial ran me off his property a couple of days ago, braying the usual stuff about half-breeds sullying his courtyard. But it wouldn't hurt for you to visit. Marisol may already be living there. And you could also find out when the caravan is planning to leave and this town can get back to normal."

The tallow candle had become a puddle of grease and the fire had dimmed to nothing. We said goodnight and went to our new rooms, they to cozy sheets on a raised bed, and I to a pile of sheepskins in the dirt. Never mind, it was my own place, something I hadn't had in a long, long while.

Smack In the Eye

I awoke in the dark. Where was that moon that had blinded me the first half of the night? I stuck a hand out to pull my blankets over my head and grabbed a handful of freezing snow. Damnation! I felt for my moccasins and turned them upside down, then burrowed deeper into the sheepskins to wait for light.

The day came, gray and frosty. Where the roof was still open to the sky, the snow on my floor lay three knuckles deep. Winter had arrived. I rose to build up the kitchen fire.

The earth on Francisco and Luisa's new roof had barely begun to settle. Melting snow would stream into their room like rain through plowed earth. I woke Francisco to tell him to start covering everything.

While they scrambled, I got my chance to corner Luz, who sat by herself at the kitchen table, small, erect, and with a defiant look on her face.

"Nando," she acknowledged me.

"Luz." I did the same.

I set my elbows on the table and leaned over, ready to get down to the problem that had arisen between us. I started out strong.

"That's my child Marisol is carrying. I'm going to marry her. I'm going to bring her back to our family where she belongs. In spite of you."

"How can you know any of that?" the old woman sparred.

My stepmother's words enraged me. I bristled at the implied image of Marisol lying beneath her oaf of a husband, the late Arsenio, possibly creating this child within her.

But other images arose. Marisol hearty and eager, joining me in bed for a long weekend last spring. Marisol playfully jumping on me and saying, 'Make me a baby, Nando!' And if I was wrong about that time, there were other nights last summer, when she came to me in the hay barn, or surreptitiously slipped between my blankets—which I had carefully placed where only Marisol would find me.

I looked my stepmother smack in the eye and to answer her said, "I know. That's all that's necessary. And you'll be sitting here aloof in your chair, sticking to your principles, ignoring a child who looks just like me, and a lot like your beloved husband Benito."

I made her strain to hear my voice when I added, "And all the while aching to play with the baby, I should think."

I leaned even closer. "Luz, what did you do to Marisol? She was in love when I left, eager to become my wife. I went to the salt lakes so I could make enough money to pay for our marriage. It was under your roof, Luz, that Marisol changed toward me. Such as that roof is," I added, as a drip sprang into life and snowmelt began pooling on the table between us.

Luz, relieved for an excuse to escape my inquiry, stood to fetch a bowl. I clapped a hand on her shoulder and pushed her back down.

"Let the water pour, Luz. I need to know."

As direct and bold as any warrior, my stepmother wasn't about to apologize or become meek. "Ours is a noble family, Nando. Our men do not marry the serving wenches they impregnate."

I forced my fists to remain on the table. "There's that noble side of things, believe the fantasy if you must, and then there is the other family, Luz. My half-breed family, whom you brought up under your own roof. Your Indian friend Nan, and me her first-born, and Nan's other babies by your husband. Half Utes, every one of us, and all beloved by you and Benito. When did you suddenly get so fancy that you forgot that?"

Luz wasn't going to give up after only one salvo. "Marisol is a different kind of half-breed. She is nobody, Nando. She doesn't have anything like the lineage you carry, in spite of your broken line."

I leaned back and folded my arms. Water from the growing drip spattered my face. I reached for a bowl without rising and set it under the stream.

"What exactly is making you so prickly, lady? I'm puzzled. How has Marisol ever hurt you, Luz?"

While Luz adjusted the bowl between us with exquisite precision, another point occurred to me.

"Did you know this baby was mine? Or did you suspect one of the pureblooded sons in the household? If either Francisco or Carlos gave you a half-breed bastard, that would upset your sense of propriety. Maybe it really isn't so terrible if it's only Nando's. True?"

"True," Luz replied with reliable candor. "I admit it, because in this case, the Aguilar bloodline is not corrupted. The problem I have concerning Marisol's situation, Nando, is that you cannot be sure this child is yours. You don't know if you'll be pouring your whole life, and a great deal of your family's assets, into supporting a child who came from that ignoramus Arsenio. You tell me you're certain, but who ever is?"

"Not saddling me with another man's child," I mused. "That's more or less what Marisol gave as her excuse for leaving me."

I turned on the old lady. "You told her she wasn't worthy, Luz. You told Marisol she shouldn't be pulling the wool over your boy's eyes, and you told her not to set her sights on trapping any of the Aguilars, didn't you?"

Luz's silence was all I needed to hear. I slammed another piece of piñon on the flames.

"No wonder Marisol prefers to live with witches."

My stepmother tried to glare at me, but the look didn't come across right. She averted her eyes.

"I don't have what I need yet, Luz."

"I know you don't. I'm thinking." Her eyes turned toward her little wooden Virgin in the niche, and I knew Luz was praying. The fresh log popped and snapped in the fireplace. I waited until she was ready to speak.

"Not Carlos's child, though I admit that wouldn't have surprised me. Certainly I am relieved it isn't Francisco's. Yours then? You are so sure? You may be accepting a babe that isn't yours, Nando, but I can see you have taken that into account." She looked up in question.

"I have. It's Marisol I love and want to support. I don't believe it's her husband's baby, but even if the child is Arsenio's, all children can be loved. Luz, give up this pretentiousness. Apologize to Marisol. Invite her back."

Luz turned away, and when she looked at me again, the old woman's eyes were moist. "I believe I owe an apology to both of you."

"I'll let you off on mine if you just go to Marisol. The baby's getting closer, February, I think. It's already snowing. She needs us."

"Sooner than February, by the looks of her."

"Luz! I'm telling you!"

The woman was gazing through the one tiny pane of glass we had. Brightness pouring in told us that the sun had burned through the clouds. I rose and opened the door. Warmth soaked into the snow, melting it so fast the yard was a bog.

"Think of your name, Luz," I said, standing beside her. I took her hand and my stepmother let me hold it. "You can be warm, and you can soften too. You loved us all, no matter where we came from. I need that from you again."

Luz stood with me in the doorway, her free hand against the jamb. "What a mud-hole!" she exclaimed. "What if I'm too late? Does Marisol hate me?" she asked, looking straight out into the brilliant world to avoid facing me.

"I honestly don't know. She's only spoken privately with me once, and then she was harsh. I think there's hope, though. There has to be."

Luz spun back into the room and grabbed her woolen shawl. "I'm going to find the girl. I can only pray she'll let me talk to her. But before that," Luz was really talking to herself now, "I'd better have a moment with Padre Miera. He'll tell me how best to handle this. He may even forgive me." She dashed out the door, splashed through the puddles and squished her way up the road to town.

I was finally free to work for Sebastian. I saddled Rosinante and left by the road to Pecos. By noon I reached the Galisteo and was climbing up the narrow cart path through the canyon. I turned off where Deer Creek curves into the river.

This morning the stream was running frothy and fast with melting snow. Oaks burned red against the tumbled rock of the canyon walls. Deer Creek was a cheerier place than when I had walked here little more than a week ago.

I tied the mare in a tight grove of young firs and went on by foot. It was easy to find the pink granite side canyon and from there, the old ramada where I began to cut for sign in widening circles through the woods.

Within minutes I was on a trail, studying a pulled back limb and a well-placed rock, neither of which an animal could have caused. The path paralleled Deer Creek, but wound high on the rock ledges.

I moved warily. Not long before, murderers had traveled this route. The trail stopped where white, crumbling rock gave way to a thirty-foot drop off into the water below. I doubled back and found a slight side-trail on the other side of a fallen tree, revealed only by moss scraped off a log.

The campsite was ancient and discreet, next to a half circle of piled stones built under the overhang of a cliff, where Pueblo hunters slept when staying out for the night. There was still a pile of charcoal and ash from old fires inside the little room. I drew my fingers through the debris of the fire pit and turned up splintered bird bones and burned fragments of corncobs.

Outside the shelter I found evidence of a more recent fire, a blackened ring in the grass and the surrounding shrubs singed. I moved out from the place in another series of circles and found a heap of fresh dirt where a bear had torn up the earth. I knelt in the mud and plowed my fingers through the loose soil. Catching the edge of a piece of fabric, I pulled it out of the ground.

In my hands was a shirt of coarse-spun wool, unraveling at the sleeves. The clothing was charred and it crumbled easily. I held my breath, looked around and listened. Nothing. Not even wind, just a faint sound from the running creek below.

I unsheathed my knife and digging deeper, dug up leather trousers, greasy and stained with blood. These were the clothes the dead man had on the night I found him hanging. The pants had been partly burned, the shirt shredded.

I would need these to convince Sebastian and the governor I hadn't made up the whole story. Before bundling the garments to take home, I tore off a piece of the shirt and reburied it. I piled the dirt back into place, but left some cloth showing. I hoped, if the killers returned, they wouldn't notice someone had unearthed the clothes.

There was no point in looking for the body. The remains of the man had been decomposing when I first encountered him and by now, cougars or coyotes would have found it.

I scuffed around the fire pit some more, then crawled into the little rock shelter and trailing my fingers across the ledges of stone, caught a delicate cord of spun wool. A curved piece of sparkling sea shell hung from the string.

I carried my find out to the sunlight. The shell was a gleaming pendant, pretty in its silvery whiteness. The shape reminded me of a glistening half-moon. The necklace was a simple thing, not valuable except that the shell came from so far away. The twisted end of the thread showed it to be well made and lightly oiled. It had mattered to somebody. I slipped the ornament into my bag and made another careful search of the area. Finding nothing more, I turned toward Santa Fe.

It was late when I returned to town. I hadn't pulled the saddle off Rosinante when incoming soldiers on lathered horses created a ruckus in the streets. I hurried to put my mare away, shoved the victim's old clothes into the crotch of a peach tree and went out to the road to look. Carlos and I nearly knocked into each other rounding the gatepost in the dark.

"You're back!" I said, giving him a friendly thump.

"Thank heavens, but not for long. We leave again in the morning for a fast run against the raiders in the west."

"Miguel!" My friend was there, hard on Carlos's heels.

"It was good, Nando, that you sent this boy with the news of Francisco's eviction," Carlos said. "Your information let me dance around Salazar's lies. Are Francisco and Luisa in Santa Fe yet?"

Francisco answered for himself, rising from the table as we came in and clasping his brother's hand. "Welcome home."

The wine jug passed from one brother to the other. "Drink this and then come view our lavish domain. You're back early. Did you abandon Salazar?"

"Someone attacked a string of wagons on its way to join the main caravan in Sevilleta. Fearing for his millions, Salazar raced for Santa Fe. I'm sure he got here ahead of me.

"The palacio's giving me fresh troops to find the thieves and hold them off until the main caravan gets past the area."

Carlos was on the bench, tugging at his filthy boots. "I get one night in my bed and then I head for the pueblos out west. I want Miguel to ride with my troops. Can you round up gear for him?"

"Of course. Give Estrella those clothes to clean," Luz commanded, tugging Carlos's jacket off his back. Food was put on the table and everyone sat down to eat.

"Then what?" I asked. "Are you and ten men taking on all of Zia and Zuni?"

"The raiders weren't Pueblo. Witnesses tell us they were Navajo. And no, not if I can help it. Chasing riled-up natives all over their own countryside is senseless, though it's reasonable to protect the caravan while it passes through that region. Depending on what we find, Anza will most likely send soldiers out to Navajo later to raise holy hell, maybe in the spring."

"Is Sebastian staying in Santa Fe, or going with you?" I needed to know, because the sergeant should see what I'd found earlier today above the creek.

"Sebastian stays in Santa Fe."

Carlos tried to laugh as he munched through a slab of pork. "Salazar seemed overly eager to get back. Thanks to the gossip you sent with Miguel, now I understand why."

Salazar back already? If he should read his bill of lading before his merchandise goes south, I could be a pauper again. There was some comfort though in thinking Celedonia might be as anxious as I to keep my salt hidden from her husband.

All hands hurried to serve Lieutenant Aguilar, clean his clothes, heat his bath and make up his bed. I left the bustle of the household and went into the dark garden, where I retrieved the corpse's stinking clothes from the peach tree. I took them into my new room and shoved the rags on the ledge inside the beehive fireplace, reminding myself not to kindle a fire anytime soon.

Healing

Bright morning beckoned like a prayer. The curandera chose the digging stick with the horned point and blue feathers that twirled from the shaft, slung her leather bag over her shoulder, and started up the lane in the direction of the mountains. The cat on the doorstep blinked and stretched as Juliana stepped over her splendidly furred friend. The golden-eyed goat, sitting atop its stone pen, bleated as the woman walked by.

The medicine woman had all day and she would need it. On waking, she had dedicated this sunny day to prayer and seeking herbs. After the attacks ten days ago on women of her kind, she wanted to be alone to nourish her strength and her gift for healing.

The snow of the day before had melted into the ground, loosening the roots the woman needed to complete her supply of medicines for the winter. She was short on Inmortal and Valerian, and other remedies might come to hand.

An hour later the woman turned onto the track along the tiny creek that was shaded by overhanging ledges. There it was, Valerian, growing out of damp moss, its fragile stem dried out now at the end of the year. She bent low and raked the soil off the slope beneath the plant. Small, nubbly roots lay hidden there, brown as nuts.

Juliana plucked them from the ground, raised the treasure to her nose and sniffed the earthy smell; a scent that verged toward tobacco, she thought, though she hadn't much experience with the real tobacco from the south. With bent back, she traversed the ledge, scraping and plucking, leaving the roots intact on every second plant.

Sleep, that's what these roots would give, or sedation for a woman in labor, or relief for an old person choking for breath. She patted the rounded bottom of her bag, satisfied with the weight of the medicine she'd found.

Turning back, she broke into laughter. Her cat and her black and brown goat trotted in a small parade down the path toward her.

"Tchhhhh. What are you doing here?" The goat blinked in innocence and lowered its head into the bent grasses. The cat rubbed against the woman's skirts, purring in the sun.

The other side of the canyon was cold. There the ground was moist and dark under the blue spruce, perfect for Kinnikinnik. Juliana found the low-lying shrub and gathered leaves off its trailing stems: sitz baths for women after childbirth, or for the brides who'd been too strenuous in their lovemaking. Hah! Juliana remembered that.

She sought the healthiest, shiniest leaves and put them in a side pouch. She'd smoke these in her pipe, later when they'd dried. Agapita liked Kinnikinnik too. The curandera found more of the shrub, shoved the goat aside, and gathered handfuls of the tiny leaves.

135

Juliana found a flat rock and stretched back on her elbows to watch the valley below through the bare aspens. The cat sunned beside her on the boulder, studying a thin column of smoke out to the northwest.

The curandera ate apples and a cheese, thank you goat, and scanned the ground below her perch for other useful plants. Was that Inmortal? A banner day!

Juliana took up her digging stick. The root was deep and it tunneled beneath the rock she'd been lying on. The curandera set to work, using the pointed stick, her hands, and finally her knife, to cut the brown fist of root. Useful for stimulating the heart, clearing the sinuses, or helping a mother's milk to come in. Inmortal was good for everything, but not very easy to find. Juliana was careful to leave a chunk of root untouched under the ground, knowing it would grow again next year.

The procession of Juliana, goat and gato, made its way down the stony path. It had been a perfect day, alone with the plants and the sky. The medicine woman stopped to wrest out a bright, golden Barberry root, in case a baby was born with skin too yellow. She snapped leaves off the last of the showy Bee Balm to sprinkle on her family's meat.

Where the creek burbled and grass still grew in green clumps, Juliana sidetracked, knelt by the water, dipped her fingers in the stream and dabbled water on her brow. She thanked God and the spirits for the medicine; thanked them for this day in the beauty of the hills.

A young man hiking up the trail, throwing stick in hand, saw the woman beside the stream. He heard her talking to something mysterious in the pool, and to her goat and bristling cat.

Juliana felt his presence and turned. Before the man could make the sign to ward off the evil eye, the witch put her finger to her lips and warned, "Shhh!"

With a wild swing, Toribio hurled his stick and spun to flee. Juliana bent to retrieve the aimless missile and couldn't keep from laughing, as she watched the ridiculous man run full-tilt for town.

Three Women

Sebastian wasn't impressed by the singed and greasy clothes I handed him.

"Frankly, Nando, these don't prove a thing. Anyone could have worn them. I'm far more interested in the fact that someone went to the trouble to construct a life-like effigy, drag it to the woods, and string up a replacement corpse in the ramada. Nevertheless, I'll keep your rags back there with our twiggy friend in the north room."

I stood silently in his office. There wasn't anything to add.

"I do believe you," the sergeant said, "when you say there was someone real up there. What you've found is a start. I'm sure more will come to light, and soon. When it does it might be less obscure. Stay alert and you'll pick up on it, whatever is."

I fingered the necklace in my pocket and decided not to hand it over to Sebastian, since he was decidedly not interested in my finds.

"It's settled. Vial has declared the caravan will leave in three days now that Governor Anza has provided more troops. Carlos and his soldiers are already on their way to Navajo country. There's too much going on right now for the governor to give this witch murder much thought, but he's counting on us to squelch trouble with the ladies while he's handling these other crises."

A heap of papers on Sebastian's desk reached the tipping point and fluttered to the floor.

"Why they put them here, I'll never know," he complained, "when I can't even read."

I said good-bye to Sebastian's backside, as he bent to pick up the spilled pile of orders and reports.

I went out to mingle in the market place. The town was packed. The din of preparation for the caravan had increased five-fold since the previous week. The plaza was one big corral. The weather had turned warm again after the quick snow. Piles of sodden dung swarmed with flies and every railing had a dozen animals tied to it.

Men hoisted boxes and bags into wagons, boys ran with hanks of rope and women sorted heaps of potatoes and onions. Just three more days and all the mess of the gathering herds and wagons would clear out, leaving behind only a handful of men, a short supply of soldiers and many lonely women.

I scanned the groups of ladies selling food and wares, but saw no one from the Casa Juliana. I wandered to the place in the stream where women do their laundry, but the water was too cold and muddy for washing, so no one I wanted to find was there. At a loss, I drifted by the Salazar's compound, thinking I might catch a glimpse of my salt bags being loaded.

Salazar's warehouse was long and high, built of adobe blocks on a solid stone foundation. The stout double doors stood wide open and a dozen Pueblo men ferried cargo to a long string of wagons and carts waiting in the street. I envied the carters. I had never left the colony. After my years in

Abiquiú, and the time among the mountain Utes, Santa Fe was big enough for me, but someday maybe I would find a place on the caravan and make the long trip to Mexico.

I rounded the building and came to the place in the wall where the warehouse ended and the merchant's private residence began. Just as I passed the arched side gate, Melchora, Celedonia Griego's Indian servant, came into the alley. When she saw who stood outside their doors, she chuckled.

"What's so funny, woman?"

"Couldn't resist could you? Had to see if your salt was all right."

This Indian could make me mad if I let her.

Instead I flashed her a smile and asked, "Well, is it?"

"Your bags went onto the wagons yesterday, bundled under oiled skins."

Good news. There was no way Facundo Salazar would be unwrapping completed loads.

Suddenly the woman caught my arm and pressed it to her chest. "Don't worry about your salt, Nando. I'll see you come out all right."

She was a little over-eager, the way she clung to me and let my arm graze her bosom, but I was shameless when it came to gaining access to the merchant's inner lair.

I looked at Melchora's black hair, shining in the sun. She must have been the same age as Celedonia, but on the Indian's head there was no gray to be seen and her skin was smooth, except for a few lines at her eyes.

"Melchora, you're Pueblo aren't you?"

She nodded.

"Which one?"

When she laughed, I saw her teeth were whole and white.

"That was a long time ago. Pecos, and I don't miss it."

Now here was a different story. I heard that most of the Pueblo women who had been transplanted to town hadn't come willingly. They'd been forced to work in Spanish households and used for God-knows-what. From the stories I'd heard, the God-knows-what part was especially true for girls who had been sent into service at the palacio.

It flashed through my mind that perhaps Melchora had been one of those, one who had quickly been impregnated with a Spaniard's child. What I didn't know was if the Pueblos would take their girls back with Spanish babies in their bellies. Even though Melchora was a tough one, there was something I liked about her, and the woman was pretty in her way. I felt us becoming friends.

"Do you have family here?" I asked.

Melchora remained airy and was smiling. Maybe she had a liking for younger men.

"Oh, I had a baby or two, also long ago. The Salazars are my family. Look at this house. Why would I want to live in a smoky hole in the pueblo again?"

The roofs of the Salazar hacienda stood proud and tall above the sturdy adobe wall which stretched two hundred *varas* along the lane. Why indeed?

On a whim, I pulled the little necklace out of my pouch. "Is this from Pecos?"

Melchora looked at the shell ornament, then at me. She fingered it on my palm, but when she tried to pick the necklace out of my hand, I clamped my thumb down.

"Where did you get this?" Melchora let go of my arm, all the sunshine in her voice gone dark. She looked me in the eye until I answered.

"I found it in the woods."

Melchora was dead serious. "Someone will need this. Yes, it's Cicuye. I'll take it back."

She tried again to grasp the necklace, but I kept my grip on it.

"Seriously, why would anyone miss this simple thing?" I asked.

Melchora put her index finger gently on the pearly shell.

"You shouldn't have this."

"Come on!"

Melchora looked into my eyes. "There's power in this."

"Melchora, don't get dramatic with me. People have been bringing shells to New Mexico from the oceans forever. They're not that rare."

Melchora's dark eyes were sharp and commanding. "Either give it to me or put it back where you found it."

"What will you do with it if I decide to give it to you?"

"Not let anyone see it. Return it to its owner."

"In Pecos?" I asked.

"Yes."

"You know who owns this?"

"Someone at the pueblo will know," Melchora replied.

"There's no rush. The owner of this trinket is dead."

Melchora's finger lifted off the shell.

"I thought it might be interesting to find out who killed him," I said flatly.

The Pueblo woman's eyes shifted to the side. Our friendly encounter was over. I used the moment to shove the necklace into my pouch

An empty oxcart rounded the corner and banged down the alley. We separated to let it pass. I was glad to get distance from the Indian. Across the roadway, Melchora put her hand on the gate and looked at me one last time. The flirtatious sparkle was gone. There was tension in her face.

"Don't get mixed up in Pecos business, Nando. If I were you, I wouldn't show this amulet to anybody. Throw it away. Far away."

If what Melchora said was true, surely I'd be feeling the necklace burning through the leather of my pouch. Instead it was cool and benign.

"We'll see," I said. "Perhaps I'll take it to Pecos myself."

Melchora burst out laughing, high and unnatural.

"Do that," she said. "Do that and see what happens to you."

She pulled the blue gate open and disappeared into the walled gardens of the Salazar estate.

A Pecos man then, a Cicuye man with power, despite his greasy clothes. Hung by his elbows to die, and his bones dispersed over the hills between Santa Fe and the pueblo. This was getting interesting.

I had another chance encounter with a woman on my morning's tour. Miss Beatriz, sublime and dressed in silk, sat on a stone bench behind the church in the little garden near the priests' quarters. It was a quiet place and out of the way. By all appearances, Beatriz was waiting for someone, dressed for the occasion, and pleased with herself.

"You're looking lovely, Beatriz. Waiting for a friend?" I couldn't resist.

She twinkled at me. "What do you think?"

It could be either the recently returned Salazar, or the about-to-depart Vial, but I didn't have enough information to place my bet.

143

Instead, I inquired in an off-hand way, "I saw you walking to Aurelia's with Marisol. Is Marisol going to live there?"

Beatriz answered with genuine innocence, "Aurelia thought it would be a good idea and she would love to have a baby in the house."

Wouldn't we all, I thought? "Aurelia not getting any babies of her own?"

Beatriz examined her soft leather shoes. "It seems not yet. We're working on that though."

"How do 'we' do that?" I asked, laughing at her.

"Not what you think. Nando, you know what it's like to be a young man, but you have no clue what happens to a man when he gets older."

"And you do?"

"My sister is a medicine woman. Wives come to her for tonics all the time."

"In secret and ashamed, I suppose."

"We are discreet." Beatriz let a small frown mar her pretty face.

"Beatriz, let's be frank. There are many forms of tonic for an older man." I grasped a dangling flounce on her sleeve and rubbed the silk between thumb and forefinger.

"Whatever you choose to do is your own business, my friend, but I don't want anyone putting pressure on Marisol to become such a tonic for Señor Vial." I hung on to Beatriz's sleeve and looked into her eyes. "I need your help protecting my girl."

Beatriz shifted to remove her sleeve from my grasp. She glanced down the street, hoping to see her lover arrive, but there was no sign of anyone yet.

She spoke to me softly. "Marisol is lost right now; lost, pregnant and sad. Her stubbornness has gotten her where she is, but she isn't a fool. She won't let anything hurt her child.

"Maybe she'll change her mind, Nando, and come back to you. But, I have to tell you, there hasn't been a word of that from her. Marisol is learning about herbs from my sister, because she wants to have a trade to make her way. She has a knack for medicine. Juliana is already letting Marisol prepare some of the tonics, and now Melchora's tutoring her too."

"Doña Salazar's Melchora?" I asked.

Beatriz nodded, but added, "Melchora's Melchora. Not many people can boss that woman around. Not unless she decides to let them."

"Why isn't Juliana doing this work herself?"

Beatriz laughed. "My sister prefers to work with the after-effects of Melchora's art: the midwifery, the birthing."

Beatriz added, "In love matters, Juliana comes to Melchora. Melchora prepares mixtures that she guarantees will bring a husband back to his wife. Women run to her when they realize they've been abandoned for someone new."

I noticed Beatriz didn't blush at the concept.

"The Pueblo woman can also blend tonics to make a man fall in love, which are very popular with ladies. Melchora's been over at the Vials, because she knows what works for an old man, particularly one married to a young wife who still wants to have her children."

"And Marisol's in the middle of all this?"

"She was showing interest in herbs earlier this summer. She'd come to our house whenever she could get away."

"Christ almighty, Beatriz, midwifery, birthing, that's one thing. But love potions for the elderly and rich? Tonics and philters? Little clippings of the adored one's hair, I'm guessing,

145

mixed with a dash of urine? Get Marisol out of this Beatriz, before she's associated with the devil's arts."

Beatriz tried to defend the curanderas. "The remedies aren't just for the rich. Poor women need these things too."

In mid-thought she stopped and lifted her head. We heard the clopping of horse hooves coming around the back of the church.

"Go, Nando! Go fast! I don't want him to see you sitting beside me." She started to push me away, but suddenly clutched my hand. "I wish I were in love like you and Marisol!"

I stared at her, surprised. Beatriz saw my astonishment. To soothe me she added, "I'll do what I can to protect her, my friend. Hurry!"

I laid my finger gently on Beatriz's cheek and left quickly, slipping like a coyote into the old orchard and from there down to the bosque by the river. As I slid on fresh fallen leaves down the embankment to the water, I could hear a horse and light carriage moving smartly along the road. My head poked above the bank, but I could only make out the back of a two-seater swinging into the church gardens.

Beatriz said she didn't want her lover to see me, but she'd succeeded in not letting me see her lover either. I was glad to be screened by the golden trees. Beatriz's affairs were too complex for me.

There was one more woman I needed to see that day. After the mid-day meal, I found Luisa Piña Diaz in her room sorting dresses laid out on the bed.

"Hello, Nando. What brings you here?"

"Hello Luisa. Feeling better now?"

My sister-in-law nodded and gestured for me to have a seat on a bench.

"With all the commotion of Carlos's brief return, did you ever get to visit Aurelia?"

"I did, Nando. I paid a call on Aurelia today before Mass. I invited her to walk to church with me. You'll never guess whom I saw at the Vials.'"

"Never in a hundred years."

"Sitting near Alfonso's wife, packaging little bundles of herbs and chatting like a magpie."

"Marisol! Does she live there now?"

"I'm not sure of the details, but in any case, she's got a friend in Aurelia. Beatriz was there too, keeping them all entertained. I can't say Marisol looked unhappy. Her face was a great deal more relaxed than yours, Nando."

I cracked some sticks between my hands and fed the fire, before I said, "Luz was going to talk to Marisol yesterday, to invite her to return. From what you told me, it doesn't sound like that happened."

Luisa shook her head. "I didn't hear a word about Marisol coming back to us."

My sister-in-law sat down on the bed facing me, then said, "I wondered what was going on with Luz. She was so quiet yesterday when she came home from church. She'd been gone a long time. When I asked her where she'd been, she made herself very busy cutting vegetables. After a long silence, she asked if I knew a woman named Melchora, from the Salazar household.

"I hardly know anybody in Santa Fe, but when Luz described the woman, I realized that when I visited Aurelia today, I'd seen an additional person there. It must have been this Melchora Luz was so concerned about, working in the room with Beatriz and Marisol. The Indian woman didn't say a word. She stayed in the background, occasionally passing herbs to the girls.

"I know Melchora. Why is Luz worried about her?"

Luisa shrugged. "Luz was quiet and uneasy, and I think Melchora was on her mind. That's all I can tell you."

The Stone

Working in the cold until well after dark, I finished the section of roof over my own room. I slept in the newly enclosed space as though it were a womb and had a hard time regaining consciousness when soldiers woke me at dawn. They hauled me out of bed and house before the morning's meat was grilled.

I chewed on my half-raw breakfast, hurrying along beside the soldiers to the palacio. Once there, Sebastian shoved a cup of chocolate into my hand saying, "This might be nasty."

I wasn't sure if he was referring to the watered-down cocoa or the mission he'd called me for.

The groom had saddled two horses that stood shoulder-to-shoulder, blowing steam into the cold fall air. Sebastian pulled himself onto the better-looking animal. Still half-asleep, I wedged myself between the wooden ridges of the saddle on the other. The mare was a long-legged, piebald sort of beast I'd never met before.

The sun hadn't made it over the mountains yet and there was ice on the edge of the river when we rode the horses through.

The road was wide enough that I could pull up beside Sebastian. I was hoping he would explain to me, over the stomp and rumble of the horses, what this mission was all about. But he didn't. He rode steadily upstream toward the canyon where the river comes out of the mountains and he wasn't in a good mood. Sebastian kept checking his surroundings in the way common to scouts and countrymen, scanning both the horizon and the near ground, without seeming to turn his head.

I began to enjoy the early morning ride, once the piebald shared some of her heat with me. I watched the rising sun strike the last few yellow leaves and turn them to fluttering gold. But Sebastian wasn't moved by beauty.

"The Comanche who found her didn't know who she is, but I've got a hunch," he finally said. "I need you to help identify the body and get it ready to bring in."

So it was a woman and she was dead up there somewhere. I sat bolt upright. My gut knotted. The roar of the river surged in my ears, or was it my own pounding blood? Marisol?

I found my voice and shouted ahead to Sebastian, "Did the Comanche say, could he tell, was the woman pregnant?"

Sebastian didn't hear me. His powerful back and the rump of his horse moved steadily up the trail that was now stony and steep.

"Sebastian!"

The sergeant pushed on, but at the top of a rise he turned and waited for me. "Was the dead woman pregnant?" I yelled again.

Sebastian couldn't fail to notice my panic. Carefully he replied, "The Comanche gave me many details. The Indian didn't say anything about pregnant."

I took a breath. The creek churned below and the rough green hills rose around us. A raven clipped the sky. I dug my heels into the piebald and continued up the hill.

It didn't take us long to get to the place where a twisted juniper tree lay fallen across the trail. Sebastian pulled up and said, "Tie the horses."

He opened the leather bag on his saddle. "Do you want something in your stomach, or not?" he asked, offering me a piece of jerky. I took it, not knowing if it would be better to do this one empty, but when anyone gives me the choice, I lean toward eating.

Cold sunlight filled the valley now. Sebastian worked his feet into the soft earth of the steep slope, forcing his way straight up toward the granite ledge that capped the hill. It wasn't breath he was stopping for. He was hesitating about the trail and the footprints he'd been following. They weren't entirely making sense, having multiplied.

"I'll follow the Comanche. You take the other."

The prints I was supposed to track became more complicated: a well-defined boot heel, a smudge from softer shoes or moccasins. The path they took separated me from the sergeant, but we both moved toward the gray ledge. My trail ended on top of the outcropping, and Sebastian's came to a stop fifteen feet below me, at the cliff's base. I could hear him forcing his way through the oak brush. Then he swore. The oath he let out wasn't about snagging his pants on a branch. It sprang from revulsion.

The woman lay tipped over sideways, where she'd been sitting when the huge boulder smashed onto her from above. The black rock had bounced and rolled, pinning her beneath it. The woman's head still hung from her neck, but the neck was broken and lopsided, half torn from her body. One side of her face was a slab of raw white bone, caked with dark blood. I won't describe the eyeball, but if it had been in its usual place in the smashed, ripped-off face, it would have leered up at the sky. She had been dead for hours, probably all night. She, if you could call this horror 'she'.

I stood beside Sebastian now, neither of us knowing where to start. I picked smashed blue flowers off the woman's

151

fingers. It took both of us to roll the heavy stone off her mangled arm. Then Sebastian put his hands on the rigid corpse. He lifted it up and around, tipping the body to the other side, so we could see what remained of the ravaged head. Gray-skinned, with huge purple blotches around the remaining eye, thick hair gluey with gore, it was the face of one of the prettiest women I had ever known.

It was Beatriz, who had been the first love of my life, she who had waited in her pretty silks for her lover only yesterday, and who had promised, so believably, to look out for Marisol.

A Forest Grave

It took the rest of the day to bring the body down. I stood guard on the hillside while Sebastian rode to the palacio to requisition a cart and some Indian laborers. That took hours, during which I lay in the dried grasses under the cool sun, a safe distance from Beatriz's festering body. I chose a place on the ledge where I didn't have to look at her, but I could make sure no animal or unsuspecting person came upon her.

Of course, as Sebastian should have realized, the Indios refused to touch her, knowing her unsettled spirit was hovering nearby, so Sebastian and I did the work ourselves of wrapping her corpse in a makeshift shroud of rough muslin.

Beatriz made an awkward bundle. We couldn't straighten out her limbs. The sergeant and I half-carried, half-dragged her down to the trail, slung her sideways across the back of a mule, and once at the road, rolled her onto a cart. None of this improved Sebastian's mood.

Two of the workers took off, having no intention of traveling alongside this woman's ghost. The third should have, because Sebastian cuffed him and shouted him into submission, so that he would stay with the cart at least long enough to help us get the rig down. Even the mules were upset by their freight, and the whole trip back was a fight to keep the team in line.

The fleeing Indios must have spread the news about a body on the mountain. Even though everyone in Santa Fe was preoccupied with moving the caravan's wagons to the edge of town, it seemed half the people of Santa Fe just happened to be near the canyon road as we drove in late in the evening. Everyone had managed to find tasks outside in the streets, unwilling to miss the spectacle our passage provided. I was relieved when we rolled under the portál of the palacio, into the protection of the courtyard.

The authorities spent little time on the body. Not only were they overburdened and rushing to get all the presidio's wagons loaded, but a dead woman of the lower classes wasn't of importance to them.

The neatly uniformed surgeon quickly pronounced his verdict without ever touching her. "An accident, terrible, but clearly an accident. She was resting under the ledge when the boulder fell. Not this woman's lucky day."

I'd always known this medic to be faster with his saw than his brain, but in fairness, he hadn't seen the assortment of footprints on the hillside.

The surgeon wanted nothing more to do with the hideous mess that had been Beatriz. He made sharp, dismissive movements with his arm. "Take her to her people. They'll want to pray over her tonight and get her in the ground first thing in the morning."

He ordered his servants to rewrap my friend. When they lifted her onto the cart, someone muttered a word a lot like *puta*, then they all disappeared into the complex of rooms that were both infirmary and jail, leaving me in the darkness to do something with the corpse. The cart was still there, but we were down to one mule.

I looked for Sebastian, but the sergeant had been summoned to more important matters. The lone Pueblo man who'd traveled down the mountain with me had also vanished.

I took hold of the mule's halter and pulled on it. I wasn't about to ride in the cart with that body, even if it was Beatriz, so I led the animal around the last few wagons still parked on the now-dark plaza, waded the shallow ford at the river, and began to thread my way through the tight lanes of the Analco.

We rolled past the old church of San Miguel. At the place where ghosts hung thick in the street beside the church's cold, stone walls, I thought I heard my dead passenger groan. Could her spirit be calling out to the other unfortunates who had burned to death here, long ago, when the Pueblos attacked the town?

Although the Indios spread the word that a woman had met her death up on the mountain, nobody knew who she was. People waited in their faintly lit doorways. A few came outside and began to follow the noisy cart as I poked my way down the narrow alleys. When we passed beyond each cluster of houses, I saw women turn and go into their homes, their relief plain to see. A boy ran beside me and tugged on my manta, "Who is it? Who's the dead one?"

I shrugged him off. "You'll learn soon enough."

Though I knew the way to Juliana's, I had to concentrate on making no wrong turns. At the point where I left the last homes behind and headed down the short lane to the curanderas' house, the people following held back, for it was clear now to whom this tragedy belonged.

A chilly night wind snapped my manta about me as I pulled to a halt. Juliana and Agapita stood at their front gate, stoic and silent. To my relief Marisol wasn't there. This, a pregnant woman shouldn't see.

155

Juliana, certain now that the cart was coming to her, bent to Agapita and spoke. Her sister went indoors and came back holding a lighted brand. Agapita held it above our heads, as Juliana and I bent to unwrap just enough of Beatriz so the women could be sure. I prayed that the side of Beatriz's face left whole would be the part revealed, and mercifully, it was, though ghastly enough.

Juliana reached out a gentle, brown hand and stroked what was left of her sister's ravaged face. Flickering light silvered Juliana's cheeks where tears trickled. "We'll bring Beatriz indoors. Tomorrow we will bury her."

I misunderstood. "Shall I return with the cart to carry her to the church?"

Juliana's voice carried to the onlookers in the lane.

"No church exists where my sister will be allowed rest. There is no holy ground that will receive her." More quietly she added, "We will bury her ourselves in the holy woods, where she'll never be mocked or cursed again. Beatriz will find peace beside the water."

It was the most awkward thing I've ever done, carrying that contorted form into the women's house. I couldn't imagine where they would put her, or how they would sleep under the same roof with the body, but Agapita showed no reluctance as she carried the light ahead of us down a short passageway and through a low door. Juliana helped push and prod the awkward load inside. She had me lay Beatriz on a mat on the floor of the storeroom, beneath the bundles of drying plants that hung from the low pine beams. I had to duck to keep from being smacked by the herbage. Juliana was about to show me out when Agapita began to take off the shroud.

"Wait! You'll want your sister with you when you do that!" I knew what she was heading into.

"My sister is here," Agapita said with stubborn calm.

"Please wait, Agapita." Juliana agreed with me. "I'll see Nando to the door and then we'll prepare her together." In the end, Agapita came too and they walked me to the lane.

"I'll return in the morning," I said, "and help bury your sister."

Juliana touched my hand, turned and went inside. I stepped into the cart and snapped the reins. The government mule stepped lively, as eager as I to turn its back on this tragedy. A few people still waited in the shadows, wanting to know more. I drove past them without speaking. Why on earth did I offer to help tomorrow?

Not only had I offered, but I had also made up my mind to approach Padre Miera, first thing in the morning, before I returned by the forest path with my shovel.

The body had relaxed during the night. Beatriz lay straight, wrapped in an embroidered linen shroud that would have done justice to a far nobler lady. Juliana took me through the back gate, down the trail to a place not far from the edge of the river. She pointed out the grassy opening she had chosen under the cottonwoods. I looked around for a minute, figuring where to dig between the roots, then started in with my shovel. I had brought a pick too. I had recently replaced the precious strip of iron on the blade, and before Juliana departed, I'd grubbed out the first four inches of sod and was into the rocky soil beneath.

It was hard work once I hit the subterranean riverbed stones. Through the thud of my pick, I heard my name called,

157

and Sebastian, the first time I'd ever seen him in civilian clothes, came through the woods, accompanied by another man. Without saying much they picked up my tools and took over, digging the hole down another foot and widening it as they worked.

Another man came up the path from the south, and another filed in from the direction of Juliana's. Not all of the men had their own tools, so we took turns, sending sparks flying off the stones, prying out the bigger ones with a strong oak stick.

No one talked much while the work was being done, but we shared smokes when we were out of the hole, and it was a proper grave by the time we were done: deep, dry, and wide enough, with straight, hard edges.

I had thought I'd be on this duty alone, but there was more sympathy for Beatriz than I'd realized, at least among the men. Sebastian too? Beatriz's death wasn't a situation to cheapen with jealousy, but it was lucky I wasn't a lovesick juvenile any more.

"This do it, you think?" I threw my shovel to the side.

Sebastian stood on the rim looking down into the grave. He gave me a lift out of the pit and all of us sat on the edge, sharing a cigarette.

"It's too hard." An older man with a sad face voiced what we were all thinking. "She's little and her bones will feel it."

"There's no coffin, is there?"

"No boards, no coffin, no money and no time."

"How about leaves?" This came from the older man. It was a good solution, so we scooped up armfuls of the spicy golden leaves that lay deep all over the grove and tossed them into the hole.

Sebastian left to tell Juliana we were ready and I dropped down into the grave again and smoothed out the leaf piles making a comfortable place for the dead woman to rest. This time, to my surprise, Padre Miera was there to help me climb out.

I almost hugged him for coming to pray at the burial of a woman who in almost any language would be called a whore. Oddly, Padre Domingo stood at his side, quiet for once and comporting himself with dignity. Had they given him some calming drug, or was Padre Miera keeping the volatile priest close, restraining the man?

Juliana and Agapita led the small procession through the woods. Four men carried Beatriz on a pallet of cut poles they had hastily lashed together. Sebastian eased himself into the grave and caught the fragile bundle, slipping her off the poles and laying her down in the fragrant leaves. He sprinkled a few more over her, and then the men hooked their hands under Sebastian's shoulders and lifted him out.

Padre Miera said the prayers and gave the blessing, doing all he could to ease Beatriz's precarious future. The red-haired padre stood behind Miera, head obediently bent, moving his lips to the familiar words. Beatriz's sisters didn't cry in front of us, but stood with their shoulders touching. It was clear as we worked together in the brittle fall air, that the women were grateful for our support. All told, there were twenty or more people at Beatriz's burial, which was graced by sunshine and the reaching branches of the huge cottonwoods.

We sprinkled dirt over the body and made our shovels fly, filling in the hole, and to finish, set the largest of the river rocks on the mound. Suddenly we were done and we didn't know what to do next.

Usually after a funeral there would be drinks and food at the family's house, but Juliana knew no one would come to her home. She simply moved among the group, conversing quietly with the men. She knelt and kissed Padre Miera's ring with everyone watching. The padre then placed his hand gently on her head. After Juliana and Agapita left the grove, the men silently departed by various paths in the woods.

Padre Miera, with Domingo, came over and suggested I walk with them back to the plaza. At first we had to go single file, but when the track widened I came up beside the priest, and Miera said, "Nando, are there truly people in this town who would murder a woman for what she is?"

I stopped, and so did Domingo. "You think she was murdered? No one at the palacio mentioned foul play." I didn't bring up the size of boulder or the footprints all over the hillside.

"No doubt the authorities dodged that," the padre muttered. "But there were many women who resented Beatriz."

I threw a look at Padre Domingo, he who had shamed the woman who was now dead in front of everyone at the church. He stood still, his face unreadable, deep within his cowl.

Miera went on, "And I suspect every one of those men digging her grave left home without his lady knowing. How about yourself?"

I felt my face turn hot with color. The old padre watched this evidence and, satisfied that his point was made, turned, clasped the arm of Padre Domingo, and they walked on ahead of me. My eyes stayed fixed on Miera's stocky ankles, which his cassock didn't quite cover.

"The wives wouldn't do that to her," I mused aloud, trying to convince myself. "They could, I guess, gang up on her and deliver some sort of beating, but to drop a boulder on her! It would take a bevy of women to move that stone."

Padre Miera turned onto the dirt lane that would take us out of the woods, and other than muttering 'if a lever's long enough it can lift the world,' he paid no attention at all to my noisy cogitation.

Right=Hand Man

Never before had a boss invited me to get drunk with him. Sebastian and I sat in the dark drinking at the wine shop, the same cantina Paulina inherited when our friend Rosa died. Sebastian paid for our cups of sweet red wine, which I considered fair payment out of Anza's coffers for having to deal with the body of Beatriz the past two days.

"No one's paid much attention to her death," the sergeant said, "because her funeral was the Indian kind in the woods and the church bells didn't ring. Not that anyone had time to look up, even if the bells had tolled."

Sebastian's face sagged with fatigue. "I've been staffing meetings all day. When I came in after the burial, Anza told me to fetch caravan master Vial. During lunch the head investigator Crespín arrived with his men. They're finally here, undaunted by the long ride from Sonora, itching to unravel the alcalde's affairs. Crespín Olivas had sufficient escort and they got through in spite of the fighting on the trail. Of course, it's up to good old Sebastian to find housing for all those men." The sergeant paused to drink again.

"Then this afternoon," he went on, "after taking packets of letters to where the caravan is assembling, I was ordered to summon Facundo Salazar to meet with Anza. The governor was furious at Salazar for abandoning his assignment to close the missions at the western pueblos.

"Are you sure, Nando, that Salazar was an acquaintance of Beatriz's? The man showed absolutely nothing in the way of grief. I wonder if he even knows she's dead?"

"He knows," I said. "The Salazars' servant, Melchora, told him. I saw them talking on the plaza."

"And how did she know?" the sergeant asked.

"By the time I'd crossed town to drop off the body at Juliana's, everybody in town knew. It was like leading a parade."

"I watched Salazar when he waited for Anza in the anteroom," Sebastian said. "Whatever concern was on his face, was not about the death of a girl. Doesn't really hold with what you told me about his night with Beatriz in La Ciénega, does it?"

"The man's a player," I answered. "The news of his lady friend's death was spreading as fast as plague throughout the town. I followed Salazar out of the plaza. Part of my job, I figured. He went straight home, making a beeline for his beloved Celedonia; under the circumstances, a diplomatic move."

The sergeant and I pulled steadily at our wine. Sebastian had made sure we were sitting in a dark corner, behind the warm beehive oven. He held an important position in this town, but I could tell the man needed to get drunk tonight.

"You should see Vial's set-up for this journey," Sebastian snorted. "I went to get him, to bring him in to meet with the governor. He'd outfitted his *carrossa* like a bordello; wool mattresses from end to end, even ruffled silk. Vial's got one wagon for his bedroom, one for his office, and another for his servants and supplies. The man's a fop."

I'd formed an entirely different opinion of the caravan master when he'd poured my salt into the dirt and called me a half-breed bastard, but the sergeant continued.

"Vial can afford his excesses. This caravan's his show. Has been for years. I'm sure Señor Vial believes it's in his interest to arrive well rested, and to make it clear who's the patrón."

Sebastian signaled for a refill. "But I've got to say it looked more like the chief was outfitting a boudoir to attract females, than running a large commercial enterprise."

Aha! Evidence that Melchora's herbal miracle might actually be working, but even though Sebastian had urged me to come out and drink with him, I wasn't about to tell him all my secrets.

We slipped into silence and together let the fuzz of alcohol soften the memory of Beatriz's death. While Sebastian quietly drank away the stresses of the day, I ran through this morning's encounter with Luz. I hadn't been able to avoid sitting down with her even though I'd just gotten back from Beatriz's funeral.

I tried to weigh what the old woman had said to me at the table today against the words Beatriz had told me just before she died, words that indicated Marisol still loved me.

But Luz had said, "You're wrong about the timing, Nando. Marisol is eight months pregnant. She's due in a few weeks. This is no baby formed in May, son; though I can see it is painful for you to hear that. I'm very sorry."

Sorry, my ass.

Luz had gone on, perhaps a bit more gently, "I invited her back, but she didn't accept my offer."

"Because," I shot at my stepmother, "you undoubtedly made it obvious that you believe the baby isn't an Aguilar,"

"Of course. We need to keep that very clear, Nando."

"By all means. And what did Marisol say?"

"That until after the birth she'd be living with Aurelia Inez, Vial's wife. When the baby comes, Marisol will return to her farm up north. Aurelia has agreed to send helpers along, to put the farmhouse back in shape. That's to be the payment to Marisol for becoming Aurelia's companion while Vial is away."

"Generous," I replied stiffly. "The lady must think highly of Marisol."

Luz didn't sniff, but still made it known how she felt about the whole situation.

Luz reported the conclusion of their conversation. " 'Say hello to Nando for me,' Marisol said politely. 'Tell him not to worry. Everything's worked out well.' "

I couldn't wait to be gone, hearing those words from my stepmother, gone from Luz, her household, Santa Fe, and the whole damn lot of them. Maybe in the spring I'd sneak through Marisol's window one night and invite her to run away with me and join the Utes. I bet she'd jump at the chance.

Given Luz's attitude, I didn't bother to give my stepmother any details of Beatriz's death, nor the manner of it, nor what the surgeon said; neither did I discuss the presence of padres at her funeral, and of course I didn't mention how many men gathered to bury Beatriz in the grove. Luz could go whistle. She would have to glean the gossip from someone other than me.

In the gloomy tavern, I turned the cup of wine round and round in my hands trying to divine the future in the dregs at the bottom. Sebastian was talking, but for the past few minutes I hadn't heard a word he'd said.

"Vial was in Anza's office, complaining as usual that there weren't enough soldiers accompanying the wagons. He accused the governor of willfully jeopardizing the enterprise. Anza, hornet-mad, retaliated that the merchant consistently concealed his profits, so tax money wasn't available to benefit the garrison.

"I almost went in to break up the argument, it was that heated, but Vial stormed out before I figured out how to interrupt them, and within minutes here came that simpering investigator, Olivas, wearing his fancy badges, saying he apologized for being early to luncheon, and waving in his six companions. Christ, I'd rather be demoted than put up with all that bullshit, have my old job back saddling donkeys."

"There's no way that will happen, Sebastian. The colony would collapse without you."

"I know. But donkey shit isn't as bad as bull shit."

The sergeant drank some more and I wondered what life Sebastian had outside the palacio. A woman in a little house somewhere behind the government buildings? Married even? Did Sebastian own land or have children? His whole being was so caught up in managing the governor's business that no one knew anything about the real man. Except that I'd found out in the woods this morning he'd once had an affair with the late Beatriz.

Sebastian added, "Ever since Vial financed the protesters who rode to Arizpe, Anza's hated him. But the governor's in a bind. Commander General Croix supports Vial in everything he does."

I put in my two *reales* worth. "Vial's a thorn in the governor's side, but Anza's far too decent a man to give the paymaster what he deserves."

Sebastian shook his head. "Vial's robbing the colony blind, but the commanders in Arizpe and Mexico depend on Vial, so Anza can't budge against him."

"Anza has friends among the Comanches. Capable ones," I hinted brazenly.

"Right. And no one would ever guess," Sebastian slurred as he emptied his mug.

"Sebastian?"

"Huh?"

"Where's Toribio?"

The sergeant looked up. "That red-faced punk? Why?"

"Beatriz," was all I said.

Sebastian's face twisted. "No longer in custody. We didn't have enough on him, but I told Toribio if he showed his face in Santa Fe anytime soon, I'd lock him up for years. No sign of him since. Down in Agua Fria probably."

I let it drop, though I made a note to ride down the river one of these days.

As good as the wine made me feel, and as fascinating as it was to be sitting here drinking with my boss, who was a lot more entertaining than usual, we both would be hard at work by dawn. We unstuck ourselves from the benches and moved unsteadily into the dark.

Paulina put a hand on Sebastian's arm as he moved out the door. He stopped, dropped a piece of a silver peso into her palm, then bent and kissed her lovingly.

Minute by minute, I was learning more about the governor's right-hand man.

When Wailing Starts

Strange noises woke me. I pulled my face out of the springy wool of the sheepskin to listen. Running, booted feet passed down the dirt lane outside our doorway, then a man yelled from somewhere close by. I was out of bed, trying to see through the lattice-covered window. In the faint light just before dawn I could make out people moving fast and horses cantering down the road along the river.

Luz bumbled into the sala, wrapping her lanky gray hair onto her head, pinning it fiercely with a needle-like bone. She might be tiny and old, but she was alert as a hare. Luz stopped and peered into the shadowy corner where I lay.

"Nando? Is that you down there? Why are you sleeping on the floor?"

I remembered stumbling to the first mat that offered itself to me.

Luz opened the door. A rush of leaves blew across the earthen floor. "Wind again," she grumbled. "Why's that woman yelling?"

I pulled on my pants, snatched a handful of small apples, shoved one in my mouth and, grabbing my manta said, "Save breakfast."

I stepped into the flow of townspeople moving down the lanes toward the bigger road beside the river. It soon became clear the crowd was headed toward Vial's hacienda.

Something must have happened about the caravan, something that threatened our lifeline to the south.

Awake now, I picked up to a trot, ducked into the bosque and took a side path to get around the throng. The overgrown trail brought me to the edge of the small stone corral at the back of Vial's house, the yard that held his goat pens and piggery. A fat little Pueblo woman had gotten there ahead of me, but she was the only one. We recognized each other; Agapita, Juliana's sister, and she moved over to give me a view. I was in position just in time to see men wresting a body from the outhouse.

The family's servants were attempting to find a place to grasp the dead man's flesh, to unwind the body out of the privy in order to place it on the narrow bed frame they'd pulled from the house to use as a makeshift stretcher.

A man is old at fifty-eight and Vial's white, flabby flesh, gone slack, was mountainous and disgusting. His skin was a sallow color and there was a smear of something on his thigh that I didn't care to know more about.

Aurelia Inez tried time and again to throw a blanket over her husband to hide the shame of his nakedness, but as the men dragged the corpse onto the litter the cover kept slipping off. Vial's skin was scraped and bleeding by the time they were done. Aurelia whined, wailed, and wiped her nose with her hand.

Vial's stiff face was frozen in a horrified look, made worse by the fact his eyes were still open. I thought I heard him grunt. Maybe he wasn't dead after all, but then I'd known cows that sometimes made that noise after they'd been slaughtered.

At last Vial's household servants managed to get the ungainly body, with its pallid legs and bulbous knees, stretched on the ground, and Aurelia succeeded in getting the blanket spread over her spouse. Then, in a swirling turn, Aurelia Inez collapsed onto the dirt beside her husband and lay there dead to the world.

A woman rushed from the house to the young wife's side. It was Marisol. She began dragging Aurelia toward the doorway. Working alone, Marisol wasn't able to extricate the collapsed widow with any delicacy. In the minute when the unconscious Aurelia was bounced over the dirt, I was able to tell that the wife's bare legs were much finer than the husband's. It was hard to imagine those beauties tangled up with his.

I called out to Marisol and started over the wall to help her, but a neatly dressed man rushed at me waving his cane. "Get out of here! This is none of your business," he screeched.

Other women hurried to bring Aurelia into the privacy of the house, and amidst the cluster of maids, Marisol disappeared from my sight. A frenzy of shrieks rose from Vial's home; apparently Aurelia was conscious again and going to live.

I retreated a few feet from the man with the flailing cane, but Agapita and I still had the best seat in the house. The merchant Facundo Salazar, out on his morning ride, had heard the cries and seeing our vantage point in the woods, he'd joined us. He couldn't have been riding very long before he'd been drawn to the commotion, because his Arabian was still cool. Atop his well-mannered horse, Salazar had an even better view than we.

His greeting was congenial enough, considering our last encounter. "What a shock," he said. "One can hardly fathom it."

Soldiers held the crowd back when officials from the palacio entered the barnyard. The surgeon and his assistants poked at Vial's body every which way, examining his skin, prying back an eyelid, peering beneath it, before pushing both lids closed. Soon they pulled the drab blanket over the man's face. With that act of closure even the animals turned away and resumed munching hay at their mangers.

When the soldiers picked up the litter to take the corpse into Vial's house, the only part of the merchant that remained visible was a fat hand protruding from the blanket, bearing an enormous, now pointless, gold ring.

When wailing starts, I leave. Agapita scurried off too. Salazar had already ridden into the woods.

I had plenty to tell my family. Señor Vial's demise would turn this town on its head. The caravan, with all its political scheming, plots and sub plots, would screech to a halt. Within seconds of the word of the caravan master's death getting out, business ventures would teeter and collapse. The critical replenishment of the colony's supplies was in question.

Santa Fe would be reeling, and men eager to become the next master of the caravan would rush to line up their moves. I expected we would see Facundo Salazar, alongside most of the region's alcaldes, hurrying to the palacio within the hour.

Luz stood in the first rays of sun in her garden wrapped in her woolen shawl, waiting for me to accompany her to the plaza. Neither of us was about to miss the feast of rumor the marketplace would offer, so we forged a temporary truce. I confirmed what she had just heard: Don Alfonso Vial, responsible for the importation of all of the presidio's supplies, richest man in town, and the sharpest thorn in Governor Anza's side, had died, and he had done so ignominiously, while going about his first business of the day.

We placed ourselves in the center of the gathering crowd. Jokes about the deceased merchant began to circulate before the sun had warmed the plaza's dirt. The humor was ribald and surprisingly cruel, and coming so soon after Vial's death, both Luz and I were shocked. After all, Don Alfonso Vial had died less than an hour before, and the manner of his going proved that he was human like the rest of us. But this was the town's first chance to get even with the person whose business practices had milked them dry for years.

"Died on the throne," the indelicate rumor flew.

"Easier than facing up to that young wife."

"Marriage to Señora Aurelia Inez, that's what did him in. No one over fifty could stand up to that."

"She had to be good at something," giggled the wags whose singsong verses glorified Alfonso's large posterior and the way he toed out when he walked. "Like a goose!" they were free to proclaim. "That goose is cooked," laughed others. "*Alfonso el ganso, ya se torció!*"

A neighbor lady told how she had found Aurelia, distraught and shrieking, standing in the muck of the byre outside the privy, screaming to the dead man inside that she was sorry, oh so sorry. No one could figure out what Aurelia could be sorry for, and why she'd be telling that to a man who'd clearly had a heart attack. Everyone agreed that Vial had proven to perfection that he was mortal after all, no better than the rest of the populace whom he had robbed and belittled.

Luisa Piña joined us on the plaza. When I told her about seeing Marisol helping Aurelia at the scene of the death, Luisa offered to go to the hacienda and bring Marisol away from there. My brother's wife, being gentry, would be granted access to the hacienda at once. Grateful, I guided her there and waited in the lane.

The procession of officials who traipsed into the widow's home was impressive. If I hadn't been so anxious to get Marisol back, I would have enjoyed watching their attempts at appearing properly grave, when their true mood was probably delight. It seemed forever until Luisa came out of the gate. She shook her head when she found me.

"Not there. Marisol left right away, as far as anyone can tell. Aurelia doesn't even remember Marisol dragging her inside. I cornered a woman in the kitchen to make sure there was no game being played here. Gave her a coin. She told me Marisol walked out the back door an hour ago. She must have gone to Juliana's."

"Why doesn't she just come home? She must know Beatriz is dead. What's left at Juliana's for her?"

"I'll find out," Luisa offered, patting my fisted hand. "Let me go home and fetch Estrella. She can take me to Juliana's."

I nodded meekly as Luisa departed for Luz's.

Suddenly horses sprinted around a bend in the lane. I stood aside to let the riders pass and recognized the governor in the midst of them, heading to the hacienda. The cohort jingled as it passed, capes fluttering, brass gleaming, in a flurry of heavy hooves and swinging manes. I caught a quick glimpse of Anza's face, stern and business-like, but with perhaps a touch of relief. Now that he was rid of Vial, he could begin to run things the way he liked.

When the governor came near, he spotted me standing there between the river and the road. As his troops flashed by leaving me spattered with wet earth, Anza turned his head in my direction and launched a wink.

Widow's Remorse

There was more grief for the wife when Anza and his men paid their condolence call at the home of the deceased. Once through Aurelia's doors, and given access to her courtyards, they couldn't help but discover the piles of hoarded supplies in every corner of her hacienda, valuable merchandise ranging from superior English guns, to the simpler provisions of woolen capes and salted meats that had been sent in Don Alfonso's care to supply the struggling garrison.

It was now clear that Alfonso Vial had made money for himself at every turn, first during negotiations with the merchants in Chihuahua, and then by tripling prices when he sold to the garrison. Meanwhile, the caravan master stole any items he could unload elsewhere for a better price.

His thieving was apparent the moment the governor's men pulled open the doors of the sheds in the yard behind Vial's home. A mound of shiny saddles, bales of beautiful blue-dyed wool, and boots made in Toledo lay under coverings of coarse homespun cloth. Anza's men uncovered trunks full of metal parts needed to repair broken weaponry, lance heads, tips for spears, and even the outlawed hawking blades. There were ingots of lead for ammunition that had never reached the colony's fighting men.

Doña Aurelia Inez's shrieks began all over again as heaps of what she thought were her own possessions were carried out the big gate of the hacienda and loaded into government carts. The widow's sorrow increased yet again when soldiers took her into custody for being an accomplice to defrauding the king. The crowd in front of the palacio gates reported they saw Aurelia's worried, tear-streaked face for a brief instant, when the wind snatched back her shawl.

Rumors flew that even if the government refrained from hanging Aurelia on the plaza, at the very least, Vial's wife would face banishment from New Mexico.

My family spread through town to take the measure of these events, and each of us later admitted to having searched for Marisol. In my own explorations, I didn't come across one person who thought Vial's widow should be placed under arrest, and though I looked everywhere, there was no trace of Marisol. One by one, we returned to the house at the close of the day.

"Marisol wasn't at Juliana's," Luisa Piña told me over supper. "Juliana and her sister were both home and neither had seen her. The curanderas said Marisol moved her belongings to Aurelia's the day before Beatriz died, and she hadn't been back.

"Francisco looked all over this side of town, and Juliana spent time searching the Analco. Agapita thought Marisol must be hiding somewhere at Aurelia's."

"Why would she hide?" I asked.

"They're finding contraband all over Vial's property. It's as though the hacienda is being looted. There must be men in every room, poking into every barn and byre. Any sensible woman would hide."

Luz looked up from her plate. "Did anyone think about asking Melchora where Marisol might be? After all, Marisol worked with the Indian woman over at Vial's."

"I did ask the curanderas," Luisa promptly replied, "but Juliana told me Marisol didn't like Melchora, so I felt there was no point in going to Salazar's."

"Even so, I'll go ask Melchora directly, in case she's seen her," I said. I shouldered my manta to go into the streets.

Luz stopped me by the door. "Melchora's not at her home."

"How on earth do you know the whereabouts of Salazar's Indian servant?" I challenged.

But before Luz could answer, Francisco swept into the yard. We went out to hear the latest news.

"The caravan's going to leave tomorrow, even after all that's happened. Anza has appointed a trio of scouts as temporary leaders; experienced men including Tito Bustamente, Vial's trail captain. The governor wants the caravan moving south, Vial's death properly investigated, and the man buried, before he chooses a new caravan master."

"That's an odd way to do things," said Luz, "sending the wagons before the master."

Francisco tried to explain. "The carts and the huge herds lumber along so slowly the new man can overtake them in a few days, probably before the caravan reaches Sevilleta."

"I suppose Anza needs to take his time, to avoid appointing the wrong sort of person, but trusting the colony's wealth to scouts?" Luz looked doubtful.

Francisco brushed off her concerns. "It's a wise move on Anza's part to get the wagon train out of here, particularly since it could snow again at any time. After the caravan's gone, he can slow things down. Local businessmen and most of the nearby alcaldes are already clamoring for Vial's job, but trust me, this time the governor will find a way to put his own man in there. No more wrangling with merchants who thwart his every move."

"So how are the odds running?" I popped an apple in my mouth and turned to Francisco. "Was Vial's death by gut rupture or murderous means?"

My brother warmed to the subject. "Half the men in Santa Fe wanted Vial dead, because they know he swindled them every chance he got. The other half would kill to get his job."

Luisa Piña turned to Francisco. "Why are you talking about the man's death as though it were murder? Can't a man's heart simply stop?"

Luz shook her head. "No one is sure. Inquiries are being made. Anza ordered Vial's body into the palace right away. The Indian woman was there, ready to prepare the corpse, but Investigator Olivas held her off."

Luz glanced at me. "Melchora. That's why I knew she wasn't home. The government uses her for laying out the dead. Herbs make the process less distasteful."

Luisa lifted her dark eyebrows. "Are you saying the palacio's no longer certain Vial died of natural causes? Are you suggesting the merchant was murdered?"

Francisco nodded.

"Come on. Give us the prevailing theory," I probed. "Did the governor somehow give Vial a heart attack while the merchant sat in his outhouse?"

Francisco's demeanor made me quit joking. "Even though the stolen goods in the hacienda proved the governor was right to distrust the merchant, Anza wouldn't dare kill Vial. The governor couldn't get away with murdering Croix's favorite New Mexican."

"Okay. If not Anza," I pressed, "perhaps they're thinking it's the wife who sped up Vial's departure."

"It's true they found her sobbing about how sorry she was," Luisa added.

"Yes, but sorry for what?" Francisco rejoined. "That her husband's heart quit? Maybe Aurelia was sorry she fed him a breakfast that upset his stomach, and on the morning of the grand departure too. Aurelia had no motive to kill her husband. With Vial dead, Aurelia's a much poorer woman."

"No doubt," I added, "but I bet they hold on to her, just in case."

Luz broke in. "Living with that man, any wife would have doctored his drink! Personally, I can't imagine going to bed with Alfonso Vial."

Francisco's eyes dared me not to laugh.

Loosened up, Luz fed us more bits she'd gleaned. "If it *was* foul play, and, boys, they aren't certain of that yet, the men examining this are expected to rule Aurelia out. The woman is beside herself with grief. It appears Aurelia was truly attached to her old sybarite."

"Many actresses have been paid less, and for better performances," Francisco suggested.

Luz would have none of it. "Accusing the wife is too obvious. Everyone in town points their finger at the weakest person, this silly woman who's not much more than a girl. Aurelia Inez had everything to gain by hanging on to her husband. Meanwhile, all the gentry, every merchant and every landowner, everyone including the governor, had his reasons for wanting Vial eliminated. They should let that poor girl go at once."

"They're not brutalizing her, mother, they're only asking her a few questions," Francisco offered.

"Probably, but the men interrogating her were Vial's rivals, the ones who wanted him out of the way," Luz added. "They'd do anything to turn the attention away from themselves."

Luisa Piña gave us a look you'd direct at squabbling children. "You're all grasping at straws."

But Francisco kept on, "If Vial's death was murder, Anza has to be under suspicion. The governor had more motive than most."

"Don't talk like that, Francisco! Don't say that out loud again," Luz whacked him. "You've gotten yourself in enough trouble already."

My brother held her off with a stiff arm. "Mother, you'd better believe that Don Crespín's men, who've traveled all the way to Santa Fe to protect the king's interests, will take the possibility of Anza's involvement under grave consideration."

Luisa was right. We were speculating wildly. I needed to get back to the plaza and look hard for Marisol before it was completely dark. Where was that woman hiding herself? This was making me crazy.

Beatriz died for reasons we could only guess at, and Marisol had been her friend, working at her side concocting forbidden love tonics for rich clients. The most powerful of those clients died today. The number of deaths in Santa Fe was mounting. Tension was in the air. In this shaken town, I needed to find Marisol fast.

"If murder is what they're suspecting," Luisa said, wrapping herself more tightly in her shawl, "I pity the man who's supposed to discover who did it. Finding Vial's murderer will be a thankless task when all of Santa Fe is grateful for the deed."

Luisa was right. This was something I wanted no part of, but because I was only a beginner in the spying business, I doubted Sebastian would add that job to my list. Still I'd have to steer clear of him as long as I could.

My stepmother picked the cigarette out of Francisco's hand and took a deep draw. I accepted the proffered punché, enjoyed one last puff, and threw the husk to the ground.

"Another hour or two of standing around talking like this and you'll figure out if it was murder or not, and maybe even who did it," I said, "but right now I need to look for Marisol. I'm off."

Prime To Vespers

Santa Fe was deathly still. The last wagons for the caravan had trundled to fields on the south side of town in preparation for taking off at dawn. The streets were empty, the stars shone brightly overhead, and the only sound was the metallic clang of a bell in the church tower.

Spicy piñon smoke traveled on the light wind. Here and there a pale yellow glow from a fireplace seeped out of a doorway or through the barred windows of a home. There were lights in the window at the palacio, but the plaza was as empty of living people as a tomb.

I crossed the log bridge to the Analco and went down the lane as far as Juliana's. There was no point in going in. Juliana would have sent word if Marisol had come to her. I slipped past the house and out to the barn behind, the one where I had found Celedonia spying. It occurred to me that Marisol knew about the place and could have hidden there.

I slipped inside. The barn was dark as death. This time there were no sounds of breathing. My eyes were used to the night after my walk through the unlit streets, but I made out no shape, no human form. I stooped to peer through the same gap I'd used before, the place that gave me a view into Juliana's house. I rested my fingers on a hewn log to lean forward and look.

I touched something dry and sharp. Someone had dropped empty piñon nuts there. The pile of cracked shells was deep, carelessly left by the last person who chose to stop and peer for a while into the curandera's home. I trailed my fingers through the telltale litter and decided I should visit the sisters after all.

Juliana took a long time to answer my knock. Her hair was down and she held a comb in one hand. I'd interrupted her on her way to bed. There was no sign of Agapita or the child.

"Nando?" Juliana held the door open a crack.

"Sorry ma'am, but I need to tell you something."

"Come in." Juliana ushered me inside, offered a seat by the hearth and encouraged the fire back to life.

"I've been wanting to talk to you too," she told me.

"Marisol?" I asked her.

"No, nothing from her. Are you worried?"

"Of course I'm worried. The last time I saw her she was dragging an unconscious woman across Alfonso Vial's yard, and no one has seen Marisol since. She's pregnant, most likely terrified, and who knows if she's found a place to sleep tonight."

Juliana put her hand on my arm. "Sit with me a while. Let's see if we can figure this out."

The mestiza settled herself on the bench opposite me and began to shell corn with her strong brown fingers.

"Remember, Marisol is healthy as a horse and good at taking care of herself," Juliana tried to assure me. "Also, she does not want to be dependent on your family."

"She *is* my family."

Juliana picked up another ear of corn and shook her head from side to side. "Not yet, she isn't. Not in her mind anyway. You know, my friend, she's not like you Spaniards. Marisol is an Indian girl."

"Do you have any idea which people she came from?" I asked.

"Probably Comanche. That's what she thinks, anyway."

"Marisol is part Comanche?" My voice rose in surprise. How could I be so dumb that I hadn't realized this basic fact about my woman?

Juliana went on. "The life Marisol used to live was nothing at all like the one Luz expects her to follow here in Santa Fe. Marisol was a free spirit for many years. That couple up in Abiquiú tried to tame her, but they couldn't, and in the end they sold her to Arsenio. You know how successful that arrangement was."

I nodded glumly, staring into the yellow flames.

"Arsenio may have been the kind of man who had to purchase his wife, but even so, living with him Marisol had a life closer to what she once knew; a way of life that's very different from what she's living now with you Aguilars. Married to Arsenio, she was in the country. She ran her own home. He was often away with the militia and her days were her own. She far out-witted Arsenio and could arrange matters as she pleased. Marisol told me she hates to wear shoes. Even moccasins bother her. Luz is after her all the time, trying to turn her into a well brought up Spanish woman, something Marisol is not."

"Luz bosses all of us around. It's her way," I granted.

"By Marisol's customs, the baby belongs to her alone and not to any man. She is not married and she doesn't want to become a servant or an unpaid retainer in a city home. Marisol knows she needs to birth this child where there are people nearby, but afterwards she'll hurry back to her farm in the country."

Juliana watched my face. What she saw in my eyes told her it was time to give me better news.

"I believe Marisol is fond of you, Nando. If you're the child's father, she'll be glad. But she's told me she hates the thought of living in a Spanish family, with all the rules for proper behavior and the religious rigmarole. Prime to Vespers! Prime to Vespers! Marisol resents having to behave in the way Luz, a woman of an almost died-out generation, expects her to."

There was silence. I picked up an empty cob and used it to scrape blue kernels off another ear of corn. Juliana moved her basket over where I could reach it.

"If Marisol would talk to me, she'd find I agree with her about every part of that."

"I suggested as much," the curandera said, "but Marisol said no, that life in Santa Fe was different for you. She said you were attached to your family, even beholden to them, in ways you would never back out on."

"But Juliana," I protested, "my plan all along has been to get us back to the ranch in Abiquiú. The family would let me be its overseer. The place is remote enough to please any Comanche girl, and Luz will probably never return there. My stepmother's too old."

Juliana's face was pleasant in the firelight when she turned to me. "That sounds like it would work. Why haven't you gone back to Abiquiú? What's stopping you?"

"The Governor. The King of Spain. Anyone else you can think of. My father built that ranch in the wilderness with his own two hands. Before I was born, Spanish officials banished my father to the barren country above Abiquiú, but Benito Aguilar turned the Piedra Lumbre into his own paradise. After many good years, the Comanches flared up, the Navajos added their firepower, my father died of a long illness and Governor Mendinueta pulled us off the grant. We don't know yet if the current government will let us go back. No better right exists than ours, but we're told there are now other claimants petitioning for the land. So here I wait, stuck in town, unable to take Marisol to my own home.

"It's less of a hardship for my brothers, " I continued. "Francisco's a city boy by nature, and Carlos has an important role that keeps him busy in Santa Fe. Getting the ranch back matters to me, more than to the rest of them."

"I see," Juliana said thoughtfully. "Why did you come here tonight? What did you want to tell me, Nando?"

"All of this, I guess. I've needed to talk about Marisol, to get some reassurance. When I went looking for her I thought she could be in your cowshed. The truth is, Juliana, I went into that barn once before. There's a way to watch your house without being seen."

Juliana raised an eyebrow. "Is this how you treat your friends? You spy on them?"

"I went to your barn the evening Marisol arrived to stay with you. I was desperate to see if she was all right and I was looking for a chance to talk to her."

"I think I understand that."

"Juliana," I blurted, "there was someone else inside your barn that night. She'd been watching your window, too."

The woman set the basket of corn on the floor and looked at me squarely.

"A woman who hated Beatriz, who was jealous of her. She called your sister a bruja. She said Beatriz had used curanderas' tricks to bewitch her husband."

There was a long silence. "Are you going to tell me who?" Juliana asked.

185

"I'm not sure that I should. Not to be stubborn. I'm thinking of your safety, Juliana."

"Knowing my sister, I'm not surprised it was some man's wife. A scorned woman, figuring out her revenge," Juliana calculated.

"You're right, and a woman of means as well. Someone who could harm a girl she thought was in her way. Though she assured me she wouldn't."

"How long ago was that?"

"A week ago Sunday. Five days before Beatriz died."

"But now everything's changed." Juliana's voice was bitter. "Beatriz's threat to the married women of Santa Fe is over. My sister is dead and her beauty rots in the ground."

"Tonight I went back to your barn, because I thought Marisol might hide there. When I stood in the place where you can see your house, I found a pile of piñon shells piled on the ledge. There were lots of them. Since the night I'd been there before, someone else watched your place for a long time. Maybe that person had been watching Beatriz? Or you? Given that Beatriz died, I thought you should know."

Juliana didn't respond for a long time. She busied herself lifting a pot onto the trivet in the hearth. She pushed the flaming logs to one side of the fireplace and spread live coals around the sides of the pot. She took time to add more sticks to keep the larger fire bright. By the light, I saw her face and it was troubled.

After a long time she asked, "The rich woman called my sister a witch. What are the ways to kill a witch, Nando?"

What a question. I rummaged around in my brain. There was one way I definitely knew. I had seen it only two weeks before. I hesitated, wondering whether or not to tell Juliana about the man on Deer Creek. She took my hesitation for ignorance.

"Well, there's no reason you should know, but since half the town thinks I'm a witch, I've made a list of things to look out for. Beatriz missed one and someone got her." Firelight sparkled on Juliana's cheeks.

"You drop a large rock on a witch," she said slowly. "That way, her soul can't escape; it stays trapped and broken. The death is so sudden, there's no time for the witch to cast a spell on you, to transform herself, or escape."

"Is that what they're saying?" I asked softly. "That Beatriz's death wasn't an accident?"

"On this side of the river, yes, that's the rumor, never mind that the surgeon at the palacio wrote off her death off as an herb picker's unlucky day."

I thought for a few moments. "You'd need to have a perfect rock in mind, one that could be moved, but was also big enough. You'd have to know when the witch would be sitting there, right under it. You'd have to be in place, get your trajectory right and the degree of drop. Then you'd have to move a huge boulder."

"I know. It wouldn't be easy at all. The part that works is Beatriz had a place she went to often. There is a seep on the hillside, in a place where the sun warms the ground all day long, and the ledge holds the warmth, even this late in the year. Beatriz often brought living plants home from there that had already frozen elsewhere. If someone had been watching her, was trying to get her, they would learn she lingered below the rock outcropping on that steep hill."

"How would one thin lady, already beginning to age, move that boulder?" I mused.

Juliana's eyes burned with firelight when she said, "Lady? No wonder you're afraid to name her! Salazar's wife."

My eyes searched the curandera's. She lowered them and whispered, "I know Beatriz had been seeing Facundo

Salazar. He was far too dangerous for her, but my sister had a weakness, some great longing, and certain men matched her need better than others. "

I didn't say anything.

"I do know where Beatriz's talents lay," Juliana acknowledged.

"So, using a hefty length of oak, or more than one person, the rock could be moved," I said, realizing I had heard this theory from Padre Miera at Beatriz's burial. "Men could be hired. 'Get rid of that witch for me. She's a threat to the town.' " The blustering Toribio rose in my mind.

Juliana's face remained solemn.

"Still, the rock might have tumbled on its own," I offered. "Freezing and thawing could break it loose. The ground would be soft along there, from the seep."

"That's possible," said Juliana. Then she turned with a desperate look. "As though I could bring judgment against Celedonia, or anyone of her class!"

"Celedonia did tell me she wouldn't hurt Beatriz, that she would try to talk to her. I took her at her word, and Juliana, Beatriz was a threat to other wives as well. I've got to tell you, I know there's at least one young man with damaged tail feathers. He called Beatriz *puta* and *bruja*, because she rejected him."

We mulled that over while Juliana extracted the pot from the fire and poured hot liquid into two mugs. We blew on the tea until it was cool enough to taste. After a few sips I said, "There's another way to kill witches."

When Juliana stayed silent I said, "You hang them to die, by hooking their elbows over a roof beam."

Juliana shuddered.

"I've seen that done, and not too long ago," I confessed to her.

Juliana set her mug down, questioning me with her eyes.

"It was a man. He'd been strung up that way in an old ramada on Deer Creek."

"Dead when you found him?"

"Long past," I replied.

"What did you do?" she asked.

"Ran away. Threw up. Told the palacio. They sent a crew out there to investigate, but by the time they got to the place the corpse was gone."

"I didn't know you'd been in on that. The town went mad," said Juliana.

"I'm the one who discovered the body. A few days later I found the dead man's clothes, half-burned and buried. It's been about two weeks now since he was killed."

Juliana drifted into her thoughts, assembling the pieces. She was wondering whether more danger was imminent, whether she, her surviving sister, and the child who lived with them were safe. If people were using the old ways to kill witches, it was a sign trouble was brewing.

"Do you know who the man was?" Juliana looked up.

"A Pecos man."

"Are you sure?"

"It's likely. Along with his burned clothes, I found a necklace with a half-moon shell. Melchora identified it; said it came from her pueblo. She asked me to give it to her, so she could return it to Pecos."

"Did you?"

"No. I told her I'd take it back myself. That made her cross, but in the end she calmed down. She urged me to take care."

"Melchora gets mad easily," Juliana said before we slipped into silence.

There was much to think about. After a while I took my leave, begging her to be even more cautious than usual, and walked through the quiet lanes toward home, wondering where in the cold, silent town Marisol had found a place to sleep.

Cruzita's News

The caravan lumbered down the Camino Real just as the sun's light poked over the mountains. The carts and wagons rolled away to the south, carrying skins, tallow, rugs, salt, socks, nuts, buffalo hides, Apache baskets, and the countless packets of the government correspondence required by Mexico.

With the caravan over the horizon, Anza could now take as long as he needed to wrangle with the businessmen, the assorted alcaldes, and the investigators sent by Croix, to choose a new master of the caravan. On a good horse, it would be easy for the appointed man to catch up fast with the cumbersome wagons and surging herds of dirty sheep.

The sun shot rays into the plaza and the church bells started to ring. The priests were beginning their work for Vial's soul.

I hadn't found Marisol last night and had barely slept. For the moment there was nothing more to do but get back to work. Sebastian's charge to me had been to get on it, to discover whose body had been hanging in the ramada, and "Hurry up," he'd ordered.

Sebastian also asked me to shed light on the troubling effigy, and above all, I was to staunch the rising reference to the word "witch," which was being used now in the matter of Beatriz's death. I hadn't been doing a very good job. The jittery town was spinning every owl sighting, headless rat, and batch of cheese that soured, into proof that witchery pervaded Santa Fe.

Prowling around on the job for Sebastian, I might turn up Marisol, and if by luck I discovered anything about Señor Vial, I'd surely get a bonus. I headed into the underbelly of the town to glean any recent accountings of murder and witchcraft.

My path led past the Analco's gloomy church into the surrounding cluster of houses and hovels. The *castas*, all those people whose veins did not run with pure Spanish blood, didn't get to have haciendas on the north side of the river. Here in the barrio, homes were pieced together out of anything at hand. Dwellings were stacked room upon room, with ladders leading to the upstairs quarters. It was hard to tell where one house ended and the next began.

I was crossing a courtyard, watching boys feed logs into an outdoor oven when an old woman croaked at me, "Nando! Come home to your own?"

Cruzita sat in front of her tiny hut made of juniper palings and brush, in the hovering stench of her torched pig shed. Usually, I tried to avoid this crone, but today I was glad to find her. Cruzita and I were going to have a discussion. She'd never liked it one bit that a half-breed, the same as she, wound up bedding down with gentry. Fortunately my run-ins with her were rare. Cruzita kept to herself, mostly traveling through the back alleys among the trash heaps and privies. Once I watched a cleric turn the old woman away from the church. Cruzita left, but not until she spat on the man's sandals.

"Cruzita, you're looking better than ever," I lied.

Her face seemed as though it had been crumpled up wet, then left to dry. Craggy wrinkles pleated the skin around her mouth and draped her neck like rotted silk.

There was still a spark in her obsidian eyes, but she looked like that stuffed effigy in the palacio: an abandoned pile of homespun rags, bundled and dark, with a protruding foot so thin I thought it was a twig. When she spoke I had to bend down right in front of her face to catch the dry wind of her words.

She wheezed, "You're heading to the curandera's house again, aren't you?"

Did Cruzita keep track of my trips to Juliana's? Those old eyes saw everything that happened in the barrio.

"Maybe."

Cruzita became fascinated with a patch of dirt on her fingers.

I needed something to get her talking. I rummaged around in my pocket until I found the little bag that held my smoking gear. I rolled a punche cigarette and inserted it, unlit, into Cruzita's mouth.

"You can light this in a minute. What I need to know, Cruzita, is who did it? Who killed Beatriz?"

She cocked her head at me and smiled sideways, enjoying her secret. Cruzita extracted the cigarette and peered intently at it, as though it were a crystal ball, then laughed. Was that white stuff in her eye milk?

"Look around you, Nando. Bad business living near witches."

"Cut it out," I commanded. Cruzita was feeding me nonsense; besides, she was the closest thing to a witch I'd ever seen.

She sat there scowling.

"All right," I said, retrieving the cigarette from her hand. "I'll get a light for you, but then you've got to tell me what you know."

There was a glitter, maybe a twinkle from an eye at the edge of the old woman's ratty shawl. I stepped away and pushed aside the skins that kept the autumn winds out of her hut. A dim bit of fire glowed on a mud hearth. I lit the cigarette with a burning splinter and puffed to get the cornhusk burning. Returning to Cruzita, I held it a couple of inches from her mouth. She tried for the prize.

"Someone everyone knows, but you don't see on this side of the river any more."

"I need a name, Cruzita."

She shook her head, more stubborn than I'd reckoned.

"You're sure you're not telling?" The bundled old woman nodded with vigor, so I put the cigarette in my own mouth and turned to leave.

Watching her chance at a smoke walking away, Cruzita gave in. She patted the ground beside her, inviting me to sit. I did.

"How old are you, Nando?"

"Twenty-three, I think."

She laughed at the very thought of a person so young. "Then know this took place before you were born, boy, and I never told anybody, not in all these years." Her ancient lips pulled on the cigarette, and she smiled. She grabbed a fold of my manta and pulled me close.

"There was a rich girl, spoiled, supposed to be marrying soon, but eight months pregnant by another man. They hired me to serve at the birth, helped by one of the family's Pueblo slaves. Trust me, the pay was good. The young Pueblo woman who helped knew her life was worthless if she talked. We had our orders."

Cruzita paused to suck on the cigarette. She drew her shawl back from her face and spoke more clearly now, excited to be back in her past.

"*Ay de mi*, what a hot night it was, but that young rica wore all her clothes. I'd draped her fine shawl over her upright knees. She was drenched from labor, lying on a woolen blanket in the straw. That girl was struggling and her face was as white as the candles that lit the room.

"Toward the end, blood ran down the Pueblo woman's arms, mixing with her sweat. We gave the girl a knot of cloth to bite on, to silence her screams.

"This birth was hidden away in a filthy granary. Mouse droppings lay in piles on the floor. We couldn't stand upright under the low ceiling."

Cruzita's voice dropped off. Just as I was wondering if the old woman had fallen asleep, the hag turned her smirking face to me and pronounced, "The gentry will turn on you, Nando. You should stay with your own kind."

I ignored the warning, but took the hint, and poured more punché into the old woman's cupped hand. "Who was the girl, Cruzita?"

"Wait," she barked. "You'll get what you want."

I laid another square of cornhusk in her dirt-black palm. All she'd told me so far was that someone rich might be involved, someone from the other side of the river. I leaned against the adobe wall, tilting toward the crone so I wouldn't miss a word, but once Cruzita started up again, I wasn't sure I wanted to be hearing any of this.

Cruzita's old voice croaked, "The girl shrieked. I clamped my hand over her mouth. She heaved her hips and the infant's head and shoulders came out, then the rest of the tiny body straggled onto the spread-out hay, slick and shining in the candlelight. The mother didn't look at her child, but lay without moving, exhausted.

"The Pueblo woman held the child up, let it yell once, then took out her knife. By all the blessed saints, I thought she was going to kill that baby and maybe even the mother, but the Indian drove the knife into the earthen floor. She was only cleaning the blade before she cut the two beings apart.

" 'It's a girl. She's whole,' I informed the rich girl.

" 'Get rid of it,' the new mother ordered.

" 'I know what you want,' " I shushed her. " 'I'm about to. But we've got to finish with you first.'

"A few minutes later the delivery was complete and the Indian pulled the girl's skirts down.

" 'Sleep,' she told her. 'I'll take care of this and be back before daylight. Don't you at least want to see your child?'

" 'No.'

"That Indian and I looked at each other. For a new mother to turn away from her babe was unbelievable, but the girl rolled onto her side, jammed her hands under her cheek and went to sleep.

"The Pueblo woman wiped the yellowish cream off the baby's skin, spat once in each of the infant's eyes and dried the child. She wrapped it in her shawl, stuck the bundle under her arm, pushed open the door and ducked into the hot summer night.

"My share of the work was over until dawn when I would bring the rica back home. For now the girl was asleep. I looked out the open door into the night. Part of my duty was to make sure the Indian got rid of the baby in a way that no one in this town would know it ever existed.

"I left the sleeping girl and followed the Pueblo woman. With the baby under her arm, the Indian ran through the dark and turned into the dung-strewn alley that runs behind the big houses in the town. I barely managed to keep her in sight. She came to the rear wall of the church and quickly took the stone stairs up to the priest's private quarters. It was occurring to me that she was about to defy orders and leave the infant on the church steps.

"I hurried to catch up, to stop her, but the woman didn't hesitate outside the convento, or even knock. She shoved her way inside and called, 'Padre!'

"I stood on the little porch in the dark, peeking into the room, trying to figure out what this Indian was doing.

"The priest sat up on his cot, his nightshirt twisted on his body.

" 'Oh! Already?'

" 'Of course. Did you think I'd let her go the full nine months?'

"The padre grunted and swung his feet to the floor, not minding that he stood naked in front of the Pueblo woman. He started to pull on his cassock, then yanked it back over his head and threw it on the bed.

" 'Suffocating. Anyway, I need proper clothing for this work.' The priest bent to a chest by the door and took out trousers and a shirt.

" 'Do you have a manta or a cape?'

"The padre turned and looked at the woman, 'Why? It's hot.'

" 'You've got to conceal this one,' the Indian said, unrolling her shawl and laying the naked baby onto the priest's bed.

He stopped dressing and looked down at the infant. 'Another little miracle from God,' he said with a twist in his voice. 'Did the mother survive?'

" 'Of course. Selfish and sturdy. She'll be on her feet by noon.'

" 'Remorse?'

" 'None.'

"The Pueblo woman wiped a little scum off the baby's flesh. The child began to cry. The woman put the infant to her own full breast.

"The priest laced on his moccasins and said, 'I understand this babe was conceived by rape, but even so, I've never known a mother who would order her baby to be killed.'

" 'She believes the disposal of the child is all arranged. When I return, she won't ask questions and she'll never mention any of this again. The midwife was paid well. She won't talk.'

" 'For a pagan, you surprise me,' the priest said. 'I understand the woman's need, but I could never condone this baby's murder. Thank you, my girl.' "

Cruzita chuckled at the next memory that arose before her eyes. The crone lowered her voice still more and put her lips against my ear.

"The priest leaned down and kissed that Indian woman right on the lips. The poor baby got stuck between them and let out a howl.

" 'All right, all right, I'm off,' the man said. 'There's nothing remarkable about the padre visiting the neighboring pueblo once in a while. The second house as I enter the plaza, right?'

" 'It's the first two-storied one. The family is ready and one of the daughters has a baby, so there's milk.' "

Cruzita leaned closer and declared, "I was beginning to understand. The Pueblo woman was going to let the baby live. She had planned this out, and with the priest! Lovers, they had to be. You decide, Nando. Listen."

Cruzita's voice grew animated. "The priest pulled aside the round neck of the woman's blouse and kissed her breast. 'Your own milk is still in,' he whispered, 'and so nicely.'

" 'Fine man of God you are,' the woman laughed, gently pushing him away. 'Take this urchin and hurry,' she said. 'If my mistress or the baby's father ever hear their daughter lives, my life's worth nothing, and you'll be sent as far away as Zuni.'

" 'I expect that's soon to happen, in any case,' the man admitted, his face glum. 'I'm the kind of priest they'd love to get rid of, but lacking a way, they'll bury me alive instead. It amounts to the same, being sent to Zuni. I'll be back from this task two nights from now. Can you get away then?'

"The Indian woman threw him a bright smile. 'Since I know her secret, I'll have more freedom now. The mistress won't dare deny me favors. I'll come.' She put her arms around the man's waist and for a moment he dropped his face against her hair.

"The priest tucked the baby under his arm and turned to the woman. 'Be careful, girl. If you push your mistress too hard she may take measures. A woman who would send her infant off to die won't hesitate to silence an Indian slave.'

"The Pueblo woman listened, but then chuckled, 'Not to worry, Jesus-man. I have powers too.'

" 'So I noticed,' he whispered, brushing her lips with his own.

" 'Come,' he said, pushing open the door that connected his rooms to the church. 'This urchin needs to be baptized.' "

The old crone went silent for a long time. I'd gotten stiff, sitting on the cold dirt in front of Cruzita's hut, watching her pulling on her cold cigarette. I shifted my position and since I'd been on the verge of hearing a name, I gave in and relit her smoke with mine. Eventually the rolled husk lit and the woman smoked a few puffs. I thought her story had slipped back into the cobwebs of her brain, but I underestimated Cruzita's staying power. Her voice came back and creaked on.

"I moved closer so I could see inside the church," she continued. "By then nothing would have stopped me. The priest carried the baby to the altar. He lit a candle, took the veil off the holy water and spoke the ancient words, brushing the baby's forehead with his finger in the sign of the cross. The padre looked over at the Indian woman. 'You're the witness if I ever need one. Has she got a name?'

" 'A name? You must be joking! Her mother sent her out to die.'

" 'Hurry up. Give me something. Anything will do.'

" 'Bella?'

" 'Fine. La Bella. Father unknown.'

" 'Mother dead. Can you say that?'

" 'I could write that, but I still have to name her. The mother's always known.'

" 'Padre, isn't there any way around identifying her? Just say the baby's a child of the church. Left on the steps.'

"The priest sprinkled an extra dash of water on the baby's brow. 'Perhaps this one won't get written in the book, though I like to keep count of the souls I've saved. It looks good back in Mexico. *In nomine patria* . . .' he hummed. 'Delivered from the fires of eternal damnation by this little drop of water. Here, wrap this creature in her blanket.' I watched him replace the baptismal implements, preparing to leave.

"I crept back into the vestibule and pushed through the door, while the priest and the Pueblo woman gathered a few items for his departure.

" 'Give her another sip,' he cajoled, easing the woman's breast from her blouse. 'See, she craves it.'"

Old Cruzita grinned at me. "I saw that holy man wink.

"The woman put the baby to her breast, but the child was too small to drink much. The Indian wiped the tiny mouth with a corner of her sleeve and ran a hand over the high, fuzzy forehead before she yielded the infant to the care of the priest.

"I slipped into the garden and watched the padre stride away into the night, carrying that baby girl to the people in the pueblo. Growing up beside the river could be good for a child. It wouldn't be the same as living in town and learning Spanish ways, but the priest understood that God in his mercy would watch over this baby.

"La Bella's mother," Cruzita whispered to me. "She always wanted that baby dead."

Cruzita clutched my shoulder and used it to stand. She heaved herself up, shuffled over to a patch of sunlight and lay down in it. Her voice was giving out, but I could hear her say, "When you find the lady, give her Cruzita's regards, will you? She must have learned her daughter survived."

"A name, Cruzita. Damn it, give me the mother's name."

I was practically on my knees in the street trying to hear her, but the old woman shook her head.

"Vial, then! What do you know about the caravan master?"

Cruzita strained to look up at me. "It's all one," she hissed. "The dead, the deeds, the dying."

The oracle had spoken. She fell asleep. I returned the cornhusk to the woman's blistered lips, tucked her moldy blanket around her naked feet, and pushed on.

Hustle

An hour later, I'd turned up only a few more fragments of information, all of them as useless as the duff Cruzita fed me. I'd asked her about Beatriz and crazy as ever, the crone had wasted my time talking about someone named Bella. Fed up, I crossed the river. I took a side lane that led me past the priests' garden where I'd last seen Beatriz alive. I stared at the bench where my friend had sat and tried to recall her prettiness, to rid my mind of the awful images of her death. I hadn't been there a minute when the gate to the garden opened and Padre Miera called out.

"Nando! Glad you came by. I've been wanting a word with you."

"Yes, Padre?" What would this turn out to be?

"Do you have plans for the next few days?" The portly priest stood in the middle of the flagstone path, pleased I'd wandered into his web.

"I'd like to find Marisol, for one. You haven't seen her, have you?"

"I'm not talking about your love adventures, Nando. Those can wait. I have a job for you."

"Father?"

"I'll give you a load of firewood if you'll help me."

It was a beginning. I waited to hear more.

"I can't make it to Pecos this week, because of Señor Vial's death," Miera said. "It's past time a priest went to the church there. We have an obligation to say Mass at the pueblo at least once a month."

"The *visita*, yes, I know."

"I've decided to send Padre Domingo in my stead. He isn't needed for Don Vial's funeral, and frankly, it would be nice to get him out from under foot."

"I understand."

"Can you leave Friday? I'll provide mules. You can make it to the pueblo in a day, stay three nights, and return Monday. Domingo can hear confession, teach catechism classes, and say Mass a few times over the weekend."

I groaned inwardly.

"Can't you send Brother Severiano instead of me?"

"Not possible. The lay brother sneaked off with the caravan. I wasn't all that surprised. He made no secret of hating New Mexico. Too wanton and witch ridden for him. I need you to do this, Nando."

It sounded like a lot of church to me, but then I remembered I had a reason to go to Pecos, something about a half moon shell and an unexplained death on Deer Creek.

"How much wood, padre?"

"Don't get pushy with me, Nando."

"And if I'm to represent the Church, I'll need a new shirt, and a manta that isn't frayed and full of stickers."

Miera looked me up and down. "I see the necessity. Those I can provide. New clothes and six panniers of split wood. Delivered by donkey on the day of your return, if you get Domingo back here in one piece, without letting him damage the reputation of the Order of St. Francis."

"The shirt and blanket in advance of the trip, please. Besides, I know what you're asking. I'm to keep Domingo's nose out of the wine."

"Precisely. He's better though. I keep him on his knees half the day, and at my side the rest of the time, but now I have to launch a major appeal to heaven to get Vial's sentence mitigated. I thought of you to be the padre's caretaker, since you've already experienced the heat of Domingo's vocation."

Padre Miera had no idea I had another paid assignment, working for the governor, but it wouldn't be hard to convince Sebastian this trip would further our investigation into the death at Deer Creek.

Then I'd only have the problem of a roof that leaked like a sieve and the missing mother of my child. There were still three days before I was to take Domingo to Pecos. I figured if I hustled I could get things under control.

Miera leaned toward me and asked in a much quieter voice, "What more have you heard about Beatriz?"

"I've been checking the barrio," I told him, "to see what they're saying there about her death."

"Good, good," Miera muttered. "What did you learn?"

"To the officials, Beatriz is dead, buried, and no longer of concern. No one at the palacio is giving her a thought, but people in the barrio are muttering that a jealous wife did her in."

"Consistent with my own dark thoughts," Miera reminded me.

"I do, and most of the gossip sides with you. But wives aside, there was also a man named Toribio who hated her, said she was a whore and a witch. Sebastian took him into custody after Cruzita's shed was burned, that day they tried to drown Margarita Chacon. The sergeant was afraid not just Beatriz, but other women, might be in Toribio's sights. But last night

Sebastian told me he'd had to let the youth go. Hasn't seen him since."

"A tough kid from Agua Fria?" Miera asked.

"Do you know him?"

The padre nodded, as he figured something out on his fingers. "How long ago did Beatriz die?"

"We found her body three days ago, but she died the day before."

Miera shook his head. "Then Toribio didn't kill Beatriz. He was busy fighting for his own life, laid low on his pallet. His whole family was down. A little sister got sick first, twisting with pain in her belly. Toribio had the same fever and pains, but he was stronger than the child and Domingo thought he might make it. The padre was too late to baptize the child before she died. Domingo dragged back in, dejected, just before we buried Beatriz.

"Toribio told Domingo he'd been cursed. A witch in the woods struck him with the evil eye and he fell into bed that same night."

"Was his little sister with him when that happened?" I asked.

"No. The girl had been ill for days."

"When Toribio's on his feet, we'll have to watch out for him, Padre. He's mean enough to go after the supposed witch in revenge."

"It will be a while. The youth was very sick," Miera replied, keeping his demeanor grave.

Too sick to get out of bed the day Beatriz died. That seemed to eliminate Toribio.

"Padre, do you know that dropping a boulder is a way to eliminate witches? Juliana thinks some woman rolled a rock on Beatriz to get even for bewitching a husband."

Miera raised an eyebrow. "A rejected wife could easily jump to that conclusion about a rival with access to love philters, but I believe few women have what it takes to murder their rivals. Still, if this is how the town's talking," he mused, "I should find a way to move Juliana's family out of Santa Fe for now."

We both stopped to consider that. "Padre, how can people rely on curanderas to heal them, and then revile them for being different?"

The priest replied, "One of the devil's signature acts is to befuddle reason."

Like any good churchman, Miera had sidestepped my question. The bell chimed in the bell tower. The padre turned to check the position of the sun and said, "There is so much to do, so much upheaval. I don't want that poor girl's death to be forgotten because of Alfonso Vial's demise. No one's certain, but she may well have been murdered, while Vial's death appears to be what happens to a fat old man."

Miera managed a laugh as he hitched his belt over his bulging stomach. "However, Beatriz's proclivities didn't help the situation. Beatriz personified the word *bewitching*."

If only he knew, I thought, but then, being male, perhaps he did. I let the intriguing thought drop.

"They're sure that's how Vial died? Of natural causes?"

"It's official. Heart attack. The woman who laid him out said nothing was present to indicate otherwise. I spoke with the Indian myself. It was very late. Croix's men made her wait while they did their own investigation." Miera started toward the door of the convento.

"Friday to Pecos, then. First light?"

"First light," I agreed. I knelt and kissed the padre's ring. He gave me a pat and waddled into his lair.

Four days with Domingo. Maybe I could lose the drunk in the canyons, or maybe he would run into that fleet-footed lady on the mesa top and never trouble any of us again.

I loaded sacks of grain onto Luz's old cart, which squeaked all the way to the mill. I loved watching the water slide through the sluices and hit the paddles on the wheel that turned the stones.

"Wheat? Okay, Nando, dump that sack in here," the miller said.

While the millstones were clunking away, saving our women weeks of work, I asked the miller what he knew.

Manuel wiggled the little dancing damsel, making a slight adjustment to the mechanism with his snow-white finger, and then tested the grit of the flour. Bending to check the flow, he said, "They say she poisoned him."

I managed not to lift my eyebrows before I said, "That's not what the padre told me."

"Vial's wife had been working a few drinks into him at night, special ones. Trying to get a little manliness out of him, 'cause she wanted a baby. They say she kept his cup full for him and then one night adjusted the ingredients."

This miller was full of tripe.

"Have you seen Señora Vial? Aurelia Inez isn't that type of person at all," I protested. "Where did you hear this?"

"My woman," said the miller flatly. "Check with yours. They're all babbling about it."

My woman, I thought, wishing I still had one. Wouldn't I love to have a chat with *my woman*? And didn't Luisa Piña tell me she saw my woman sitting there between two curanderas, adding fresh herbs to Vial's bedtime drink?

I left the mill as soon as our wheat was ground and drove the cart downstream toward town. It should have been a pleasant ride through the golden forest, but with my worries about Marisol and the rash of unexpected deaths, a shadow had fallen over the streamside beauty.

A Confession

There was scant heat in the early morning sun, but I tried for what I could get. I sat outside in the work yard where the kitchen wall blocked the running ground wind, cutting leather into thin strips. I wasn't doing it well, since my hands were cold and my knife needed sharpening.

Then, as though she hadn't been missing since Vial's death, as though she hadn't refused to have anything to do with me for weeks, Marisol suddenly came through the gate. She walked straight to me, her red skirt snapping around her ankles. My sweet girl was as lovely as ever, but, as much as I wanted to, I couldn't reach up to her right away.

I didn't dare soften, just because she had suddenly decided to appear. She knew it, and when she stood before me, she held herself stiffly guarded.

I'd been sick with worry when I couldn't find her, but now I tried to remind myself this was the woman who had turned me down in marriage. First Marisol pushed me away and then she hid from me. Why had she come today, and how did she know where she could find me alone in our bustling household? I was afraid she was about to stomp on my heart again and then walk out of my life forever.

I paid close attention to weaving thin leather thongs into a net, waiting to find out what this was all about. A curtain of Marisol's hair blew over her face, and then she caught me off guard by lowering herself to the ground and sitting in the dirt right at my feet. Marisol kept her back to me, but she leaned against my legs.

I felt the warmth of her through the soft blue folds of her manta, but I couldn't see her face. I was scared to talk. Whatever this sudden appearance meant, the woman was braver than I. While I waited, I noticed the red glints in her dark, thick hair, remembering how in times past my head had spun watching them catch the sun.

"Nando?" Marisol's voice was shaky. Was she afraid of me?

"I'm here." I laid the net on my lap and dared to place a tentative hand on her shoulder. She let it rest.

"What I have to say," she whispered, "is hard. How you hear me will matter forever."

Had she come to tell me she was leaving, for someone else, maybe? I didn't want to turn into a statue of cold stone, but that could do it. Marisol pushed a little pebble around in the dirt with her forefinger. She leaned forward so she no longer touched me.

We were silent. Marisol remained intent on the pebble. I had to strain to hear her next words, because she talked so quietly.

"Nando," she whispered, "I killed Señor Vial."

I set aside the tangled netting.

"I'm responsible for his death. Aurelia is under arrest and everything she owns has been taken from her. But *I'm* the one who killed him!" Marisol hurled the pebble across the courtyard. It hit the trunk of the cottonwood tree, ricocheted and dropped with a clunking sound into a hide bucket. "Good shot," I muttered, before I could stop myself. Marisol's face hung down and tears dripped off her cheeks.

"How could this possibly be?" I asked.

"For weeks now, even before you went to the salt lakes, Beatriz and I carried medicines from Juliana's house to Señora Vial. Aurelia Inez was trying to bring life back into her husband. Imagine the richest man in town, the caravan master, and he has nothing to give his wife. During the visits, Aurelia and I became friends.

"I had happy times with Beatriz and Aurelia. Sometimes, when Beatriz was busy elsewhere, I'd go in her place, and sometimes Melchora came and showed me how she made the tinctures.

"Aurelia was pleased. The medicine was working. Alfonso Vial became lively. He'd tease Aurelia, flirt with Beatriz, and try to cuddle me. When I got back from La Ciénega, Aurelia asked us to step up the dose, so she could have a chance at making a baby before Vial left for the winter. Melchora and I ground roots and boiled plants and then Aurelia dropped our mixtures into her husband's wine."

I fingered the netting for a moment before saying, "I didn't know you dabbled in love tonics, Marisol."

Marisol started crying again.

"Melchora gave you her latest recipes and you passed them on to your new girlfriend. How sisterly!"

Marisol gulped back a sob, recovering herself enough to retort, "I didn't expect you'd be mean, Nando."

I leaned my forehead on her shoulder by way of apology. "Please go on."

She waited a moment, deciding whether or not she could trust me. Finally she said, "At dinner his last night home, Alfonso started to get stomach pains. Something had changed. He fell asleep right at the table. Aurelia begged me to set it straight; to fix whatever had happened because of the drink. She shrieked that witches knew how to undo the evil they caused, but I had no idea what to do. I ran to look for Melchora, but couldn't find her. Then I hurried to Juliana's, carrying some of the bad tonic with me.

"Thankfully, Juliana and Agapita were home. Juliana asked about Alfonso's symptoms, his breathing, his pallor, and then the two of them disappeared into their back room. Quickly they made a fresh tincture. I ran to Aurelia's with what Juliana called an antidote.

"When I got back," Marisol continued, "Aurelia met me in the hall and told me her husband was better. It turned out, she said, he was only taking a nap, worn out from the last few days of assembling the caravan. When I showed up, husband and wife were on their way to bed, to spend their last night together before he left.

"Still, I begged Aurelia to give Juliana's herbs to Señor Vial. Aurelia said she would if she got a chance. I don't know that they ever got into him, because the next morning he was dead."

This was a long speech. Marisol trembled beside me.

I held my lady tight. "Marisol, you didn't kill the caravan master. Women toying with love tonics killed him. All you did was play into their hands, and only if these women knew what they were doing and the drugging was done on purpose."

Marisol was silent, thinking over my words. After a time she asked, "They don't hang a woman until after her child is born, do they?"

Sweet Jesus! It was time for this to stop.

"Marisol, did you know that Beatriz was flirting with Alfonso Vial?"

Marisol's head turned and she looked at me directly for the first time. "Flirting? You mean . . .?"

"Precisely. I learned that Beatriz decided she knew better than anyone how to help Alfonso revive his abilities. No herbal mixture was needed. Beatriz was famous for having a way with husbands."

Marisol sank against me. Again, I had a view of the back of her head for several long moments.

Without looking up she asked, "Has Beatriz practiced her arts on my man?"

Noting that I was once again "her man," I answered carefully. "Not in recent history."

Marisol's rigid shoulders let me know she took my meaning, but mercifully, she let it be.

"Beatriz and Vial? Do you think there was something between them?"

I nodded and watched Marisol as she decided to confess something she knew about this.

"Aurelia told me she surprised Vial and Beatriz kissing in the sala, but how could I take her seriously? Beatriz adored Aurelia. The girl wouldn't steal her friend's husband."

"You're telling me Aurelia caught them?"

Marisol nodded. "A businessman came to see Vial. Aurelia led him through the house to the sala. She and the guest caught a glimpse of Beatriz sitting on Vial's lap. Aurelia laughed when she told me about the look on the visitor's face— so shocked, and clearly embarrassed for Aurelia. But Aurelia believed that Vial was only being playful. Aurelia was very sure of her husband."

Marisol turned and looked at me, wondering if something about this parlor drama could possibly give her a reprieve.

"Who was the visitor?" I asked.

Marisol shrugged. "Some *rico*. How would I know?"

There were a dozen candidates for the role in Santa Fe. I took a deep breath.

"Consider the possibility," I suggested, "that Beatriz, the woman who prepared potions for the wife, secretly ached for the husband's attentions, and quite possibly his money."

"How can you be so dim, Nando?" Marisol blurted. "If that were the way of it," she insisted, "Beatriz would be trying to get rid of the wife, not poisoning the husband."

"You're right," I granted, though mostly because I didn't believe Beatriz was capable of killing a moth, much less a man.

Marisol whispered, "Beatriz had men wrapped around her little finger. Powerful men, who gave her affection, presents, and the feeling she mattered. But so what? Beatriz is dead."

"And now, so is one of her lovers."

We looked at each other, eyes wide.

Marisol and I sat together, closer than we'd been for weeks. When I'd imagined the reunion between us, I'd planned to tell her that even if the baby did come from her former husband, I would accept her child and love it. I'd intended to smother her with kisses, but this wasn't the time. I settled for wrapping both arms tight around her.

"Perhaps it was Melchora who changed the mixture," I said, "working dark magic for her own reasons. Or it could have been Juliana, trying desperately to save her little sister. Or maybe it was Aurelia after all, paying the curanderas to rid her of her faithless husband."

Marisol shook her head vigorously from side to side but I went on, "Or it could have been a big, dumb mistake. Maybe the tonic was too strong for a man of Vial's years, under the strain he carried. Or maybe Aurelia pushed too hard that night and it was a natural death after all."

"Lord preserve me," Marisol cried, "I was only trying to help! But I'm the one who steeped the drink that night and poured it into his cup."

My thoughts strayed to Crespín Olivas and the rest of Croix's investigators, far too close for comfort. I pulled Marisol's head and shoulders into my lap. Could anyone who knew Marisol possibly imagine her capable of murder?

She softened into a sobbing heap and wept all over my leather trousers. I stroked her hair, her back, and when the heaving of her shoulders subsided, I held her work-worn hands fast in my grip.

"I suppose if you're looking for a responsible party," I offered, kissing those chapped fingers, "I could be considered a candidate. I'm one of several men in town who was snubbed by Vial. Any of us could have slipped silver to a woman who knew how to choose her herbs."

"Now you're being silly," she said into the depths of my lap. "I know it wasn't you."

"And I say the same to you."

"Who's going to agree with you? I brought Aurelia the poison."

"You may have been the messenger, but not the murderer. Anyway, who can prove it?" Marisol sat up. I tried to get her to look into my eyes, but she turned her face away.

"Aurelia?" I pressed. "She who ordered the drugs and stood to make a fine profit, while divesting herself of a quarrelsome old man . . ."

"A man, who in spite of everything, she happened to love."

"That was her mistake. And then there are the women at the Casa Juliana." I held my fingers up, counting suspects. "The town has always thought of them as witches, and few would believe Juliana tried to undo the damage. Certainly the women there have more skill with herbs than you."

"Don't forget Melchora," Marisol added, sitting straighter and looking directly at me now. "The Indian played a part. All of us took whatever plants she handed us and tossed them in the pot."

"Many a woman has mixed up her medicines. Though, once Melchora realizes she's a suspect, she might finger you. Even so, hers would only be the word of an Indian servant against yours."

"Which would be the word of another Indian servant," declared Marisol.

Correct. Again. "But if it comes down to the two of you, there would be no contest. The Aguilars would vouch for you, Marisol."

"Would Luz?"

Marisol felt me wriggle, but she didn't back down. "The Salazars would support their own woman to the end, and in case you hadn't noticed, the Salazars have a lot more money than the Aguilars."

The alleged murderess wiped her nose, brushed dirt off her favorite skirt, and clumsily tried to stand. I stood and offered my hand.

Together we got her off the ground. I lodged her against my side. "Our servant days are long behind us, Marisol. If you still think of yourself as anyone's *criada*, you're being foolish. No one else does. It's time to let it go."

"Have you?" she asked, putting her hand in mine.

I laughed and squeezed her. "Almost."

We slipped out of the kitchen courtyard and were walking hand in hand now, behind the barn, down to the stream. There was fresh laundry hanging on the rock wall by the riverbank. Marisol felt for the dryness of the linen. She folded the smaller pieces with particular care, then looked up and said, "What if Aurelia *is* convicted? Then I would have no choice but to come forward, to try to help her."

I grabbed her. "By the saints! Marisol, stop! None of this will happen. Not if I have a breath left in my body." Pulling her into my arms, I felt her heart pounding. I spoke with my lips pressing into her hair.

"We'll help her if we can, but it has to be done without implicating you, or anyone at the Casa Juliana, or in a way that turns Melchora against us."

Marisol's voice was stronger now. "Aurelia won't hold up to questioning if they treat her harshly. She could easily break and drag any of us in, and she probably won't accuse the Indian woman. Even Aurelia's afraid of Melchora."

While Marisol was summing up the variables, a thin band of clouds covered the morning sun, turning the world somber.

I shivered and said, "You're right that Aurelia might try to pin the blame on someone else. But I don't think it would be you. Why not her husband's late mistress, conveniently six feet underground? That would be more likely."

Marisol said simply, "Aurelia won't blame Beatriz."

We sat together at the river's edge. It was a miracle to be talking like friends, touching and taking comfort in each other. I could see she'd returned to me because of the extent of her fear, but even so I was grateful Marisol and I had a future again.

"And if they do accuse me?" she asked. "What will we do then?" She stared into the gray river and became quiet.

If only I could promise her the worst wouldn't happen. I stood to shake off the chill and tried to reassure her.

"Francisco is often at the palacio and he's watching closely. He's told me they've already interrogated a half-dozen people. Croix's agent has called for a wider investigation and witnesses have been ordered to stay in town. So far, there's been no mention of a villainous Marisol. I'm told Aurelia is being held, but mainly because of her husband's pilfered supplies."

Maybe Marisol was hearing me. Maybe there was more light in her eyes.

"Marisol, is this why you have turned from me?"

She must have heard the pain in my voice, because she reached up and placed her hand on my cheek. Marisol stood on tiptoe and kissed me softly at the edge of my mouth, then on my lips, asking nothing, only giving what she could to signify a truce.

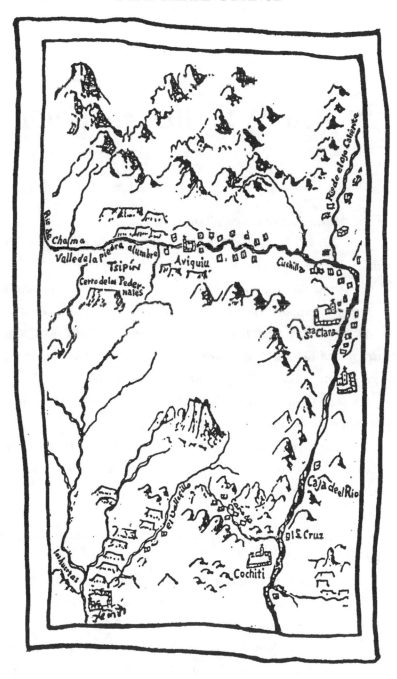

In Bed With the Governor

"Juan! You've stolen all the covers."

"Sorry," Anza muttered sleepily as he slung a piece of quiltover Anna. He rolled his body toward the wall.

Anna Serrano lay wide-awake, staring at the embers of the fire in the hearth in the corner of their bedroom. The man beside her didn't fool her. He was as alert as she was, and twisting and tossing. Every time she thought she might drop off, he pulled the covers off her on this late October night.

"Maybe if you'd explain what you're worrying about, I could calm down this whirlwind beside me."

There was a grunt. A hand fumbled to reach her. Their bodies shifted into spoon position, she at his back, ready to whisper whatever comfort she could offer.

"I'm trying to sleep, wife."

"No, you're trying to decide who's to be the next caravan master."

Her husband let out a groan through clenched teeth.

"You're not getting anywhere on your own. You ought to tell me what you're thinking."

"All right then, but remember, you asked. Whomever I choose is going to change the complexion of the colony. When I pick the man, I put incalculable wealth at his fingertips. I also give him the means to unseat me, to overpower my administration. That said, there's only a handful of reprobates and rascals to select from, and I need to make the decision within two days."

Anna's arms tightened around the governor.

"Whoever it is, love, won't be anywhere near as criminal as Vial, and he'll be indebted to you, not to a former administrator," she offered.

Another groan. "You decide. Ruybalid? A scoundrel, hard on his people, hoarding wealth out west of here. But also, tough and effective. Not intimidated by the Indios. Not liked by them either."

"Next choice," said Anna.

"Salazar. Capable. Highly competitive. The only man with enough experience in business not to make New Mexico look idiotic in the markets down south. We both know Facundo has always hoped to unseat me."

"Keep going."

"Your brother. He knows the men in Chihuahua, but . . ."

"But he's not reliable," the candidate's sister admitted.

"And screams of nepotism would be heard all the way to Arizpe."

"Right," conceded Anna. "But at least you would know whom he served. Go on. Who else?"

"Vial's oldest son? He traveled with his father. He knows the players."

"And would continue his father's legacy. The son undoubtedly profited by his father's theft."

"Yes, Anna. I'd concluded that myself. Have I explained my whirlwind adequately? No sensible solution exists. Will you allow me to go to sleep now?"

She poked him. "Not quite yet. Who would Croix appoint?"

Anza flung his arms over his head. "Anyone he could be sure would ruin me. The Commandant General used to extol everything I did. Now he schemes to get rid of me."

"By sending Don Crespín Olivas here, among other things."

"With a regiment of investigators."

Anna sat up and began stroking her husband's temples in the dark.

"How much do you care if Croix forces you out, Juan? Haven't you served your king longer and harder than any monarch has the right to ask?"

Anza gave a minimal sound of assent.

"You're right. I don't care really." He spoke to the dark, beamed ceiling. "At least, not if he'd let us go home to Sonora in peace; if maybe for once he would absolve a retiring governor from the Residencia. *How fair is it, anyway, to have a tribunal in Mexico judge my work; opinionated men who never took an arrow, who never rode farther than their hometown church?"*

Anna eased the taut sinews in her husband's neck. "Residencia and Croix notwithstanding, it would be good to go home. New Mexico wears on us. We're not getting any younger Juan. It's a long, hard trip back to our ranch."

"And what does this have to do with choosing the next caravan master?"

"*You only need to pick a man who is able to do the job. He doesn't have to be perfect. He just has to be adequate for a journey or two. Someone who lives nearby, so you can keep an eye on him.*"

There was a long silence, as both minds considered the candidates.

"*Salazar,*" they said in unison.

"*At least he's a gentleman.*" Anna bent forward and kissed her husband's brow.

"*And he understands business,*" Anza added. "*Taxes from Salazar's factories contribute greatly to the colony's coffers. I only wish I liked him better.*"

"*Not important,*" Anna said. "*It's only me you have to like.*"

Anza gathered Anna into his arms and nuzzled his face against her. "*I think we've got our man. I'll keep it to myself for another day or two, in case anyone better comes to mind. Anna, excuse me, but you've got the whole quilt on your side of the bed.*"

"*Every man for herself,*" she chuckled, pulling the quilt all the way off him, so he had to wrestle with her to get any covers back at all.

The governor was a much more relaxed man by the time the battle ended.

On My Knees

I couldn't find Marisol later that day, or all during the next. Had she disappeared on me again? It began to seem like I'd made up our encounter, with its promising ending.

To get through the hours waiting for her to show up again, I kept busy. There was plenty to do working on the house and preparing for Pecos. Miera sent over a neatly packaged bundle for me of a shirt, new manta, and a pair of too-long, but useable, trousers.

I had a minute alone with Luz the night before I was to leave, and got the chance to ask her about the story Cruzita told me. Did my stepmother have any memory from the old days of who Beatriz's mother was?

"Why?"

"Cruzita implied Beatriz's own mother once wanted her dead. Where did Beatriz come from?"

"Cochiti Pueblo."

"Pink-cheeked, slight of frame, Spanish to her core."

My stepmother turned her hands up and said, "As far as I know she spent her childhood in the pueblo. When she first came to town her Spanish was rough. She was a quick learner though, in many ways."

"You've heard no stories about her origins?" I persisted.

"There are always stories, but Nando, don't aggravate yourself about Beatriz. She was one of the lucky ones. Children born out of wedlock are often left in the fields to die. I can tell you that happens to unwanted babies more often than being left in a basket at the church. This town is small, and when the infants grow up, their parents risk being recognized in the features of the illegitimate child.

"You truly have no idea, have heard no rumor, of whom Beatriz's parents might be?"

"Why would you bother yourself about Beatriz?" Luz asked.

"If you haven't guessed already, I'm working for the governor again. Anza's intent on discovering who killed the woman. I've been following a few leads and finding out that lots of wives wanted Beatriz dead, or at least out of their married lives."

Luz listened with evident interest. "Back with Anza, eh. *Sub rosa* or above ground?"

"Above ground, but discreet. Officially I'm an assistant to Sebastian."

"I see. Well then, back to your case. What makes you think the girl was murdered? People do die in the mountains, you know."

"And a rock smashes down on them with precision and is surrounded by footprints in every case."

"Anza cares? With all that is going on, the governor is interested in the death of a tart?" Luz quizzed.

"Anza doesn't like what was implied by the method of her death. He doesn't want rumors of witchery rekindled in his territory and he's too modern to allow women to be accused of witchcraft, and murdered for it. The Commander General's investigators are in Santa Fe now. They have their eyes on everything. Anza's position as governor is shaky enough without that kind of trouble."

Luz was at the table, stuffing punché into her pipe. I took it to the hearth and lit it for her.

"I may have overheard something once about Beatriz, Nando. Some little thing is niggling at the back of my mind. Let me sleep on it and see if it floats to the front. Smoke?"

I could tell that my honorable stepmother was lying through her teeth, but she'd made it clear I would have to wait. I sat beside her, took a turn at her pipe, and wondered when she'd see fit to tell me what I most needed to know.

I finished with the animals after supper, locked up and returned to my room. A warm glow came from the corner, where a small fire flickered in the newly built fireplace. The kiva's smooth beauty was repeated in the shadows that played against the walls and the timbered ceiling.

My random pile of sheepskins had been shaken out, added to and arranged into an inviting place to sleep in front of the fire—just out of range of sparks. Tallow candles, carefully placed in clay dishes on the floor, framed the bed, two at the head and one at the foot. There was a pottery basin of warm water on the stone hearth. A beautiful blanket, deep red and dark blue, one I had never seen before, covered the tidy bed.

Mesmerized by the flickering lights and the mysteriously inviting scene, I washed in the warm water by the fire. When I slipped naked under the blanket, a linen sheet, old and soft, greeted my skin.

What was happening to me? A feather pillow too? I pulled it around my neck and shoulders and sank onto my back, deep in the piled skins. Firelight moved in shifting patterns across the wooden latillas of the ceiling. I crossed my arms behind my head and rested, wondering if there would be more of this magic.

The door to the room opened and softly closed. I barely heard the footsteps on the new earth of our floor. In the near darkness, Marisol walked to the head of the bed and kneeling down, laid her warm palms against my temples. I held my breath, not sure if this was real. Her fingers lingered on my eyelids, touching them lightly. I reached up and cradled her head and pulled her face down to mine. I couldn't believe that what I had dreamed of was actually happening. I turned my head toward her warmth and our lips met, hers pliant and partly open, mine hard with sunburn, but eager.

I rose, and on my knees, reached for her with both arms. Marisol leaned into me with her forehead resting on my shoulder. Her hair fell over both of us and I slid my cheek over the silkiness of it, holding a handful against my mouth. She smelled like roses.

I reached for the hem of her blouse and gently pulled the shirt over her head. Marisol moved back and unfastened the waistband of her skirt. It slipped down, leaving her naked in front of me. I drew her onto my lap, so she would have the fire and me to protect her from the room's cold. I held her in the curve of my body and pressed the side of my face against hers. We were still and said nothing, watching the yellow and red flames. Marisol had placed a basket of piñon and juniper sticks on the hearth. Now and then I reached out and added one to keep the fire burning.

Marisol must have braided her hair right after she'd washed it, because loosened now, it flowed in waves down the length of her back, until the glossy blackness met the floor where she sat. Rogue strands of copper flashed in the firelight and reminded me of the halos I'd seen on angels in the paintings in the church.

I moved a little apart, to comprehend this woman who had overwhelmed me in the dark. Marisol's back was strong and straight and her shoulders broad, yet taken altogether, she was small. Sitting behind her, there was no sign of a baby, but when I reached around, her smooth moon of a belly pushed hard against my hands. I ran my palms over the fullness of her, and on my knees, leaned down and nuzzled her, kissing both her and our baby at the same time. I pressed my forehead lightly against what I imagined to be the forehead of my child.

I was running kisses up and down her spine, and with the light of the fire playing against the lids of my closed eyes, I was finding her, finding Marisol again, with my tongue and my hands, with the inside of my arms and with the skin of my belly. Her breasts were larger than before, full, gorgeous, and dark like berries at the nipples. I plunged my face into their softness and she clutched my hair, pulling on it gently.

When I could wait no longer, I lifted the dark wing of her hair away from her ear and whispered, "Yes?"

"Sí." she whispered.

"The baby?"

"Yes, like this." Marisol lay on her side and her hands invited me into her. She twined her legs with mine to pull me closer.

I wanted to be tender, but she met me with the full force of her own desire. Marisol moved beneath me, her body warming, melting, pouring forth love. We found the ways we could to meet flesh to flesh and still be careful of the baby. We sank into the deep bedding, twining legs and arms. Hard against each other, we met and rose like wild animals in arched and aching joining.

Our lovemaking ebbed and flowed throughout the night. Marisol's skin sparkled with moisture and my own felt vibrant with touch. Where the fire's warmth found us, we gleamed and were warm. I pulled the new blanket over our backs to hold off the night air. She lay against me, motionless at last and I folded myself around her, wrapped my leg over her hips, and rubbed her feet with mine.

Now that we were peaceful, my fingers began to explore the curve of her pregnancy, and when I prodded a certain place I found a hard, bony resistance. The baby rolled against my fingers and I felt a knocking under the skin. I opened the palm of my hand and pressed evenly, finding the shape of the child. The baby was awake, and no wonder.

It surged and kicked inside Marisol so vigorously she laughed, "Be careful of this one! He's going to fight you for every inch of me."

"Let him! I'll give him lots of practice," I replied, pulling her still closer. Marisol wiggled her bottom against me.

We let the fire die down and when there was no hint of moonlight remaining, we finally fell asleep. We had covered all the elements needed for a proper reconciliation: fire, tears, tenderness and quite a lot of tickling.

Lying there later, touching as much of my lady as I could, the recollection of the fear that had sent her back to me coursed briefly through my mind. In case Marisol was remembering it too, I whispered to reassure her once again that no one could hold her responsible for Alfonso Vial's death. "But even so, even though I've found you again, we may need to get you out of Santa Fe for a while, until this investigation settles down."

"But not too soon," she whispered. "Not any time soon."

I stayed silent rather than argue with her.

I slid my arm under the hollow of her neck to position us for what was left of the night. Marisol gave me a love-nip saying, "Good night, my love, my amorcito."

The Grandmother's Blanket

Padre Domingo barely spoke a word all the way to Pecos. His face remained grave and his demeanor frozen. The man rode beside us hidden in his cloak, in shock maybe, or else he felt just plain dismal at being returned to the Pueblo world, even for a few days.

Padre Miera had sent along a boy of fourteen or so to help, one of his young servants who lived and worked at the church. Gabriel was the liveliest of the three of us and did a man's share of the work loading and leading the animals. Bemused by the night with Marisol, I rode in a trance, as silent as Domingo. The only good thing about leaving Santa Fe was escaping the spectacle of the burial of Alfonso El Ganso, the late Señor Vial.

We rode up to the pueblo walls moments before dark and took the southward track over to the mission. Pueblo men came out of the convento to greet the padre. They helped the cleric from his mule and handed him a cup of wine. Domingo entered the stone walled convento flanked by a sacristan and the porter. A servant led the priest's mule into the nearby corral.

Gabriel and I stood in the forecourt, looking at the closed door. Smoke lifted gently from the mission's chimneys high above us into the starry sky. I was glad to see the guardians of the Pecos church had welcomed the priest and prepared a warm room for him. I was at a loss, though, to figure out how to stay at Domingo's side, as Miera had ordered, since no one invited us to go inside with him.

Gabriel circumvented my dilemma. "Let's get out of here."

"What?" The boy's voice jarred me.

"They don't need us any more. My mother's family lives here. They'll be glad to put us up."

"You, maybe. I'm supposed to take care of the priest."

"That door's shut and you weren't invited to supper. Neither was your mule, by the way."

I followed Gabriel when he turned his animal and headed up the wide backbone of the mesa toward the old part of the pueblo.

"Is your mother here?" I asked.

"She's dead." The boy was matter of fact.

"But your mother was from Pecos?"

"Yes, but she left a long time ago."

"Before you were born?"

"Yes. I don't know who my father was. Maybe Comanches killed him."

Orphaned, I realized, after his mother, for some reason or other, moved to Santa Fe. When she died with none of her people nearby, the good Padre Miera must have taken in her baby.

"But you still have family here?"

"My grandmother. She came for me when she learned of my existence, but she saw I had more to eat with the priests and after a time sent me back to them. Comanche raiders steal our horses and raid our fields, making hard times in Pecos, times when no one can even plant the corn. There have been years when almost all of the young men were killed and no one was left to hunt. My grandmother tried to keep me here, but living at the mission was safer. Miera was always good to me."

Gabriel talked to the guard at the gate in Towa. A nod from the boy in my direction, and I was allowed to pass into the pueblo. Gabriel and I crossed a courtyard open to the stars. We threaded between small cook fires and by their light, climbed a pole ladder. Gabriel led me the length of a long balcony, ducked through a hanging curtain of hide and ushered me into one of the many small apartments.

Humans are similar in many ways, no matter their color or tribe, proven once again by the reaction of Gabriel's grandmother to this unexpected visit.

After she'd smothered my embarrassed companion in hugs and kissed him on his nose, the old woman pulled a roasted squash from the ashes on her hearth. She rekindled the fire under the pot of cornmeal and wound a strap of fresh elk meat around a stick. The old lady turned the sizzling meat over the snapping flames. We sat in her small room, in a semi-circle around the raised earthen cooking place, gorging ourselves on hot food.

From there to our blankets was a short step. Lying down, I watched the firelight make the silhouettes of Gabriel and his grandmother jump on the old walls. I heard my friends' quiet voices quietly speaking the Pecos' Towa. I heard juniper sticks popping on the fire and a low drumbeat somewhere deep in the pueblo.

My responsibilities for the day were over. Padre Domingo was probably already drunk and snoring over at the convento. With my hand wrapped around the pouch that held my fire kit and the shell ornament, I sank into a sheepskin on the earthen floor and after a time, I slept.

I was wrong. Domingo had not gotten drunk. I attended Mass in the morning, along with the Pecos people. The baffling priest comported himself with unexpected dignity. He drew in the parishioners with the mystical pageantry. Afterwards, he met with the Pecos elders, and over the next two days taught catechism classes for adults and children. The priest said Mass each morning, noon and night. I joined the villagers at the rail and made my lips move along with the litany.

There was no sign that Domingo either wanted or needed me, so after Mass on Sunday, I found Gabriel and we rode out to the Río Pecos through the rattling corn stalks in the early winter fields. At this time of year the river was too chilly to swim in, but trout like cold water, so we dropped our hands under the overhanging banks and felt for fish.

I lolled in the grass like a carefree puppy. The sun was warm enough that we could lie patiently on our bellies and Gabriel threw two fat, silver trout onto the grass. I wandered along the banks looking for sprigs of onion or mint.

The Comanches had been on good behavior since Anza bested them in '79. They were enjoying the advantages of being included in the Spanish Empire's array of riches and enterprise. Peace was building, and the Pecos people who lived at the edge of the Comanches' vast plains were enjoying the respite.

We sat on the grass warming our hands in the sun, and I suddenly had a notion. I pulled the shell necklace out of the pouch. It glinted in the light, spinning slowly as it dangled from my fingers. Gabriel saw it and reached for it. I let him take the ornament in his hand. He held the half moon up, squinting and lightly touching the smoothed edges in admiration of the work.

"Is this yours?"

"No."

"No?" he queried.

"I found it. I think it might belong to a Pecos man." I hesitated. "Maybe a dead one."

Gabriel dropped the shell on the grass. "What are you telling me?"

"I don't know exactly. I was wondering if this looks like something you've seen here. On a dancer, or a woman, or around the neck of a cacique, maybe?"

"I suppose. It looks like it could belong to a shaman, but remember, I don't live here anymore. I live in Santa Fe. I haven't been to Pecos in over a year. You saw my grandmother's tears all over her face."

With a curious finger, Gabriel stroked the shell necklace where it lay on the brown grass next to me. At last he asked the obvious: "Who died?"

"I don't know. A woman in Santa Fe said the necklace belonged in Pecos. She told me to be careful, that it would bite me." I leaned back on my elbows and laughed. The boy looked at me like I was odder than he'd realized.

"It bit the man who had it, that's for sure. They killed him like he was a witch." Gabriel's big eyes fastened on me. "Hanging by his arms," I added for emphasis. "Pinned behind him. Tortured to death."

I turned to look at Gabriel, who didn't move.

"And the day after I found the dead man, someone tried to kill my horse."

Gabriel backed a little away from me. "Did you take this shell off the neck of the dead person?"

"No, Gabriel. I found it a few days later, lying in the dirt not too far from where he died."

"Then the shell could be anybody's. Not the dead man's at all."

"Might be. But I found the victim's clothes buried in the dirt, and this shiny necklace near them lying on a ledge."

"The man was naked?"

"Not when I first saw him. By the time I returned with some soldiers, his body was gone. Disappeared. A bear ate him, maybe, or whoever hanged him came back to get rid of the evidence, probably because they knew I'd found him. They could be sure the Spanish would investigate and there'd be questions, making trouble for everybody."

"Dios! Get rid of that thing!" Gabriel snatched the talisman by the string and flung it into the river. I was in the air, catapulting toward the water, trying to save the half moon shell. Gabriel, on his knees, began shouting. He seized my ankles to keep me from plunging into the green, cold Pecos. The pendant hung precariously by its thread from a red willow twig bobbling in the current.

The boy was over his fit. He held my feet with care, and I extended my reach and plucked the shell off the branch. I slid backward up the bank on my belly, while Gabriel hauled on my legs to keep me moving in the right direction.

I wiped the river water off the shell and caught my breath, then pointedly replaced the necklace in my pouch.

"You and everybody else," I muttered.

"At least I kept you from falling in," Gabriel puffed.

"That would have been all right. I can swim. But this? What if we'd lost it? Who knows? Maybe this piece of shell is going to tell us who made that man die so horribly."

"It might even tell us who that bear ate," the boy said.

After cooking the trout on his grandmother's hearth, Gabriel touched the pouch where it hung around my neck and looked over at the old widow. I took his hint and decided to ask her about the shell.

The woman gathered up the bowls, then came to sit beside us. She bent to pick up her smoking pouch, and I handed her the necklace without explanation. Not that I could speak Towa anyway. In exactly the same manner as Melchora, the grandmother laid the shell in her palm and ran her thumb over it.

Gabriel spoke a few words to her and she nodded and said something in reply. Her eyes filled with water and tears sped down her cheekbones, glittering like the shell. I waited and finally Gabriel spoke.

"Grandmother says this belongs to Tuqué."

"Who's Tuqué?" I asked, trying to show more patience than I felt.

"Everyone's old uncle," Gabriel translated for her. "The one who bosses all of us, who has the most horses, who didn't get killed in the raids because he wasn't there when they happened. Tuqué comes from the strongest family in the pueblo and has the most to say to the Spanish over at the visitor's house by the church," Gabriel explained. I saw the grandmother watching her boy carefully. She added something more in Towa.

Gabriel nodded and said, "Except Tuqué isn't the big one anymore," she says. "He's gotten old. He's a little man now, and no one trusts him. There's still a lot of noise from Tuqué, but he doesn't have the power he used to."

The grandmother spat on the ground. I swear she was following every word her grandson said in Spanish.

"Your grandmother doesn't like Tuqué, does she?"

"She hates him," Gabriel stated.

Then why had she cried, I wondered?

"What's she got against the old uncle?"

"I can't tell you. Not now anyway."

More words spilled from the woman in sharp outbursts. She turned and looked at me, her eyes brimming. She let out a burst of Towa and reached for the pendant.

I held the shell back from her hand. By now I knew not to let anyone get hold of the thing, because this simple necklace created strange reactions in everyone I showed it to. I stowed the necklace out of sight.

The woman grasped Gabriel's arm and shook him. Reluctantly, the boy translated his grandmother's words.

"Tuqué took my daughter. By force. I was not willing to let her go. When Tuqué rode away with my child, he threw a coin at my feet. One coin for my beautiful girl!"

"I took the coin to Tuqué's mother. I waved it in her face and accused her of joining her son in this. The woman showed me her back. To this day we don't speak."

It was strange to hear this woman's story coming from her young grandson's mouth. She reached over and took his hand, stroking it fondly. I could tell Gabriel was embarrassed to translate what she spoke next.

"The fine Spanish man who got my daughter never married her. He wouldn't even let her stay under his roof to have her baby. My daughter died. Gabriel survived, but only by a miracle. Some rude Spaniard has no idea what a good son he has.

"Soon after my daughter was taken to Santa Fe, I watched Tuqué ride a new horse into our village. Over the years, he rode many horses much finer than the rest of us have. I am not the only woman whose daughter disappeared in Santa Fe. Women got hungry. Some traded their girls to Tuqué for food. Tuqué took their children away, always promising marriage to a fine Pueblo man, but the daughters were sold to Spaniards instead."

I turned toward the jumping flames, hoping their heat would dry my face. Was the irrepressible Gabriel crying too? Maybe he had never heard this story. Or did it hurt every time?

The grandmother abruptly pulled her blanket over her head and became silent. The atmosphere in the little room turned grim. I went out to the balcony and down the ladder to the latrines. The friendly life of the pueblo didn't look so perfect any more. I sensed divisiveness. The communal friendliness I had always imagined was a chimera. Now I saw that hierarchies and factions formed here. There were victims and abusers, once again displaying the whole sad array of human behavior.

Outdoors again, I found the air had chilled and light from the remaining fires now reflected off low clouds. The wind picked up, coursing in from the mountains. Snow might hit us on our trip back, but even if a storm was on the way, I wanted out of this place. I suspected Padre Domingo would agree with me on that.

When I went back into the apartment to my blanket beside the fire, the grandmother and her grandson looked to be asleep. But after I lay down, Gabriel whispered to me, "Sorry. Sorry for the story she told you."

"I'm sorry I ever took that cursed necklace out of the bag. In fact, I'm sorry I ever found it."

"She told me she was glad you did, because it means Tuqué lost it, that he became separated from his power.

"Is he here? Does Tuqué still live in the pueblo?"

"When you went out I asked her if she knows where Tuqué is." Gabriel kept his voice down.

"Did you tell her about the dead man? Because it could be Tuqué, you know."

"I know, but I didn't tell her. When I asked, 'Where's Tuqué?' she told me he went to Taos. She shrugged, and said he hasn't come back yet. She acted like Tuqué's whereabouts didn't matter to her at all. Anyway, it's hard to talk to a woman who has her head under a blanket. Are we leaving tomorrow, Nando?"

"If the Gods let us, yes. Clouds are racing in, but Padre Domingo will be in a rush to get away from here, even though it's going to snow. Me too, I'm ready to be home."

Father Domingo's Lament

We made easy leagues until the snow came on hard in the early afternoon. Padre Domingo, Gabriel and I had reached the highest point of the trail when the light went flat and then quit on us altogether. Huge flakes blasted out of the north, thrown by a blustery wind. The snow was wet and it balled up under the mules' hooves, making us stop to knock off the clumps with the points of our knives.

Always, the padre stayed mounted, while Gabriel and I worked to keep us moving forward. Now I understood why Domingo left Zuni as soon as they took his servants away. The man's huge blue cape was wrapped over his head and face, and his skirts swirled against the animals' legs, sometimes snapping into our faces when we knelt to tend to his mule's hooves.

We weren't going to reach any known shelter before dark. We'd be lucky to find any place at all that would prevent us from being buried alive. Domingo muttered prayers. Gabriel and I alternated breaking trail, cleaning snow off the animals, and warming our hands in our armpits under the wool of our mantas.

Through pelting snow, I began to look for a thick stand of trees, or a rock overhang. I felt for my fire kit and worried about finding twigs dry enough to start a fire.

241

The padre kept his head down and went on crooning incantations. Except for beseeching his God, he wasn't about to bestir himself over our predicament. His two servants would have to figure out the solution.

No obvious shelter appeared, and by now, anything we might find would be filled with snow. There was nothing to do but ride on through the storm, and if we couldn't ride, we'd huddle under trees, remaining on our feet until daylight so we wouldn't freeze to death. I could do it, but could Domingo? Could Gabriel, who was young and didn't have a man's weight yet?

We finally arrived at the trail beside the frozen creek and Domingo came out of his trance bellowing, "Set me down!"

"What?"

"Set me down this minute. I've told you three times! I have to relieve myself."

Well hell, I thought, the imperious bastard has to pee.

Gabriel leaned against the mule and let the padre use his body to slide to the ground. I untangled the priest's cloaks and batted off lumps of snow.

Domingo floundered off the trail to the edge of the winding creek and became uncharacteristically silent. I was knocking snow off his saddle and saddlebags, realizing just how close we were to the entrance to Deer Creek, when I heard the padre yell, "Never underestimate the power of prayer! This will do perfectly."

By the grace of whatever, he had found what we so badly needed, a high rock wall that had been undercut by the little creek over the centuries. The alcove carved by the water had a low ceiling that slanted ten feet or more deep into the hill. Back in the cave there was a pile of dry brush and branches, washed up long ago, that I could plunder for something to burn.

The mules achieved a little shelter by standing at the mouth of the overhang. Inside I still had to fight against the wind to get a spark off my flint and light the tinder. Finally, with all of us, even the priest, huddling around the makings, we started a fire. In time the flames roared and we were warm. We didn't have much food, only dry provisions, but what was in the bags was enough for one night.

My private prayer came true. True to style, Domingo carried liquid sustenance. A wineskin hid under his cloak. When he figured out he couldn't conceal it in the close quarters of the shelter, he pulled the bag off his shoulder and squeezed a long stream into his mouth. After a few long swallows, he passed it to me. Did the priest have a generous heart after all?

The fire warmed the air and bounced heat off the rock walls. The wineskin changed hands and the three of us got so potted on stolen vestry spirits that we forgot to be miserable.

Domingo was downright chatty and after a while asked me with a glint in his eye, "Nando, that girl you were having such a fine time with on the road from La Ciénega, what do you know about her? I noticed you were one of the men who dug her grave."

"The one you called La Bella? I don't know much about her, Padre," I lied, "except that Juliana of the Barrio Analco called Beatriz her sister. Beatriz moved up to Santa Fe from Cochiti quite a few years ago."

"Not one drop of Indian in her," said the padre. "Except her mores."

"Beatriz had a unique outlook on the sanctity of marriage," I replied. A particularly fond recollection of Beatriz momentarily took hold of me. I couldn't keep from smiling.

After a time I remembered to ask, "Why did you call her La Bella?"

"When? On the plaza?"

"Yes. Bella isn't Beatriz's name."

Domingo hesitated before explaining. "The girl reminded me of someone, someone about Beatriz's age, but long ago. Seeing your friend touched a long-lost corner of my brain. It's gotten so I get the years mixed up." The muscles in his battered, stern face wobbled. "She was so beautiful, that little one. I couldn't call her anything but Bella."

His lament sounded as though he'd had a crush on some young girl back in the days before his lonely years in Zuni. Was the padre truly celibate? Hadn't there been a hint to the contrary a few weeks ago when we rode together into Santa Fe, some mention of a lump under his garment?"

Domingo downed more wine and slurred, "Dead now. Doesn't matter." He leaned back on the saddle blankets I'd spread on the sandy floor.

"I warned that Indian woman. Told her she'd better stop Beatriz before the girl and her father committed a mortal sin."

The padre tried to shoot another stream of wine into his mouth, but missed. The sacramental liquor trickled through the scraggle of his red beard.

He burped and lay down, adding, "Had to put a halt to it somehow. Can't be in this profession and overlook something as grave as mortal sin."

Domingo didn't notice when I took the wineskin away. Gabriel reached for it, but I pushed his hand off. There'd be no more wine for any of us this night.

God almighty, what was this drunken cleric implying? That Facundo Salazar was Beatriz's father? For certain Salazar was old enough to have fathered her, in which case, by Jesus, Domingo wasn't joking about the sin.

Yet, what did Domingo mean when he said, "*Before* they committed a mortal sin?" Maybe, because he'd only just

244

returned to civilization, Padre Domingo didn't know just how much had gone on between Beatriz and Salazar.

The priest mumbled and fumbled with his rosary. I dragged more branches out of the sand, building up a woodpile for the night. Of course, it wasn't necessarily Salazar. Beatriz had other paramours. Many another gentleman could have fathered the pretty Spanish girl, then sent his bastard child off to a pueblo to be reared out of sight.

The priest kept babbling. "You should have seen the look on that lady's face when I confronted her. Told her I'd found that baby she threw away, alive and all grown up now, and that the girl was standing across the marketplace, watching her mother. First chance I got, I made that hypocritical woman face her sin."

The priest had a smug look on his face when he lay back on the blankets and shut his eyes, confident that Gabriel and I would keep the fire blazing for him throughout the night.

In his own strident way, the padre had tried. Hadn't he beaten Beatriz in the streets when he noticed her making moves on the man who might be her father? And a priest who sat in the confessional in Santa Fe many years ago, might just know who Beatriz's father was.

The padre groaned a few last words, rolled into the fetal position and slept. Had this awkward cleric, returning to town after twenty years in the wilds, stirred up old bones under the beds of the town's finest? Had Domingo, with his incessant tongue and the memory of some ancient confession, triggered Beatriz's death on the mountain? Was it even possible that the holy man in his zeal had committed the crime himself?

Hem Stitching

It was dusk when I brought the padre back to Miera's convento. Riding in, I saw Cruzita through the gloom, teetering on a fence rail, pulling frozen apples off a tree in the church's spindly, old orchard. Cruzita had spoken the name 'La Bella' too, right before she'd implored, "Look to the mother!" Pieces were beginning to fit together.

I hurried through the crusted snow to the priests' quarters. It would be a relief to unload Domingo and Gabriel, to be home again, finished with this assignment. What joy to think of Marisol waiting for me in our fire lit room! My family would be glad of the pile of firewood, but the new clothes Miera had given me were already dirty, torn and frozen solid at the cuffs.

Just as I sat down to supper, Francisco stomped in out of the snow. "What are you doing eating here, Nando? Sebastian's waiting for you. There's a meeting at the governor's. Leave that bowl of beans. You'll feast at Anza's table tonight."

"No one told me." I pushed back from the table and struck a pose in my muddy garments. "Am I expected to dress for the occasion?"

Luisa, Marisol and old Luz rose at once to raid Francisco's chest. I could have passed for a gentleman when I stepped out the door, as long as one didn't notice that the slim woolen trousers had been rolled under and hemmed with a few quick stitches.

Luz was the one who fixed them in the privacy of my room. It was more appropriate for her to see my naked legs than the two young women. If only she knew. But then, being Luz, she probably did.

My stepmother knotted the thread and reached for the trousers. "I remembered what was perplexing me before you went to the pueblo; your question about Beatriz's mother," Luz said looking prim.

I needed to hurry to Anza's dinner, but I slowed to pay attention, knowing this could be important.

"And don't look so eager. I don't have a good answer for you. I never knew anything about Beatriz's origins, but something else has come up.

"I went to speak with Padre Miera after you confronted me with not being kinder to Marisol. You know, Nando, I do try to get along with you. That was many days ago, weeks even, before Beatriz and Alfonso Vial died. I wanted guidance from Miera about how to approach Marisol, and I thought perhaps he would hear confession from me.

"I had to wait to see the old padre. He was talking with someone in his office, so I went into the church and sat down on the bench in the back where I could be alone with my prayers. No such luck. I was quickly interrupted."

Luz motioned me to hold the candle closer so she could see her stitches. She pushed the needle through the thick material and went on with her story.

"I'd only been there a few moments when Padre Domingo came in through the street doors, clutching the servant Melchora by the arm. As soon as the door shut behind them that reprobate priest bent over the Indian woman as though he would kiss her. To her credit, Melchora tried to twist out of it, but the man clung to her.

"I wished with all my might, and you'd better believe what I'm telling you, Nando, that I could have transported myself from there. This was no scene I wanted to witness. Melchora broke free and actually slapped the priest. 'I don't want any of this!' she told him.

" 'Too bad. Too bad you're too fancy for me now, but you *will* hear this from me,' he responded with his red face turning even redder. 'You'll see,' he hurled at her. 'Beatriz is the Baby Bella. And thanks to you, she's drawing her own father into bed with her!' Domingo grabbed Melchora's arm again.

"The Indian woman stopped pulling away. Melchora stood still in front of Domingo and looked up at him.

" 'What you're saying is the truth? You're certain beyond any doubt that Beatriz was that baby we saved?'

"The Indian woman searched the padre's face and saw he believed every word of what he'd told her.

"Melchora whispered, 'I'll see that Beatriz won't be a problem any more, and I can promise that Vial won't go near her again, but you must never let the lady, her mother, know. She will be furious if she learns that we failed to kill her daughter. We won't be able to walk the streets of Santa Fe ever again without fear of her reprisal.'

"Padre Domingo clamped his bottom lip between his teeth. It looked like he was stopping himself from saying something more. Then he sighed and reached out a comforting arm to Melchora, who yielded and leaned against him. They stood clinging to each other.

I tell you, Nando, if I weren't so old I would have slid under the bench to hide.

" 'Are you sure, are you completely *sure* Beatriz was that child?' the Indian woman asked Domingo.

" 'Coming upon her as I did,' the priest explained, 'seeing her for the first time since she was an infant, it was as though I approached her mother—so young and fresh, and impetuous, just like her. And like the mother, sexually volatile as well.'

" 'I see, I see how it happened,' Melchora mourned. 'Over these past few years I watched the girl Beatriz become a woman, but the change happened gradually, and I was too close to her. I didn't notice the resemblance to her mother. I never guessed.'

Luz's fingers stopped driving the needle through the cloth. "Melchora huddled against the priest, clutching his robe in her fists.

"Padre Domingo patted her and said, 'I am asking myself if I ought to have saved that soul, only to have her turn into a wanton whore. I came out of exile and found this girl I'd kept from death, all grown up now and carousing with every man in town. You cannot guess my sickness of spirit when I watched her set her claws for her own father. I should have left her to die!'

" 'Melchora, I had to talk to you. I had to warn you so they don't burn in hell.' The priest pleaded with the Indian, 'Stop the girl from sleeping with Vial, if it isn't too late.' "

My eyes were riveted on my stepmother. Here was pain beyond belief. Our beautiful Beatriz was the abandoned baby of Cruzita's tale. I listened as Luz's story went relentlessly on.

"With that the padre flung Melchora's arms away and sped from the nave. The Indian woman was left there alone and, I swear this is true, Nando, Melchora began to laugh. She stood there and laughed until she had to prop herself against a wall. Then, to my amazement, her laughter turned to sobs. The woman fell to her knees and bending down to the earth, she cried and cried.

249

"I didn't move until Melchora left. I waited several more minutes before going to the door and tapping for the priest."

Luz was lost in thought, barely seeing me at her side, certainly not checking the length of my borrowed trousers. She looked up with a confused and gentle face.

"Does this help you, Nando? Does this awful story tell you anything at all useful to your work?"

"What you tell me is horrible, but yes, important. Luz, do you remember which day this took place?"

My stepmother frowned as she concentrated. "It had to be soon after the first snow, because my shoes left mud all over the floor of the priest's office. It was the day Carlos departed the second time for Zuni. You left the house in the morning and I decided this was my chance to talk to Padre Miera. It was early the following morning that Sebastian sent soldiers for you."

"By all the saints, mother, they came for me because they'd found Beatriz dead on the mountain. Beatriz wouldn't have gone to the mountains in the dark. She must have been up there that same afternoon you heard Domingo and the Indian woman talking in the church. Most likely Beatriz was already dead by the time the padre told Melchora who Beatriz was."

Luz added the final touch. "And Señor Vial, who apparently fathered her, died three days later."

We stopped, because Francisco was coming through the doorway. "Nando, hurry up. How long does it take to hem a pair of pants?"

I whispered in my stepmother's ear, "Be thinking, Luz. Try to remember. What family was Melchora serving twenty years ago?"

She shook her head as she handed me the trousers. "That's too far back."

I cinched the belt tight to hold them up, then bent and kissed Luz lightly on her papery cheek.

"Gracias," I said, certain she would understand that my gratitude was for far more than a few stitches in my pants.

Francisco dropped me off at Sebastian's office, tipped his hat, and went on to Anza's dinner by himself. The sergeant wiped the agreeable smile off his face the moment he turned to me.

"What took you so long?

"Mules couldn't make headway in the snow. We slept under a ledge during the storm last night, if you can call that sleeping."

That elicited no sympathy from the sergeant. "Did you learn anything of use at the pueblo?"

"There is, in fact, a man missing. Someone called Tuqué. They say he rode to Taos, but he should have been back by now. People became very quiet when I brought up his name."

"Tuqué. Horse trader? Family members among the caciques?"

"Same person. Tuqué also sold Pueblo girls when he needed a boost to his income. What's this dinner about? Why am I included?"

"You're going as my secretary. Everyone knows I can't read or write. Don Crespín has no idea who you are. We might learn something important, and I think the governor's going to need plenty of friends at his table this evening."

Sebastian, naked from the waist up, strained to pull a clean shirt with frills over his head. He buttoned a vest saying, "We have a couple of minutes before we go. What else have you found out? How does the overall situation look to you, other than wagons attacked, witches hanged or crushed, and the caravan master falling over dead? The colony's a disaster. It's a god-awful time for Croix's investigators to be here, if Anza expects to keep his post."

I passed the sergeant a brush and began to summarize.

"In the matter of the murder of the Indian man and the girl, several similarities. Each was made to look as though a witch was being killed. Doing a service to society sort of thing. Everyone accepts that it's no crime to rid the world of a witch.

"People in the barrio all have an opinion about Beatriz's death, but no one at the pueblo is talking about the hanged man; stolid faces, shoulders locked together in a wall of silence."

"Enough of that. Anything on Vial?"

"There are plenty of rumors, all contradictory, and no facts. I say leave Vial to the formal investigators.

"Then tell me more about Pecos."

"The man in the ramada was probably this Tuqué. Initially Pueblo business, but the effigy changed everything. At that point we were gifted with a missing body and a fake, castrated Spaniard. The murder changed from personal to political, which eliminated some suspects, but added others."

"I agree, so what about Beatriz?" Sebastian bent to smear tallow on his boots.

"She was marked for murder; probably sleeping with both Vial and Salazar. No wonder she didn't have time for a lout like Toribio, though we can't rule him out. Plenty of motive for several men there, and a few wives, too. It was hard work to set up her death. Someone really wanted Beatriz dead."

"That's true about Deer Creek as well," Sebastian added.

His fingers smoothed his hair one last time. "Is there anything, anything in these, shall we call them 'lesser' murders, that would shed light on Vial's death?" asked the sergeant.

Now was the moment.

"I learned today that Beatriz was fathered by Vial."

Sebastian stood straight up and looked at me.

"By damn! Jesus, Nando, how did you find this out?" For once I had every ounce of the sergeant's attention.

"It's a long story when we're rushing off to a dinner party, but I got the information from three different sources."

"Father and daughter dead within the same week." Sebastian let out a low whistle. His lips stayed pursed. He tapped them with a finger, watching me.

"We may have a woman on the suspect list. Twenty years ago Vial raped a rich girl, who ordered her servant to throw the resulting infant away. The servant balked and gave the baby to the local padre. Back in those days the town priest was Padre Domingo. He spared the child, sending it to live in a nearby pueblo.

"Now Domingo's back in Santa Fe after twenty years away. I'm guessing the padre's reappearance alarmed the mother, who sprang to protect herself."

"Who is she?" Sebastian's voice was sharp.

"That's the missing piece of the puzzle, but there are people in this town who could tell us. I think both Padre Domingo and Cruzita know which Spanish lady threw her offspring on the dung heap. Probably an Indian servant too, someone who was just a girl at the time."

The sergeant gave me a long look of appraisal. "Good work, Nando. So far, anyway."

Sebastian bent to wipe his boots before adding, "Does this revelation about Vial and Beatriz contain any possible clue to the matter at Deer Creek?"

"Slight at best, and only because the effigy wore Facundo Salazar's cape. Everyone knows he and Beatriz were lovers."

The relevance of what I just said eluded me. I was beat. I sat down for the first time that day and let Sebastian do the brainwork.

"The effigy was designed to be a threat," the sergeant said. "We have to wonder if the fake corpse looked like Facundo Salazar only by coincidence, or on purpose, to warn that he was next. Somebody went to trouble over the details of the officer's jacket, the mock ring and, of course, the implied castration."

Sebastian mused, "All rich Spaniards wear fat gold rings. Vial wore his to the grave. The governor wears one. So does every padre in the land, so while there may be meaning in that ring, it alone doesn't suggest the effigy was Salazar.

"Think wider, Nando. Who else could the effigy represent?" Sebastian was blowing out the candles now.

"I'd say any Spaniard with riches and power. Any man who would wear a big gold ring and a blue jacket with silver filigree and silver buttons on it. Governor Anza, maybe."

Sebastian stopped moving around the room and sat down with his hands on his knees. He looked up with his big, worried face and said, "Or any one of our leaders, any one of our aristocracy. Nando, do we have another revolt brewing? One in its earliest stages—where someone, Pueblos probably, are setting fire to imaginations, sending the message: 'These intruders can be brought down. These Spaniards can have their whackers cut off, can be murdered, can be driven all the way to Kingdom Come, just like we did before.' "

At a loss, I shook my head. Sebastian's fear was warranted. Ninety years ago the Indios had set aside their differences and joined forces to drive the Spanish out of New Mexico. Hundreds of people died, including dozens of priests, and the Spaniards had to retreat to Mexico for more than twelve years. The colony could not possibly go through that again and hope to survive.

Sebastian rose, and pushed me through the door. We crossed the courtyard to the governor's quarters.

"What's this gathering about?" I whispered.

"It's billed as the ceremonial supper to follow this afternoon's business meeting, to prove that everyone came out the day's work still friends," Sebastian stated.

"I'm not sure I understand what Don Crespín's game is, Nando. I can tell that Anza hasn't got the investigator figured out either. Perhaps Olivas's intent will become clearer during dinner. Watch closely and mind your manners; everything that fierce, old stepmother of yours ever taught you."

Dinner Knives

The room was long and the ceiling high. Wheels of candles lowered from the vigas lit the feast. Half a dozen uniformed men flanked the governor. There were women present too, Anza's wife, Anna, and Celedonia Salazar, who sat peacefully beside her husband.

Don Crespín Olivas, sporting a tall lambs wool hat, his medals gleaming, sat at the governor's right hand.

I suppose, now that Anza had named Facundo Salazar as a candidate to become the next caravan master, the governor couldn't avoid inviting the merchant, for there he sat, hawk-like and supercilious. I watched Facundo's nose visibly narrow when he saw the likes of me enter the room. My chair was tucked in at the bottom corner, like an afterthought. Paper and a pen were next to my place.

"Cover. Use it," Sebastian mouthed and I picked up the quill.

Don Crespín ate serving after serving of roast buffalo. There were platters of corn and eggs, chili sauces, plates heaped with turkey, a giant pudding of golden squash, and hot, round loaves of bread. Finally, a huge apple cake. It was a New Mexican feast, rough compared to what these men were accustomed to, but after the hard trip up the Camino Real, Don Crespín knew better than to quibble. His fork flew.

When the head investigator had achieved his fill, he wiped his mouth and jutting beard. Resting both fists on the table, Don Crespín commanded silence and started in.

"I should like to share with your guests, Governor, some of the discussion we enjoyed earlier today."

The governor graciously extended his hand.

"On behalf of the Commandant General, my esteemed friend Teodoro de Croix, I wish to express our profound regret at the passing of Alfonso Vial, a formidable contributor to the wealth and stability of New Mexico.

"It is a fortuitous coincidence that my associates and I arrived here at this moment. You all know the purpose of our visit was to investigate the treasonous acts of Alcalde Duran. That shall be done, in due time, however, given the circumstances of the death of Alfonso Vial, remarkably on the very eve of the departure of your annual caravan, we find ourselves obliged to veer from our previous course in order to investigate the caravan master's death.

"I decided to apply my expertise to the task of ascertaining the reason for Vial's death. There is no doubt that Commandant General Croix would require it. In his absence, I have made the determination to proceed."

Anza leaned away from Don Crespín to observe him better, which he did with a bland expression. Anza had been listening to this man all day.

"Because Vial held a high position in the colony, one could presume there were people envious of his station. Therefore we summoned men and women from Señor Vial's household, as well as from every stratum of this community, to give witness. So far, each and every one of them testified that at the time of Vial's death he had not received any threats, nor had there been any person of whom Vial had recently expressed concern.

"It soon came to our attention that his wife, Aurelia Inez, might have been in a position to be jealous, but throughout our interrogation of her, the woman exhibited profound sadness at the loss of her spouse. My colleagues and I have ruled out any role of Aurelia Inez in the matter of her husband's death. She has been released from the Casas Reales and remanded to house arrest for the duration of the investigation into the purportedly stolen goods."

While the dinner guests whispered excitedly at this news, I detected a tightening of Anza's lips. *Purportedly* stolen goods?

Don Crespín turned again to the governor. "Señor, will you please give your account of the report by the Indian woman who laid out Alfonso Vial's body?"

"Certainly," Anza said, his calm voice masking his surprise at being ordered around by this man. He cleared his throat and began.

"A Pueblo woman prepared the body for burial. I often call her to do this work. The Indian is knowledgeable in local medicines and her herbs are useful for such procedures.

"Because of Vial's rank, I asked her to expand her process, to examine the corpse in a more thorough manner than usual. In addition to preparing the body for burial, she was to look for things like broken skin, hidden wounds, the condition of the eyes, or food particles in the airway.

"Of course, this type of inspection had been performed by the surgeon from the presidio, immediately after Vial's death. Still, I wanted a second report, one not prepared in haste and under strained circumstances."

Don Crespín's eyes were fixed on Anza. Every guest leaned forward to hear the details of the laying-out woman's account.

"When the Indian's assessment of the late Señor Vial was completed, she told me that Vial's body was whole and showed nearly normal color—given that the man was dead. There was some redness in the mouth and under his eyelids, but nothing to suggest trauma. She assured me that Vial's death was from natural causes, which corroborated the first report suggesting he'd suffered a heart attack."

Don Crespín waited until he was sure Anza had finished, then inquired, "What was the woman's name, Governor?"

"She is known as Melchora."

"And where is she from?"

"Santa Fe. Melchora has been here most of her life."

"The Indian woman is from a nearby pueblo, if I am not mistaken," Don Crespín contradicted the governor. "Which one?"

Anza looked to Doña Celedonia. "Señora? Are you able to tell us? The Indian lives in your home."

Celedonia, wearing her jewels, didn't mind having all eyes turned her way.

"Melchora came from Pecos. She was past childhood when she arrived in Santa Fe."

"Where did she acquire her medicinal skills?" Don Crespín asked.

Celedonia didn't know. "Isn't that the type of thing women learn in their pueblos? The Indian has always been useful to my family at times of sickness."

Don Crespín turned to the governor. "Is this Melchora what you would call a *curandera*?"

The governor explained. "I know the church suggests we avoid curanderas, but there are women in this town who are useful healers to the populace, and yes, some of them come from the pueblos. Women's skill with medicines has been handed down over many years."

Just then, one of Don Crespín's associates, a short, intense man named Montenegro, whispered something urgent in the head investigator's ear.

Don Crespín's voice tightened as he asked, "Governor, to your knowledge, do any of these women say prayers or incantations while they administer their medicines?"

Anza shook his head. "I have never witnessed such practices," he lied.

"Are you aware if these women perform any kind of ceremony as part of their healing technique?

"Not to my knowledge," responded the governor with gravity.

Don Crespín scanned the rest of us in the room. Though we'd all undergone plenty of ritual and singsong from curanderas while they mended us, to a person the dinner guests gave no indication that ceremony or incantation were ever involved.

The investigators conferred on their side of the table until their bowed heads bobbed in unison, at which point Don Crespín told the assembled guests, "In that case the work of curanderas in Santa Fe is not a matter we must pass to the Inquisition. This investigation will remain within the civil sphere."

With that, Don Crespín resumed his interrogation. "Who summoned Melchora to lay out Señor Vial's body?"

"I did," Anza responded.

"Did you pay her?"

"Certainly. Preparation of a dead body is not something one undertakes for free, particularly in governmental cases like this."

"How much she was paid?"

Anza looked toward our end of the table and queried, "Sebastian?"

Sebastian replied promptly, "Melchora received a pair of stout leather shoes and eight *varas* of imported linen."

There was a satisfied smile on Olivas's face as he said, "While in your employ, Governor, and paid generously, I should like to note. Señor Montenegro, please tell us what you have found."

Montenegro's voice was the thin kind that makes you wince when you hear it. "I must inform you that my report is inconsistent with that of your laying-out woman," he piped.

Sebastian leaned toward me and whispered, "Watch how Don Crespín's knife cuts."

"Upon examination of the body," Montenegro intoned, "and of other types of physical evidence at the scene of Vial's death, my associates and I found strong evidence of rapid death through acute poisoning. The inside of Vial's mouth and nose were red and raw. The man's face was oddly contorted, as though he had been violently sick just prior to his death. Vial was so weak he had fallen over in the privy. There was evidence in the red streaks on his body that he had raked his skin raw with his nails, the heat of the poison having caused fierce itching.

"I submit it remains remotely possible that Vial died of a heart attack. But if so, his heart stopped because of difficulty in breathing and slow movement of the blood, both of which are reactions to poison."

Don Crespín asked his man, "These symptoms were clearly evident?"

"Yes sir. So much so that we became obliged to initiate a more thorough examination of this case. After studying the corpse, we questioned Aurelia Inez again. She told us about the nightly cup of supposed 'love tonic' she administered to her man."

I shifted uncomfortably in my seat. Here it comes.

"The drinks were prepared by local curanderas, and had been given for many nights. Tearfully, the young woman claimed she had poisoned her husband, though unwittingly.

"Inspection of their kitchen areas and scullery offered interesting evidence. Fragments of the blue flowering plant, easily recognizable as monkshood, were found swept into the cracks between the flagstones of the stillroom floor. Monkshood, genus *aconitum*. Also called Wolfsbane. I am told the plant grows seasonally in the mountain meadows above Santa Fe. Monkshood has a very beautiful blossom in the shape of the cowl of a monk's habit, nevertheless, you will have heard how rapidly it causes death."

"Tell me, Señor Montenegro," Don Crespín asked, "what would it be like to die from this plant?"

"Monkshood can cause intense vomiting and diarrhea, burning of the skin, paralysis of breath, loss of vision, convulsions and, after ingestion of even very small amounts, death within hours."

"And there was evidence of all this on Vial?"

"Yes, sir, there was."

The room became still as the assembled party considered the tortured manner of Vial's dying. Don Crespín let the silence linger before he questioned Montenegro further.

"How likely is it that a laying-out woman versed in local herbs would *not* know of the poisonous qualities of this plant?"

"Not at all likely. Children are warned off the purple monkshood early in their lives. Even grazing animals know not to touch it."

"Does there exist any possibility, whatsoever, that Melchora could have missed the reaction Vial's body had to this poison?"

"Not if she handled the body at all. The governor said just now the Indian woman checked the airways. Those tissues were highly inflamed, one of the many signs."

All eyes were fixed on the two adversaries seated at the top of the table, the Governor of New Mexico and Croix's head investigator, Don Crespín Olivas. I could hear the candle flames flutter on their wicks.

Don Crespín offered his sharp profile to the rest of us, as he faced the governor squarely. "I say that your Indian woman chose to ignore these most apparent signs of poisoning. Or failed to disclose them. I suggest sir, that was because she had been well paid not to."

"By me? Surely you are not suggesting . . ." Anza was groping to catch the investigator's meaning. Everyone at the table watched in astonishment as Don Crespín closed in on our governor.

"Shoes and Belgian linens. Superior presents to give an Indian," Crespín pursued. "How convenient, if one wishes to cover up murder, to have the laying-out woman within your control."

Francisco leapt to his feet.

"Too fast! You rush into this! Melchora is influenced by other men besides the governor."

At that, all heads shifted to view Melchora's master, Facundo Salazar. I cast a quick glance at his wife, whose eyes locked for a split second on mine.

Francisco plunged ahead. "Men who had more cause to eradicate Vial than our governor did!" my brother concluded hotly. The burly officer next to him seized Francisco's jacket and yanked him down.

Scarcely anyone noticed, because now one of Anza's sub-lieutenants was up and yelling.

"Don't accuse a good man like the governor! Olivas, you said yourself that Aurelia Inez hired curanderas to concoct that love potion. The colony is rife with women who deal in poison and Melchora is expert in these skills. Interrogate her! And don't do it gently. It's the word of a witch woman against the word of our governor. And while you're at it, round up all the other brujas in this village. It's time to bring their obscene arts to a halt!"

Governor Anza grimaced at this burst of support. He stood and banged on the table with the butt of his knife.

"Enough! Don Crespín, I put myself at your disposal. I can see that your investigation must head in my direction. My innocence will be proven, but duly, in the courts. And it is in the courts that any suspect in the death of Vial will be tried."

The governor turned to his vehement lieutenant, "While I appreciate your words on my behalf, sir, there will be no torturing of women in my colony, as long as I am governor."

Anza next bore down on Don Crespín, "And I *am* still governor of New Mexico, while you, Don Crespín, are a very long way from those who might support you in this."

The warning, sternly given, was sourly received. Don Crespín rose stiffly and gathered his cape around him. "We will proceed in a civilized fashion, Governor. As deputy to the Commandant General, I require that you stay within the villa of Santa Fe, Juan Bautista de Anza."

Don Crespín turned to the table full of men. "A proper tribunal will be formed to ascertain the truth in this situation. Meanwhile, hold that Indian woman in close confinement. We believe this Melchora and her collaborators will be able to speak to many of our concerns."

Collaborators? It was time for me to grab Marisol and run.

Sebastian, without instruction, headed for the door. "With your permission sir," he bowed hastily toward Don Crespín, "I will bring Melchora in before she has a chance to flee."

Anza gave a curt nod and left the room. Stuck to his heels was one of Don Crespín's men. Olivas called his colleague back.

"Leave the governor be," the head investigator ordered. "There is no place Anza can go without being instantly recognized and apprehended. He is effectively a prisoner within his own territory."

Flight

The dinner party broke up in haste, everyone hurrying to spread the news. Because I gathered the papers and pen to keep up Sebastian's ruse, I was nearly the last through the door. I broke into a run.

Marisol was implicated in Vial's poisoning. She had to leave, now, tonight, but the fact she was more than six months pregnant presented a problem. She could still ride, but not hard, nor long, nor fast. My Marisol now had something in common with Governor Anza: there was nowhere in this territory she could go and not be recognized by the authorities.

Her flight was dangerous in every way, yet I couldn't leave her here to be interrogated as Melchora's assistant, to be accused of whatever scheme this was. It didn't matter whether the poisoning was Melchora's doing, or involved the governor, or any other troubled soul in this wretched kingdom. Marisol was at risk.

Who could I count on as allies? Francisco. Luz maybe. Possibly Padre Miera. Sebastian had to back the governor, no matter what, and he'd be riled that I skipped town in the middle of the job. Never mind that the death of a lone Indian had lost all importance, now that the caravan master was dead, and as for me squelching witch frenzy, the governor now had the excuse he needed to round up every suspicious woman in the land.

Did taking Marisol away give notice of guilt? Seal her sentence? Probably, but not necessarily. I had to think it did not. For now, I was going to remove her from sight, get her somewhere far from Santa Fe before they began questioning Melchora and the other women.

My mind raced as fast as my feet. Where to hide her? The grandmother's house in Abiquiú, where Francisco had stashed Luisa's share of the alcalde's possessions? Forget it. It was smack in the middle of the row of houses surrounding the plaza. Unless Marisol hid in the barn alongside Francisco's hams and sofas, she'd be fodder for gossip the minute she opened the door.

Her farm on the Chama? Better. Not great. Neighbors would notice her there too, and the house had to be a shambles after the night early last summer when I'd extricated her naked and bleeding, leaving two dead men sprawled across the floor.

What I needed was to find Nan, my birth mother, the only person I knew who could spirit Marisol out of the colony into the mountains, keep her safe, and oversee the delivery of this child. Nan I would trust absolutely, but how to reach her? How to get word to her? Our tribe would be settled somewhere for the winter by now, but how long would it take to find them, dragging a woman in delicate condition through the snows and storms of the north on the bony back of a mule?

If we could get at least as far north as Abiquiú . . . It came to me. The ranch. I could take Marisol to the family's ranch, far away though it was. Forbidden to us, and in ruins, no one would imagine we would dare go there.

Our hacienda wasn't entirely uninhabitable when I visited it last summer. Water flowed year round in the creek. Several rooms were still almost intact, some with functioning hearths. With my silver I could engage a man in Abiquiú to travel north to find Nan. My mother would hurry down with horses and a party of Utes to help us. We'd make do at the ranch until Nan arrived.

I started to laugh. Wouldn't Anza like to come with us! Get out from under that overreaching Don Crespín and have a few good days of riding, with a promise of peace at the other end.

Francisco interrupted my first light moment of the day, striding out of a side street and grasping my sleeve.

"Melchora's gone. Sebastian went straight to Salazar's for her, but the woman's disappeared. That triggered a round up. They've brought in Juliana. They're arresting all known curanderas and are putting them under guard at the palacio."

"It's only been twenty minutes! If Melchora has already fled, she must have had her ear pressed to the dining room door." Feeling more desperate by the second I added, "Melchora can't have gotten far. She has to still be in town."

"Trust me, Sebastian's working on that."

I grabbed my brother's arm, spinning him around. "I need a cart and two mules, with the axles as well greased as before." There wasn't time to explain my urgency.

Francisco stopped in the road and stared at me. Something in my face kept him from arguing. He caught on. "With hay spread thickly on the floorboards, sheep skins, blankets, food for several days and a chamber pot."

"Hurry!" was all I said, dashing for the house.

Marisol was asleep in our room. I knelt and gently woke her. I told her what happened; I told her my plan.

"I'm sending you out of town in my brother's cart. Tonight, now. Put on your warmest clothes, extra socks, and wear mittens. Francisco's gone to find his driver and get the cart hitched to the mules. We'll have you out of here within minutes, but before I can leave I've got to talk to Padre Miera."

"You're not coming with me?" she asked with a troubled look.

"I'll catch up with you the moment I'm done. Tomorrow afternoon at the latest. We'll be together before you get to Santa Cruz. Depending on how you feel, we'll either keep the cart, or saddle the mules and ride. Do you think you can ride?"

"I'm healthy. I can ride. But the cart's best for getting out of Santa Fe. Won't that be noticed though, a cart leaving at night? "

"Not one as sly and sneakily outfitted as Francisco's. He's had practice."

"They'll suspect Melchora's hidden in it. Every cart or wagon leaving Santa Fe will be searched."

I blustered to make Marisol think I had these problems solved. "Not yet they won't. They think Melchora's here in town, and most likely she still is. We're going to beat them. You'll be out of Santa Fe before the search really begins."

Marisol was dressing while I explained, and throwing small possessions in a bag: a knife, flint, her comb, a piece of soap. I followed her into the kitchen and together we gathered whatever bread, meat and cheese we could find.

"We'll be rid of the cart and riding mules by the time the authorities are searching the roads. That way we can take to the woods and skirt the checkpoints. We've done it before, haven't we?"

I could see aching tiredness in Marisol, and sadness.

"Aurelia's back home. They've declared her not guilty," I offered.

"And Juliana's in a cell," she retorted. "Did they take Agapita and the child as well? What other women have been arrested?"

I couldn't tell her, because I didn't know. With two bundles, our new blanket and a water gourd, we left the house and moved across the dark, frozen yard to the barn. Francisco was there talking with his former manager.

"The cart's ready," my brother said. "Amado will take Marisol down the hill toward the Río. Remember that arroyo a league past Tesuque, the site of one of my less glorious undertakings? That's where you'll find them, as early tomorrow as you can get there."

Amado nodded, "To hide the rig we'll be waiting down in the channel. Marisol can rest while you catch up with us."

He and Francisco helped Marisol into the cart. I pulled the sheepskins carefully over the hay and wrapped my girl in the new blue and red blanket, tucking in her feet. I put the bag of food by her hand and the gourd. Our kiss was discreet, because my brother was standing right beside us. Francisco patted Marisol's hand before Amado pulled the hides over his load.

"Quietly, quietly, now."

They were off in near silence. I stood in the lane, my hand lifted in parting, thinking how important it is to keep your getaway cart in good condition.

"Just a few hours," I said after them, by way of prayer.

"Come in and sleep." Francisco clapped his hand on my shoulder.

I blew the breath out of my cheeks. "Sleep? You're kidding. I have to talk to Miera, quick, before I leave."

My brother raised his eyebrows. "Miera doesn't want to be bothered this late. The priest will be up early. Better see him at dawn."

"I don't think so. There's something important from the trip to Pecos that I never got to tell him, because of the dinner at the palacio."

Francisco put his arm over my shoulder. "Sleep. You'll be better at all of this if you rest a few hours."

I nodded, then backed out of his grasp. I told him, "Be careful, big brother. When you took on Croix's men in the palacio this evening, you forgot the investigators are here primarily to steal Luisa's inheritance. Don Crespín and his men would love an excuse to remove you from the list of claimants to the alcalde's wealth. By whatever means."

The look on Francisco's face might have been contrition. My brother however, would never be able to damp down his excitable spirit. "I forgot the danger to Luisa, you're right, but I couldn't bear sitting there, hearing Don Crespín smear Anza. And Anza, the polite host, blindsided."

Francisco the way I love him, I thought. "I liked the jab you got at Salazar. The investigator took it seriously, don't you agree? And, Francisco, thank you for your cart. You'll have to explain our disappearance to Luz and Luisa, because by morning I'll be long gone."

"I'll tell them. They'll worry about both of you and light lots of candles. By the way, Luz said that if I saw you before she did, to tell you she remembered it was the Greek family. Whatever that means."

I filed the information for a more rational time.

"I pray to our Mother in Heaven you're making the right move, Nando, and that Marisol gets safely out of Santa Fe, because I think it will go much worse for her if they catch her fleeing. What's your intention?"

"Get her to Nan. Let this calm down. Meantime our home will be the Piedra Lumbre for a while, the ranch."

Francisco let out a low whistle. I'd finally managed to impress my elder brother.

I was at the padre's door by first cockcrow. The sky was still dark when Miera let me in. Amazingly he was welcoming, even this early, and he listened with care as I poured out the events of the night before.

Then I backtracked to the murder in the ramada near Pecos, and the likelihood of the victim being a man called Tuqué. When I told him that Vial, the third in succession to die, was the father of the murdered Beatriz, the padre was incredulous.

"Your Padre Domingo knows," I pressed. "He's known all along that Vial was Beatriz's father. I'm beginning to wonder if it's a coincidence that both their deaths occurred so hard on the heels of Domingo's return to Santa Fe."

Miera was looking at me like my brain was spiraling out of control, but I wasn't finished yet.

"I'm convinced your crazy priest holds a piece of information crucial to the governor exonerating himself, information that could also free Juliana and the other curanderas they've arrested."

Trained to listen, the padre regarded me gravely.

"There's a connection between the deaths. I can smell it, and Don Crespín smells it too. Santa Fe's a scared town after the murder of Vial. Salazar's Indian, Melchora, figures in that death somehow, and they're after her. Last night, when Don Crespín craftily linked the governor with Santa Fe's curanderas, Melchora disappeared and Sebastian tore the town apart looking for medicine women."

The padre's silent attention encouraged me to tell more.

"Olivas's attack on Anza was so blatant, it's hard to ignore his real motive: unseating our governor. He claims there's evidence Vial was poisoned by the monkshood plant. Says Anza was behind it. That means Sebastian's best maneuver to prevent Anza from being indicted is in charging any and all females who have knowledge of herbs. Sebastian's desperate to protect his man."

The padre grasped it all. "Where's Marisol?"

It had been a long time since I'd been to confession, but telling him about Marisol felt like one.

"Marisol isn't in Santa Fe any more. Being here is too dangerous for her."

Micra slowly nodded and laid his hand on my shoulder.

"Do you remember when I wondered if we ought to be getting Juliana and her family out of here?" the padre asked. "I was wrong not to have acted. I fear for the women confined in the palacio. It's so easy to take out a village's troubles on a few helpless females. I'm glad Marisol has gone."

I bowed my head. "We didn't help Juliana back then and now it's too late for her. But maybe Marisol will have a chance."

After a moment I looked up. "What do you know, what can you tell me about Melchora, Father, now that she's the principal suspect?"

"Strong. Smart. Manipulative. She's made herself comfortable at Facundo Salazar's. She serves Celedonia Griego in every aspect of the household, including Facundo's business. Not bad for a Pueblo girl who showed up in town at the age of twelve.

"Melchora didn't come to Santa Fe willingly," the padre admitted. "She was kidnapped out of her pueblo. At first she was one of the kitchen girls at the palacio. She was traded into private servitude and became pregnant. After that I noticed her from time to time in different households. I have no recollection of what became of her babies. She has little use for the church.

"At some point she attached herself to the Salazars. Even that good family hasn't been able to get her to Mass very often. Melchora's her own mistress. The woman possesses a casita of her own now, out at the edge of Salazar's cornfields, unusual for an Indian servant. However, nothing in her background points toward her poisoning Vial, and she's set up well enough not to have done it for the money."

"Could she be so loyal to Salazar that she'd help kill off the merchant's competitor?" I asked. "Or so loyal to his wife, that she'd remove a woman named Beatriz, who threatened Celedonia's marriage?"

Miera stepped back and took a good look at me. Then he shook his head. "Melchora is loyal primarily to Melchora. The woman is a consummate survivor. She has learned to do whatever she must to take care of herself, and she's positioned herself well. Why would she put anyone else's interest ahead of her own, if it were to endanger all she's gained? Melchora's made herself indispensable to people in this town with her herbal skills and has earned a considerable degree of freedom.

"But back to Domingo," the padre said. "I will ask him what he knows. That much I can do, and I will let you know what comes out of it."

Daylight was beginning to illuminate the room. Padre Miera pinched out the solitary candle flame.

"Please, Padre, bring up Melchora's name with Domingo. Watch his reaction," I asked, then added, "I may not be in Santa Fe for a while. If what you learn is significant, you should tell Sebastian."

The padre smiled that I should be giving him orders. "As you say, my son." Watching my face he added, "I was fairly certain you were working for the governor again. Thank you for confirming it."

"I've never felt I needed to conceal that from you, Father," I said, giving him a level look before I resumed pushing my point. "If Domingo hesitates, if you can tell he is covering up something to protect himself, will you go harder on him, Padre?"

"I will have no problem getting the truth out of Padre Domingo," Miera asserted.

"You're so sure?"

The portly priest smiled. "The man will tell me. If he refuses, all I have to do is threaten to send him back to Zuni."

The Merciless Stars

I dug my silver coins out from the under the hearthstone. I still had on my brother's turned-up pants and found that I could slip a dozen coins into Luz's thick and hurried hems. I replenished my fire kit, loaded my pistol, and put a few small tools into a bag. I rolled two more blankets into a bundle, wrapped them in a hide, and tied them onto the back of Rosinante's saddle. Strips of jerky and dried apples went into one leather pouch, cornmeal and piñon nuts into another. I filled two water gourds and grabbed a fresh cheese.

At the last minute I decided to appropriate a mule from my neighbor Guillermo's corral. Rosinante already had enough to carry and I might need a mount for Marisol. I strapped baskets on the purloined animal, telling myself I'd settle with Guillermo later, though how much later I couldn't tell.

Sunbeams were showing over the Sangres and a few people were already out in the cold morning beginning their work. I rode slowly through the plaza. No one could tell that my empty-looking baskets were jammed two-thirds full with the supplies Marisol and I would need to make a start at the ranch. I'd left the handle of the hatchet showing so they'd think I was going for wood. I waved at Gabriel who was pulling the day's first bucket of water from the convento's well.

I was relieved to get past the Casas Reales without encountering Sebastian. A little farther out I picked up the pace and headed north. Sure enough, where the road narrows near the top of the hill, a patrol of soldiers waited to scrutinize whoever was coming or going. I would have no trouble passing, but I didn't want any of these men to know my business. I lost time cutting behind some cow pens before I could duck into the woods. I was nearly in Tesuque when I rejoined the road.

An hour later I found the empty cart. It was not, as Amado promised, tucked into the deep, dry channel of the arroyo, but abandoned in the chamisa brush at the side of the road. No driver, no mules, no sheepskins or gear, and, worse, no sign of Marisol. I tried to swallow, but my throat had closed.

The wagon tongue rested on the dry dirt of the road. Silvery wisps of hay on the empty floorboards fluttered in the wind. I knew it was Francisco's cart, because of the great gobs of tallow used to silence the wheels.

Stay calm, I told myself. The only way to figure this out is to stay calm.

I dismounted and checked for signs. A flurry of footprints, hastily brushed over. Shod mules following each other into the arroyo of the Tesuque Creek. No scrap of cloth, no lock of hair hastily left in warning, nothing but dry hay clicking in the wind.

Had there been an accident? Had the cart overturned and the animals fled? Did travelers on the road gather up the injured and take them to safety at Tesuque Pueblo? The upright, undamaged cart told a different story.

A patrol. A patrol of Anza's soldiers looking for Melchora must have apprehended Amado and Marisol. They'd taken them into custody and returned them to Santa Fe, to interrogation and probably prison. I'd missed them because of the circuitous route I took out of town. But would soldiers have left two valuable mules to wander away in the arroyo?

Maybe the soldiers had no choice. The mules had probably broken loose and the men had no time for chasing livestock. Returning a fleeing witch woman, suspected of having a hand in the death of the mighty Vial, would take priority over recovering runaway animals.

I circled the cart once, and then again, creating a larger arc. The only point of exit I found was the one the mules took, so I kicked Rosinante harder than I meant to and we plunged down the arroyo bank, following torn up ground beside the streambed.

I didn't stick to every twist of the meandering creek, but took a beeline over the swales, avoiding jagged arroyo cuts. The tracks of panicked animals were easy enough to find whenever I was back beside the water.

I'd gone around three long bends in the channel before I found the mules. They stood grazing on a sunny point of land where green grass still grew. There was nothing other than the dragging harness to tell me these were Francisco's mules, borrowed from his father-in-law's estate. No human was in sight.

I cried out in fury. I'd ridden half a league to a dead end. The mules would survive, but Marisol might not. And the baby within her? I turned Rosinante toward the road and forced her to run.

The sigh I heard was a deep one with shudders in it. The sound came from a dull yellow clump of chamisa down by the streamlet, a place I had by-passed while taking a shortcut. I rode over and found that the moaning came from beneath two bushes. All that was visible were boots and an arm that flailed in the sunlight.

The man appeared to be in one piece and judging from the noise he made, was alive, but there was something wrong with the way he was hooked together—a major part of him was broken. I couldn't tell if it was his pelvis or his spine, or maybe the thick bone of his thigh.

"Amado?" I queried. "Amado, is that you?"

"Go to the devil and the saints with you!" Francisco's manager boomed. "Goodbye and goddamn you," he rolled away from me in his delirium.

I squatted beside him.

He railed, "Yep, they took your big bellied lady and left me and the mules to die out here."

"The mules are fine. You're the one who's a wreck."

I poured water into my kerchief and wiped bloody sand off his face. That calmed Amado some and he told me, "They hit us when it was still dark. It happened fast. Marisol came out from under the blanket with her knife and went for the woman, but a man grabbed her arm and wrestled her onto his horse. Another one slashed the mules' traces, seized the bundles and the raiders were gone, but not until they'd thrown me down and stomped on me. Their horses took a turn jumping on me too. Damn me for being stupid. I had the reins wrapped around my forearm. Got dragged this far and then dumped into the rabbit brush."

I saw fresh green bruises on the side of the man's face and believed every word he said.

"They wanted the mules, but those animals don't work for any one else but me. They spooked and didn't choose to be rounded up. What in Christ's name is the matter with my leg?"

"Broken for sure. Here, drink this." Amado winced, then upended my gourd and let the water surge down his throat.

"I've got to find Marisol, but I can't leave you lying under a bush. What do you suggest?"

"Leave me here. Tell the Indians at Tesuque. Tell them Francisco will pay them. Leave me that gourd is all, and hurry up."

"Was it a patrol from the presidio? Soldiers?"

"Not by any chance. A hell-raising woman and two Pueblo men. That's who I saw, anyway."

"Which way did they take Marisol? Which way did they ride?"

"I can't give you directions. I was upside down and banging along the ground. Speed I can estimate. About as fast as first-rate horses can run."

"Marisol double-mounted with her captor?"

"A tight fit."

"That will slow them."

"Not much. They had damn fine horses."

"I looked all over. I looked carefully. All their tracks were brushed out." I was getting to my feet, ready to ride for the pueblo. "I'll tell the Indios to come get you and where to find your mules."

I put apples and jerky into Amado's kerchief and left a gourd of water by his hand. "It won't take me long. They'll get to you in an hour I'd say."

"Hour's long enough for a coyote to get here. Hurry the hell up."

"I'm gone."

Saving Amado put me behind another two hours, and that didn't count the half-day's advantage Marisol's captors already had on me. It was long past noon when I found the tracks they hadn't bothered to erase. Six horses. Two not carrying riders. One double-mounted.

I didn't let myself think about the baby. If Marisol hung onto this child it would be a miracle. If I could get to her while she was still alive, in time we'd make lots more babies, and the town wouldn't have any excuse for chattering about who the father might be.

I was more mad than scared. I pressed Rosinante harder than she'd ever been ridden, following the kidnappers' tracks a long way over to the wide fan of the Rio en Medio, then down to the Rio del Norte. I crossed the cold, green water, then rode up the sand hills on the other side and down into the brittle leaves and brushy bosque of a side canyon. The sun dropped into the Jemez and the air took on a hard chill. It wasn't long until dark.

The people who had Marisol weren't making for Santa Cruz and they hadn't turned back to Santa Fe. They were riding brazenly across pueblo land, in a westerly direction, into an unpopulated region across the Rio. Who in God's name were Marisol's kidnappers?

By the time dark fell, I was in country I hadn't ridden in for years. I could scarcely find their tracks and there was no moon.

I rode as long as I could, dismounting often to feel along the ground for holes in the sand made by the animals' hooves. The only advantage I had was there were six of them, so they churned up a wide track of earth. Except when they were riding on rock. That was where I had trouble. My eyes were good in the dark, and even without a moon there's enough faint light given off by the stars that you can make out a trail. But not on rock.

I stopped at a pothole to figure things out, and let Rosinante and the borrowed mule drink. The moment they'd taken on water, both animals lowered their heads into the rustling grasses.

Great rock cliffs rose in the dark on either side of me. We'd been moving up a long draw between two massive walls of stone. For certain these people weren't riding over the tops of those cliffs. I climbed back on Rosinante and nudged her into the sloping center of the canyon. I no longer held the mule's lead rope. The animal knew to stay close, being afraid by nature of coyotes, cougars, bears and wolves. This mule was smart enough to stick with friends.

A light wind rolled across the ground from the west, and it was this wind that warned me. The moving air carried sounds down the canyon, long before Marisol's captors could hear my approach. I heard a woman's voice. Amado said there had been a woman. I heard men talking too.

I slowly drank a few swallows of water, listening and deliberating. I chewed through a slice of dried meat and ate a handful of little apples and some piñon nuts. All the while I listened. These people were arguing. For a second, I thought I heard Marisol's voice. Maybe something muffled? Had they gagged her?

I tied Rosinante, but loosely—not so tight she couldn't break away if she had to, and I did the same to the mule. The pair had grass there and stars aplenty. I checked my knife and pistol, slung my water gourd over my shoulder, and took off uphill.

I smelled smoke from a fire, which let me know the raiders had stopped for the night. They weren't going anywhere and I had time to make a wide circle, to climb the cliff and move along the ledges until I could see down into their camp. I would do a lot of studying before I would begin the business of extricating Marisol, because there was only one of me.

Quietly leaping across a steep, narrow side ravine, my gourd swung and knocked against a rock. The noise seemed louder than a fiesta drum. I dropped low and waited a full ten minutes until the talking resumed and I knew the people down below had figured the noise for the movement of some wild animal. To wait was frustrating, because I was just one small canyon away from being able to see who was there. All through my traverse, particularly when the other voices stopped, I could hear a low, muffled sound from Marisol.

I traveled the last thirty yards on my belly and finally reached a vantage point between boulders. Squatting between two huge rocks, I blended in with one and got cover from the other. I looked into the camp below.

Small flames lit up a woman's face and graying hair. She leaned over a bundle of blankets. It was strange to see Celedonia Griego sitting in the wild, but hadn't I already learned that Salazar's wife was adept at transporting herself through the night?

The Spanish woman's face showed strain, not unlike the time I discovered her in Juliana's barn, but this time she didn't face the night alone. Two sturdy Pueblo men sat on rocks nearby, pointedly not paying attention to what was in the blankets.

That's when I understood that the bundle was Marisol, and the muffled noises her moaning. By the look and sounds down there, my girl had started childbirth, brought on by the hard ride and the terror. Too early by months for a living child. It was anger, not the cold running wind that froze my face into an unmoving mask. I got ready for the work at hand.

"I can't stand listening to this! Kill her," one of the men said. "She's going to die anyway. Get it over with"

"Maybe," responded Celedonia. "But not unless we have to. We need a hostage and she'll do. She's worthless to us dead."

"Put her out of her pain," the other man sided with his partner.

Celedonia kept looking into the fire as she said, "Maybe she'll live. Maybe she'll die. Who cares? But don't count on her dying. These girls are tough. She's young enough; she'll be able to ride tomorrow."

Celedonia Griego looked up then, out into the night, and stared in my direction. I was fairly sure she couldn't see me, because the fire made the surrounding night too black to fathom anything. What troubled me more was that all day I had followed four horses with riders. Where was the other person?

I held still as death when I heard Celedonia say, "Anyway, it will be easier to bury a small baby than a grown woman."

One of the men rose and walked away from the firelight into the dark. The other Indian remained near Celedonia, a musket across his knees. He leaned forward, picked up a stick and prodded the fire. Celedonia slowly drummed her fingers on her thigh.

Marisol let out a screech—still muffled, but a cry nonetheless. I rose to standing, silently preparing to leap.

The stone crashed into my temple. That much I felt. My knees hit the rock wall. I bounced off the side of the canyon and the ground slammed into me. I rolled over and over, careening down the hill. I saw a thousand merciless stars and then nothing.

The Death Cave

I heard the pinched, tentative wail of a newborn babe over the drumming of hooves. My belt buckle dug painfully into the flesh of my stomach. Someone had drawn and tied my hands behind me, so my chin banged and rubbed on the coarse fur of an animal. Darkness, edged with deepest blue, engulfed me. Black of night.

Nan came. She laid me on the ground and placed her warm hands on my legs, my shoulder, my burning head. I felt the urge to live rise in me, but only for a moment. Light burned, and then that deep, dark blue.

My mouth tasted like red arroyo sand. My dry tongue found a hole where I remembered teeth. I couldn't swallow. Still, Nan poured water into me. I rolled over and retched.

A woman said, "Your captive is alive."

It was not my mother's voice. Someone yanked a blanket up to where it snagged my raw chin. Rough wool; burrs in it.

"Nobody will want this dying half-breed as a hostage. Too bad we lost the girl."

I squeezed my eyes shut until they hurt, tightening against the anguish. Lost the girl. That bundle. Marisol's moaning sound. Where was the baby?

The hard ache at the back of my head rose yellow behind my eyes. Surely both were dead. A crackling light, then darkness.

Something wet was put between my lips on a wooden stick. Soup, salt. I slept.

Morning sun on the backs of my hands. I moved my fingers. They worked. I flexed my wrists, and then, still prone, I stretched my legs and made my toes move. A room, a place with walls. Smooth stone, curving up to the cave's roof. Smoke in sunlight, wavering oily blue. A woman out there on the sandstone ledge, watching the valley below. Nan? Is that you?

Cold. Cold wet ground. How come it's wet? Did I pee? I shift my body. Someone comes inside and stands over me. I see the muddy hem of a skirt, red moccasins. The button on one is bone, the other, tarnished silver. I have seen that black button before.

Is it better to play dead, or to let this woman who is not Nan, know I am awake? I keep my eyes closed. I command my eyelids not to tremble.

Darkness. The rough blanket on my face again. Will they ever leave their fire, go to sleep? Now I really need to pee. I don't want to urinate where I'm lying any more. My guards, my captors, are speaking.

By now I've figured out who they are: Celedonia and Melchora.

Why is Celedonia here? Is the merchant's wife under some threat from this masterful Indian? Why else would a woman of her station be hiding out in a cave, why else would she be a participant in Melchora's desperate flight?

My mind seizes at scraps of their conversation and twists the words inside out, looking for an explanation of this partnership. Does the Indian woman hold her mistress in some sort of grip? I remember the ugly bruise on Celedonia's face the night I found her in Juliana's barn. I wonder.

Oh, my poor girl. My poor Marisol.

Drifting in and out, listening for hours, I realized I was wrong; that Melchora wasn't the strong one, the perpetrator. The Indian actually seemed contrite.

"Nobody suspects you, Celedonia. It's me they're after," Melchora told her companion. "You can tell the authorities that Juan and Eloy abducted you along with Marisol; that you know where their half-breed informer is. Celedonia, you have a way back. You have a husband to return to. You don't have to hide out with me forever. Just give me enough time to get out of the colony."

That was when I learned all my guesses were wrong, because Celedonia reached out to the servant woman beside her and took her hand.

"I'm not leaving you, Melchora. You followed my orders; you poisoned Vial for me. Let's not have any pretense about that. If they catch you, they'll hang you on Santa Fe's plaza, friend, but we won't let them, will we?"

Melchora remained quiet while Celedonia spoke, but not nearly as silent as I. It was not Anza, nor any man at all, but two angry women who had killed Vial.

The merchant's wife snarled, "And do you really think I would go back to Salazar after his infidelity? Never! Beatriz's bouquet provided enough monkshood to kill both men. Such pretty blue flowers! We should have gotten rid of Facundo too. No, Melchora. You and I stay together. It's God's will that neither of us goes back to the colony. Ever."

So it was sweet Beatriz who provided the means of the caravan master's death. But did she pick the poisonous plants knowingly?

Melchora nodded slowly before she asked her friend, "Killing Vial seems right to you then?"

Celedonia's voice went hard. "I haven't had a moment of remorse. Vial's deserved punishment for a long time, and throughout all those years how many other women do you think he preyed upon?"

Celedonia Griego paused and moved to look into the back of the cave where I lay. I didn't breathe.

Returning to Melchora, Celedonia asked, "And what about you? Do you feel remorse about Tuqué? That was a horrible death for Tuqué."

"What was a young girl's life to Tuqué?" Melchora flared. "He saw us as meat for men, nothing more. Girl-children were his trade items, so he could have a mighty stallion to ride whenever he wanted.

"But the girls grew older and became wise," the Indian fumed. "The women waited a long time. They honored me when they asked for my help.

"Every grown woman in the pueblo understood what Tuqué's disappearance meant. They heard how he died, and not one woman opened her mouth. I helped commit the most longed-for crime in decades. No one bothered to search for Tuqué's killers."

"That's because it's no crime to kill a witch," Celedonia added. "Making Tuqué's death look like witch-kill sent a message, and everyone kept their distance, at least until Nando blundered onto it.

"At first we women thought it was enough to put Tuqué to death, with just the right degree of torture," Melchora confessed. "But then Nando discovered the body and hurried to tell everyone in Santa Fe. That could have undone us, but we saw our chance to strike fear into the guts of even more men. Surely Spaniards used us as hard as Tuqué ever did. Believe me, the way the women tricked out that effigy . . ."

Melchora laughed aloud at the memory of their handiwork.

"Could things have worked out any better?" she gloated. "God was on our side when it was Nando who fell off the cliff into our camp, valiantly trying to save his poor Marisol. If soldiers corner us, we'll use him as a hostage, or if you say so, we'll kill him here and now."

Forget hostage. If they knew I was hearing all this they would murder me for sure.

I let out a groan, as though I were waking up. There was no way I wanted them to realize I'd heard all they'd just admitted to. Melchora strode inside, pointing my own pistol at my hurting head. She pulled back the blanket and ordered, "Time you got up. Stop pissing on yourself."

I blinked, pretending I was just opening my eyes. I held my head, rolled onto my knees and tried to rise. Not much was play-acting. I literally crawled out of the cave to the brink of the ledge, and without caring which woman saw me, got to my knees and peed over the side of the cliff. I was weak as a kitten, but was relieved, that after the beating I took, everything worked. I lay down on smooth stone in the feeble sunlight and immediately went back to sleep.

When shadows fell across the cliff face, and the aerie became gloomy and cold, I crept back into the cave, pulled the blanket over my head and lay there wavering in and out of sleep.

One or the other of the women stayed guard over me at all times. Water was brought from the creek below, in my own gourd, I noticed. Occasionally a bowl of mushy meal was set beside me. I sat part way up, but only long enough to eat. I saw that the hem in my pants had been slit open and my silver was gone. Celedonia hadn't had to pay for my salt after all. Another score for the house of Salazar.

I would like to think I was watching the women's every move, planning my escape and shaping my strategy for bringing Melchora and Celedonia in custody back to Santa Fe. It wouldn't be true.

Except for intermittent moments of lucidity, I was mostly not there at all. When I awoke and remembered Marisol and the baby, tears streamed from my eyes. The women never said another word about her. I ached all over knowing that Marisol belonged to the past.

I could differentiate between night and day, because daytime held warmth. Sometimes I dragged myself outside without prodding and lay in the sun. The nights were brutally cold. I often couldn't tell whether it was Melchora or Celedonia speaking.

I wouldn't be worth two *reales* as a hostage. My head pounded. There was a sizeable gap in my teeth over on the right side of my mouth. When I was conscious, I picked at caked blood on my face. There was something seriously wrong with my shoulder. I was finally able to stand up to pee, but my right arm hung half a foot lower than the left. And Marisol was dead.

In the one truly clear moment I'd had, when they'd talked about killing Vial and Tuqué with so much compassion for themselves and none at all for their victims, I knew these women had no mercy. A girl screaming in childbirth would only be in their way.

The Darkest Cold

If I wanted to save my life, I knew I'd have to let my captors think I was well enough to serve as a hostage. Other times, I didn't care to try. Then I'd fall asleep again.

It was dark, sometime well into the third or fourth night, not long before dawn I guessed, when I overheard the women talking quietly. The fire had gone out and I woke up quaking from the cold.

"Can you get us to Mexico?" I heard Celedonia ask the Indian woman. "Could we make it to El Paso?"

I don't know if Melchora nodded or was taking time to think. Huddled beneath the rough blanket, I couldn't see them as they talked.

Then Melchora said, "We would stay on the river. Never leave it, even though the road does. In the beginning there would be Pueblos who would provide for us. We would avoid the Camino Real."

She paused. "On the other hand, maybe it would be better to head west toward Zuni and get someone there to take us to Arizpe. Whichever way we choose, it's a long, hard journey, Celedonia."

"You forget I have money," the merchant's wife responded. "We can buy fresh horses, and once we're farther away from Santa Fe we can hire men to help us."

Celedonia's voice suddenly dropped and became hoarse. "Why wasn't that cursed baby killed, Melchora? Until that hateful Padre Domingo came back to town, I didn't even know my child existed. How did she survive to come back and ruin our lives like this?"

The silence that ensued was so long and so total that I thought the women had vanished from the cave.

But then I heard deep sobbing, and the crumpling of skirts as the Spanish woman flung herself flat on the sandstone floor. Her outpouring of grief went on a long time, and throughout I heard no movement from Melchora.

When at last the crying subsided, the Indian spoke and her voice was gentle. "We've been through this again and again, Celedonia. The way it happened, Beatriz lived many happy years."

"But you don't understand!" The sand of the cave floor muffled Celedonia's voice as she cried out, "I ordered the death of my own child. Twice!"

"Yes, you screamed at your husband about his lover, you shrieked orders at all of us to get rid of the witch, and you poured out a list of ways to do it." Melchora's voice was tired, without the strength I was used to hearing in it. "But screaming and murdering are two different things. You were a woman in pain, Celedonia, and you didn't know Beatriz was your daughter."

"She died because of me," the lady whimpered.

Melchora again kept silent.

"You cannot know!" Celedonia sobbed. "There will be no respite, no mercy, no relief from what I have done, ever, until the last fires of hell burn out."

"Maybe I do know," replied Melchora. "Maybe I know all too well what you feel."

There she was then, Celedonia Griego, the mother I'd been told to find. A daughter of the Greek family. Beatriz was this woman's child, and Beatriz died because of Celedonia's jealousy. Even so, the mother's tears were real.

At last I heard the swish of hands brushing off skirts. Celedonia must have risen from the ground and moved toward the ledge. She spoke out into the night. "I'm consigned to hell no matter what I do. We might as well try for Mexico. I'm willing to go, if you'll come with me."

Melchora stood next to Celedonia. "I think we can get through," the Indian said. "If you want to make the journey, we should leave right away. The weather won't be getting any better here in the north."

"What about Nando? Do we take him or kill him?" Celedonia asked.

I held my breath while Melchora deliberated my sentence.

"We'll keep him, but only until we clear the Spanish settlements. If we need a hostage, it will only be in the first twenty leagues."

I exhaled deep inside the blanket. Would Celedonia agree? Apparently she did, because I heard her flesh out the rest of her plan.

"In his condition, Nando will be a problem, but we'll roll him in his blanket and get him on a horse somehow. At first, he may be all that gets us through, but after we pass the towns, putting up with an injured hostage will be pointless. We cannot let Nando return to the colony knowing where we're traveling. When we don't need him any more, it will be easy to kill him with the bit of monkshood we have left."

Melchora said, "I wish we still had Juan and Eloy to help, but no matter, I was glad to see the last of them."

There was silence. I imagined the women were pondering how they would prop me up for the trip, and how they would dispose of my body once they were safely past the villages.

After a long moment, Celedonia spoke softly. "Melchora, bless you for helping get rid of Vial. Without you I couldn't have done it right, but I would have tried because I was so undone by Beatriz's death, and I'd be hanged for it by now."

Melchora whispered words I couldn't hear and then Celedonia went on.

"The pain of her death is so terrible I can't bear it, but how was I to guess it was my own daughter who stole my husband?"

Celedonia's voice softened to a plea. "We need new lives, Melchora. Does God give new lives to women like us?"

But her remorse was short lived. I heard no more tears in the woman's voice when Celedonia said, "The only solace I have comes from knowing Vial is dead. Alfonso's vileness is what set this tragedy in motion. First, the rape that gave me a daughter I could not possibly keep, and therefore did not know. Then Vial's sickening advances toward Beatriz, that drove her into the arms of Facundo. My daughter's death was a grievous error, Melchora, but Vial's wasn't. My honor, and the honor of my daughter, required killing Vial."

I had slowly slipped the blanket off my face so I could hear them better. I could see Celedonia lean her head against Melchora's shoulder. Melchora opened her blanket and wrapped the smaller woman in with her. They were played out now, quiet, and glad for the comfort of each other.

"Thank you, Melchora," Celedonia said, holding her friend tight. "Bless you for all you have done for me."

Right then I sneezed. I knew as the urge raced to my nose that this would cost me my life, but I couldn't stop it. I sneezed, once, twice and a third time. Everyone knows you can't sneeze in your sleep.

Celedonia and Melchora were on me before I could fake anything. The pistol was cocked and in my face. They strapped leather thongs around my arms and yanked them behind my back until my injured shoulder screamed. Images of Tuqué hanging by his elbows raced in front of my eyes, and the maggot-bitten smell of him rose in my throat.

The women kicked me until I rolled over. They bound my ankles, then jerked my blanket off and threw their few possessions into the center of it. They took the water gourd I'd carried, my knife and my gun. Within minutes they had fled from the place, and I was an aching, bound man lying abandoned in a cave, a long day's ride from anywhere.

They left without killing me. Why should they take the time, why bother? Death by starvation would be slower, harder, and wouldn't add another outright murder to their long list of killings.

With their strong horses, the two would be quickly gone from this plateau.

At first I lay still, exhausted with pain. Then I became frantic, trying to free myself, but for all my lame thrashing, there was no splintered bone or sharp rock I could work into position to cut the thongs. The closest water was over the ledge, down the steep cliff face in a stream in the canyon. If I tried to roll there, I would kill myself.

Food? If I could get my hands free, the best I would find to gnaw on would be the leather thongs. A couple of days and a couple of nights and I would be dead. Probably sooner. All it would take was one bear returning to her favorite lair, or this pack rat that sniffed at my bloody chin.

It turned out I was simply next on the women's list, the one right after Marisol and the unborn babe.

Between the two of them, the Indian servant and the rich Spaniard's wife, they had enough will and craft to make it out of the colony. It didn't matter that I'd found out who had killed Tuqué, Beatriz and Alfonso Vial, because no one would ever know what I'd heard tonight. Innocent women in Santa Fe, some of them my friends, would be hanged as witches, and Governor Anza would be convicted for conspiring with the curanderas to kill Vial.

Lying on the sandy floor of the cave without the use of my arms, I was utterly spent. I felt the dark, deep, cold saturate my bones. I came to understand I had no more business with this world.

Sweet Humming

I never expected to find myself in heaven. My arms moved without pain. My unbound legs sprawled on a soft woolen blanket. There were no more stinking pants and even though I was naked, I was warm. A fire blazed against the wall of the chamber and a clay jar next to it bubbled audibly.

I blinked at the light. My throat was moist and my lips were soft with smooth tallow on them. A beautiful, brown-skinned woman leaned against the yellow sandstone walls and smiled into my eyes. She reminded me of Marisol. Then there was nothing.

Except humming: a sweet song with a beating drum. A hand lightly slapping a thigh.

I raised my arm to touch the singer and clasped a bundle of thick Indian hair. Lips met mine and I lay there, marveling at tenderness. At life. And meat, softened with her teeth before Marisol gently fed me the roasted strips.

It was a long time before I tried to talk. By then I had noticed that my love still moved like a woman who carried a baby on her small, strong frame. My smile felt awkward. I fingered a place on the side of my mouth where my tooth had once been.

Marisol moved steadily and well, doing everything for me, keeping the fire lit and cooking whatever was in the pot. She fed me with her fingers. But she also took her turn at resting, leaning against the wall watching me, or lying next to me in the same blankets I'd long ago strapped to the back of a borrowed mule. Had that happened in another life? Was this truly heaven I was in and the two of us had made it here, notwithstanding all the priests' predictions year after year?

I slept through the night without waking. In the morning I sat up and ate real food. Corn meal, nuts and apples.

"This is what I stowed on the mule, isn't it?" Actual words spilled from me at last.

"Yes," she said, tears springing to her eyes when she heard me speak.

"Nando!" She knelt and hugged me gently, which was good because I could hide my own wet eyes. "My kidnappers took the supplies you put in the cart, but later while they were hauling you into this cave, I found Rosinante and the pack mule, exactly as you'd left them."

I touched her round belly, marveling. "How did you get away? And this child?"

"The baby lives. I pretended I was in labor and the women had the mercy to untie me."

Experiencing unmanly tears, I turned my head away. We both waited a long while before we talked more, then through the rest of the morning we slowly told our stories.

"When you fell into camp, everyone ran to see if you lived, to capture you if you were still alive. The Pueblo men fled the moment the women's backs were turned. They paid no attention to me.

"I ran into the night, carrying only the blanket they'd draped over me. I ran downhill faster than I'd ever run before. When I figured the hunt must have begun for me, I switched to stealth. I found your horse and mule, huddled together waiting for you to return. I praised you for the knife, blankets and cornmeal you'd left behind.

"Then I hid. I couldn't go to help you because I had no idea where Juan and Eloy were, and because of the baby, I was no match for the two women."

I stroked her arm, enjoying the warmth of her skin, wanting to tell her how clever she'd been to feign the birthing.

"I was aching down there, after being bounced across the valley and up into the mountains. The ache was turning into real pain. I was desperate to rest, to stop, which is how the idea came to me. My cries must have worried them, because the ruse worked. I scared the devil out of Celedonia's two hirelings, that's for sure."

Marisol laughed and I tried to join her, but I couldn't, not yet.

"How many days has it been, Marisol? How long have I been like this?"

"Three nights with Celedonia and Melchora, now two with me. That cut on your head is deep. Thank God you were unconscious, because I was able to put your shoulder together. There's no way I could have pinned you with my foot and yanked on your arm if you'd been awake."

To picture that took more than my bruised mind could handle. In a while I asked, "And the rest of the time, before you got to me?"

"After I hid the animals, I tracked Melchora and Celedonia. I saw that they took you to this cave. It was two days until you came out and peed over the ledge. What a relief that was."

"You're not kidding." This time we laughed together.

"I found a cave for myself farther up the canyon. I made do without a fire. By day I hid in the woods and watched the cave from below. I kept an eye on the women's horses, but decided it was best not to drive them off. Who knew if we might need them?"

I lay back. I'd heard all I could stand: Marisol, alone in the woods, watching over my captivity, carefully planning her moves to free me as soon as she could—handling the horses, cautiously protecting the baby. And where did she come by fresh meat? I'd have to remember to ask her that. With what remained of my energy I gave her a little pat and rolled away to sleep. I was overwhelmed.

"Before you go to sleep, Nando, I need to say that I wanted to get to you sooner, but it was too dangerous when the women were there. When at last I saw them leave, I came to the cave as soon as I dared. You were still alive, though at first I couldn't tell. It took all of two days and a night before I was sure you would live. Last night I knew you were mending. When you looked at me today, when you spoke at last, I was sure."

There were tears in Marisol's voice. Without opening my eyes, I reached out from under the blanket, found her hand, and squeezed it, before succumbing to a few more hours of sleep.

The decision about whether to leave that day ended the moment I tried to stand. I was dizzy and confused. It was clear I wasn't ready to move yet.

"Where do you think we should we go?" Marisol asked after she lowered me to the ground.

"Santa Fe," I asserted. "Back to Luz. Get the facts to the authorities and have them track down the women."

But Marisol would have none of it.

"Santa Fe's too dangerous. Nobody's going to believe your story, Nando, and they'll still suspect me. Celedonia and Melchora will try to defend themselves if they're caught, and they'll do it by blaming Juan and Eloy, or me, or possibly even you."

Marisol's brain was working much better than mine.

"Remember," she pressed, "it won't be just your friend, the governor, judging your words. That man from Mexico is sticking his nose into everything. The moment we show up in Santa Fe, Nando, I'll be taken away from you and put in jail. There'll be no bed or good food for me. And remember, in the government's eyes, you abandoned your duty."

I rolled away to face the sandstone wall. "How far are we from Abiquiú do you think?"

"With you in this shape, about a month."

"No, truly."

"Two or three days gentle riding."

"I can do it," I mumbled.

"Maybe after another day or two you can," she conceded.

"And then another hard day to get up to the ranch. What if we skip Abiquiú? Go cross-country over the barrancas and reduce the chances of being seen."

She shook her head. "I think we should move down off the mesa and stay on the west side of the Río. We'll travel by night, but I'm not sure we can get as far as your ranch."

"Can you ride?" I stupidly asked, forgetting she'd been on a horse all the way from Tesuque where the cart had been ambushed.

"More to the point, can you?" she retorted. "And we've lost most of what we need to winter at the ranch. Your pistol, for instance."

"As well as all our money. I was going to pay someone to go north and find my mother, but Celedonia stole my silver."

"I'm sure she'll find it useful out past Zuni."

My sweet-natured girl was becoming testy.

We compromised. We decided to make for Marisol's old farm on the Chama. Though it was close enough to settlements that we'd risk being seen, the odds were against it. Marisol's place was remote and it had only been half a year since the house was occupied, so there might be some supplies left. The roof would be intact and the river ran year round. Best of all, it wasn't as far as Abiquiú, so we would be able to make it there with only one or two nights of travel, depending on how I held up. And, it was in the right direction: north, toward Nan and protection among the Utes.

I mulled over my other obligations. In this battered condition there was no way I could track down Celedonia and Melchora, but I doubted they would get far without an escort and traveling in winter. They would have to be expert and wary to evade the Navajos to the west, or the Apaches who kept an eye on the corridor of the río. I trusted that the fate the women deserved would soon catch up with them.

Without my information, Anza would have to pick his own way through the maze of Croix's investigators, personal enemies, and all the conflicting powers in his kingdom, but he'd manage. I could only pray that witch fever had subsided in the town and no women were being interrogated cruelly.

Marisol made one last dinner out of the grouse she'd struck with a throwing stick. Her Comanche upbringing was serving her well. I watched her use two sticks to drop hot stones into the clay jar, to heat the remaining handful of cornmeal and meat. We ate what there was, slept soundly under the same blanket, and were strong enough the next day to attempt the slow trek back to the valley.

Brother Bear

Rosinante whinnied when I emerged from the cave, and all the while we were loading she kept pushing her muzzle into my back. In spite of her eagerness, I moved so slowly it was mid-morning before we'd packed our few supplies. I took one last nap before we left to fend off the dizziness that mounted the longer I was on my feet. By early afternoon, my seven days in the cave came to an end. Marisol and I descended the mesa, guiding the animals down a gentle slope through ponderosa pines. Cloud shadows raced over the distant foothills of the Sangre de Cristo Mountains in undulating waves of darkest gray.

A heap of storm clouds rose in the north. Until now, we'd been blessed with warm autumn days, which was one reason Marisol and I were still alive. No storms had come in yet to soften the canyons with snow. The rock cliffs held enough heat to keep our bones warm at night, but from the weight of today's purple sky, we knew our Indian summer was about to end.

Marisol led us across the flats, through the sparse piñon and juniper. It didn't require much from me to follow along and Rosinante seemed to take extra care with her steps. I was alive, we were free of the women who had tormented us, and soon we'd be sheltered by four walls. I relaxed in the saddle as we crossed the last broad expanse of mesa.

From the looks of it, the storm would catch us about the time we would reach the dense woods of the bosque. The wind kicked up and vanguard raindrops spattered the dirt, so we put more hustle into our passage. The season changed from autumn to winter as we hurried into the shelter of the cottonwood forest.

We pulled long, dead branches up against the trunk of a living tree, so they fanned out in the shape of a teepee. It was the kind of hasty shelter my mother's Ute people built on their journeys. Smaller branches and brush served as a roof lattice. We carried no skins with us, only our blankets. We would need those to sleep in, so we found a way to layer slabs of loose bark over the framework. At least a part of our hut would shed water, and the smoke from our fire would leave by the holes we didn't have time to cover.

Marisol worked with my fire kit, deftly striking the flint with the iron until she ignited a spark in the little ball of dry grass she carried under her manta. I broke dry twigs off the lower parts of the juniper trees and handed them to her to feed the growing flame. We sat beside the fire, eating the remainder of last night's grouse and some dry old apples, scant, but enough.

The animals found water at a dark trickle that pooled in the woods and grass on the lush forest floor. Knowing we had truly begun our journey home, we let our bones sink against the saddle blankets on the ground and waited for sleep.

I had to keep shifting to stop my shoulder from hurting. Marisol had put it back in place, but even so it throbbed. One time that I awoke, I heard the velvet silence that told me snow was falling. I reached out and sure enough, my fingers patted a cold drift next to the hut.

It wasn't my shoulder, but the crunch of dead leaves and men's deep voices that woke me in the thin, gray dawn. Someone was coming toward us through the light snow.

There was no way anyone would miss our bark-heaped structure, even if they had failed to notice the horse and mule. Marisol's eyes opened and I put my finger on her lips. Could we have camped near a village by mistake? I peeked out from under the blanket to make sure the fire was dead and not wafting smoke. My hand felt silently along the ground for our knife.

The men had spotted our camp and came stomping toward us. Probably not Indians then, though I think I would have preferred a Ute or Comanche right now to Spaniards from one of the towns. God, let it only be farmers looking for their cow.

I rolled up from the bed as quietly as I could, pulled the blanket over the top of Marisol's head, and holding her knife, crouched at the side of the gap we called a door. Two more booted footsteps and then a bearded face peered into the gloom of our shelter. I couldn't be sure if the Spaniard saw me. Neither of us moved. The man's eyes roamed over our water gourd, the saddle, and the lump that was Marisol.

I was tensing to leap, ready to drive the knife into the man's throat, but stopped in mid-lunge when someone yelled from the forest, "Rosinante!"

My fist that gripped the knife twisted to the side, as Carlos's shout rang through the morning woods. "This is my brother's mare!"

My feeble strength gave out and I tumbled back to the ground. Marisol sprang out of the covers and wrapping herself in the blanket ran out calling, "Carlos! It's us! Help me with your brother!"

Men moved out from behind the trees as I set a naked foot into the snow. My great, good bear of a brother lunged to my side and wrapped me in a hug that made everyone in the clearing laugh.

"Sweet mother of God! What are you two doing out here? Nando, you are a filthy, degenerate, marvelous sight for sore eyes. Christ, Marisol, do you always treat him this badly?"

Marisol was giggling and crying at the same time. Even though she adored my brother, it was my hand she held while we stood there being appraised by a half dozen blue-caped soldiers from Santa Fe's presidio.

"Get that fire going, spread some hides. This is the thinnest little brother I've ever seen, though with a rather wide woman beside him. Has he married you yet? High time, I'd say."

Using care, Carlos examined the yellow and blue wound at my temple. I winced when he lightly fingered the edges of the cut in its center. Finally I grinned. By God it was good to see him.

"Nice teeth," my brother said, pulling my lip to the side so he could examine the damage. "What you have left of them. At least you still have the most visible ones. Am I correct this has to do with the abandoned cart, Francisco's driver with a broken leg, and a flying witch who's led us to hell and back up and down this valley?"

"Sí."

"Any idea where Melchora is? We thought we finally had her. A farmer reported he smelled smoke in the night. He thought someone might be camping in the woods here, trying to shelter from the storm. But instead of the witch, I found my little brother."

"The farmer's got a good nose," I commented. "We'll talk about witches in a minute. Have you got anything to eat?"

"We're working on it," replied a soldier next to the fire. "Here, hold this for now." The man I had almost knifed handed Marisol a cup.

She sipped and passed it to me. It was manna from heaven, hot, spicy chocolate. The men watched while we took turns drinking. One of them placed a roll of blankets on top of a deerskin and led Marisol to it. I followed, and we sank back together. We began to tell them what we'd been through. Not all of it, not even most of it, but what a group of soldiers hunting a suspected killer needed to know.

"You say that Salazar's wife was with her?" Carlos asked. "It fits. Two women, or maybe a woman and a man, were spotted yesterday in San Ildefonso. They were getting their horses shod at that renegade smithy's at the pueblo."

Carlos sounded weary as he went on. "By the time we were told of the sighting, they were several hours ahead of my men. We've been patrolling the roads, but that Indian woman is smart. When we realized how sly she was being, we were certain it was the runaway. The roads are under surveillance, but we've come up empty, so we started hunting her in the bosques."

Carlos turned to me. "Is Salazar's wife all right? Has the Indian been hard on her?"

His line of thinking caught me off guard. I stalled. I needed time to understand our situation before I told Carlos everything.

I gave him this much. "Celedonia appeared to be cooperating with the Indian."

Marisol shot me a sideways glance that I hoped no one else saw.

Carlos seemed troubled by what I said. "My assignment is complex. Anza says, 'Bring back the Spanish woman. Show her every respect. Yet do whatever it takes to capture the

Indian. Anza named Don Facundo head of this year's caravan, but until Celedonia's safe, there's no possibility the man can take the post. He won't leave town with his wife missing."

Lord help me. Getting everyone set straight on this was going to take perseverance.

Hot food was served in wooden bowls. My brother's troops dined well. Meat, yeasted bread, squash, corn and chili were among the benefits of traveling with the lieutenant. I hid my confusion by busily eating my breakfast. Marisol did the same, but she went faster, not needing to work the food around a painful jaw.

Sunshine began to filter into the woods and clumps of wet snow fell noisily from the trees. Men set to work, staking out their horses and even hanging our blankets over limbs to dry. Their own gear was sorted and cleaned after a fashion.

Carlos saw that someone tended to his gray, then took advantage of the bustle to sit next to me and explain things.

"Anza and the investigators believe that Melchora is using her mistress as a hostage. Celedonia's life is in danger. The fact the Indian fled in this manner substantiates the charges against her. If we could only find them, we'd get the Spanish lady out of the Indian's hands and safely back to Santa Fe. You have to agree that jumping you before sunrise shows how hard we're trying."

Marisol kept her head down as she ate. She knew how big a mistake they were making.

Where was the truth here? What I'd overheard spoken between two women in the mountain cave? Or did truth lie in the testimony of witnesses in Santa Fe, as part of an investigation needed to exonerate a sitting governor? Anza and Don Crespín must be relieved to have fingered a mutually acceptable culprit.

This version of the truth might be convenient for them, but by now I, and a handful of others, knew differently. Shouldn't Celedonia be held accountable for conspiring to poison Vial? His death I might forgive her, given the rape and its consequences, but not her role in the murder of my friend Beatriz.

I had personal reasons, too, for knowing Celedonia was guilty of attempted murder. There was about to be an unforgivable miscarriage of justice if I didn't find a way to clarify the situation.

"Carlos, is anyone considering the possibility that Celedonia left with Melchora willingly?"

"No, not that I've heard," my brother said.

"Consider this, will you? The two women have known each other all their lives. They work closely together. Anyone with a brain might guess that Celedonia was furious with both her husband and Beatriz for their love affair."

A frown settled over Carlos's face, but I didn't care. "There could be more to this situation than meets the eye. Celedonia could have gotten away from Melchora a dozen times this past week. I watched them operating together for days. They seemed like friends. She was right in there kidnapping and tormenting Marisol. She beat me up and left me for dead. She's not as innocent as you and the governor think."

Carlos was listening, so I pushed one more possibility.

"Maybe Celedonia and Melchora killed Vial together. When I was working for Sebastian, I learned Vial once raped Celedonia. Long ago to be sure, but as a result, she gave birth to a child. Melchora was her attendant at the time."

There, I had managed to give my brother the critical nugget. Was it enough to make him question his certainty?

But Carlos shook his head.

"You mean to suggest that a Spanish woman, one used to every luxury, would flee with her Indian servant just as winter threatens? Celedonia Griego is far too high born for any of the mischief you suggest. You're daft, Nando. Daft. But because of that knock on your head, this time I'll forgive your error in judgment."

I'd tried. What else was I supposed to do?

"Whatever, Carlos," I said with a submissive shrug. "I was only wondering. I'm sure the authorities know what they're doing. Have you heard if they've come to any conclusions about Beatriz's death, or that corpse at Deer Creek?"

"Nobody's talking about them anymore. A whore and an Indian. Both probably witches. Who cares?"

I turned away to avoid showing the shock on my face. But how could Carlos know better, if he wasn't informed? I set down my plate and stood to face him. "Would it give any more credence to what I'm saying if I told you that Beatriz was the child Celedonia produced as a result of that rape?"

The lieutenant turned and looked straight into my eyes. I had gotten his attention.

"So there's the explanation for Beatriz's exquisite Spanish beauty," the lieutenant mused.

"Melchora delivered the child in secret and was told to dispose of it, but unknown to Celedonia, the Indian sent the babe to Cochiti."

Carlos filled in the rest. "And Celedonia's bastard daughter, as well as the man who forced the child on the woman, died within three days of each other."

I nodded. We'd moved to the edge of camp, to get away from the listening soldiers.

"What's your source?"

"Mainly Padre Domingo," I answered, "who had a hand in hiding the infant. And Cruzita, who was at the birth. Also your own mother, Luz, who always knows what's going on."

Carlos winced, but I continued.

"It's significant that both deaths happened within days of Padre Domingo's return to Santa Fe. Padre Miera knows about the connection. He was beginning an inquiry of his own when I left."

The cast of characters impressed Carlos. I gave him one more piece of evidence.

"Celedonia's own words, though heard only by me. I know that's not good enough in court, even if corroborated by my wounds."

We'd reached the string of horses. Carlos reworked a knot on the tie line before saying, "I take what you tell me seriously. I believe your information to be solid. Sebastian knows?"

"Everything but what I overheard in the cave. There's more than what I just told you, but I'll give you the rest while we travel."

Carlos stroked his gelding's dappled neck. Then he told me what I least wanted to hear.

"Marisol is not out of trouble yet. I was told to bring her in if I found her. The investigators weren't clear if she ran away with the two women, or escaped on her own. I'll do what I can to allow her to be held under house arrest, but given the heat around this matter, it might be safer for Marisol to stay within the palacio."

My shoulders slumped. Anything but this.

"Nando, please trust I'll do what I can for her."

Carlos and I started moving back to camp. I stalled. "I'm not much good for travel at the moment. We're trying to get to Marisol's house, which isn't far. I need serious rest and a curandera."

"You have no choice but to return to Santa Fe." Carlos's voice was firm. "The curanderas there are all under lock and key, but Luz can put you back together. I'll send enough men along with you to make the trip manageable. You'll be home by midnight."

Marisol's eyes had never left us and she'd read the situation. I reached for her outstretched hand and groped for a solution. There wasn't one. Soldiers were all around us. I bent to pick up our horse blankets, but the lieutenant got to them before I did. I was glad, because leaning over made my head pound.

Pooling Darkness

Restoring us to the grip of government in Santa Fe took longer than anyone expected. First Carlos had to report to the garrison at Santa Cruz. A farmer, hat in hand, had come in that morning to report two of his sheep had been slaughtered, with the best of the meat hacked off.

The settler's news spurred the soldiers' hunt for the woman in a new direction. Carlos rode north to check the report, leaving Marisol and me behind at the garrison. We were given a small room to ourselves at the end of the barracks. It must have been the extra sleep, platefuls of good food, and sunlight blazing on fresh snow. Somehow, by afternoon, the world was brighter and my head hadn't hurt since breakfast.

Carlos and his men raced back late in the day, in a rush to catch Melchora down by Black Mesa. We headed out with them, knowing we'd have to camp at least one more night before Santa Fe. Clouds blocked the sun as we left Santa Cruz and light snow began to sift out of the sky. It was getting on to mid-November and winter had a more earnest presence.

Toward dark, big wet flakes fell thick and fast. I could almost grab a handful out of the air. Carlos's soldiers gave up and made camp as soon as we came to the banks of the Rio Grande. A hundred feet off the river we huddled under buffalo skins while the men set up a tent. They weren't as good at getting the fire to light as Marisol, but she kept quiet while they fussed at it.

To show them I was on the mend, I took my turn hauling water. The evening was ghostly white and gray, with mist rising off the river. After scooping the buckets full, I stood by the río and swung my arm back and forth to loosen my shoulder. Two mallards caught my eye, bobbling in an eddy downstream. I lingered on the riverbank watching them.

That's when I noticed a person standing in the winter willows and a second approaching the water's edge. The two hesitated in the mist; I think deciding where to cross. In the near darkness, they hadn't seen me. I stood stock-still.

When they backtracked into the brush and began untying their horses, I dropped to the ground. Leaving the buckets, I crept back to camp. A soldier had finally achieved a tiny flame, but I clamped my hand over it, pointing to the river.

"Women. On the point below us. Trying to cross," I whispered.

The men reached for their weapons. A soldier put an arm behind Marisol and hurried her deep into the woods, slinging a blanket over her shoulders to keep her warm.

We mounted bareback. What sounds came from the moving horses were muffled by the river and softened by the snow. I turned to see if I could spot Marisol, but she was gone from sight.

We nudged the horses toward the bank and waited in a hollow where a small creek joined the Río. The renegade women entered the current on their mounts, pushed through the cold water, and crossed to the western side. It was when we urged our horses down the gravelly bank that Celedonia and Melchora finally heard us. They whirled to look. Seeing horsemen in the gloom, the women drove their booted heels into their animals' flanks and raced toward the west.

We did the same, eight men in near darkness, whipping our horses and pushing them into the breast-high waters. We surged up the western bank.

In the lead, Carlos began to close on the fugitives and yelled with all he had, "Celedonia Griego! Turn to your right! Get away from the Indian. We are here to protect you!"

All I could see was a spark off a shod hoof and the dark shapes of riders in billowing capes, riding fast as goddamn hell into the twilight of the west.

Carlos yelled again, "Halt! We will shoot! Celedonia Griego, fall aside!"

But the women were widening the distance between us, and Celedonia Griego, if she heard the orders, paid no attention.

A militiaman who rode behind with me, following more slowly in the rear, exclaimed, "No way that bitch is coming back. She's leading them! Oh Christ, look out!"

Celedonia's horse saw the deep arroyo chiseled across the land. The panicked beast drove its forelegs into the earth, trying to avoid plunging into the ravine. The woman shot over the flying mane.

The soldiers' horses were running so fast they almost ploughed into the chasm themselves. I hauled on Rosinante's reins and whooshed as she skidded to a stop. Two men rode right over the edge, maneuvering wildly to keep their beasts upright, barely avoiding landing on the flung body of the señora. The rest of us jumped to the ground and slid into the deep arroyo. Sweating and out of breath, we stared at the broken body of a lady.

Blood poured from the hole in Celedonia's chest, pooling darkness onto the churned up snow. A shattered branch of scrub oak penetrated her lungs, piercing her back and driving through her breast. Celedonia's pale legs were splayed bare against the even whiter ground.

Carlos and the militiaman, still panting, knelt beside her. Carlos pushed his fist into the center of the pulsing wound, trying to staunch the flow. The other man groped for her wrist, to feel for a sign of life. Carlos laid his cheek next to Celedonia's, but stood up quickly to face the rest of us.

"Dead, goddamn it!" My brother blurted, "That's it. The governor's going to be pissed." The lieutenant was so angry I thought he was about to kick the lady's corpse. Instead, Carlos reached out and pulled a corner of Celedonia's cape over her gray face.

Looking at the black hole of wilderness where Melchora had ridden, I asked, "What about the other woman?"

My brother let out a curse I'd never heard before, then added, "That witch is long gone and I'm not riding any farther tonight. We'll never catch her anyway, I can promise you that."

Carlos bent and pulled the rings off Celedonia's stiffening hand. "Identification. In case there's any question." His soldiers straightened out the woman's limbs and wrapped her in her cape.

That gave me my chance to pick up her leather pouch where it lay at my feet. I tucked the bounty out of sight, even though I wasn't stealing. Most of the silver in her bag had once belonged to me.

DEAD LIZARD'S DANCE

The storm had quit during the tragic rush to catch the fugitives. Ragged clouds opened and closed high above us, in front of a rising moon. It was fattening tonight, half-full, lifting off a pointed hill in the east. The air was still. Numb with disgust, I kicked fresh snow on top of Celedonia's blood and went to find Rosinante.

My mare and I rode over the snowy ground until we found Celedonia's blown and heaving horse. Slowly, I led it back to camp where I gave the news to a very cold, but secretly relieved, Marisol.

~ 1760 ~

The Love Child

The serving girl sat on the dirt near the turkey pens. She leaned against the warm adobe wall in the back courtyard of her master's hacienda, looking down at her newborn child pressed close against her breast.

Her daughter was the tiniest of little girls, with skin the color of light chocolate and blue-black hair already visible in a straight fringe at the top of her precious head.

For two days they had rested in the small room where the female workers slept. Today the serving girl was ready to be outside, to enjoy the sunlight and sit with her baby in the fresh, fall air.

The master had allowed the new mother to remain in the back of the house to recover from the birth. There was every likelihood he had fathered the child, because he had ordered this servant to his bed almost every night; his gift to his wife, he explained.

Once the patrón decided his servant's belly had become too big and he'd stopped using her, the man's wife soon quickened, but that pregnancy ended early. The servant girl remembered the wife sobbing in disappointment and the woman's reproachful eyes following her through the dark rooms of the hacienda.

Ever since that morning at the pueblo when the servant girl's mother had sold her, she had kept her head down and done what she had to in order to survive. She squeezed her eyes tight, fighting back rough images.

A squawk from her infant returned the servant girl's hand to her baby's back. To the devil with all of them! She had been relieved to get away from the patrón during the months her belly was big. The master, who bedded her night after night, had rarely approached her gently. The servant woman's slim body shuddered. The reprieve was almost over.

She kissed the baby's tiny feet and brushed her lips over the strange little birthmark on her daughter's arm, as she wrapped the naked child in a blanket. The baby quieted. The mother's finger traced the strong pulse beating at the edge of her daughter's forehead.

The Pueblo woman smiled. This time she had bested the patrón. Her daughter's perfect skin was fairer than most Indians', but still far darker than the skin of the Spanish master. The moment the mother had seen the fine structure of her child's Comanche face, she knew this infant was her own, a child made by love.

She shifted her daughter to her other breast. This baby had a Comanche father. One day, handsome, laughing Tosapoy, the second son of a Comanche warrior, began talking to her behind the market stalls. The girl didn't know his language, but they could sign, and the next time he came to Santa Fe, he found *her again. They lay down in a wooded place by the river and made up a language of their own. The servant's face brightened at the memory of the only true pleasure she had ever known.*

From then on Tosapoy sent word to her as soon as he arrived in town, when his Jupe Comanche clan came to trade. Tosapoy would put a jay's blue feather on a path the girl was certain to take.

To steal an hour or two with her Comanche, the servant girl maneuvered for jobs that took her beyond the walls of the patrón's house. She delivered messages, fetched food and medicine from the market, or escorted the master's daughter to her friends' houses. Had the patrón found out about the love meetings, he would have killed Tosapoy.

The young woman raised the baby to her shoulder. The child's skin was lighter than her father's, but that was because the servant's own blood was mixed. Someone francés, her Pecos mother once told her.

Her face grave, the young woman bent and kissed her baby's perfect forehead. This babe was no offspring from rape. This babe was Tosapoy's and hers.

The patrón would never accept this infant as his, not with skin this warm shade of brown. He would surely beat the mother, but after he'd punished his servant, he wouldn't hesitate to accept the baby into his household. The patrón might be angry, but he wouldn't pass up a free house slave. As the child grew he would use her, blood, bone and heart for his own needs until she died.

The young woman shook her head slowly from side to side. She would never do to her daughter what her mother had done to her. Her daughter would not be enslaved. Not the daughter of Tosapoy.

She clutched her child, fighting tears. If Tosapoy would only come, she would flee with her baby and go with the Comanches, but Tosapoy had not returned for months. He never knew she carried a child. For whatever reason, his life had gone in other ways.

The young mother had overheard that a Comanche delegation was in town, parleying with Governor Tomás. The Comanches brought their families when they came. She would find their camp. She would look for the right woman, someone who would take Tosapoy's daughter.

The patrón? When he asked to see the child, she would tell him the baby died. The other women in the sleeping room would help her with her story. If the patrón looked into her face, he would have no trouble seeing grief.

Her baby slept. The mother's tears streamed onto the cheeks of her beautiful daughter. She bent and kissed the tiny lips. She knew the priests believed in baptism in a church, but what could bless an infant more than a mother's tears, a mother's desire for her child to live a happy life?

The sun was warm, the milk good. The woman unwrapped her baby and cleaned her carefully with soft lamb's wool. The child slept while her mother tucked her tightly into two small blankets.

The serving woman rose to go look for the Comanches' camp in the hills behind the palacio. It was siesta, when the patrón's household slept. Now was the best time to go. The new mother wiped her eyes on the corner of her baby's blanket and left by the rear gate of the courtyard.

~1782~

Blue Dust

Carlos and his men accompanied the dead lady into Santa Fe, who'd been strapped across the back of her horse. Marisol and I, dangerous fugitives, were under subtle guard. The procession wound through the ice and dung covered lanes to the wagon gate at the back of the palacio. Carlos dismounted, went in and returned with Sebastian. The two officers talked low and fast between themselves.

Sebastian cast a quick look at Marisol and me, then walked over to Celedonia's wrapped body. Carlos unfastened the folds of the cape to expose her face. Sebastian looked, but only for a moment. The two men nodded, Carlos swung into his saddle, and we began to move again, this time to Facundo Salazar's hacienda to bring him his wife's remains. Sebastian stood to the side, his hat in hand.

"Nando," he said as we rode past, "Marisol stays here. Help her down."

It took everything I had not to grab the reins out of Marisol's hands, spur both horses and run for the mountains. Struggling against that instinct, I dropped to the ground hoping Sebastian didn't notice my shaking legs. I looked into Marisol's eyes and whispered, "Eat and get some rest. I promise, this won't last long."

323

I think she nodded before she slipped to the ground, leaning against my body to steady herself. I grasped her hand and squeezed it, before passing her to Sebastian. He seemed kindly enough, the way he put an arm around her to help her the first few moments off her mule. I stayed there watching while they walked together through the wagon gate, but my brother gently called, "Nando!" I climbed back on Rosinante and rode to Carlos's side.

The Salazar family's servants took Celedonia's body from her horse. They carried her between them into the house and shut the solid door of the hacienda. We were told Facundo Salazar waited within.

Luz could see the wreck I was, and the sadness that deadened me at leaving Marisol a prisoner at the palacio. Francisco and Luz heard my whole, long story while they doctored, fed and bathed me. Carlos came in, leaned his elbows on his knees and listened to it all for the second time. My brothers promised to carry food, clean water, and extra sheepskins to Marisol, and to ask Sebastian to let me speak with him at the first opportunity.

The ancient dog down our lane had a bark like a creaking gate. For hours the noise wove through my dreams of bloody snow and a fat grouse trying to flap its broken wings.

It must have been near dawn when I awoke. I fumbled to light a lamp, drank water, lay back and thought about how close we'd come to escaping, to getting to Marisol's house, maybe even to the ranch. Marisol and I had been running toward a life of our own, beyond the confines of the city. Now, we'd been thrown back into the worst possible situation and she was a prisoner. At least we were both alive.

Carlos slept on sheepskins near my bed. I leaned over and tried to tell if he was awake, hoping he might talk for a while. Then Celedonia's pouch caught my eye, lying amid my pile of clothes. I undid the bone button and poured the contents onto the bed.

The jingling of coins woke Carlos. He rose on his elbow and muttered, "What's going on? What's that?"

"I was trying to be quiet. Sorry. Celedonia's purse. I found it in the snow."

Carlos sat up and looked. "I saw that lying near her. I wondered where it had gone. Figured a militiaman lifted it. Never thought my brother would steal from the dead." His voice was froggy from sleep.

"Not stealing. That's my silver she took. And here's a dolly's buckskin pouch." Carlos watched through puffy eyes while I undid the thong and held the smaller bag open next to the lamp. I poked around, trying to pick up a fragment of whatever was inside. I didn't get much, so I licked my fingertip, stuck it back in and held my findings under the light.

Blue powder!

"Their monkshood. The poison Celedonia and Melchora used." I sucked in my breath.

Carlos squeezed his eyes with his fingers. "You sure?"

I mimicked the Spanish lady. " 'When we don't need him any more, it will be easy to kill Nando with the bit of monkshood we have left.' Celedonia's exact words to Melchora in the cave."

"And now she's probably done it, too." Carlos said leaning forward and pointing to the blue finger I'd put in my mouth.

I filled my mouth with water and spat onto the dirt floor. Twice. I dipped my neck cloth in the water beside my bed and carefully wiped my whole hand.

325

"I couldn't have gotten much. Don't worry, Carlos, I've beaten death so many times this week, I suspect I'll do it again."

Carlos was wrapping the thong around the top of the little bag. "Let's keep an eye on you, even so, and take this to Sebastian as soon as it's light."

"Well why can't Marisol come home?" I blared at Sebastian. "Why are you still holding her and all these women? You've had Juliana for almost two weeks." I stood in the sergeant's messy office with Carlos at my side.

"For one thing," Sebastian grumbled, "Don Crespín Olivas demands it. For another, Anza doesn't want any more suspects tearing out of here and disappearing into one void or another. Chief Merchant Vial was poisoned and every one of these women played a role in it."

"You're as sure of that as you were that Celedonia had been kidnapped, aren't you?" Carlos said without budging from my side.

My brother knew he was safe with his words. Carlos and I had talked until the sun rose, and he told me how he had already informed the palacio of the details of Celedonia's complicity with her Indian servant. The soldiers who rode north with my brother confirmed to a man that Salazar's wife had ridden in the fore, leading Melchora in the women's rush for the hills.

Carlos told the officers at the palacio that I'd spoken earlier with Padre Miera about this case. Hearing that, yesterday Governor Anza had summoned both Miera and Domingo to come forth at once with their piece of the puzzle about Celedonia Griego.

Carlos assured me Padre Miera had done his part well, getting the history of Celedonia and her unwanted baby to spill out of Domingo. The vagabond priest admitted he had indeed told the Spanish lady, and later her servant Melchora, that not only had the child from her past survived, but grown-up now, she had become the mistress of Celedonia's own husband. Padre Domingo eagerly pointed out that Beatriz was about to commit a mortal sin with Señor Vial, as well. Everyone, from the governor on down, could see that Celedonia had motive aplenty for the deaths I'd overheard her confess to masterminding.

Sebastian concentrated on rolling his hat brim into the proper shape and didn't look at us when he said, "Many questions have been answered, but these women we're holding were also involved. We're keeping them at the palacio until the investigation is complete."

Sebastian face was haggard when he said to me, "Your girlfriend may be sweetness itself, Nando, but she mixed tonics and brought them to Vial night after night. She did everything Melchora told her. Being that close to the crime, there's no possibility the Commandant General's man will allow Marisol to go free. We had a hard time talking Don Crespín out of confining you as well."

Carlos persisted. "What will it take to satisfy Anza and the investigators that these women are not criminals?"

Sebastian threw back his head and laughed at what a futile proposition that was. "Bring the governor proof that Vial was not poisoned. And you'd better believe that Anza, as fair as he is, has no interest in Don Crespín Olivas reviving his suspicions that it was New Mexico's governor who engineered the death of the merchant. Anza finds it convenient to have these women on the hook."

I leaned over and spat in disgust, which made me remember the blue powder I'd tasted in the middle of the night.

On a wild hunch, I handed the sergeant the little buckskin bag. "All right, then. You want proof? Start with this. Here's some of the poison. Carlos and I found it in Celedonia's pouch. Try it on a goat or something and see if it does the trick."

Sebastian screwed his head around to look at me as though I were cockeyed.

"You are in possession of the poison that killed Vial?"

"I picked up Celedonia's purse at the scene of her death. Carlos and I opened it last night. The silver she stole from me was in it, and so was this little bag."

Sebastian started to tip it onto his desk.

"Careful!" Carlos put his hand over the bag. "Nando did that last night and got it on his fingers. Licked them too. Granted he didn't get much, but here he stands before you, hale and hearty."

Sebastian stepped back from the bag and was staring hard at me when the governor walked in. We stood at attention.

"Stand easy, gentlemen. Hello Carlos, Nando." The governor appraised my green and yellow face and hunched shoulder. I didn't flash him the smile that showed the gap in my teeth.

"Looking better, Nando. Coming along, coming along. What are you all up to so early in the morning?"

Sebastian pushed the little bag toward Anza.

"Nando found this in Celedonia's purse. Convicts her once and for all. It's the remains of the poison she used."

The governor tried to peer into the bag, careful not to touch its contents.

"We need someone to verify what's in here. Luckily, the best person for the job is right under our roof. Sebastian, send for the curandera Juliana," the governor ordered.

"Should we call Don Crespin?"

"We'll leave His Excellency's minion out of this for now, until we're certain what we've got."

The soldier came back with not only Juliana, but also Cruzita, Marisol and Margarita Chacon. Marisol looked as though she had gotten some rest, but the growing child was slowing her moves. The other women seemed well enough, but weighed down too.

Sebastian and Anza stepped back to let them all cram into the room. After a nod, Sebastian asked, "Juliana, can you identify what is in that purse?"

Juliana handled the bag with care. She recognized pouches like this; maybe it was even one of her own. She cleaned off a patch of Sebastian's desk, poured a few grains into a mound and examined the material with her trained eye. She poured out more, building a small pile of the powder. Juliana looked up and gestured for something to stir with. Sebastian handed her a new quill. Carefully the Pueblo woman picked through the pile, spreading out the light blue dust.

"Cruzita, look," Juliana murmured. I didn't think the old crone could see much, but she brought her face down almost to the surface of the desk. She sniffed.

"Can I have some water please, in a cup?" Juliana asked. The cup was brought. She drank off some of the water to lessen the amount, then sprinkled in a pinch of the powder. She swished the mixture, smelled it and held out the cup to Cruzita. "What do you think?"

The old woman eyed the solution, methodically turning the cup in her hand. She stuck her nose into it and inhaled. Then the wry old bruja lifted the cup to her mouth and gulped the mixture down. She glared at the astonished onlookers and laughed her croaky laugh.

"Gentian. Good for the stomach. Do you have any more?"

We stood stock-still. Governor, sergeant, spy and all the alleged witches stared at Cruzita, waiting for her to drop dead. Or start writhing, itching and moaning. Instead she sat in the sergeant's chair and smiled at us all.

"Have a taste?" She stuck the mug under Sebastian's nose.

He pitched back and shook his head so hard his jowls waggled. "Are you all right?" he managed to say.

Cruzita giggled. The sergeant looked at Juliana and asked, "So how did you know?"

The younger curandera explained. "First of all it was too pale to be monkshood. This is blue, not blackish purple, and we could smell the gentian bitters.

"Next, you have to travel very high in the mountains, or a good ways north, to find monkshood, while gentian can easily be picked in the meadows of our nearby mountains. I admit the differences are subtle, but I'm certain, because I recognize this particular mixture. The powder here is a remnant of the blend I made for Marisol the night she ran to me for an antidote. I decided early on not to try the love tonics on the caravan master—Vial was too old and they might have sickened him. The night that Marisol came, I knew it was best to soothe his stomach. The caravan master only had a bellyache."

Anza fixed his bushy brows on the Pueblo woman. "Melchora and Celedonia didn't poison chief merchant Vial?"

"They did not. Not with this, anyway."

Anza interjected, "You say that, but if the two women were innocent, why did they flee?"

"What choice did they have?" Juliana's voice had spark in it. "The case was decided against all the women the moment Don Crespín Olivas produced the blue petals, declaring them aconitum. No official there knew his botany and every man in the room seized upon that as convicting evidence, even though Melchora had examined the body and found no signs of poison. Don Crespín's men, for whatever purpose, made their condemning judgment. Those of us who know medicine were not consulted," Juliana concluded.

"And Celedonia?" Anza's voice was low. "The woman died, but you are saying she had no hand in this?"

"All that's certain," Juliana offered, "is that Celedonia had no knowledge of herbs and had to take someone's word about what was in the drink."

I cleared my throat to get attention. "Sebastian?"

"I know what you're going to say, Nando," the sergeant was dismissive. "That you fled with Marisol for the same reason, that she was about to be convicted on the word of the Commandant General's men."

"Yes sir, that, but something more."

Sebastian looked impatient, but Anza nodded for me to proceed.

"The evidence all pointed to Melchora when she fled Santa Fe, but at that time no one suspected Celedonia. Yet, for some reason, the Spanish lady believed she too had committed a crime and would soon be found out. What else explains why she rushed into the wilds with Melchora?" They were listening, so I pointed to my face.

"These wounds came from my time in captivity at the hands of Melchora and Celedonia. They nearly killed Marisol and her child. The driver Amado had his thighbone broken when they attacked his wagon. We have each experienced the evil these women can do.

"And Celedonia participated in everything with her servant. Kidnapping Marisol, tormenting both of us, making plans to run to Mexico with Melchora.

"You've probably heard this from Carlos, but when the women didn't think I was listening, Celedonia confessed to ordering the deaths of Beatriz and of Vial. Everything she said confirmed what I had already learned back in Santa Fe: that Vial fathered Beatriz by raping Celedonia many years ago. Celedonia claimed that honor required avenging the death of her daughter. In Celedonia's rage, that meant murdering the child's father.

"The two women realized I was beginning to figure this out. They congratulated themselves at having me at their mercy. I overheard them say that when I was no longer useful to them, they'd use the little bit of monkshood left to get rid of me."

I drew my finger through the remaining hillock of blue powder on Sebastian's desk. "Why would the women rely on this to kill me, if they knew it was only blue gentian? Melchora and Celedonia were convinced this powder was poisonous. They fled because they believed they had in fact murdered Vial."

The room was quiet. My brother stood unwavering at my side. The governor spoke.

"So if the women didn't do it, then how *did* Vial die? The failure of an old man's heart?" Weary to the bone, the governor searched the faces of all the people gathered in the office. "And whatever the actuality, do any of you disagree that Don Crespín went out of his way to make sure we all thought this death was done by poisoning, and by a woman I employed?"

Heads nodded in agreement, though no one said a word.

"It would be useful to confer with Melchora again," the governor said. "There might be more she could tell us, something she might have been afraid to say under the circumstances of that investigation. On those occasions when she worked for me, I had respect for her skills."

"She's somewhere in the Jemez Mountains, a woman by herself," I said, "and it's mid November. I doubt she'll ever be seen again." Did I mind how final that sounded? I thought of Melchora tormenting Marisol, and of her part in Tuqué's death.

Anza snapped out of his mood. "After we've overcome the next hurdles, I'll send men to look for her. Right now I have an apology to make." The governor turned to Juliana and the other women.

"I have been in error. I am in your debt. I regret my eagerness to believe the accusations made by Croix's investigators.

"Still, I must ask you one last favor. It is necessary that you stay inside the Casas Reales for at least one more night. All of you. It is not time for Don Crespín Olivas to know what we have discovered. I have serious inquiries to make, and I want the investigators to think we are still holding the same set of beliefs. Ladies," and Anza turned to include old Cruzita, "will you be my guests at the palacio for a little longer? Not in cells. Real beds, and a decent dinner. It is the least I can offer, but I need your help."

The women managed to keep their longing to be freed from showing on their faces and once more their nods indicated they would comply with the governor. Marisol and I exchanged a glance. Just one more night.

"Facundo Salazar?" Sebastian asked. "He was informed last night that his wife was implicated in Vial's murder. Should we tell him it is not so?"

Anza turned to the others in the room and raised his voice.

"I will choose the time to inform Salazar, and I'll tell him myself. Not yet, not at this moment. There are still too many uncertainties. But I agree, for the comfort of the man's soul, he must be told."

The Windlass

Sebastian told me which room in the palacio the women were now occupying. In the darkness that came early at this time of year, I made my way to the western wall of the Casas Reales and paced a certain number of steps until I was under the slatted window where he told me Marisol would be. The opening was high on the wall, too high to see into.

I whistled low. Whistled again. A small brown hand showed, wrapped around the posts in the window and there was Marisol's smiling face. Due to the thick adobe and the smallness of the opening, I could barely make out the muffled sound of the other women's voices.

"What did you have for dinner?" I asked.

"Roast lamb."

"Elegant fare for witch women."

"The governor sat with us at dinner. Anna Serrano too."

"Are you comfortable?"

"Three sheepskins for each of us. Good Navajo blankets."

"Stay warm, my sweet. Carlos will tell me when they're about to let you go. I'll come at a run."

"It must be cold out there, Nando. Go home and get warm. Don't worry about us. We're fine. It's only until tomorrow."

The hand gave a little wave and was gone.

335

"Hasta mañana," I sang back to her. Marisol was in the clear. The governor was our friend. The baby lived and we would be together soon.

I stepped lively around the corner of the Casa Reales, crossed the plaza and slipped through an alley, taking a short cut to Luz's house. The temperature was dropping to a deeper cold than we'd known yet this season. I pulled my manta close and put some hustle in my stride.

I was hurrying past the wall of the convento garden when I heard a booming splash. The noise was the one a full bucket makes when the rope snaps and the pail plunges back into the well. It seemed strange for someone to be drawing water in the dark, after everyone's in bed, but I heard nothing more and didn't pause. Then came a deep cry. Just one.

I vaulted the low wall and ran to the well house behind the church. I noticed the bucket still hung high under the roof, held tight against the windlass. One more splash and a choked-off moan, then nothing. Someone had fallen into the well. A drunkard?

I peered into the black hole. Moonlight glinted on a distant circle of rippling water. I cast a quick look for anything I could use, a ladder, or a pole. There was nothing, so I yanked a length of rope down from the windlass. I knotted a loop for my foot, and pulling the rope hard against my thigh for friction, praying the windlass frame was sturdy enough, I inched into the well. I rode on the bucket, lowering myself deeper and deeper into the dank hole.

Jesús! A fierce hand seized my foot. Fingers gripped my ankle, clawed up my leg.

"Wait!" I yelled, and using my arms, held my weight to take pressure off the rope, which gave me a slack piece to wrap around my middle. That done, I could reach down. Icy fingers seized my own I bent lower and a hand locked onto mine.

I pulled. Whoever it was not only lived, but possessed an insane strength that threatened to drag me under. Using my foot and my one free hand, I heaved him over the bucket. My sore shoulder screamed, but I had hauled out a choking, spluttering man. His weight drew me downward. I didn't have the strength to hoist us both, so I bent my head back and yelled at the top of my lungs for any passing being to extricate us from this moss-walled grave. My voice couldn't rise out of the clammy hole. I felt like a drowning lizard thrashing in a pail.

The man, half on the bucket, still clinging to my leg, scrabbled his feet against the juniper logs that cribbed the well, got purchase, and began to help. I worked my knees higher on the rope and together we gained another foot.

Weak as I was, and with my injured shoulder failing, I couldn't hold out long, but this fellow and I got a rough rhythm going and we were gaining ground. His head was well above the water now and he coughed, inhaled great gulps of air and began to yell in chorus with me. Water streamed off him, plastering his dark hair over his eyes. I drew in two more lengths and moved us a foot higher.

Praise the Great Spirit and all the saints and angels, we were heard. I felt a tug on the rope. And another. Someone called and more voices echoed in the well. Priests! I recognized Miera's and hoped the fat old man had help up there.

He must have, because a rope flailed down from above. I secured it under the arms of the stranger and in a shot he was moving skyward. Twirling in space, he ascended toward the lurching moon.

The rope whipped down a second time. Fumbling with numb fingers, I looped it around me and gave a tug to signal I was ready. Slowly, I spiraled upward. Clutching hands dragged me over the stone lip and dropped me in a sodden heap beside the half-drowned man. The bell in the church tower clanged, as a convento boy rang for help.

The man shuddered and rolled away from me. We both sat up, and there I was in the milky moonlight staring into the dripping face of Don Crespín Olivas.

Bucket and ropes lay tangled between us. Padre Miera leaned over to unwrap the coils and, seeing me, yelped, "Nando!" Padre Domingo reached among our jumbled limbs and gently raised Olivas to his feet.

The dazed man shook himself like a wet dog, before sputtering a command. "Take me to the palacio! I must speak with Anza at once."

Miera gestured, and the night watchman left at a run to alert the governor. Boys hurried with blankets from the convento.

Olivas peered at me, trying to tell if he recognized me or not. "This man saved my life. Do any of you know him?"

"Of course," the old padre said. "That's Nando. You're a lucky soul this is the man who heard you fall."

"I did not fall. I was thrown!" spewed Olivas. He huffed as a blanket was wrapped around him, then took a few shaky steps toward the palacio.

"I am grateful to this person named Nando. There will be a reward. Now hurry up and get me to the governor."

The governor had dressed in haste. His blue commander's jacket couldn't conceal the nightshirt under it, tucked into his breeches. It scarcely mattered since Don Crespín Olivas was draped in a water-soaked blanket, as was that high-ranking sleuth of the northern provinces, me.

The two priests, Miera and Domingo, stood to the side in their blue robes, looking exactly as priests always do. Did they sleep in their garments to be ready to tend the needy at any hour? Men had been sent to uncover which widow's house Sebastian was favoring this night, and to bring in the other chief officers.

The head investigator accepted a mug of hot wine, slumped into a chair and proclaimed, "Vial's murderer has become known to me, because the donkey's son tried to kill me too."

Anza waited, his eyes intent upon Olivas's battered face. The next few words would tell him much.

"I was taking a turn around the plaza, enabling my dinner to settle, when that insufferable merchant Facundo Salazar comes raging out of the night. Storming toward me Salazar says, 'Good Evening Don Crespín,' and without further niceties, grabs me by the throat."

Anza and the priests bent over Olivas, listening. Padre Miera, moved by the fright in the man's voice, laid his hand on Olivas's shoulder, but the investigator steadied his eyes on Anza.

"Why do you look so astounded, governor? Because Salazar was the man who was about to lead your caravan?"

The investigator winced before he continued. "Salazar dug his hands into my windpipe. Pressing with all his force he drove me to my knees and clamped his fingers around my neck, trying to shut off my air. I had no way to protect myself. In that lunatic's grasp I was a puling kitten.

"You sent my wife to die,' Salazar cried as his hands bit deeper, 'calling that blue *mierda* monkshood!'

"My only defense was to pretend I was done for. I sank to the ground, but Salazar's hands stayed locked on my throat.

"Salazar might have broken my collarbone, the way he tightened the vice of his fingers, as he spat into my face, 'This is how I stopped the stinking bastard who raped my Celedonia. There was no woman's poison involved! Celedonia had nothing to do with Vial's death, but you convicted her anyway, didn't you?' "

Crespín's voice trembled. "Salazar fell on top of me, slamming my face into the dirt. Then he rose and stepped back, watching to see if I was finished. He pushed me around with his foot. Because it was dark, he wasn't certain.

"Crazed, Salazar hoisted me in his arms and set me on cold stone. Still pretending, I didn't dare open my eyes, but I smelled water and heard the man rage under his breath, 'Here's a hole. As good as the last hole.' He lifted my body above the well and hissed, 'Vial died for raping Celedonia, and now you die for killing her!'

" 'Beatriz, you witch!' Salazar sobbed, sweat dripping off his brow, as he heaved me over the side. 'My wife was right. You stole my soul!'

"My hand flung out, groping for the edge, so Salazar knew I was still alive. I yelled as I tumbled against the sides. That well isn't deep. I bounced off the bottom and rose into the air. Fell back under the cold water. Another time, and another. Then a bucket crashed down and in came a foot. This man here, whatever you called him, climbed into the well after me."

I saw something like tears on the head investigator's face; outrage on Anza's.

"Facundo Salazar is a madman and a killer," Olivas finished. "I do not know what his reasons are, or if his wife or their Indian Melchora assisted him, but I can tell you that Salazar's the murderer afoot in your town."

Olivas sank against the back of the chair, so weak from exhaustion that I took his cup to keep the wine from spilling.

The governor locked his hands behind his back, planted his feet wide and leaning down, addressed the shivering investigator. "Have we achieved a new understanding, sir?"

Croix's emissary, looking sheepish, mumbled, "We have, governor. I extend my apologies."

"And mine to you," said Anza. He looked the investigator in the eye for a moment, then turned and placed more wood on the fire.

"It fits," he explained to the priests. "Much of this squares with what Nando has found; the love triangle of Salazar, Celedonia and Beatriz; Vial and Beatriz dallying with each other, a troubling combination; Celedonia's uncontrollable jealousy. Then, to bring it all to a head, you, Domingo, came home and informed the town who Beatriz really was."

Padre Domingo's face receded deeper into his cowl and he moved so Miera's bulk blocked him from Anza's view.

The governor's hand massaged his jaw. "Salazar and Vial were always in contention, even without a woman coming between them. Facundo coveted Vial's position and damn near got it too.

"But even with Facundo's outburst against Don Crespín, we still don't have hard evidence that will convict the man of murdering Vial."

Everyone in the room fell silent.

"Sir?"

"What is it now, Nando?" Anza was out of patience.

341

"The morning of Vial's death, I ran to his home just like everyone else. I found a spot for myself in the woods behind Vial's goat pen. Another person had gotten there ahead of me, the little Indian woman called Agapita."

Recognition flickered in Anza's eyes. "Go on."

"Pretty soon Facundo Salazar showed up on his horse. He'd been on his morning ride and he'd heard the uproar at Vial's hacienda. But there was something wrong."

"Yes?"

"Agapita pointed out that the horse was dry and cool, but Salazar was all in a lather, even his clothes were wet. He'd pulled his cloak off and bunched it at the front of his saddle. It was as though the man, not the horse had been doing all the running."

The governor recognized the significance of this. "I will see if Agapita can confirm that Salazar, in an agitated state, was at the scene of Vial's death."

Don Crespín nodded his head, eager for us to find sufficient evidence to convict Salazar.

I could tell them more, about a rich merchant stumbling upon Vial and Beatriz kissing, for instance, or that Facundo's wife had suddenly been told her daughter lived.

But it didn't look as though anything more would be necessary, because the head investigator from Arizpe drooped in his chair, stunned and silent. None of us needed further convincing that what Olivas told us he'd experienced at Salazar's hands was the truth.

Sebastian had been found and stood in readiness by the door. Seeing him, Anza commanded, "Go arrest Facundo Salazar. Shackle the merchant and bring him to the palacio."

Sebastian caught my eye and swung his head toward the door. There was yet another job for me this night.

Crescent Moon

I pulled a dry shirt over my head while I ran through the streets toward Salazar's, barely keeping ahead of Sebastian and his armed soldiers. I led them through the blue gate where I had once shown the shell to Melchora, weeks and weeks ago.

Under a starry universe we entered the courtyard of the Salazar's home, unseen and unheard. It was so late even the dogs were asleep. A light glowing through one window was the only sign of life in the hacienda. The presidio soldiers stood guard while Sebastian and I tried to peer inside, but it wasn't possible to see through the oiled skin that covered the windows. Sebastian knocked with his gloved fist on Salazar's solid back door.

In seconds, the door opened and there stood the gentleman of the house, lamp in hand, with old socks on his feet and a gentle look on his sleepy face.

"It's late, you know," Facundo Salazar mentioned civilly.

Sebastian blocked the door with his booted foot and waved his men forward. I stood aside to let the armed soldiers enter ahead of me, then followed behind.

A leaping fire on the corner hearth warmed the room. Light glowed on the long, round vigas. Salazar's Bible lay open on an ornate table beside his chair. His boots, pistol and sword waited in readiness on a bench beside the door. The man was at peace, ready for bed. All that seemed odd was he gave no protest at being walked in on by armed soldiers from the garrison.

"Facundo Salazar, I am under orders to arrest you," stated Sebastian.

Salazar had already resumed his seat in his armchair before the fire and was bending over to pick up the weighty Bible. He looked at Sebastian with a question on his face, so intently innocent that at first not one of us noticed the pistol in his hand.

The hammer was back, Facundo's finger hooked the trigger, and before anyone had time to react, a brutal explosion hurled us against the walls. Black smoke billowed around Salazar, obscuring his face. A young soldier took the shot. Bending double, the man collapsed onto the floor. In the seconds it took to realize what was upon us, Salazar was no longer in his chair, but stood towering over us on the thick oak table, a rapier in hand, daring those of us still on our feet to approach his steel.

"Come forward, you cowards!" Salazar roared, throwing open his arms, revealing two more pistols jammed into his belt.

He held the soldiers at bay with the lunging sword. Because I'd entered the room last, I was close to the door, jammed against a rack that held old cloaks.

Sebastian broke the stunned silence. "It's no good, Salazar," he shouted. "There's a whole troop out there poised to bring you in." My groping hand landed on a shaft, some sort of pole, leaning hidden beneath the coats.

Salazar reached for a pistol. The soldiers sprang toward the former Commissioner to the West, who raised the gun and fired. Smoke swirled in the air, sulfur stung our eyes, and another soldier twisted to the floor, writhing and groaning, clutching his knee.

In that second I gripped the pole and swung it forward. Catching a glint of curved steel, I raised the weapon and went for Salazar. The quarter moon of an illegal hawking blade bore toward Facundo, making him leap backward off the table and collide with the wall behind. Without missing a beat, Sebastian seized the shaft in front of my hands and caught Salazar at the throat. The winged edges of the blade nailed the man to the wall, but the perfect arc kept the honed steel just off Salazar's gullet.

Sebastian and I leaned on the weapon, holding it steady against the man's throat, pinning him there. Salazar's eyes bulged and a stream of sweat poured down his face.

The only soldier still on his feet moved in to disarm the merchant. The clearance between the steel and Salazar's Adam's apple was so scant that the merchant didn't dare speak. Instead he watched with hatred as the soldier stripped him of the remaining pistol and pulled a knife from a scabbard under Salazar's shirt.

I could smell Sebastian's breath and feel his heat as we continued to hold the hawking blade unyielding and level while the soldier, careful not to jolt Salazar against the blade, worked a rope behind the man's back and bound his arms tight to his sides. With one soldier still moaning on the floor, and a second clearly dead beneath the table, the lashings were made taut and strong. Only when Salazar was immobilized did the sergeant and I let up. Though my weak shoulder quaked, I held the hawking blade at the ready, in case this monster came to life again.

The gunshots had alerted the palacio. Anza, Olivas, Carlos, and the priests strode into the room, followed by more soldiers who went straight to attending the wounded man and holding back Facundo's neighbors, who choked the doorway. Carlos relieved me of my grip on the hawking blade.

Sebastian shoved the bound Salazar into his chair, but when Facundo saw Padre Domingo, the merchant reared up and shouted, "Killer!"

Sebastian's fist shot out and slammed into Facundo's chest, knocking him back to sitting.

Salazar sat still, his head hanging forward, his arms bound against his sides, while the dead soldier was carried out, onlookers were forced into the night, and the heavy door was drawn shut.

When the room was quiet again, those of us still inside, governor and priests, sergeant, soldiers and I, found ourselves staring down at Facundo, waiting to hear this man speak.

The merchant scanned the rank of faces that encircled him. His red eyes settled on Padre Miera.

"Father, Bless Me." Salazar startled the priest with his plea. The good Miera stepped back.

Facundo's voice rose in a wail. "I have rid the world of evil. I have scoured the earth and cleansed it. The witch woman is dead by my hands. I wouldn't have known, I confess I wouldn't have recognized my duty, had not my good Celedonia brought me to my senses. For this, I beg you to assure my wife her place in heaven, Padre, for she has earned it."

Salazar's chin dropped onto his chest. I stared at a small bald spot on the top of the man's head.

"The madness is on him again," whispered the governor.

"I did all that my wife asked," the accused man moaned. "The whore and I picked the blue flowers together, the exact flowers Melchora described for us. Beatriz and I lay on the mountainside until I knew the time was right to remove the witch from this world. After I strangled her, I rolled the stone to pin down Beatriz's dark soul. I did everything Celedonia requested."

I was incredulous. Salazar killed Beatriz because he believed loving her was a satanic act? I stepped toward the murderer, but my brother gripped my arm and held me by his side. The mad man went on talking.

" 'The flowers. I need them.' Celedonia implored, when I'd returned in my cart. 'Did you bring me the blue flowers?' I thrust them proudly between my wife's hands, telling her I'd done all that she'd asked, but as soon as she clutched them, Celedonia began to weep and rant, and said we'd been wrong. In a choked voice, my wife explained that the witch, Beatriz, turned out to be Celedonia's own daughter."

Salazar thrust his chin at Padre Domingo. "This killer priest, this red-haired devil who dares to stand here in my bedroom, told my wife who Beatriz really was. Celedonia at long last confessed to me that Vial had raped her before our marriage, leaving her with child." Salazar's tears flowed down his cheeks. With his hands bound he could do nothing to brush them off. Sniffing loudly, he persisted with his story.

"Celedonia began to strip the petals off the plant to brew a tea. 'Facundo, you and I are not at fault,' my wife whispered. Her lovely hands were shaking, so I pressed them to my mouth. 'We will give this tea to Vial who raped me, who ravaged women all his life, who even tried to take his own daughter to his bed. It's to Vial we will bring these poisonous flowers, and let their beauty sing him to sleep.'

" 'Melchora, arrange for these petals to go into that brew you make for Vial each night,' Celedonia commanded her servant before she took my arm and drew me off to our bed. Celedonia and I slept once again in each other's arms, in peace that night, relieved of the witch's curse."

Facundo's wet eyes searched the faces of those of us standing in his room. He seemed not to recognize anyone now, neither Anza, nor Olivas, nor either of the priests.

"I rose early the next morning," Salazar told us, "and watched for Vial, to make sure Melchora had obeyed my wife and the monkshood had done its work. But singing and spry, Vial walked into the yard behind his house, unfazed, a man satisfied by sleep and ready to enjoy his day."

Facundo tipped his face up to the speechless Miera and writhed his wrists against the ropes. "You must bless these hands, father, for they put an end to a fornicator. These hands flung my old cloak over Vial's head; they pressed heavy folds of cloth against the rapist's face. This fist," and Salazar turned his clenched hand in front of his eyes, "this fist forced the fabric into his mouth. That morning, behind the chief merchant's house, I honored my Celedonia and her daughter. I rid the earth of Vial's sin."

Miera shuddered.

"I had to send my wife away," Facundo let out a painful sigh. "So soon after we were joyfully reunited, Olivas with his broom and dust pan found the monkshood and declared it the cause of Vial's death. In front of everyone he accused our Melchora.

"Celedonia believed Olivas would quickly discover it was she who had ordered Vial's death and that she would hang for it. At the governor's dinner party, I watched Celedonia's beautiful face wither when Olivas said the death was by aconitum. I alone knew those flowers hadn't killed the man, but Olivas said for certain they had, so my poor Celedonia had to flee, and you bastards ran her into her grave."

Impatience tensed the governor's face. "You could have confessed to Vial's death and saved your wife's life," the governor interjected. "Did you ever think of that?"

"Confess? But there was no sin." Facundo slipped out of the chair onto his knees. "The death of a rapist, the death of a witch, these are not sins. They are God's work. I had nothing to confess."

Facundo's forehead was on the floor and a mewling sound rose from him. Miera moved closer to put his hand on Salazar's hunched back, but Anza drew him back.

The governor turned to the armed soldiers in the room, and said, "Get Salazar out of here. Lock him in jail. I can't stand to be near this madman any more."

Pleased With His Beneficence

Carlos and I sat in the sunshine in the courtyard of the palacio, our backs against a warm brown wall and our boots in the mud. This morning we'd struck a deal about outfitting Marisol and me for the winter ahead that made it possible for us to move to her farm. My brother agreed to provide new boots for each of us, blankets, two iron pots, and supplies of dried corn, apples, and squash to go in them. Also, one musket, an axe and a shovel.

With Olivas's reward money I'd bought two fine mules. We now had an outfit that far surpassed what I'd thrown into the cart the night I'd sent Marisol fleeing to the north. All we lacked were baby clothes.

With my new mules and my woman all chomping at the bit to be gone, I wouldn't be lingering here if Carlos didn't have me well in hand. Sebastian came out of his office, gave me a nod and asked Carlos to come inside.

"Wait here, Nando. We'll send for you shortly," ordered my brother. I nodded at the lieutenant glumly and tapped my feet to pass the time.

Something niggled in my brain, something not quite right. I thought about the mad merchant Salazar incarcerated in a cold stone cell. There was more to this. Insanity seemed a cheap defense, particularly coming from a successful businessman, a person appointed to high positions in the colony. I rummaged through my weakened brain, trying to remember certain things, like how many sets of footprints I'd seen around Beatriz's body on the mountain. Who had told what to whom, and when? Maybe the governor sensed something unresolved too, which was probably why I'd been called to the palacio. But hadn't I done enough? Hadn't we both, Marisol and I? Couldn't we just be finished with these troubles and get started on our life together?

Carlos knew I would be impatient. Within minutes he and Sebastian were at my side, propelling me into the office, where, it turned out, the governor sat on the bench behind Sebastian's desk.

"Nando!" Anza rose and extended his hand. I shook it like a man who expected to greet the governor on a daily basis. Carlos and Sebastian sat down on a banco against the wall to watch the interview.

"Sit down, sit down, Nando." Anza inquired about my injuries, praised my speedy intervention with the hawking blade the other night, and then asked for all possible information about the Indian woman, Melchora. This is the piece, I thought. The piece we haven't settled.

"Other than what the padres told you, that Melchora was at Beatriz's birth as young Celedonia's helper, only this. In the cave last week, Melchora said she'd had a hand in the death of that Indian over on Deer Creek. She claimed she was glad to help the other women string him up, because Melchora was one of the Pueblo girls Tuqué sold to Spaniards in this town."

After a long silence Sebastian got off the bench and went over to the governor's side. They conferred in mutters, before Anza spoke.

"It sounds as though Tuqué's death was Pueblo business. Out of our jurisdiction. The Pueblos are entitled to mete out justice in their own manner. But what about the effigy? Would Melchora have constructed and hung the fake corpse all by herself?"

I shook my head. "No. She said she admired how the Pecos women tricked out that effigy, though for certain, Facundo's cloak was Melchora's contribution."

"But why an effigy? A *castrated* effigy?" Anza asked.

I stood when I told him, "The women wanted to send a signal to all men, sir, Spanish and Pueblo alike, that they weren't going to put up with brutality from males any more."

The governor and I looked at each other. After a moment he nodded slightly. He muttered so low I could barely hear him, "Perhaps we shouldn't have tried so hard to keep the details of that murder secret."

Anza shifted his attention to Sebastian and let his voice return to its usual strength. "It isn't a crime to create an effigy, though it might be one to steal a body. Given the circumstances, we'll never be able to indict Melchora, or any other Pueblo woman, for that hanging. Also, we know that although Melchora may have tried to kill Vial, the caravan master in fact died by Salazar's hand. And if I can keep my botanical facts straight, Melchora didn't use aconitum; she dealt in blue flowers, not purple, putting only gentian in her brews. We will not find the Indian woman guilty of a punishable crime without endless work to prove conspiracy."

"Is it certain then, sir, that Facundo Salazar murdered Vial?" I asked.

"Beyond all doubt. Imprisoned, the man confessed it all again and in greater detail," the governor replied. "As though it were a bedtime story, something about people in the distant past. The man is insane and his wife was mad with jealousy. It is a hideous tale. When soldiers took Salazar away from the interrogation, he bowed to me and walked off like an actor on a stage."

Anza summarized, "Facundo has been incarcerated and Celedonia is dead. Melchora's crimes against you and Marisol were repugnant, but she has fled from civilization. Winter in the mountains will dispatch her soon enough. Do you concur, Nando?"

Anza started to move a weight of papers across his desk, not seeming to notice that I didn't reply.

He called Carlos to his side and they bent their heads over something written, amending a word here and there. How the men could turn in an instant from this murderous business to their daily work was a puzzle to me, but there they were, absorbed in their papers. Apparently the loose ends of the two investigations weren't troubling them after all. I wondered if I could leave. There was still time enough in the day to start for Marisol's farm if they'd let us go right away.

At last they each took up a quill and signed vigorously, with Sebastian serving as witness, laboriously printing his own name.

The process ended with a ceremonious handshake. Carlos resumed his place beside me on the bench. There was silence as Sebastian drifted sand over the signatures and Anza restored the desk to order.

The governor cleared his throat. "Should I tell Nando now, or would you like to?" the governor asked Carlos.

Carlos bounded to his feet. With a careless slap on my sore shoulder he said, "Nando! The ranch belongs to the Aguilars again. The governor has restored our holdings on the Piedra Lumbre."

My battered noggin swirled. The governor, pleased with his beneficence, hurried to fill in the details.

"These past three years the principal opposition to restoring your grant came from one claimant, Facundo Salazar. Because of Señor Salazar and his process in Mexico to acquire the Aguilar's ranch, I have not been able to return the lands that should rightfully be yours. Your father, Benito, served this colony long and well. He held that ranch for nearly two decades, lending strength to the settlements around Abiquiú. His wisdom established security in the area for many years.

"You men," and Anza included me with his glance, "fought at your father's side to protect the peace. I have noted that since being remanded to the capital, you have each continued Benito's legacy of service to New Mexico. Now that Facundo Salazar has been indicted, and his conviction is inevitable, Salazar's claim is no longer valid.

"With my signature," and the governor flourished the valuable deed before us, "those lands once granted to Benito Aguilar, now accrue to Benito Aguilar's widow and all Benito's sons. You may return forthwith. You are commanded to restore order and productivity to the holding, to enforce the peace, and once established there, to pay your tithes and provide your fair share of armed men to the local militia. It will be my pleasure to travel north in the spring to conduct the traditional ceremony, and I'll throw the dirt with my own spade.

"I recognize that your absence has been protracted. The depredation upon the property by Comanches and Navajos has been considerable. It is within this government's means to provide you with a sum sufficient to build new herds and to make some of the buildings habitable."

During this announcement, I had risen to my feet. The ranch! We could go home at last.

"There's just one problem," the governor said.

There was always a hitch.

"Carlos is too valuable to my command. I cannot allow him to leave his posting to become a rancher in the wilds.

"Further, until the proceedings against the alcalde are finalized, Francisco is required by law to remain with Luisa in Santa Fe."

The governor leaned back in his chair and grinned.

"Francisco doesn't seem cut out for ranching anyway. No matter. There's nobody better suited to run the ranch than you, Nando. Carlos and Francisco already asked weeks ago, when they petitioned yet again for reinstatement of their rights, that you be appointed manager on their behalf. But then you went missing in the service of the crown, at great expense to your well-being, and, I might add, at considerable risk to your woman."

Anza rose and stepped over to me. He scanned the wounds on my face. "My clever lizard almost met his death serving our king. Evading witches, hauling the head investigator out of the well, trapping Facundo Salazar with a hawking blade. Such selfless action does not go unnoticed by your governor. I'm glad you came through, my friend."

I wasn't used to praise. Embarrassed, I did the slightest jig to answer him. "Still dancing, governor. Your beaten-up lizard's back on his feet."

Anza laughed and shook my hand. "It is with pleasure, Nando, that I turn the ranch on the Cañones Creek at the southern end of the Piedra Lumbre over to your management. I have every confidence you will step into your late father's shoes with ease."

Who was I to argue? The governor decreed it. By God, Marisol and I had a home.

The Winter Trail

The governor never intended for us to go north to the ranch at once, what with winter approaching and Marisol large with child, but we insisted. Seeing our determination, Anza lent us four soldiers to transport us and to help get part of the old hacienda livable as quickly as possible. Sebastian scrambled to augment our provisions and we left the next day.

With extra men to work on the ranch, the repairs happened fast. It wasn't I, but Marisol who needed care now. I could see her belly expand by inches every day. Her breath didn't come easily and it was impossible for her to get comfortable at night, no matter how many sheepskins I piled beneath her.

Anza's soldiers were a godsend. With their help we secured two rooms against the cold, patching the cracks, mudding the chimneys, and stretching oiled skins across the window openings. We pulled dead branches, mud and stones out of the well, bitter work in wintertime. The men brought heaps of firewood from the forest; easy, since no one had foraged here for years. We took turns hunting and on many days ate fresh meat. Marisol dried strips of venison over the fire to feed us later on.

I remembered our ranch as an impressive place. Our family once lived in several houses, the main one boasting seven rooms. There were barns, fenced gardens, lambing pens and a long stone corral we used when we brought the sheep down from the high country. Most of the original structures were still standing, but crumbling now. Mud, sticks and stone don't hold up long without constant effort from human hands.

I longed to have our helpers stay all winter, but the soldiers kept their gear in good condition, ready to ride. They eyed each storm that rolled through, gauging what kind of winter we were getting into.

The soldiers left exactly two weeks after arriving. Their orders had been to stay a fortnight, no longer. As Marisol and I watched them ride away down the valley, back to the main road that would take them to Abiquiú and on to Santa Fe, I wondered if I were up to this task. I held Marisol's hand in the frail sunshine, watching the empty trail.

"Never mind," I said, trying to sound stronger than I felt. "Nan will be here soon. The man I hired in Abiquiú promised he would leave for the north right away. He's half Ute too, and he's familiar with Cedro and the Capotes."

Marisol stayed silent, unusually so, while I kept talking, trying to cheer her. "Knowing my mother, she'll hurry down with half the clan and a herd of horses too. I bet she's here before Christmas, and that's weeks before this child is due."

Marisol nodded and stood stoically beside me. In the silence that lasted a little too long, we both remembered a question that remained between us. Whose child *was* this?

If the baby was born before late January it could not be mine. The way Marisol's body was changing, I had a suspicion that would be the case. If she held out until at least mid-February, I could trust the child was my own.

"We've come this far," I told her, giving her hand a squeeze. "Things are good. Neither of us died at the hands of the women in the canyon, and now, by Anza's great gift, we have a home."

Marisol's fingers stroked the back of my hand. "Yes, but still it's hard, watching everyone leave," she said softly.

I agreed. All we could hear was the slight gurgle of the creek in the ravine and a high wind in the tops of the pines.

"We'll have a healthy baby," I said, holding her close, "and soon we'll have lots more children. We'll be lucky to be alone with each other, ever again."

"The quiet's nice," Marisol said. "Do you think Benito and Luz ever got to be by themselves up here? Before Carlos was born?"

"I hope so."

Two mornings later one of our mules was missing. The signs told us someone had taken the animal from the barn, even though we had pulled rails up for the night.

"If you need a watchdog, get yourself a good mule," Benito used to say. But it hadn't worked this time. The missing animal had not brayed. This robber had skill.

Six inches of new snow had fallen the day before, so tracking was easy. The moccasin prints went around the point of the mesa to the east and then disappeared. Whoever took the animal had ridden upward toward the dense woods in the foothills. I lost the track when they traversed the band of slick rock that capped that part of the mesa.

I'd figured Navajos would begin to prey on us, once they learned people were living at the ranch again, but this seemed soon. When I got back to the house, Marisol told me a sack of corn had been taken too.

Day by day there were other signs: the bucket missing from the well. Someone had walked down by the creek. I followed the footprints into the woods and, not far from the back of our barn, found something that almost made my heart stop. A dead raven, just like before, lying on the snow, its feathers ruffled by the wind. I had little doubt that the woman who'd attacked Rosinante had left her mark again. It felt like she was daring me now, drawing me on to her. I threw the bird into the bushes and didn't tell Marisol.

Marisol no longer wanted to stay in the house by herself, so together we ventured a short distance along the creek. Using brush and a fallen log, we set up a blind back from the water. It became the place we went every sunny day. Wrapped in three mantas, Marisol sat near me, while I did some lazy hunting. With my arm around her, we watched for a deer, or maybe an elk to come to the water's edge. Occasionally I would drift away and set snares, which netted us some grouse and after much practice, two turkeys.

Late one afternoon when we returned to the house, two blankets were missing from our bed. The thief had not only stolen something we badly needed, but had come right into our home to do it. We searched throughout the labyrinth of rooms, our own and the uninhabited ones. When we were sure the robber was no longer in the house, I went out to check the livestock. All our animals were still there.

I came back from the barn, stomping the snow off my boots, and found Marisol waiting in the doorway. She said, "Are you thinking what I'm thinking?"

"Are you thinking Navajos?" I asked.

"No," she said.

"Are you thinking Apaches?" I continued.

"No." Marisol shook her head again.

"Are you thinking a woman named Melchora, desperate and alone in the snow?" I asked, as I checked the blade of my knife.

"Yes," said Marisol.

So she knew. "We have more blankets, don't we?" I asked.

"One more and the horse blankets, but if she keeps this up things will become hard. Nando, we need more people up here. Why haven't any of your cousins come?"

"I don't know. I guess they're waiting until we have the place all fixed up, with clean beds ready for them.

"Marisol, I can't leave you alone while I go to Abiquiú to recruit more family. Do you think you can still travel?"

Doubting it, she shrugged. In her condition it would take two days and the world was frozen solid now.

"Could you make the journey down to Abiquiú if I lead you on a horse, or would it be better in the cart?"

"I don't know." Tears were in the offing. "I'm so big I can hardly walk."

Damnation! I took her gently by the shoulders and looked into her eyes. "I'm not going to let that woman terrorize us any more. By all the kachinas and saints, Melchora's done enough damage to us. Our supplies are easy pickings and she has all those reasons in that dark mind of hers to want to hurt us. The woman must have come to roost not far from here."

Marisol watched my every gesture. What I decided mattered to her a great deal.

"Be brave for me, Marisol. Agree to stay alone in the house for a couple of hours at a time and I will hunt her down. Melchora isn't any smarter than we are. Meaner, for sure, but I'm feeling mean enough myself to take that woman on."

I looked at Marisol for a sign of assent and she gave me what I sought. She took up my knife and the sharpening stone. Without looking at me, she started working the edge.

"Go get her, Nando. She'll pick at us until there's nothing left, or she'll stage some frantic attack. She's sick enough to kill and she's got nothing to lose. Hunt her down. There's nothing else you can do."

"Are you sure you're willing to be here by yourself?"

Marisol face was set. "I'll stay here and I'll be fine. It's still weeks until the baby's due. I can ride Rosinante to Abiquiú if you don't come back, or to come find you if I think you need help."

"If you ride out, take a mule. Much better footing."

"Be quiet, Nando. I know what I'm doing. But you'll come back. I'm not worried about that."

My fingers rested gently at the tip of her chin. "If you think I need help, Marisol," I sought her eyes with mine, "do not ride into the mountains. Do not come after me alone. Return to Abiquiú and get help. Promise me."

She looked at me for a long while before she finally said, "I promise."

Marisol turned away and finished sharpening my knife. She found whatever blankets she could to make the bed, and lay down. Without saying goodnight, she turned on her side. When I climbed in beside her, she pretended to be asleep.

She had sent me to the mountains to confront Melchora. I might as well leave at first light, because our life couldn't go on until I'd returned from the hunt and the woman had been dealt with once and for all.

Tsipin

On the birthday of the Virgin, I ascended the south side of the mesa as fast as I could go, traveling up a deer path. The days were the shortest of the year and although I'd left early, the sun was about to drop behind the edge of the Cerro Pedernal.

I knew the woman was here. I hurried faster than my body wanted, determined to get to the abandoned city of the ancients on the mesa top before night. The ruins of Tsipin were enormous, the surrounding mountains vast. In darkness I would lose Melchora.

Once Melchora realized I was coming for her, she could sneak out of Tsipin by any of the precipitous routes off the cliff face, but I doubted the woman would leave. She too was ready for battle. She had used the dead raven to call me in.

Melchora was probably peering over the rim rock right now, watching me climb completely at her mercy, no larger than an ant on the side of the endless hill. She could be hiding in any cranny next to this cliff-edge path, or waiting in the final, narrow throat of rock I had to pass through to get to the mesa's top. It would be simple for the Pueblo woman to tip a boulder onto me, to send it crashing off the crags, or she could hurl rocks from the piles of Tsipin's rubble until she knocked me off the mountain.

The path went up and up. In places the sun had melted the snow to nothing, in others I picked my way over glassy ice. I sweated in spite of the cold. The sun's rays had left my side of the hill and the air was frigid when I spotted the final slot I had to crawl through, only a hundred yards ahead.

Someone long ago had carved a corridor through the uppermost ledge, a narrow shaft just wide enough for a person carrying a burden, no more. Square chunks of tuff had been set into rugged stairs. I slipped into the mouth of the defile and leaned against a solid slab to even out my breath.

There was no clink of stone, no crunch of foot against snow, no snapping twig. I moved into the passageway and climbed the icy steps that led me straight into a blank wall, but I'd been to this cunning place as a shepherd boy, and knew that the corridor turned sharply to the right, and after a few more steps took a hard turn to the left before opening onto the mesa.

I stopped before the first turn and slipped my fingers around the corner. Nothing. I looked up at the narrow slice of sky to see if there was a crone's face leering down at me. There wasn't.

When I reached the mesa's rim, the last of the lowering sun blazed into my eyes, blinding me. At that second, a screaming shape swept past my face. I ducked, knocking my head on the rock wall, before I recognized the wide, beating wings of an owl. My heart pounded in my throat. When I stepped onto the broad, open mesa, I felt no braver than a timid rabbit ready to dart back into its hole.

The sun plummeted behind the southern flank of the Pedernal. Melchora could be anywhere in the darkening ruin, crouched in one of the rubble-filled room cells, or waiting in the dense branches of a piñon tree. She could be hunkered deep in the ground in one of the kivas the ancients had carved into the surface rock. Wherever she had gone to earth, I needed to draw her out before nightfall.

My guess that she had retreated into the old pueblo was correct. Melchora's footprints were everywhere and there was evidence she had tied my mule in different places among the trees.

As boys, we used to herd sheep up here. That was long ago, but I still knew the layout of the old city, so I moved fast and almost soundlessly across the snowfield between the deteriorated buildings. When I could, I slipped into the protection of piñon and juniper trees.

I was heading for one of the ancient sacred circles I'd found playing with my brothers. The path was easy to follow in spite of the gathering dusk. Long ago, bare feet of the Pueblos had worn a shallow gully in the surface, making a track that led me through the old gardens and down to the snow-filled sacred place. Here the stones were bigger than buffalos. I dropped into a crouch, tucked my body between two of them, and waited.

Deep in the cold slot, I leaned against silent rock and tried again to quiet my breathing. After a few minutes, I climbed higher and found a spot to wedge myself. Once more the owl surged over my head. Something skittered across the trail. Then for a long time there was silence.

A stone clattered as it rolled. The woman was coming. I heard her running over the path. She stopped and listened, hunting me.

Melchora's feet left the stone pathway and crunched over snow. She circled around behind me.

I waited in my cranny. The cold of the boulders poured into my limbs, but I didn't dare shift for fear she would hear me.

Melchora's skirts swished nearby and once I heard her grunt with the effort of climbing. Then it became too quiet. She had found her own place to hide in the rocks. We were in a standoff now, here in the black night beneath the towering Pedernal.

A sharp ground wind riffled through the stones, numbing my skin, but I didn't risk wrapping my manta tighter. For all I knew the wind was a trick Melchora had wrought, to make me shift my weight, to force me out of hiding.

I heard the owl perch on the boulder above me, its talons scratching on the granite. I looked up. Christ! The witch woman stood dark against the sky, her arms raised high to heave a chunk of stone straight at my head.

I twisted and dropped onto the floor of the slot. The rock bounced off the boulders and tumbled onto me, but its force had been dissipated. I lay motionless, the stone heavy on my chest, knowing I was luckier than Beatriz. Let Melchora think it killed me.

The woman peered over the side, trying to see into the crack. I held my breath. She couldn't reach me from on top. I heard her slide down the side of the boulder and drop into the snow.

I used the few seconds while she was moving to gather the rock into my hands. Melchora was coming. I heard ragged breath in the woman's throat and smelled the rancid onion smell of her sweat. It was too dark to see her face, but she came closer, working herself into the hole. We were inches apart.

She bent over, poked me and laughed a bitter laugh.

I shoved the rock up into her leering face. Melchora used my own trick of the twisting fall, but as she went down, I struck her again with the stone.

Melchora's right hand clutched her bleeding forehead; the other jabbed blindly, trying to hold me off. Wounded though she was, she'd still fallen close enough to the entry hole to wriggle out of the slot. On hands and knees I followed her, but Melchora leapt on me, knocking me backward. She had me now, pinned against a slab of stone, going for my eyes with a splinter of rock.

I shot out both hands to protect myself. Melchora flinched. By sheer luck I got a knee against her chest and drove her back, just enough to get my other leg driving against her shoulder.

Our hands locked, wrestling stiffly, but Melchora's palms were bloody and her grip slipped. I pushed her over and rolled to my feet, wrenching my sore shoulder. In the second when I clutched it, Melchora fled.

I could only sense her movement in the pitch black, but I heard the rustle of her clothes. I ran toward the sound, reached into the night and caught her garment. Reckless with rage, I flung Melchora down and jumped astride her. She arched her body, straining to get out from under me, but I had her pinned.

There was a trace of moonlight sliding across the mesa top now. By its light I saw Melchora's glare, the moisture in the corners of her eyes, and blood on her face. She twisted her shoulders, spat at me, and then collapsed, the air leaving her. I figured it for a ruse, but I was wrong. The woman lay on the frozen ground, limp and motionless under the rising moon.

I had no idea what to do next. I couldn't sit on this woman forever, but I also didn't dare let up, because Melchora could toss me off and hide in the old pueblo before I was on my feet.

But then my enemy helped me out. She whispered hoarsely, "Kill me."

I tightened my hold.

"Don't take me back," she begged. "Kill me here."

Melchora lifted her head off the ground, pleading with her eyes. That was when I noticed that a tiny medicine pouch, hanging from a thin cord, had worked loose from the top of her blouse. It lay just to the right of her collarbone.

I pressed the woman's arms over her head, transferring both her hands into the grip of my left. I stretched her out long and taut so she couldn't move. I reached for my knife and held it in front of her face. The medicine bundle rested on her breast.

Tears pooled on the Indian woman's cheeks. I took the fine point of the knife and lifted the leather cord from where it lay on her skin. Staring directly into Melchora's eyes, I slit the thong. Keeping my eyes on hers, I bent toward her, picked up the tiny pouch with my teeth and dropped it down the opening at the neck of my manta. The bag rolled down my chest and lodged in a fold of my shirt.

I had taken her power. From that moment, I was crushing the bones of a woman who gave no resistance. Crooking my elbow, I pushed it into her breastbone.

"You're finished, Melchora. You've lost."

She tried to pull away from the pain, but she couldn't move.

"I have your power. I've swallowed your power. You are finished."

She moaned as I dug my elbow deeper.

Melchora's eyes closed. She suddenly seemed small and weak. I lifted my body off her, but kept her hands pinned. I moved along the ground until I knelt above her head. I still held her wrists hard against the snow with one hand, and my knife gleamed in readiness in the other. When I carefully slackened my grip, Melchora didn't tense or try to move away, but lay exhausted against the ground.

"You're not going to kill me?" she whispered.

"I don't have to," I replied. "You've done it for yourself. I'm going to leave you here in the mountains, alone, in the cold. You're a clever woman Melchora, but you'll have to use every scrap of your wits to survive."

Melchora didn't speak for a long time. Neither of us did. At last her voice filled the silence.

"Get this over. Kill me now."

I shook my head. "Hear again your own words, spoken when you left me in the cave: 'A quick death is too easy for this one.'"

Melchora rolled her head to the side. "I'm going to make you kill me, Nando. I'm going to tell you the plan I made. Not even Celedonia knew it. I'll tell you and then you'll kill me for sure."

I waited above her, ready for whatever horror this would be.

"It was never my plan to use Marisol as a hostage," Melchora said hoarsely. "I was certain you would send her out of town and I was ready to catch her the moment you did. It was my intention to frame Marisol, to make it clear she was the one who'd killed Vial. I was ready with more of the blue flowers and I was going to leave her for the soldiers to find, with enough evidence on her so they would never come after Celedonia and me."

I seized the woman's hair. I clutched so hard that a clump tore from her scalp. I resisted wrapping her long braids around her neck and strangling her, because I needed to hear every word of what this woman had to say.

"You were there with Facundo Salazar on the mountain when Beatriz was slain, weren't you?" I demanded to know.

Melchora made no sound, so I shook her until she rattled.

"I didn't kill Beatriz," she grunted through clenched teeth.

"But you were up there with Salazar, weren't you?"

Melchora nodded. Barely. I shook her again.

"I helped him move the stone," she wailed. "That's all. Beatriz was already dead. He choked her to death while they were making love."

Breathing hard into the Indian's face, I forced myself to remember that Marisol was alive, the baby strong within her. Even though Melchora helped with the stone, I believed the Pueblo woman hadn't killed Beatriz, and I knew she had not killed Vial. Facundo Salazar had strangled his lover and suffocated Vial. Maybe Melchora assisted Facundo in their deaths, but from what I'd already learned, and from what I now saw on the face of the woman beneath me, that no longer seemed probable.

Slowly I released my grip on her heavy braids. The fierce Melchora rolled over on the frozen ground and wept. Maybe I was no longer trying to slaughter her, but I wasn't done with her yet.

"You tried to kill Marisol. You knew full well that framing Marisol meant she would be hanged as soon as her baby was born."

I didn't want to listen to Melchora's sobs. I grabbed her shoulder and twisted her around so she was forced to look at me.

"Why did you try to kill me on the cliff above the camp? Why did you leave me to die in the cave?"

"I didn't know it was you out there that night when Marisol was pretending to be in labor. Celedonia and I were in way over our heads. The Pecos boys were scheming to get away. Terrified, I hurled the rock. But Nando, you didn't die. And that last night I didn't leave you to die."

369

"Liar!"

"I dragged you to the cave. I fed you. I put a blanket over you night after night. Celedonia would have killed you. You need to understand something. Celedonia is the one person who kept me alive all these years. It was she who got Salazar off me, who had the decency to continue to give me a home, but without the awful obligation of serving the master with my body. I had to play along with her. But only a little."

"You're lying to me and to yourself!" I cried. "You trussed me up like a sheep about to be butchered and left me without food or water, to freeze to death in winter." My thumbs worked their way into the gristle of Melchora's neck.

I could feel her swallow. She tried to speak, but wasn't able until I eased the pressure on her throat.

"I knew Marisol was out there," Melchora rasped. "I saw traces that let me know she was watching us. Celedonia would have killed you before we left, but to save you, I told her you would suffer more if we left you in the cave. We did not kill you, and Marisol got to you in plenty of time. That was the best I could do."

"What a fine, upstanding citizen you turn out to be!" I sneered. "And what about Tuqué?" My fingers danced along Melchora's throat.

"Tuqué earned his death. Tuqué stole young Pecos girls. He traded us to Spanish men in Santa Fe. When I was twelve he sold me for one horse to an officer at the palacio. A few months later, a man named Griego won me at cards. After two babies, Facundo bought me to be his house slave. His bed slave. Those were hideous years, but finally Facundo gave me to Celedonia and the torment ended. Yes, I helped kill Tuqué, but I didn't carry out Tuqué's death alone. The hands of many Pecos women worked to hang Tuqué."

"The deft touch of Facundo Salazar's cape on the effigy? Have you just explained the reason for that?"

Melchora nodded.

I'd heard all I could stand. I lifted my fingers from her throat. I got off the woman and stood up. The iron-hard cold knocked sense back into me and the moonlight restored my sight.

Sometimes killing was justified, and Anza had decreed Tuqué's death to be Pueblo business, but how far does lenience go? I looked down at the woman where she sat on the snow, cautiously fingering the scrape on her face.

"Facundo Salazar has been jailed for the death of Alfonso Vial."

Melchora didn't move. "He admitted to killing the caravan master and also Celedonia's daughter," I finished.

Melchora's laugh startled me. A gust of wind rushed through the tree above us.

"How did they catch him?"

I watched her face. "Facundo went mad. After Vial, he tried to kill Investigator Olivas too. By sheer chance I was the one who rescued Olivas. On the strength of the investigator's testimony, Sebastian went with soldiers to apprehend Facundo. Salazar fought until he was cornered, then collapsed into his insanity. The merchant proudly confessed to all of it. He believed he'd been serving God. We'd already figured out your monkshood was nothing of the sort. Pure gentian."

Melchora laughed again. "So you caught me! Lying to the mistress and the master. Kill me for that, Nando. They would have. I made sure the bouquet Facundo brought back from the mountain was gentian, not monkshood like they all thought."

Here I was, standing on a mesa top on a December night with an admitted accomplice in the horrific hanging of the Pueblo man, a woman who could send a stone crashing onto a dead girl's body, the same woman who kidnapped and nearly killed Marisol, and to my utter confusion, I felt sorry for her.

"What the hell am I supposed to do?" I blurted.

"Do what I told you," she answered simply. "Kill me. I can't go back to the colony. People will run in fear, scream that I'm a witch. They'll make me rot to death in a dank prison."

"I understand about Tuqué, fair enough if the man kidnapped you, but after that you went too far, Melchora. You got caught by the darkness of it."

The woman groaned something low and I saw the harshness of her life etched on her tear-streaked face.

"I can't kill you, Melchora. Even after what you did to Marisol, but I ought to bring you out of the mountains, give you to Anza."

"Will you get money for me?"

"Doubtful."

Melchora didn't need to know that Anza had already decided he had no case against her without endless investigation and expense. The remaining grievance was my own.

"Because of what they did to you as a girl, I won't kill you, Melchora, and I won't force you back to Santa Fe. But if you come near Marisol or anyone in my family ever again, I *will* kill you. Other than that I'm done. Our fight is over."

Melchora sat still. For the first time tonight she knew she was going to live.

"I'm known as a witch, Nando. Witches can travel at will. I will find my way to people on the plains, or maybe to the ocean far to the west. I have the skills to make the journey.

Leave a few supplies for me by your creek, near where I killed the raven, and I will go away."

"You already have one of my mules; you have our blankets. I will leave a parcel of food and winter moccasins beside the creek. You can make a life for yourself somehow, with the strengths you have.

"You're no witch, Melchora, though you seem to revel in dead birds. I'm going to let you go, but remember, the old evil is undone and your power is gone.

"Now!" I said extending a hand to raise her to her feet. "Get going, fast, before I change my mind."

She didn't take my hand and she didn't move.

"Go!" I yelled.

Melchora slowly rolled onto her knees. I wasn't sure I was doing the right thing. She could turn on me still, and I would face Anza's fury for letting her go, but something told me this was right.

"Leave that way, over the mesa's edge," I ordered, pointing west. "If you return to the towns you will die. If you come near my family, I will take the power in this bag of yours and use it to bring about your death. This I promise," I said, my voice as cold as the wind over snow. "Are you ready, Melchora, to do as I say?"

I stepped back, secured the medicine pouch inside my shirt, and watched her rise. The woman moved shakily toward the cover of the piñon trees. For a moment, Melchora stood frozen in the moonlight, unable to believe she was both alive and free. Then she disappeared into the forest.

I was twenty feet off the trail, heading for the eastern edge of the mesa when Melchora's voice came through the darkness.

"Take care of my daughter, Nando."

My head whipped around.

Melchora's voice came from a distance. "I didn't know until too late. I saw the mark on her arm when we captured her. I have no doubt. Give her the love I wasn't allowed to, Nando."

"Melchora, what . . ."

I saw a bundled shape slip over the ledge of rim rock and vanish into the night.

"Melchora!" I cried, but Marisol's mother was gone.

Running down the east side of the mesa, I raged at myself for letting Melchora go, because it was clear the woman knew Marisol was her daughter when she stole blankets and food from us. She jeopardized her own child's life and the life of her grandchild too.

Fool! Nando, you're a fool! But catching at icy tree trunks to slow myself down, I came to realize that Melchora had only taken what she needed to survive, and she took nothing that we didn't have more of. I saw again her deep, sorrowful eyes, and I felt at peace with my decision to free the mother of my beloved.

I halted and stood where a fast-running creek gives life to the snow-filled forest of oak and pine. I opened Melchora's medicine pouch. In the silvery light I saw pieces of bone and fragments of dried herbs. And Tuqué's shell.

I pulled out the gleaming necklace that I'd stuffed into the wide hem of my pants, along with my silver, the night I'd fled Santa Fe. I held the ornament against the moonlit sky and thought about giving it to Marisol, a talisman from her mother.

I looked at the shell glowing in the moonlight and decided my family would carry nothing forward from Tuqué. Nothing.

I threw the contents of the medicine bag into the current. I tossed in the necklace, and the pouch after it. The stream would cleanse the darkness and carry every last remnant far away from here.

After a while, I knelt on the frozen snow with my hands pressing into the pure whiteness on either side of me, and took a long drink of the cold water.

~ 1783 ~

Epilogue

The babies, a boy and a girl, were born on the twentieth day of January. Nan and my sister caught the newborns. When they saw how beautiful the children were, neither of the Utes brought up the tribe's objection to twins, because with a ranch this big, everyone knew we were lucky to be making babies two at a time.

The women finally allowed me back inside. Marisol was sitting part way up with an infant in each arm, beaming. The babies had been washed and wrapped in the warm, woolen blankets Luz had sent in panniers on Francisco's horse. Little did she know we would need two of everything.

The date the children were born made it doubtful I was their father, but twins often come early. We could only wait and see if someday they resembled Aguilars. The consensus for now was that they looked neither like Arsenio, nor me, but rather like Luz, skinny, bald and toothless. These babies were decidedly tiny, but they had spunk. Feisty and roaring for life.

We were content to love them for that.

DEAD LIZARD'S DANCE

A Glance at the Times

1763-- The end of the French and Indian War essentially splits the North American continent in two, giving Britain possession of the eastern half, while Spain retains the vast region from the Mississippi to the Pacific Ocean. France keeps only two small islands in the Caribbean.

1776-- Americans upset the Europeans' tidy equation by signing the Declaration of Independence and the American Revolutionary War begins.

-- Spain's King Carlos III creates a special military command in New Spain to protect Mexico's silver mines from Apaches and other tribes in the north.

-- Juan Bautista de Anza leads the first group of Spanish settlers cross-country from Mexico to San Francisco.

1777-- King Carlos III appoints Anza as Governor of New Mexico.

1779-- Spain and England declare war against each other and engage in battles throughout the world.

-- In New Spain, Governor Anza wins a critical campaign against the formidable Comanche Chief, Cuerno Verde.

1781-- Americans, aided by French and Spanish allies, defeat the British at Yorktown.

1782, 1783
-- The time of this story

1783-- The Treaty of Paris officially ends the American Revolutionary War, as well as the war between England and Spain.

1786-- Governor Anza successfully negotiates a treaty between Spain and the Comanche nation.

1788-- Relieved of the governorship, Anza returns to Sonora and dies shortly thereafter. King Carlos III of Spain dies that same month, December 1788.

Pamela Christie

New Mexican Spanish

Acequia—an irrigation ditch

Adobe—mud bricks

Aguardiente—crude brandy

Alcalde, or Alcalde Mayor—a local headman, a mayor. The root word of alcalde is the same for "Al Qaida"—the foundation.

Alfonso El Ganso, ya se torció—Loosely: Alfonso's goose is cooked.

Amorcito—my little love

Ay de mi! —Oh me, oh my!

Barrancos—ravines, canyons, cliffs

Barrio—a neighborhood, usually of the poor

Bosque—the dense cottonwood forest that grows along New Mexico's rivers

Brujo/Bruja—a witch, sorcerer, medicine man or woman

Cacique—a religious leader of a Pueblo

Carrossa—a huge carriage or wagon

Casas Reales—The Palace of the Governors. See *Palacio*.

Casita—small house

Castas—half-breeds, or those of mixed blood

Chamisa— *Ericameria Nausea*--a yellow, brushy weed, rabbit brush

DEAD LIZARD'S DANCE

Cicuye—a native name for the Pueblo of Pecos

Cojones—testicles

Compadre—a friend, buddy, but mainly a godfather

Convento—the missionaries' house and offices, attached to the church

Criada—a serving maid

Croix, Teodoro de—(pronounced "Croy") Commander General of Spain's Northern Provinces from 1776 to 1783.

Curandera—a medicine woman, a healer

Gato—cat

Gordo—a fat man

Hacienda—a large house or country estate

Hasta Mañana—until tomorrow

Hola—hello

Horno—an adobe oven in the shape of a beehive

Jacal—log hut

Latilla—peeled poles used in ceilings

League—in Anza's time a league was about 2.5 miles. Most say there are 3 miles to a league, the distance a horse can walk over flat ground in an hour's journey.

Manta—a cape, like a poncho, also a blanket

Mestiza—a person of mixed ancestry, usually Indian and Spanish

Mierda—crap

Niyol—wind

Novia—fiancée

Palacio—The Palace of the Governors, one of the earliest government building in the United States, still in use today. Also called the Casas Reales, or royal buildings.

Patrón—the landowner, the boss

Peso—a silver coin, roughly equivalent to $36 in Anza's time, but hard to gauge. Actual coins were rare in early New Mexico, as payment was usually made in goods.

Piedra Lumbre—the area north of Abiquiú where the broad valley of the Chama is surrounded by shining red and gold sandstone cliffs

Pinché—cheap, crummy, paltry

Playa—in New Mexico, a dry lakebed

Pueblo—People. Referring to the culturally similar groups of native peoples who lived in villages in the region of the middle Rio Grande. Lower case *pueblo* refers to the villages themselves.

Punché—a locally grown, rough tobacco substitute

Puta—whore

Reales—small coins worth an eighth of a peso

Rico/ Rica—a rich person

Residencia—the formal review of a high-ranking officer after he leaves office

Río—a river

Río Bravo, Río Bravo del Norte—today's Rio Grande River

Rito—a creek

Sala—the living room

Sangre de Cristos—the principal mountain range of Northern New Mexico, literally translated as *The Blood of Christ*. Probably referred to as simply La Sierra in 1782.

San Lazaro Mountains—today's Ortiz Mountain Range, South of Santa Fe

Tse—rock

Turtle Mountain—an Indian name for the Sandia Mountains East of Albuquerque

Vara—a standard measurement equaling a little less than a yard

Viga—a log roof beam

Visita—the obligation of priests to say Mass at churches too small to have a resident priest

Pamela Christie

Historical Sources
Specific to Dead Lizard's Dance*

Brooks, James, F. *Captives and Cousins*, University of North Carolina Press, 2002.

Cobos, Rubén. *A Dictionary of New Mexico and Southern Colorado Spanish.* Museum of New Mexico Press, 2003.

Ebright, Malcom and Hendricks, Rick. *The Witches of Abiquiú: The Governor, The Priest, The Genízaro Indians, and The Devil.* University of New Mexico Press, 2006.

García, Nasario. *Tales of Witchcraft and the Supernatural in the Pecos Valley.* Western Edge Press, 2001.

Gutiérrez, Ramón A. *When Jesus Came, the Corn Mothers Went Away, Marriage, Sexuality, and Power in New Mexico, 1500-1846.* Stanford University Press, 1991.

Herrera, Carlos R. *The King's Governor, Juan Bautista de Anza and Bourbon New Mexico in The Era of Imperial Reform, 1778-1788*, A Dissertation for his Doctor of History Degree, University of New Mexico, Albuquerque, 2000.

Kessell, John L. *Kiva, Cross, and Crown, The Pecos Indians and New Mexico 1540-1840.* University of New Mexico Press, 1979.

Moore, Michael. *Medicinal Plants of the Mountain West.* Museum of New Mexico Press, 1979.

Noble, David Grant. *Santa Fe, History of an Ancient City.* School of American Research Press, Santa Fe, 1989.

Poling-Kempes, Lesley. *Valley of Shining Stone, The Story of Abiquiú.* The University of Arizona Press, Tucson, 1997.

Preston, Douglas, Preston, Christine and Esquibel, José Antonio. *The Royal Road, El Camino Real from Mexico City to Santa Fe.* University of New Mexico Press, 1998.

Quintana, Frances Leon. *Pobladores, Hispanic Americans of the Ute Frontier.* University of Notre Dame Press, Indiana, 1991.

Schmutz, Ervin M. and Hamilton, Lucretia Breazeale. *Plants That Poison, An Illustrated Guide for the American Southwest.* Northland Press, Flagstaff, Arizona 1979.

Simmons, Marc. *Witchcraft in the Southwest. Spanish and Indian Supernaturalism on the Rio Grande.* University of Nebraska Press, 1974.

~Exhibits, Lectures and Festivals at El Rancho de Las Golondrinas, a living history museum south of Santa Fe

~Lecture Series by Southwest Seminars, from 2001-2009 as a benefit for the Palace of the Governors. Lectures by, among others, José Antonio Esquibel, Orlando Romero, Dr. Stanley Hordes, David Grant Noble, Dr. John Kessell, Dr. Joseph Sánchez, Dr. Thomas E. Chávez, Joe S. Sando, Dr. Fran Levine, Dr. Robert Himmerich y Valencia, Dr. Estévan Rael-Gálvez, and Skip Keith Miller.

Thanks to Tomás Enos of Milagro Herbs for helping me clarify the differences between monkshood and gentian.

*Additional sources are cited at the back of *The King's Lizard*, Lone Butte Press, 2004, 2005.

Pamela Christie

Acknowledgements

Thank you to the secretive, steadfast and generous force of Bill Baxter, always, and to editors Ardeth Baxter and Jennifer Dewey for staying with and after me.

Thank you to my early readers Rick Shore and Cynthia Marshall, and to my waggish fan club composed entirely of Ronnie Whitman. Thank you to Dorothy Massey of Collected Works who continues to shelve my books face out.

Unending thanks to Chris Lincoln, Wendy Hitt, Edy Keeler, Mabsie Walters and Mark Kaltenbach for hiking me up canyons and creeks when needed, and of course to Cleone Stoloff, who read the manuscript four times because she's my mother.

Blessings and thank you to my son Jack Dant and his wife, Carrie McConaughy, and to my delightful granddaughters, Nicoya and Amiyah, each of whom has contributed enormously to my stories in a multitude of ways.

photo by Buck Cuddy

Pamela Christie received her education at the Catlin Gabel School in Oregon, Bryn Mawr College, Pitzer College and the University of California at Berkeley. She has lived, played and worked in New Mexico for over thirty years, in both a remote mountain village and in Santa Fe.

Lone Butte Press of Santa Fe, NM published her first novel, *The King's Lizard*, in 2004. In April of 2007, *The King's Lizard* was awarded the New Mexico Press Women's Zia Award for fiction, to honor an outstanding New Mexico woman writer.

Ms. Christie loves to explore the countryside she writes about, finding traces of ancient mysteries and hearing tales of the people who lived in the rugged kingdom centuries ago. She is currently a guide at El Rancho de Las Golondrinas, a living history museum near Santa Fe.